Born in S[...] South of France [...] animals, a dog and a cat. His debut novel, *Fever City*, was published in 2016.

@TimBakerWrites

Further praise for *City Without Stars*:

'An exhilarating and kaleidoscopic novel that will also break your heart. Baker has assumed his place among those crime writers you must read.' Stav Sherez, author of *A Dark Redemption* and *The Intrusions*

'An intense, emotive and completely absorbing read, suffused with a violent energy and an unrelenting pace.' *Raven Crime Reads*

'A powerful second novel . . . with all the moral uncertainties of an Ellroy or a Winslow. Highly recommended.' Maxim Jakubowski, *Crime Time* Book of the Month

'An intelligent thriller that moves at a breath-taking pace.' Nicholas Searle, author of *The Good Liar*

'A tour de force; stark, elegant prose that tells the story of a country in brutal freefall – and the ragtag outsiders still fighting the good fight.' Rod Reynolds, author of *Cold Desert Sky*

'Powerful, magnificent, majestic, breathtaking . . . An incredible piece of storytelling written with a brutal beauty and an incredible intensity.' *Grab This Book*

'A fascinating, immersive page-turning read . . . *City Without Stars* will sit alongside powerful novels like *The Power of Dog* by Don Winslow.' Keith Nixon, *Crime Fiction Lover*

'Baker is a huge talent. Highly recommended.' Linda Boa, *Crimeworm*

---

by the same author

FEVER CITY

City Without Stars

TIM BAKER

FABER & FABER

First published in 2018
by Faber & Faber Limited
Bloomsbury House, 74–77 Great Russell Street
London WC1B 3DA
This paperback edition published in 2019

Typeset by Faber & Faber Limited
Printed and bound by CPI Group (UK) Ltd, Croydon, CR0 4YY

The right of Tim Baker to be identified as author of this work
has been asserted in accordance with Section 77 of
the Copyright, Designs and Patents Act 1988

This is a work of fiction. Names, characters, places, incidents, and historical events
either are the product of the author's imagination or are used fictitiously. Any
resemblance to actual persons, living or dead, events, or locales is entirely coincidental.

*This book is sold subject to the condition that it shall not, by way of trade or otherwise, be
lent, resold, hired out or otherwise circulated without the publisher's prior consent in
any form of binding or cover other than that in which it is published and without
a similar condition including this condition being imposed on the subsequent purchaser*

A CIP record for this book
is available from the British Library

ISBN 978–0–571–33834–4

FSC
www.fsc.org
MIX
Paper from
responsible sources
FSC® C020471

2 4 6 8 10 9 7 5 3 1

For my wife, Julie,
and in loving memory of our mothers,
Lorel Baker and Sheila Curtis

This thing of darkness I acknowledge mine.

William Shakespeare, *The Tempest*

MEXICO, MAY 2000

I

City Without Stars

DAY 1

Victim 873 – Isabel Torres

Isabel

It arrives with the storm, approaching floodlights bruising the desert night. Yellow dogs raise their heads, their eyes glittering then going black with the passing lights. The Lincoln Navigator blasts across the wasteland, impaled plastic rustling from its passage, frantic to escape the snare of barbed wire.

The shriek of braking tires sends the dogs scattering into shadows. Trash circles in anxious eddies then disappears with the headlamps. The animals quiver in the sudden silence, pawing the ground, greedy and afraid.

Two men get out, silhouetted against desert hills that tremble with the nervous kick of lightning. They open the cargo hatch and heave something into the darkness. There is the crash of cans spilling.

Doors slam shut and the car pulls away.

The dogs nose the storm-crumpled air then cautiously re-emerge, padding silently towards the whisper of settling dust.

2

Pilar

Sunlight forces its way through the grime of the windows, disturbing a man in his sleep. His arm scouts for a companion, but finds only an empty pillow which he gathers close to his face.

A shower runs in the adjoining bathroom, steam escaping through the open door, examining the detritus of the night before: an empty bottle of tequila, a crowded ashtray; the silver foil of a torn condom pouch.

Hotel rooms.

Contained universes.

Hidden histories for everyone except the people caught within them. The man on the bed is the past. The woman in the shower is the future.

Pilar soaps her black pubic hair, the hot water running out. She turns it off to build up the pressure of the cold jet, tensing her muscles under its challenge; feeling alive again.

Another morning.

Another chance to make things right.

She stands in front of the veiled mirror, her hips tilted in contemplation as she pats her small, muscular body dry, water pooling at her feet. Toothpaste. Hairbrush. Deodorant. Her life has always been composed of modest needs combined with a desire to change the world. Paradox is not a word she uses. She glances at her watch, curses; now dresses hastily. Plain briefs, fraying bra, jeans and a tunic with a company logo on it. She pockets a pack of cigarettes and opens the door, letting traffic noise in. The man in the bed stirs but Pilar's already gone.

The room shifts with her absence, reconfigures into a dormitory, solitary with slumber. Noises retreat into the amber world of sleep – the neighboring room's radio, car horns, the hum of a distant vacuum cleaner all vanishing as he falls into a deeper cycle, lost in dreams of his childhood, of stealing watermelons from the fields before the factories came. Esteban turns away from the sunlight which does its best to wake him. The lost power of Nature in an urban environment. Proud but futile.

In an hour, maybe less, the killers will arrive.

Ten years ago, it would have been just a warning. Routine. Punches to the gut, slaps around the face. Maybe a broken finger. But that was ten years ago. Things change fast when people die for no reason. Fists had been replaced with razor blades. Knives with guns. Now they don't even bother to mask their faces. Immunity destroys prudence.

And murder becomes mundane.

In an hour, maybe less, the door will be kicked open. Three strangers will enter, will douse the bed with gasoline, flick a flaming match. The mattress will leap alive, Esteban sitting up, already dead, his scream lost in the roar of combustion, the flames inside his lungs, feasting on his oxygen. The killers will walk away, just one step ahead of the smoke.

The desk clerk will see the license plate of the blue Ford pickup and immediately forget it. But it won't make any difference. They'll come back later and kill him anyway.

3

Isabel

The sun-blistered cinder block of the *maquiladoras* stretches across the arid landscape, forming a chaotic monument to free trade, special border incentives and tariff exemptions. Like all the other raw materials they consume, the factories swallow young women and transform them into viable merchandise: sweatshop workers. The logic of exploitation is too profitable to resist. Dummy corporations are established in tax havens. Earnings are shifted to overseas accounts. Pension schemes are improvised, then plundered at will. Toxic by-products are vented into bereaved streams filled with poisoned wildlife.

Or simply dumped in communal garbage.

A janitor hoses down the front entrance of the factory, the plump gush of water drowning out the whine of machinery from behind barred windows. He hates the nocturnal dogs and leaves traps for them. Occasionally he discovers the tip of a paw or a sun-inflated corpse, but mainly he just finds tipped-over trash cans and refuse colonized by humming flies. He moves along slowly, tugging at the heavy hose, the pressurized blast loud against the wall. Normally he would never waste water like this, but the bosses are on alert. *Sindicalistas* from Europe are heading their way, to create trouble about hygiene and safety. Fire hazards and health. Profits and pay slips. *Pinche* foreign assholes, making more work. For what? There were no trade unions for people like him. Uneducated. Unskilled. Aging and aching. Lucky to have a job and angry that it can only be this: hosing down shit.

A pack of dogs darts out from behind a dumpster, the janitor opening the jet so hard that it knocks over two of the scavengers as they flee. He trains the water back on the trash, and a woman's shoe skitters away fast as a rat. The janitor peers behind the pile of garbage, then drops the hose and runs; the water snaking backwards and forwards on the ground, the dead woman's hair writhing to its punch.

4

Pilar

Just like when she was a teenager, Pilar sits with the bad girls at the back of the bus, all of them smoking cigarettes. Maria looks Pilar up and down. 'So tell us, how was Esteban?'

Pilar glances out the window, the bus slowing in traffic. 'He snores.'

Maria slaps at Pilar playfully. 'You know what I mean. How *was* he?'

Pilar pauses, the other women gathering close for the verdict. 'I only had three minutes to find out before he started snoring.'

The women all laugh. Only Maria can keep a straight face. 'But were they a good three minutes?'

'For him!'

The girls erupt. At the front of the bus, the driver stares in the rearview mirror. Laughter is like money. You hate people who have it. He grinds the gears in irritation and turns his radio up.

Pilar looks out the window, at the traffic jam swelling the way it does every morning: an exercise in collective torment. Esteban was a nice guy, as far as guys went, but Pilar had expected more from him. His selfishness in bed was something he shared with too many young men. Quick gratification on the horn tip of alcohol. She remembers the things that led her to want to sleep with him. The way he spoke to her, never raising his voice in a town full of shouts. The way he made her laugh.

He was a friend in the *cantina*, but a stranger in bed.

Pilar will be spared any guilt from her postcoital assessment of Esteban. She won't even see the first news reports of the killing, before Esteban is identified. Later the police will contact his family in La Angostura and then forget about him, the way the media will. In the old days murder was front-page news. Banner headlines rare and raw with evil. Now it is an embarrassed side-glance, a hurried step over another drunk on a crowded, ugly street. Distasteful but routine. By the time Pilar finds out that Esteban is dead, too much will have happened for her to even cry. Her main emotion will be selfish relief. She'll know what Esteban could never have known: that the killers were really after her. And she will also know that with every miss, you become stronger. Statistics don't lie. If they're going to get you, it's on the first attempt. If not; the second. This is her fourth, counting that time in Tijuana. She is on her way to becoming immortal.

In Ciudad Real, that's a very favorable condition.

Pilar leans her head against the glass of the window and is rocked into a shallow sleep. Car horns sound not with fury but with mournful resignation, like church bells at a country funeral. For a glorious moment, Pilar is able to forget where she is and what is expected of her in only a few days . . .

Then there is the lurch of arrival, Pilar suddenly awake and embarrassed, brushing away the trace of saliva from the corner of her lips.

She follows her friends out, holding her breath through the haze of diesel fumes as they hurry past rows of idling buses, hundreds of other women emerging ghostly from the clouds of exhaust, moving together across the barren fields, like soldiers in a gas attack: ready for slaughter.

The regular thump of machinery grows louder as Pilar approaches the perimeter fences of the *maquiladoras*. She breaks into a run when she sees the police cars and ambulance already circled by a crowd of women. 'We'll be late!' Maria shouts after her, but Pilar doesn't even glance back. Cursing to herself, Maria runs after her, more workers from the buses darting forwards in a spontaneous wave of curiosity.

Two municipal policemen try to keep them away. A short woman in her twenties grabs Pilar's arm, steering her to the front of the group. 'It's Isabel!' Lupita's voice is husked with disbelief. The ring expands with the new arrivals, pushing past the ambulance, outflanking the cops, who give up trying to hold them back. The workers take turns looking at the body lying between the trash cans, crying out with sobs of horror and crossing themselves when they see it.

A young detective, Gomez, takes a pen out of his jacket and gingerly lifts something with it. It's the high-heeled shoe, still dripping water as Gomez holds it by the ankle strap, displaying it to his partner, Fuentes. 'Wearing shoes like this, what did she expect?'

Fuentes looks at the young man. He feels like slapping him for the sheer fucking ignorance of the remark, but what good would that do? He is stuck with Gomez, whether he likes it or not. So far, it's all *not*. Gomez has the bullying swagger of all athletic men who come into power too early. The question is: what will Gomez do with all that power? Fuentes likes to believe the answer is up to him. He opens an evidence bag and Gomez drops the shoe into it. 'Whatever she was expecting, it wasn't this.'

It never is.

Getting off a bus at night; walking out a front door; waiting for friends who are late, who got distracted with a drink too many or an unexpected kiss in the shadows of an awning. Hurrying to pick up a child from school or do the shopping before the *miscelánea* closes. The last thing on anyone's mind when they're running for the first bus of the day or stepping outside to have a cigarette is *I am about to die*.

This is the basic fault not just of Gomez's comment but of the arrogance of his logic. Routine implies continuity, not eradication. Everyday habits, whether good or bad, make you blind to the unexpected. The dead girl had strapped on this shoe with the certainty that she would unstrap it at the end of the night. Just because she has no future now doesn't mean she didn't have one yesterday. And it is Fuentes' job to make sure that the people who stole her future will pay for it with their own. He wants to take their future out into a dark alley and execute it against a graffiti-stained brick wall. Fuentes doesn't believe in God but he believes in Yin and Yang. Light and dark. Give and take. This is why he requested the transfer to Ciudad Real. To be the one who finally makes a difference. The one who finds and punishes the killers. Who smashes their fucking complacency. And if he can teach a dumbass hotshot like Gomez how to think intelligently on the way, so much the better.

Pilar stares at the body of the young woman, at the trickle of water still coming from the nearby hose. She doesn't make the sign of the cross like the others. She doesn't retreat behind the protective blanket of prayer. She prefers the chaos of the clenched fist raised in an angry crowd. She calls out to the two plainclothes detectives standing just a few feet away from the corpse. 'It's a disgrace! You should take her away, instead of just standing there doing fuck all.'

Fuentes and Gomez turn and look at her. The intensity of Pilar's gaze unsettles Fuentes. It's familiar in its defiance. He rolodexes faces fast in his mind, screeching to a stop under *T*. 'This is a crime scene,' Fuentes says to Pilar. 'Please, just let us do our work.'

'If you did your work, she wouldn't be lying there, dead.'

There is a chorus of agreement from the women. Gomez gives Pilar a smirk of hateful admiration, like a mark who's just been suckered by a short-con artist. He nods in the direction of the *maquiladora*. 'Don't you have dresses to make?' He turns to one of the uniformed policemen. 'Get the goddamn *chicas* out of here.'

The uniformed cops begin to shove the women around the breasts, happy to hurt as they push them away. But Pilar rushes past them to the garbage cans, snatching up two lids and crashing them together, chanting with the beat: 'Protection for the women! Justice for the victims! Protection for the women, justice for the victims!'

Maria and Lupita join in, also grabbing lids. The bystanders pick up the chant. More women from the buses come running across the field. The two detectives watch the spontaneous protest growing larger and louder. They exchange looks. 'That's all we need,' Gomez shouts over the clamor. 'Fucking ballbreakers.'

5

El Santo

Three black Suburbans and a red Dodge Ram pull up outside a fancy brick house with large windows looking out onto a low wall – as far as security goes, a fatal combination. It's a snooty new neighborhood. Actual lawns. Sprinkler systems. Audis and Mercs in driveways. A setting unused to the crisp snap and click of semi-automatics being racked.

The killers are already eight hours late. El Santo had told them they'd hit the house just before midnight, but then they'd all gotten wasted at Mary-Ellen's place after the barbecue and the next thing he knew the sun was leaching through the smog and Mary-Ellen was making her breakfast specialty – not that any of them ate that shit, particularly in the morning. El Santo peered over her shoulder as she drizzled maple syrup over the pancakes or waffles or churros or whatever the fuck that thing was that she cooked. He had to think of an excuse, fast. 'Jesus, look at the time.'

'Sit down and enjoy your breakfast.'

'I'm late.' At least the coffee was drinkable. 'I'll have someone drop you at the airport.'

'No need. I'm driving it in via El Lobo.'

Driving? 'Wait a minute, the airport is secure.'

'This way I can take in forty K, easy.'

She was getting greedy. It never takes long. 'I have a funny feeling.'

'I *can* do something about that, you know.'

'Why is sex always on your mind?'

'Maybe because I hang with a crew of moron males?'

'Well, this male's no moron. Airport or drive, I want the normal tax.'

'No way! We have a deal.'

'An airplane deal. It's different.'

'Why is it different?'

'Lower freight. Higher risk. And I like you.'

'You'll make me cry. Airport tax. Besides, you just said driving over was a risk, a huge risk you said.'

'I said you have to be more careful.'

'Ten.'

'Fifteen.'

'Ten.'

'Twelve.'

'Ten! Keep it simple for Christ's sake, you know neither of us is good at math.'

Why even bother arguing with a hard-ass like Mary-Ellen? El Santo accepted ten and got away without eating breakfast.

So by the time they left, they were running eight hours late. And when they do finally arrive, in broad fucking daylight now, it doesn't feel right. 'Where are all the motorcycles?'

'Probably out being serviced,' El Feo says. El Feo is the kind of guy who makes all the other crew members feel smarter than they should.

'Are you sure this is the right place?'

'Fuck yes, positive, boss.'

It's been almost a year since El Santo participated in an operation. He hates them. It isn't the killing, or the risk he might be killed, that bothers him. It's the way everything is always the same. The stunned looks on the victims' faces; the reaching for the weapons and the break for the back door. The chaos of screams and then the simmer of silence. A video loop with the same images, the same sounds, playing over and over again. It reminds him of what that priest with the bleeding hands used to lecture about when he was preparing them for Holy Communion: 'Heaven is change, children, but hell is the horror of repetition.' Go figure: hell turns out to be *Groundhog Day*. But he needs to be here in person for this operation. This one is special: a rare chance to take out a Tijuana crew stupid enough to invade his home turf.

One, two . . .

The front door explodes off its hinges.

He makes sure El Feo goes in first, just in case they're expected.

They all stream inside after him, a toxic tide in ski masks and ballistic vests, holding gunmetal black in their hands. In the microsecond after they enter, El Santo knows they have screwed up bigtime.

It's not the *Happy Birthday* sign. Or the balloons hanging from the ceiling. Or the pile of empty Coke cans crowding the ruins of a cake.

And it isn't the teenage couple lying stoned in each other's arms on the sofa, or the boys around the TV screen, playing *World Cup 98*, or the bored girls smoking cigarettes as they watch them play.

It's the sight of the maid coming out of the kitchen, a garbage bag in one hand, a dustpan in the other. She could be his mother. She is ordinary; already tired at the beginning of the day. Pissed to find the place looking like this. And kind enough never to tell the parents.

Two words scream inside his head.

Three words actually.

Wrong fucking house.

He turns to El Feo but already there's that telltale red orb burst and then the white bloom of combustion blast.

Too late.

The massacre has begun.

Shrieks. Screams. The explosions of screens, windows, furniture. The thump of bullets through walls, hollowing craters out of the facade of domestic harmony. No one goes for a gun. There aren't any. No one even has time to run. He looks at the couple on the pockmarked sofa. They haven't even moved and they're already dead.

Fifteen seconds, give or take. Fifteen dead, give or take. The maid slumped on the floor, her dustpan still in her hand. Faithful to the end to her mission: to clean up after others.

And a traumatized boy trapped in El Feo's arms. At least El Feo has got that right: make sure there's at least one survivor they can question. 'What's your name, kid?'

The kid tries to answer, moving his mouth, but nothing's working. El Feo slaps him. 'Lay off!' El Santo says, then turns back to the boy. 'We're not going to hurt you. What's your name?'

'Tomás.'

'Okay, Tomás. What were you doing here?'

'Celebrating...' His voice cracks and he has trouble finishing the sentence. 'Gerardo's...' His face is lost.

'Birthday?' Tomás nods. 'Where are his parents?'

'In Monterrey.'

There's a burst of gunfire from upstairs and a jolt runs through Tomás' body, like someone's just hooked him up to a car battery. Plaster dust drifts from the ceiling, covering them in surly white. 'Tomás, hey, listen to me, *hombre*. You ever heard of Los Toltecas?'

For the first time Tomás looks at him. '*Sí.*'

'What did you hear about them?'

'They were like the Mayans?'

'I'm talking about the motorcycle gang. Do you know them?' Tomás shakes his head. 'Listen carefully, Tomás: when the police come, you tell them it was Los Toltecas who did this, understand?'

The kid could have nodded. Three of his men stomp down the staircase, one of them holding a fistful of jewelry. 'Do we do him?' El Feo says, pointing to the kid with a gun.

'Were you even listening?' He pushes El Feo towards the front door. 'We need the kid to tell the cops who did this.' El Feo grunts the way he does when he doesn't understand a fucking word you tell him. 'Who fed you this crap information?'

'My contacts.'

The way he makes it sound, it's like he said *my aircraft carrier*. El Santo checks the neighbors' houses through the windshield as he drives away. Not a single sign of life. There will be no witnesses. There never are, these days. Legally speaking, that is. But El Santo knows the look the maid gave him just before she died will be testifying against him for the rest of his life. Of course he's killed kids younger than these. Hell, he was younger than some of them when he first killed. But the maid looked like his mother, and the kids were . . .

He leans over and punches El Feo so hard in the face that he knows he'll need to ice his hand.

'What was that for?' El Feo whines, as though he didn't know. He probably doesn't. El Feo's cell phone rings and he stops his sniveling enough to answer it. He turns to El Santo like a dog to the master who mistreats it – forever hopeful of change. 'Good news.'

'I could do with some.'

'It's done.' The snort is supposed to be a laugh. '*Pinche* unions.'

'At least someone did their job right.'

'Come on, boss. One out of two's not so bad. They turned him into toast.'

'Fuck, did you say *him*?'

El Feo looks at his cell phone, as though it's just stung him. 'That's what *they* told me.'

'The target was a fucking *chica*!' He'd hit him again if his hand wasn't so sore. So instead El Santo steps hard on the accelerator, imagining it's El Feo's face. They roar towards the highway, the other vehicles speeding after him, fanning out on either wing, as though all of them are racing each other, trying to get as far away as possible from that fucking birthday house.

6

Pilar

Inside the hangar-like room, scores of women bend over rows of sewing machines but there's nothing domestic about this scene. It's more like something out of a military field hospital. The hum and stutter of sutures. The grind of saws. The slap and slash of retaining belts and the machine-gun percussion of automatic needles firing thread through welts of leather. The savage sounds coalesce into a furious chorus of repetitive noise made worse by the certainty of its rhythm. The torment of hell is not the pain itself, but the knowledge that it will never stop.

Sunlight lances through large openings in the roof, creating a contrasting patchwork of brilliant solar glare intercut with cubes of cold shade. Why pay for electricity when you can use desert flare for free? The lights only come on for the night shifts, when the electricity rates go down anyway.

Pilar works against the puzzle of the irregular natural lighting, passing hems through an arc of darting needles. A single slip would cost fingers, maybe the whole hand. But Pilar has the concentration and reflexes of the young. Ten, maybe fifteen years in a factory like this and then you are through, whether you like it or not. Twenty years, max. In most countries, that's a life sentence.

A uniformed guard taps her dangerously on the shoulder, startling her, Pilar's fingers almost slipping across the line of mutilation. She pulls away angrily, her shout of protest lost in the noise. The guard indicates an elevated office in the back of the building. She exchanges glances with Maria and Lupita as she's guided towards the stairs. Pilar feels like a prisoner suddenly being escorted out of her cell on Death Row. But is she heading towards reprieve or execution? The steps she's mounting sure feel like a scaffold.

The guard closes the door behind them and immediately the noise level is halved. Pilar feels like sagging with relief, but instead makes sure she straightens her back as she stares defiantly at the sweatshop manager, López. The buttons of his expensive shirt strain under pressure from a belly that has grown with the size of his bonuses.

Standing to the side of the room are Fuentes and Gomez, the two detectives from the crime scene. López points to Pilar. 'Is this the one?' Fuentes glances mildly at her, then nods. López turns back to Pilar. 'You're fired.'

Pilar stands there, stunned by the arbitrariness of the action, her face flushing with anger. She takes a step towards the desk, the security guard yanking her back. She pulls away from his touch with disgust. 'You think firing me is going to stop the killings?'

'Keeping you here isn't going to stop them, that's for fucking sure.' López nods and the guard grabs her by the arm. She tries to pull free from his clutch but he's not letting her get away again. He opens the door, noise racketing in. Pilar twists around, staring back at López.

'And my pay?'

'Fuck your pay. It'll go towards making up for all the time wasted by your little demonstration this morning.'

Pilar turns to the two detectives. Gomez shrugs. Pilar's eyes blaze with cynical confirmation. What the hell is she expecting from these two cops – support? She must be out of her mind. 'You stand by the bosses when they fire us, and you stand by the killers when they murder us.'

Gomez whistles with mock trepidation, and Pilar is yanked out of the office. She manages to slam the door hard behind her.

'Doesn't she realize there are thousands like her, just waiting to take her place? The stupid cunt.'

'Hey! She's somebody's daughter, show some respect.' Fuentes crosses to the desk, making a money gesture with his fingers. López looks at him, feigning bewilderment. 'Hand it over.'

Sighing theatrically, López pulls some bank notes out of his wallet. 'I suppose you're going to give it to her?'

Fuentes snaps his fingers impatiently. 'All of it.' López hesitates and Fuentes snatches his wallet from his hand, pulls out a wad, then tosses the empty wallet back.

López stares at the bereaved wallet as though it has a bullet hole in it. 'You're exaggerating!'

'So the fuck are you.' Fuentes shoves the money inside his jacket and leaves. Gomez blows López a kiss, following his partner out.

López thumps the table, shouting after them, 'Motherfucking thieving cops!'

The staccato of needles and heave of heavy machinery recedes as Pilar walks out through the doorway, towards a vaulting desert sky. She puts a hand up against the dazzle and heads towards the bus stop on the highway, walking across an enormous field of obliterated glass glittering like cheap trinkets in the sunlight. Without the buses, the improvised parking space outside the factories is transformed into a huge wasteland, empty now except for a cluster of a dozen cars surrounded by men drinking beer.

One of the men calls out to her as she passes. 'Hey, *chica*, come and have a beer.' Pilar moves on, not glancing in his direction. The man begins to follow her. 'Come on, baby, all I want is a black kiss.' His friends laugh. Pilar increases her pace, passing another man urinating between two cars. He turns to Pilar, exposing himself, still pissing. 'Hey, *nalgona*, want to suck me?' Pilar mutters an insult as she swerves away. She can hear footsteps behind her. She glances back. The first man is following her. 'Be nice or we'll make you be nice.'

The man who was pissing also starts following her, his fly still undone. 'We know how to make you be nice.'

Pilar wheels on them, pulling out a set of door keys and waving them menacingly. 'Try anything, you assholes, and I'll take someone's eyes out, I swear!' She glares at the other men standing around the cars. 'Whose eyes will they be?' She points to the man who was pissing. 'Yours, motherfucker?' The man takes a step back, zipping up his fly, watching her. Pilar feigns masturbating like a man. 'Not you. You'll go blind without my help.' The other men laugh and he shoves one of them angrily. Pilar surveys the group. 'Take a look at yourselves, drunk in the morning while your wives and sweethearts work themselves to death in the *maquiladoras* to pay your rent. You're fucking pathetic, all of you!'

As soon as she says it, she knows she's gone too far. Their eyes collectively harden. They're no longer lazy, dishonest men lounging around their cars drinking beer.

They're a pack.

Pilar turns and marches off, breathing hard to control her anger and her fear. One of the men shouts after her. 'Come back and suck us, you fucking whore.' Behind her is the ominous growl of a car engine starting up.

Pilar fights the urge to break into a full run. Approaching fast from behind is the sound of tires crushing gravel. She can feel the heat from the engine. The car brakes hard, sending dust blooming all around it. She picks up a rock and turns, facing a black sedan.

Two doors slam as the dust settles, revealing Fuentes and Gomez standing on either side of their car. Gomez holds up his hands in mock surrender. 'Please, lady, don't hit us.'

Pilar glares at him, taking a step back towards the highway. 'Leave me alone.'

'I'd like to offer you a lift back to town.'

She turns to Fuentes. 'Do I look stupid enough to accept a lift from the police?'

Fuentes sighs. 'All right then, I'd like to offer you a choice. Either you accept a lift, or I arrest you. But one thing's for sure: I'm not going to leave you alone with those sad motherfuckers back there.'

Gomez opens the front passenger door with a flourish, smiling sarcastically. Pilar hesitates, unable to disguise her fear. She looks from the detectives to the beer drinkers around the cars, all watching intently. She turns back to Fuentes. 'You two get in first, then I'll get in the back. On my own . . .'

Fuentes and Gomez exchange pained looks but obey, shutting their doors with exaggerated slams. Pilar stands there, not moving, listening to the tick of the engine block in the heat. She glances back at the parked cars. The man who was pissing smashes a beer bottle against the ground, staring at her.

Gomez sticks his head out of his window, slapping the door with his hand. 'Hey, *señorita*? Your taxi is waiting.'

Pilar circles around the car, dropping the rock as she climbs into the back, the car lurching forwards before she even closes the door. She turns, staring out the back window, yellow dust rising behind them, blocking her view of the jeering men. She straightens, looking ahead. Fuentes' eyes are framed in the rear-view mirror, watching her. Gomez turns, his arm across the back of Fuentes' seat. 'What the fuck is wrong with this country when a woman can't accept a ride from the police without being afraid?'

'I didn't make this country, I just live in it.'

'So do we, *chica*, so do we.' With a sigh of disgust, Gomez turns back to the road. The slur of gears tests the uneasy silence as they hump up onto the highway. Pilar looks back at the rows of *maquiladoras*, all the anger and fear now replaced with a flooding despair. How could she have let this happen – at the worst possible time?

The ring of a cell phone makes Pilar jump. Gomez speaks brusquely, then hangs up. Fuentes looks at him as he drives. 'Fucking nothing,' Gomez says. 'Someone turned into toast at a hotel. I told them to leave it for the *delegación* to handle. Probably a drunk with a cigarette. Nearly happened to my father. I woke up in the middle of the night once and the house was full of smoke, only I was too young to even know it was smoke. Know what I thought it was?'

'No, but I have a feeling you're going to tell me.'

'I thought it was ectoplasm. Some kind of spiritual shit. I was so excited, I just about pissed myself. I thought I was going to see a real live ghost.'

'Only ghosts are dead.'

'That's the trouble with you. No sense of humor.'

'Ghosts are not funny.'

'See what I mean? You're a literal kind of man. Nobody likes it when you're so fucking literal. *Ghosts are dead. Ghosts are not funny.* Technically you're right, but who cares?'

'Technically I'm wrong because there's no such thing as ghosts.'

'There you go again! Lighten up, man, I'm just trying to tell a story.'

'So tell it.'

'I will when you stop interrupting me . . .' He turns to Pilar for a response but she's staring out the window. She feels his eyes on her and glares at him, pulling out a cigarette and lighting it. 'Those things will kill you,' Gomez says, looking at her hands. They're shaking. 'Like this sorry drunk at the hotel. Like my old man.' Pilar holds onto the door handle, going back to staring out her side window. Gomez gives a fast snort of frustration. He's a man who's used to people listening to his stories. And here he is, stuck in a car with two people who may as well be asleep. Gomez sulks, the car slowing as they enter the city center.

'So what about your old man?'

Gomez stares at Fuentes, trying to decide if he's just riding him or not. 'My old man? I found him downstairs, asleep on the sofa, right next to a cushion that was burning.'

'And he was dead?'

'Why do you say a thing like that?'

'You said: *like this sorry drunk at the hotel and like my old man.*'

27

'Well, what I meant was one burnt himself to death, and one – my old man – died of lung cancer.'

'That's not the same as what you said.'

Gomez turns to Pilar. 'Come on, please, just for once help me out here. Tell him that's not what I meant.'

Pilar looks at him. 'I wasn't listening.'

Fuentes smiles. 'She's got sense.'

'And you don't – is that what you're saying?'

'I don't have a choice, is what I'm saying: you're my partner.' The car pulls over on a busy street. Fuentes turns in his seat, gesturing extravagantly to the crowds. 'Plenty of *witnesses*. You should be safe.' Pilar goes to open the door, but Fuentes taps the lock down. 'One more thing . . .'

Fuentes turns and motions with his chin for Gomez to get out of the car. Gomez is surprised but obeys, shooting Pilar a resentful look. Fuentes shifts in his seat, staring at Pilar. She meets his gaze at first, but then looks away. Fuentes reaches into his jacket and pulls out the money he took from López. He holds it out to her. 'Your pay. I made him hand it over.'

'After making him fire me . . . ?' Pilar stares at the money, not touching it. Her voice breaks with anger. 'He'd give it to you, but not to me? The person who earned it? That motherfucker!'

Fuentes waves the notes in front of her. 'Hey? My arm's getting tired.'

Pilar hesitates a moment longer, then snatches the money. 'Don't expect me to thank you.'

'It never crossed my mind.'

Pilar leafs through the bank notes. 'It's way too much.'

'Must be your birthday.'

'*Claro.*' Pilar goes to pop open the lock but Fuentes puts his hand over it. 'I used to work in Tijuana.' Something ripples across Pilar's face, then is gone. 'You're good, you know that? Real good.' She glares at him defiantly, trying to brazen it out. 'You heard what I said: I was in Tijuana.'

'What did you do there, line up girls for *gringos*?'

Fuentes doesn't react to the insult, his eyes studying her face. 'I arrested you. For organizing an illegal strike.'

'You're mistaken.' Pilar's voice wavers. 'I've never been to Tijuana.'

Fuentes shakes his head, pulling up the shirt cuff of the hand over the lock, revealing the back of his wrist. There is an unmistakable scar: a set of tooth marks. 'You left a calling card.'

Pilar looks from the scar up to Fuentes' face. She is remembering him. He smiles when he sees the recognition in her eyes. 'That's right . . .' He pops the lock and Pilar gets out fast.

Fuentes follows her, catching her by the arm. 'I want you to know. I'm not here for labor disputes.'

'What else would you be here for?'

He lifts his head, indicating the building he parked in front of. Pilar glances up at the sign. *City Morgue.* 'What can you tell me about the girl they found this morning?'

'Her first name was Isabel. She was paid less than five pesos an hour. And nobody came when she called for help.' Without another word, she turns, walking quickly away.

Gomez comes up behind Fuentes, staring after Pilar. 'Boss, you're so desperate you'd fuck a *maquiladora* girl?'

Fuentes rubs his scarred wrist. 'She's no *maquiladora* girl. She's a CTON union organizer. One of the best.' He looks up, watching her disappearing. 'She's a goddamn stick of dynamite.'

Gomez smiles, staring down the street with renewed interest,

29

but Pilar is already lost in the street crowd. He turns back to Fuentes and motions to his chest. 'Really nice tits.'

Fuentes pushes past his partner, going up the steps into the morgue. Gomez smiles. He knows he's scored. He lights a cigarette, watching a pretty young woman passing by, feeling pleased with himself for the first time that morning.

7

Ventura

Ventura drives the Mercedes 280 SL through the old town, heads turning as she passes. It's the third car Carlos has bought since they moved up here from Mexico City fifteen months ago. He got it on a whim but kept it mainly in the garage, preferring his Hummer for country trips and the Bimmer for the city. The convertible has become Ventura's by default. She loves the way it makes her work when she drives it, paying her back with reliability and a throaty purr.

The rhythmic hum of tires ribbing the cobblestones begins to cede to the fast smear of blacktop and the roar of eighteen-wheelers as Ventura leaves the colonial center for the new airport; stone, stucco and hand-painted tiles giving way to plywood, cardboard and cinder block.

Much of what Ventura drives through just didn't exist when she was born here in 1973. She spent her childhood amongst the churches and patula pines of the old town, with weekend excursions to the tennis and pony clubs out at Las Altas, a chic colony built for the new breed of businessmen arriving with MBAs, maids and Mercs. The clubs' manicured lawns with their outdoor piped music were her only memory of the outskirts of Ciudad Real before her family left for Mexico City at the height of the '82 crisis; certainly not these shantytowns she's passing – blue plastic sheeting and rusted corrugated tin fashioning a tattered patchwork of poverty across a sheet of hard yellow desert.

A shadow rushes over the road and she peers up at Carlos' plane coming in to land, dust trailing behind it, plastic bags ballooning fast into the air.

Carlos is on the phone when he comes out of the terminal, but still manages to kiss her – on the cheek. They've been together for almost three years: sufficient time for the first passion to have faded, but not long enough to stop believing it might return.

Ventura pulls away from the curb, the windsocks pointing her back to the city, Carlos alternately cajoling then pleading with someone on the phone. Neither seems to work because they hang up on him. He curses with a savage laugh. She waits in the hot silence for what seems like an eternity. 'Hello,' she says.

He actually looks at her for the first time since he arrived. 'Sorry.' He leans across and kisses her on the cheek again. 'New York is having a shitty day. Don't slow,' he says, leaning over and tapping the horn, the street vendors moving out of the way. 'A really shitty day. I should have known. The Hang Seng and Tokyo were both down five percent last night.'

'How was Culiacán?'

'Rough. Try explaining even basic fund management to morons like them. They were all shitting in my milk just because the Nasdaq is down. Big deal. Tomorrow it'll be up again, but no, they've got to panic. Did they want to pull their money last year? They were begging me to take it. They couldn't hand it to me fast enough. But now . . .' His phone rings. He glances at the number. 'Like this one, harassing me morning, noon and night.' He folds the phone. 'They're like fucking animals.'

'I know you've been under a lot of pressure lately.' His laugh's a bite. 'Maybe you should think about scaling back.'

'You sound like one of my clients. Now is exactly *not* the time to scale back. I thought you of all people would understand.'

'I'm just saying—'

'Don't interrupt. This is unique; a once-in-a-century chance. Millions are being made *right now*. And if you're not making them, you're losing them, because this opportunity is never coming back. *Never*. Take the next left.' Ventura follows the sign pointing to the border, then looks at him, not understanding. 'I have to drop by the bank.'

'Don't you want to go home first?'

'It can't wait.'

Ventura stares at the border crossing coming into view, long lines of cars stretching way beyond the bridge. She looks at her watch with exasperation. 'Well, I can't drive you across, I have an appointment in an hour.'

'Cancel it.'

'I can't. It's with Felipe Mayor.'

His phone rings. He glances at the screen. 'Who the hell is this?'

'Don't answer. We're talking.'

He hesitates, then takes the call. '*Bueno?*' He grimaces like he's been kicked in the shin. 'Señor Santiago? How are you?' A furious voice shouts across the electromagnetic spectrum, filling the car with its substantial anger. 'I'm only just boarding now . . .' Ventura glances away from the lie. 'I know, but a passenger was sick. Today? It's going to be difficult with this delay. How about tomorr—' Ventura turns, shocked at the violence emanating from the phone. Carlos looks faint from its force. '*Thirty* percent? Are you sure?' Carlos swears weakly, defeated

33

by the response. 'I understand your concerns but it's really nothing to worry about. These movements are normal. It's just part of a minor correction . . . I know I promised, but—'

The caller hangs up, the relief of silence flooding the car.

'Who the hell was that *pendejo*?'

'The person I've been trying to avoid.' Carlos curses. 'That's what I was getting in Culia-fucking-cán. They trust you enough to make them money, but they never trust you enough not to lose it.' His phone rings.

'Don't answer it.'

Carlos sees the number. 'I've got to take this one. *Sí . . . ?*' There's a long, painful pause. Then he hangs up.

'Carlos, what's going on?'

'The same shit, baby, always the same old shit.'

Ventura pulls up a block before the footbridge. 'Have you got your papers?' Carlos nods. 'Leave your luggage in the car. It will only slow you down.'

Carlos gets out. 'Look . . .' His phone rings. He answers it and, without so much as a wave, heads off towards the crossing.

She fossicks irritably for a pack of cigarettes hiding somewhere deep inside her camera bag . . . Looking up suddenly as footsteps hurry towards her; her smile already fading as he covers his phone with his hand. 'Mayor's loaded. Try and set up a meeting with me, okay.'

She watches him trotting back towards the border, the phone against his ear, then she pulls out into the traffic, accelerating away from the wail of horns.

8

Fuentes

Fuentes hurries through the keening odors of bleach and vinegar that saturate the public section of the morgue, as though death were just another microbe that could be scoured away. He stops a passing intern in a soiled smock just outside the autopsy area. 'Do you have the results from the homicide this morning?'

'Which one?'

It's always hard to hear that question. 'The female they found outside the *maquiladora*.'

The kid starts to glance down a clipboard but then he remembers. 'They haven't done her yet.' Fuentes looks at his watch, the only outward sign of how irritated he is. But it's enough for the intern to pick up on. He steps back defensively. 'It's not our fault. The first priest we brought in wouldn't perform Last Rites. He said she was a whore.'

Fuentes lets out a barely audible curse. Partly, it was the tendency to allow sentimentality to get in the way of forensic science. But mainly it was the Church itself that fed the fear and the superstition; that grew strong and rich on ignorance. The Church was supposed to be there to help its faithful, but too often all it did was torment its own believers. Most priests seemed to prefer playing devil to angel.

Millions of Mexicans were already being denied the other sacramental blessings – the communions and the confessions and the marriages and the baptisms – simply because they were using contraception or were divorced or gay, or sympathetic towards the Zapatistas. And now they were even punishing the dead. The PRI should never have allowed the Church to reacquire its power and influence. It was like a cunning henhouse thief: once bitten on the heel, he starts to wear boots – not just to protect his ankles but to better kick the guard dog next time. 'Luckily Padre Márcio came by.'

Fuentes stares at him. '*The* Padre Márcio? I thought he was in Juárez now.'

'He visits all the time.' Fuentes turns. It's Gomez. 'He has an orphanage on the other side of town. If it weren't for him, half the girls would never have received final blessing.'

It takes a moment for Fuentes to realize that Gomez is not being sarcastic. He follows Gomez through the doors to the autopsy room. The body of the victim lies naked on a stainless-steel mortuary slab, a yellow label hanging from her left ankle, marked *NN* with the day's date. A man in a black suit stands over her, his back to Fuentes, the clerical collar just visible.

The priest turns when he hears them. He is a tall man in his early sixties. Arctic gray eyes are framed by the snowy abundance of a thick beard and flowing hair that is part messiah, part Manson. He is the legendary general of the Army of Jesus.

Gomez steps forwards and kisses the ring on the priest's finger. Padre Márcio bows, more with embarrassment than approval. Fuentes goes to shake hands, but the priest only offers the tips of his fingers. The palms of both of his hands are covered by mottled fingerless lace gloves. 'Your Grace,' Fuentes says deliberately.

36

'I am a mere priest.' I know, Fuentes thinks, so why did you let Gomez kiss your fucking ring? 'But I try to do what I can.'

'Father, I need to examine the body . . .' Márcio glances back at the corpse, not stepping aside. 'I'm sorry, Father, but I have to ask you to leave.'

Ignoring Fuentes, Márcio makes the sign of the cross over the body, whispers something, and then bows down and kisses the foot of the dead woman. Gomez crosses himself, as surprised as Fuentes by what the priest has just done.

Márcio turns away from the corpse, tears warming his cold eyes as he stares at Fuentes. 'Find the man who did this.'

'We will do our best, Father.'

Padre Márcio turns to Gomez, his voice brittle with disdain. 'God does not require one's best efforts, God requires one's total, sincere devotion. Faith must be absolute or it is not faith.' Gomez bows his head, chastened. Who would have thought? The fucking kid has a soul if not a conscience. 'You must have faith in yourself; in your ability to find this monster. You must believe. Otherwise, you leave the door open.'

'Open to what, Father?' Márcio turns back to Fuentes, and his look sends a chill down the detective's spine. It's not the look of a saint. It's the look of a killer. Perhaps that's what a good priest is: a stone-cold killer of sin.

'The devil himself,' the priest says.

They both watch him leave. Gomez shivers. He must have felt it too. The power inside the man. All that pissed-off, godly wrath. 'You see those hands? He's a fucking saint. You can tell. The way he kissed her foot. Like Mary goddamn Magdalene.'

'Mary Magdalene was a prostitute. And that's what the first priest called Isabel. But she's no Mary Magdalene. Isabel was a hard-working young woman.' She was so much more than that. She was innocent. She was exploited because she was poor. And then she was raped and butchered and thrown out with the trash.

Fuentes stands over Isabel's body. 'It's just like the man said . . .'

'Padre Márcio?'

'The boss in the *maquiladora* this morning: *There are thousands like her, just waiting to take her place.*'

The doors burst open, making Gomez jump, and a forensic pathologist and the young intern enter.

Fuentes turns to Gomez. 'You can go if you want.' Fuentes puts on latex gloves, watching Gomez walking away on the other side of the glass panes in the door until the sound of an electric saw brings him back to reality.

9

Pilar

Pilar waits in a plaza crowded with buses disgorging the women coming back from the *maquiladoras*, the next shift already pushing impatiently past them, desperate to board. There are fewer buses in the afternoon, and that means many of the workers will have to stand all the way out to the factories.

Some of the women getting off the buses recognize Pilar, moving quickly out of her way lest she contaminate them with her latest condition: unemployment.

Pilar spots Maria and Lupita in the crowd and shoves her way towards them. They all embrace. 'Did they talk to you?'

Maria shakes her head. 'We're both safe.'

Pilar wants to burst into tears of frustration but she's stronger than that. She smiles. 'That still leaves two of us!'

'It's not enough,' Lupita says, too quickly to be anything but the truth.

The three women cross the square, past the boys selling cartons of illegal cigarettes and boxes of paper tissues and little bags of pumpkin seeds, and turn a corner, entering an apartment building constructed in the 1960s, when the whole town was optimistic about the future; when everyone still believed in the Mexican Miracle.

In those days, the people of Ciudad Real considered themselves fortunate. They lived on a border with the most powerful and attractive nation on earth. There were plenty of jobs on the other side too; jobs that the *gringos* would never dream of doing themselves.

Back then there was easy credit, low inflation and full employment. US politicians were focused on oil subsidies, military contracts and the Cold War, not on illegal immigration, collapsing manufacturing and the War on Drugs. That 1960s *Yanqui* optimism spread south.

Times were good.

Before the killings.

Before the *narcos*.

Before the economic crises and the currency collapse; the devaluations and the inflation and the recessions.

Before NAFTA.

Now most of the decorative tiles on the front facade of the building are missing and rust stains from broken guttering streak the exterior. Now times are not so good, and it doesn't look like they'll improve in this generation. The women take the stairs. The elevator is broken. For good.

Pilar taps twice on a door and sees the light from the peephole eclipsed for a brief moment. There is the sound of a chain unslotting, two deadlocks turning and then the door springs open, afternoon sunlight blinding them, Juan Antonio ushering them in quickly, then locking the door. Pilar tries to speak but he silences her with a finger to his lips. 'Not without a drink.'

The women look at each other as he rattles beer bottles out of an ancient refrigerator, passing them along. 'I don't know about you but, *puta madre*, I need one.'

'It wasn't her fault,' Lupita says.

Juan Antonio snaps the cap off against the edge of the kitchen table, foam erupting in outrage at the violence. He takes a long swig of beer, then sighs. 'It was entirely her fault.'

'Fuck you!' Pilar gets angry the way she always does when she's made a mistake. 'We still have Maria and Lupita in there.'

'I wanted you! That's why we brought you in from Tijuana. We need *you* here.'

'What else could I have done?'

'Shown some discipline for once and stuck with the plan.'

'They dumped her body outside – was that part of the plan?'

Juan Antonio takes another long drink, then slams the empty bottle down on the table. 'A year's work, fucked in a single morning, wasn't part of the plan either.'

'She was just lying there, in the trash.' There are tears welling in her eyes. 'I couldn't just . . .' Leave her there like that; pretend not to see her. Pretend it didn't happen. 'She was put out like garbage. You want us to ignore that?'

'Jesus, Pilar, that's not what I'm asking you to do.'

'It sounds like that to me.'

'There's only one way to stop the killings and that's to humanize the *maquiladoras*. Once the women have unions, they have protection. Cause and effect. Until that happens, they will never be safe because no one will fear harming them. You of all people know that.' Pilar gives him an agonized look and turns away.

Lupita gestures behind Pilar's back for Juan Antonio to calm down. He goes over to Pilar, putting an arm around her shoulders, his voice softening. 'I understand how you feel, but we have to be strong. We have to be exemplary at all times. We have to prioritize our actions.' Pilar nods, martyred to the logic of the Cause. Again. 'But now we have no choice. We have to bring the strike forward.'

Pilar glances helplessly at Lupita and Maria. 'That's impossible.'

Juan Antonio takes the untouched beer from Pilar's hands and pops the lid. 'Emotion renders our tasks more difficult, but it should never stop us from reaching our goals.' He pauses, staring out at the balcony, spider web phosphorous in the glare of the sun. 'We need to take the force of all that emotion and make it work for us.'

'How do we do that?' Lupita asks.

He takes a sip of beer, thinking, then smiles with the answer. 'We find out when the funeral is . . .'

10

Ventura

It's the last place you'd ever expect to find Mexico's most famous writer eating lunch. Raw concrete floors. Corrugated-iron roof; next to a wholesale automobile accessory store. Felipe Mayor is more Michelin than Goodyear.

Mayor was born into a wealthy family with land holdings in Jalisco, Sonora and Chihuahua and banking interests across Spain and Latin America. His father had profited from close contacts with dictators on both sides of the Atlantic in the period after the Second World War until his mysterious death in Santo Domingo in 1964. The trust fund he'd established for his only child kept Felipe Mayor at a safe legal distance from the origins of the family's fortune, allowing him to turn his antiseptically clean hands towards more interesting occupations than making money: writer; diplomat; international libertine. A perennial candidate for the Nobel Prize for Literature, some see him as too controversial to win, others as too commercial. He's been poured into the same middlebrow alphabet soup as Mailer, Moravia and Malraux.

But here he is, sitting in a steak house in Ciudad Real wearing jeans and riding boots, looking more like a *ranchero* than a literary aristocrat. The only outward sign of his true identity is the neatly maintained, elegant moustache – a fastidious monument to the vanity of a silver-haired man content to spend hours of his life in front of a bathroom mirror.

A flash of sunlight slaps his face as a door opens, the restaurant going quiet with the intrusion. Ventura is younger than she sounded on the phone, with long, sun-bleached hair carelessly pulled back into a loose ponytail. She wears a white tank top, the air-raid siren of jungle camouflage pants and the surprise of a gold Rolex. Taking off her sunglasses, she surrenders her eyes to the restaurant's gloom. When she spots Mayor she gives him a relaxed smile. She's been behind the scenes of enough fashion photo shoots not to be intimidated by fame.

'Ventura Medina, I presume.' Mayor rises from his seat with a courtly bow.

'Thank you for seeing me, Señor Mayor,' she says, sitting down opposite him. 'I really appreciate your time.'

'When you get to be my age, you'll appreciate it even more.' Her laugh is a relaxed caress. He smiles, pleased as any author who has found his audience. 'I was very impressed by your portfolio. Especially your portraits.' Mayor holds up two fingers to the waiter. 'You mentioned that you're a friend of Francesca Ellis?'

'We went to art school together in Italy. She was the one who gave me your contact details.'

'Of course. I spent a lot of time with her parents.'

'Francesca told me all the stories – especially the outrageous ones.' She gives him a knowing grin.

He sighs nostalgically. 'Times were different back then. Everything seemed so . . . innocent.' He leans back, nodding thanks to the waiter who places two large frosted glasses of beer in front of them. 'Every generation makes its choice about the way it wants to live – and it doesn't always have to be with war.' He raises his glass and they toast. Ventura doesn't normally drink at lunch but her parting with Carlos makes her grateful for the icy needle of alcohol puncturing her annoyance; her concern about him, and the way he has changed. She looks up, realizing that she hasn't been listening. '. . . brings you to Ciudad Real?'

'Apart from you?' He grins, pleased with her mocking fearlessness. 'I recently moved back here from Mexico City.'

'Your first mistake.'

Again that caressing laugh, a flutter of lightness in a heavy city. 'My partner's business is based along the border. I wanted to spend more time with him.'

Mayor is disappointed to hear mention of a companion so early in the conversation. 'It's a typical story, I'm afraid: a woman forced to sacrifice her own career so that her husband's can flourish.'

'I know, only we're not married, and—'

'And you are not a typical woman.' He smiles with perfect teeth. 'I can see that from your work. You mentioned an interview and taking some photos?'

'It would help me enormously.'

His eyebrows rise with feigned modesty. 'May I ask what magazine it's for?'

'It's not for a magazine, it's for a book . . . And to be frank, I need your name to help me sell it.'

He laughs, delighted by the confession. Unlike most powerful people, Mayor still values honesty. 'Splendid. That makes us partners.' Two rare steaks appear, the meat overlapping the rims of the plates. Mayor picks up his knife and fork, carving with gusto. 'My father bought land up here. Not for the proximity to the border. Not for the incentives. For this. The finest steak in the world.' He takes a bite and gives a hum of satisfaction. 'My father would cook it straight on the coals. Just toss the meat in and watch the flesh char black.'

Ventura slices through her steak, the bottom of her plate running red. She hasn't had a meal like this for years. Carlos refuses to eat red meat. There is so much stress in his life, he says, the last thing he needs is to worry about cholesterol. She takes a bite and is transported back to Sundays at Las Altas and communal barbecues around the swimming pool, juggling plates in laps and brushing away flies.

'I can see you've got spirit,' Mayor says, watching with satisfaction as she eats. 'So what is this famous book of yours about?'

Ventura glances around then leans forwards, whispering, 'It's about the murdered women of Ciudad Real.'

Mayor slowly crosses his knife and fork, his appetite suddenly gone. 'Like you, I grew up in Ciudad Real. And like you, I escaped; only to return here. So perhaps you'll understand when I say that home is the first place you ever want to leave but the last place you'd think of finding the end of the world.'

'You can trust me to get to the heart of this story,' she says, not paying the slightest attention to what he's just said.

'I don't doubt it,' he lies.

'I've already done a huge amount of research.'

He takes a sip of his beer, pausing diplomatically. 'Research is just the opinion of others, and in this case, mostly of people you shouldn't trust. If you really want to face this challenge, you must free your mind from everything you've heard or read. But most of all, you must be careful.'

Ventura has some idea of what she is up against. Over eight hundred murdered; zero suspects. Numbers that don't add up. Her instincts tell her the government is to blame, the way it is to blame for all the other massive numerical failures: the trade deficits, the exchange rates, the tax increases. The spiraling inflation. But where should she start with all these numbers? That's the real reason she has reached out to Mayor; not because it is frightening, but because it is so overwhelming. 'How should I begin?'

'The way we always do: by asking questions.'

'Who is behind the killings?'

'Think about it: the simplest questions are always the hardest to ask.'

Ventura takes a deep breath, not so much wanting to impress Mayor as afraid that she won't. She puts her fork down and tries again. 'How do I find a question that nobody wants to answer?'

Mayor drains his beer with satisfaction. 'I am so glad you asked.'

11

Fuentes

It's not the way you might imagine. No matter how many autopsy reports you read, you never become desensitized. The opposite actually happens: each new report impacts at a higher emotional level. Scientific and medical euphemisms offer no protection from the underlying savagery of the murders; from the despair of not being able to stop the killings.

Hundreds of victims; dozens of different locations, yet the specificities of the crimes are nearly always identical. Rape. Strangulation. Signature torture signs, most of them kept secret. If you let out details like that, people who would never even think of killing might be tempted to do so. Contamination, followed by compulsion. It's like Guinea worm. Once it burrows in, you can never get it out. It just keeps boring its hole until you both die.

Hardly anyone knows about these concealed acts of obscure mutilation, yet they have been performed on almost all of the victims. The most obvious conclusion is as dramatic as it is impossible: a lone serial killer, with perhaps one or two inept copycat killers to explain the occasional fluctuation that chance or circumstance cannot.

Fuentes knows what all good detectives quickly learn: that with homicides the most obvious conclusion is usually the right one.

Three out of ten murders are domestic disputes. Five out of

ten are professional criminals settling accounts amongst themselves; these days mainly about drugs. Another ten percent are the accidental outcome of spontaneous, opportunistic crimes. How many times has Fuentes heard the sobbed phrases?

I didn't know anyone was in the house.

It was an accident, I swear.

He wouldn't stay down.

Criminals rarely think about the consequences because they rarely *think*. Most do what they do because there is nothing else that they can do: they are uneducated, unimaginative; without hope. Neglected or abandoned children, crushed by poverty, often abused physically or sexually in institutions or on the street. Forced out of school. *Escape* becomes *break in*. Climbing through a window is instinctive, not logical.

Whatever the cause, the solution to the crime is usually lying right next to the murder weapon. Which nine times out of ten is covered with fingerprints.

Nine times out of ten you don't have to be Columbo. It's that ten percent margin that makes all the difference. The crimes that are premeditated. The crimes where risk has been carefully weighed against consequence. Crimes not of passion or opportunity but of calculated precision. Crimes of intent and therefore decipherable.

Solvable.

Convictable.

And then there are the black hole crimes, outside all statistical reference because of their scope and savagery.

Crimes like the murders of the women of Ciudad Real.

Over eight hundred women murdered in ten years. Not counting the hundreds who have disappeared. Argentina and

Chile didn't teach the world what the generals wanted everyone to believe: that when there are no bodies, there are no victims. Instead Argentina and Chile taught us that when there are no bodies, the conspiracy reaches to the highest levels of the State.

Whatever is happening in Ciudad Real, powerful men have to know about it; are perhaps even involved. It is the lesson of the Juntas. Fuentes chose to transfer here because he knows what so many other policemen don't: exactly what he is up against. It awes him. It overwhelms him. But somehow, in a way he never understands, it doesn't frighten him because he knows in his gut he is going to solve these murders.

Starting with Isabel's.

His desk phone rings. He picks up the receiver, listens for a moment, then glances across the room to a glassed-in office. He hangs up without a word, then gets up and crosses to the office, entering without knocking.

Captain Valdez indicates one of the chairs facing a huge oak desk empty except for two telephones and an overflowing quartz ashtray. The universal prerogative of all bosses. No work. 'Where's Gomez?'

It's not because he's his superior that Fuentes doesn't trust Valdez. And it's not even because of the way he looks – the aesthete's high forehead exaggerated by the receding hairline; the cruel inquiry of his wire-rimmed glasses that balance the weak chin, bestowing the scholarly scorn of an aging yet still canny dictator. It is the disdainful distance all foot soldiers and field men maintain from the bureaucrats; the mutual knowledge that Fuentes is in another, higher moral orbit and there is nothing Valdez could do about it, even if he wanted to – which he doesn't. Why would he? Why cross the border of that expensive empty oak desk to the seat on the other side? Where risks are measured not by press releases and signatures on cables but by bullets and booby-trapped front doors. They work in the same office but they may as well be on opposite sides of the globe.

'He's eating, why?'

'One of our men has just been picked up in El Lobo. He had forty-two kilos of cocaine inside a car.'

Every time Fuentes hears about a corrupt cop, it feels like it's a personal insult. Cops take huge risks every day and for what? Everybody still hates them. They get paid fuck all and there's so much money out there, available just for turning a blind eye. It's tempting. It's understandable.

But it's unforgivable.

Because every corrupt cop places pressure on the honest ones; puts their lives in jeopardy. Why waste your time trying to bribe someone who doesn't want to be bought? Just put a bullet in them and move on to more reasonable relationships.

'Was it an official car?'

'Be thankful for small mercies. It was registered to an American woman, Mary-Ellen González from San Diego by way of Matamoros. Fifty percent *gringa*, hundred percent good-time girl.'

Fuentes accepts one of Valdez's cigarettes, even though he hates filters. They don't stop the cancer, they just make the slow death taste drier. 'She's being held too?'

'He was on his own. We don't know where she is.' Probably dead, Fuentes thinks. Unless she was an informer? Could even be entrapment. He wouldn't put it past Washington. He keeps his ideas to himself. It's safer that way. 'Agents of the DEA are in town even as we speak,' Valdez says, 'exercising their extra-territorial right to investigate corrupt Mexicans while doing everything in their power to ignore corrupt *gringos*.'

Fuentes taps dead ash onto the floor. Valdez speaks like a politician because that's what you have to be to hold down a position like his. He waits what he considers a respectful time before asking: 'What's this got to do with me?'

'You're going to have to wait a little longer for US forensic assistance.' Fuentes swears. Valdez shrugs. That's the real difference between a field cop and his admin superior. 'This arrest has . . . well, changed their priorities.'

'As long as they're not *gringas*, they don't give a fuck about the murders. The only thing they care about is making it as hard as possible for their rich children to buy drugs.'

Valdez raises his eyes to heaven. 'They don't have a choice, you know that. They have to follow the lead of their congressmen and senators.'

'Who don't care about the kids in the ghettos.'

'And if they don't even care about their own poor, why should they care about ours? Look at it from their perspective. They didn't really trust us even before today's arrest.'

'And they're sure as hell not going to trust us now.'

'Exactly. And speaking of trust . . .' Valdez leans forwards, peering over the rims of his spectacles, his eyes alert, testing for lies. 'Can you trust Gomez?'

'Can you trust me?'

'I know I can trust you never to give me a straight answer.'

And I never will, Fuentes thinks. 'I trust my instincts. Why?'

'The cop they arrested was Paredes, Gomez's partner before you came along.' Fuentes tries not to show any reaction but

Valdez is sharp. He smiles maliciously at Fuentes. 'You're going to be tailed, you're going to be photographed, you're probably already being tapped.' He slides a piece of paper across the desk: there is an address written on it. 'So let's be careful, shall we?'

Fuentes stares at the paper, then lights it, dropping it into the ashtray. A section of the paper takes off, aflame, as though trying to escape before thinking better of it and spiraling back to earth with a bitter trail of smoke. It lands on the floor, crumpled into a fist of angry, curled embers. Fuentes steps on it on his way out, pausing at the door. 'You know, no matter what I do, I can't make you look good.'

Valdez shrugs magnanimously, pulling a sad face. 'Just don't make me look bad.'

12

Pilar

Juan Antonio is on the phone, absorbing the last rays of the sun outside on the balcony. As soon as it sets behind the hills, shadows will slither out of storm-water drains and slide off tiled roofs, staining the town with their cold gloom.

He glances inside through the glass sliding doors. The women have all showered and changed, and Maria and Lupita are trying to distract Pilar, joking about something on the internet.

Juan Antonio feels guilty about his outburst with Pilar. It's the way he often speaks to her these days: harsh and critical; devoid of any encouragement. He's only hard on her because he wants to help Pilar achieve her potential; to become not just a great union organizer, but a future political leader. A female voice on behalf of neglected women.

Besides, it was the way he was taught and it worked for him. He was trained by survivors of the Tlatelolco massacre, veterans who knew the meaning of struggle and the strength of ideology.

Thirty-two years later, it's still *Us against Them*, only the *Us* has grown in size and the *Them* contracted into something much darker and more dangerous. In the old days, *Them* was the ruling coalition of corrupt politicians who owned everything and shared nothing – except on the eve of elections. They were smug, fatuous and supremely certain of their control. Nowadays, the politicians and their allies have become a part of *Us*, the coalition of the weak and fearful; of the powerless. Now *Them* is the *narcos*. They control everything, including the *maquiladoras*. They don't just run the country, they're running it down. They are sucking it as dry as the skull of a longhorn baking in the Sonora desert.

Outside the building, a group of youths crosses the road slowly, looking up and down the street. They pause next to a black Dodge Super Bee. One of them puts his hand against the driver's window and peers inside, then quickly takes out a coat hanger bent into a hook. Juan Antonio covers his cell phone and calls out to the gang. 'Keep walking, assholes, that one's mine!'

The boys turn as one, looking up at the balcony and giving him a collective *mentada* before obediently moving on. Juan Antonio repeats a date on the phone as he cranes over the balcony, watching the gang disappear down the street.

He goes inside. Pilar looks up at him from the computer screen. 'Isabel Torres,' he says. 'She lived with her mother. In Anaprata.'

There's a sad silence. It is an added desecration. Isabel was second generation.

That was all part of the original lie when the factories first opened. Back then there had been jobs, lots of them. The problem was they were mainly for women. The women were told they could go to Ciudad Real on their own, find work easily, save up; improve their lives and return to their families with money. Everybody wins.

That had been the promise. But it rarely worked out that way. The work was regular but exhausting. The money was a little more than most places, but the cost of living was a lot

55

higher. Especially housing. It was expensive and hard to find. The factories and sweatshops went up overnight but housing was much slower. Shantytowns sprang up in a desperate attempt to keep pace with the *maquiladoras*. Basic services such as electricity, running water and sewage were lacking, as was public transport.

Almost all of the new female arrivals were young. Many fell pregnant. They needed help raising their children so they could return to work and start earning again. Mothers and sisters were drafted in. Housing and feeding one person became housing and feeding three. The numbers added up back home in Zacatecas or Durango or Chiapas. But once in Ciudad Real, they lost their easy elasticity. No matter how hard you tugged and pulled them, the numbers never seemed to stretch far enough.

Ask any *curandero*: the fever dream of fortune is easily broken with brutal but effective medicine – the ice-pack of freezing mountain nights spent in a makeshift hut or women's dormitory, followed by a hemorrhaging sweat induced by under-ventilated interiors ablaze with desert sun. The seductive mirage that brought hundreds of thousands of women up north quickly evaporated into a saltpan of tears and perspiration. And nothing grows in saline, not even bank accounts.

Anaprata was one of the first shantytowns to go up and it is still one of the poorest and most dangerous neighborhoods in town. But what choice did Isabel's mother have? Isabel Torres was born in Ciudad Real and that's where she died. She was a poor woman from an exploited class. Pilar mourns her fate but is not surprised by it. 'I'll go see her mother.'

'Do that. We're going to time the strike with the funeral. Of course we'll help out with expenses.'

'When's the funeral?' Lupita asks.

'In three days.'

The women exchange nervous looks. Juan Antonio is annoyed by the sudden unease. 'That's what you wanted, right? To bring the killings into the strikes?'

'Of course,' Maria says. 'But it doesn't give us much time.'

'That can't be helped. If we don't stay on top of events now, we'll be left behind.' He turns to Pilar. 'If we can get you into another *maquiladora*, do you think you can shut it down in time?'

Pilar stops and thinks, trying to find an honest answer: her reputation says *yes*. But what of her heart? It says *maybe*. 'I'll need an example. If Maria and Lupita can close their *maquiladora*, I know I can do the same.'

Juan Antonio puts an arm around Pilar's neck, pulls her towards him and kisses her on the crown of the head. 'It will be a triumph if only four of us can close down two *maquiladoras*!'

'How many other factories will strike?'

'At least fifty. Maybe even a hundred. This time they won't be able to ignore us. It'll be—' The air pressure swells and breaks across the room, heavy with the intent to harm. It surrounds them like an earth tremor, hammering at exteriors, before vibrating deep inside them, threatening to burst them all open with an expanding, internal traumatic shock.

Pilar sways, nauseated by its power, the noise of the blast already filling the room, consuming her with its velocity.

Then they are all on the floor, the air full of car alarms collectively screaming in panic, the rush of birds scattering shadows like shrapnel as they escape across the sky.

Juan Antonio is the first up, stepping carefully through the glass heaped around the balcony. He looks over the ledge, catching a glimpse of body parts through the black smoke. One of the youths is sobbing, propped against a wall, blood pumping from where his foot should be. Juan Antonio hurries back inside. 'Careful of the glass,' he says, helping Lupita up. 'Everyone's okay, yeah?'

Pilar helps Maria up. There is a single tear of blood on her cheek. 'Don't move . . .' Pilar removes the glassy thorn from Maria's face. It's surprisingly long.

Maria stares at it, amazed, then looks at Pilar. 'Can you smell gas?'

Pilar shakes her head. Behind her, Juan Antonio is snapping the laptop shut. 'We can't stay here tonight. We need to move.' Pilar takes a broom and starts sweeping, the glass rustling on the floor. Juan Antonio looks at her with disbelief. 'What the hell are you doing?'

'Cleaning up,' she says, her voice shaking and sounding far away through the ringing in her ears.

'We have to go.' He takes the broom from her trembling hands and holds her close. 'Don't you understand?' The first sirens are approaching in the distance. 'That was my car they just bombed.'

13

Ventura

The *maquiladoras* they pass look regimented and severe; more like internment camps than factories, with razor-wire fences and parade ground-size parking zones. 'All the victims worked in these sweatshops,' Ventura says to Mayor. 'That's why I need to get inside one.'

He stares at the industrial parks stretching off into the distance, forming a Brutalist vanishing point. 'But you have no experience.'

'Nor did any of the women when they first arrived here.' She turns her face away from the blast of a passing big rig.

'Certainly exploitation is a great equalizer,' Mayor says, waving the dust away.

They drive on in silence, soon passing smaller, older factories set between garbage dumps, fuel depots and abandoned cars.

And then there is nothing but the tan and brown countryside, with the olive sheen of vegetation in the distance, and beyond, the copper gleam of the border.

Mayor glances inside Ventura's camera bag, propped between them as she drives. All you need to know about a photographer is the type of camera they use. Nikon is professional but unimaginative; Canon is technique compensating for originality. Hasselblad is for control freaks, and Contax is for wedding photographers. But Leica is the really dangerous one. It's for disillusioned artists or overconfident amateurs. 'Leica . . .'

Ventura smiles proudly. 'Only the best, right?'

Mayor looks away. On the horizon, the ridged hills begin to rise in the south, the mountains beyond dun-colored and raw, soothed by strands of violet shade lying clever and concealed between peaks.

They are mountains that awe, mountains that threaten; not because of their height but because of their persistence, locked between the harsh topography and the blue sky, refusing to let go, to allow themselves to be eroded into more yellow and red desert, more sighing sand. They are defiant; reckless and noble as a bloodied fighter struggling to his feet on the count of eight.

'Where did you say we were going?' Mayor asks, his voice quavering as the car bucks over a stock gap.

'To Kilometer Zero.' Ventura turns back to the road, the sun reflecting off the vast whoosh of the red hood as it streaks over ancient bitumen curtained with gravel, with the slip and slide of shifting sand.

She leans forwards and turns on the radio, singing along with the song that is playing, '*Los caminos de la vida*'. Mayor watches her. She has a lovely voice, rich and expressive. He claps when she finishes. 'Do you always sing when you're afraid?'

She stares at him, both impressed and embarrassed. She decides to be honest. 'It's this countryside. It frightens me. Its isolation.' Her isolation within it. 'The number of young women who have died out here.' Her need to explore this story and the fear of where it might lead.

She pulls over suddenly, the air going quiet and hot as she kills the engine and with it the breeze. She looks around. There's absolutely nothing out there . . . Except for the place they're going to visit.

Ventura gets out her camera, changing her 50 mm lens for the 35 mm. Falling back on the routine of professional expertise calms her and restores her confidence. She takes the flowers from the back and sets off into the desert, Mayor following her along a battered path. It leads to a sandy knoll crowned by a cairn and littered with offerings broken by the elements and time. She places the flowers on the ground, securing them with a rock. Her camera whispers in the dry silence. 'This is where they found the body of the first victim.'

He leans down and brushes a cracked piece of glass that has been set with cement into the stone. Under the stained plate is the smear of what was once a photo, before humidity and sunlight dissolved it into a blistered blur.

'Have you ever been out here before?'

Mayor shakes his head in shame.

'It all started here. Ten years and more than eight hundred murdered women later, it shows no sign of stopping.'

Mayor scans the arid landscape as though searching for clues, his face cast in bronzed sunlight. She shoots him fast, the memorial in focus over his shoulder, looking ragged in the rasping wind. 'They dropped the first body here, far from town,' Ventura says, putting her camera down.

'They were afraid that they'd be seen.'

'I think they were also ashamed of their terrible crime. But over the years, as the number of victims grew, so did the killers' audacity. Now the bodies are left within the city limits.'

'Impunity,' Mayor says without hesitation.

'Somewhere along the way, they have acquired total immunity.' She crouches down, framing the sad shrine above her fresh flowers, her camera singing its song into the empty desert.

She slowly stands, staring out at the malevolent landscape, and for a second almost catches a glimpse of it: the violence like heat haze, trembling a passage towards her.

14

El Santo

Jaime Santiago was known to everyone as El Santo. He earned his nickname not because both his names belonged to the same Apostle, but because he once robbed a bar wearing a plastic version of the famous silver mask of the wrestler. El Santo was the most popular wrestler in Mexico, and when his mask was finally removed, it was he who lifted it himself to announce his own retirement.

That was class.

Santiago wanted some of that class to rub off on him and it did. He only ever wore his plastic mask once, but the name stuck.

The Saint.

Things could have ended right there in the bar. Santiago had no idea that it was owned by Amado Lázaro Mendez, the head of the Ciudad Real cartel. Amado was there during the robbery, and laughed so hard at the sight of the fifteen-year-old in the wrestler's mask holding up the till that Santiago had actually thought of shooting the mocking bastard. Lucky for both he didn't. The next day he got a message from one of Amado's henchmen: *Come work for us.*

El Santo started out as a lookout, in the unlikely event that a law enforcement official not in the pay of the cartel might stumble upon a transaction. The kid was bright, but what really led to his fast advancement was something Santiago had that most of the others in the cartel could only dream of: a US passport.

Santiago's mother came from Puerto Palomas and, like most of the women there, gave birth at the nearest hospital, which happened to be on the right side of the border in Lunar County, New Mexico. Santiago even went to school there, until his mother made him get on the bus with her and travel the two hundred kilometers to Ciudad Real. He may as well have crossed an ocean. Two years later, he was a dropout and a novice crook with a plastic mask. And then Amado came along. After a couple of weeks observing the kid, Amado gave Santiago very specific instructions: go home and finish your schooling.

El Santo had helped move over five hundred kilos of coke into safe houses in Columbus and Deming by the time he graduated. One kilo a day. He was the cartel's first *lunchbox smuggler*. In the greater scheme of things, five hundred Ks of coke was nothing – only sixty million on the streets after it had been cut. But Amado was all about planning. The little details. Five hundred kilos here, fifty thousand there. No matter how much you had, it was never enough. And each safe house was another silver stake in the greatest market on earth: the United States of Addiction. When it came time to run – and Amado was smart enough to know that time would one day come – he'd have his very own personal guide to *How to Disappear Forever* and the money to make it happen.

El Santo was rewarded the way you were in the cartels: he was turned into a killer. After high-school graduation he was driven to a house on the outskirts of Ciudad Real and handed a cut-throat razor. What he did with it was his own business; he just had to obtain a name. What was surprising was how fast that name was delivered. And the next one, and the one after that.

The thing El Santo hated most about those evenings in the house wasn't getting the names, it was what happened afterwards. Digging the graves; hard work in the bracing night air, his lungs and arms aching. It was the way he felt when he used to shovel snow in Puerto Palomas, the sweat on his body warm then freezing cold. Worst of all was the lacerating stench of the lime; the way it got up his nose or worked itself into his open pores, so that his body would itch and even bleed from its bite.

By the time the police found out, there were over a dozen bodies decomposing in the backyard. The papers called it *the House of Death*. If they only knew the real extent of the killing that had been going on. That house was like El Santo's lunchbox. A drop in the fucking ocean.

Amado came. Amado went. Now fifteen years after that first heist, El Santo was the head of the cartel. The fourth in as many years since Amado died – or staged his own death and disappeared. With Amado anything was possible. Although Santiago rarely killed people himself anymore, he still sanctioned their deaths. So why the fuck didn't he know about this car bombing?

'They were just kids heisting a car,' El Feo tells him. The nickname is not meant ironically. El Feo is one ugly son of a bitch. Just having him in the room is enough to put you off your food. 'They got unlucky.' They sure did. 'They heisted the wrong car. The bomb was meant for some CTON union organizer.'

El Santo doesn't like the sound of that. Two fucked-up CTON hits on the same day? You always have to be careful about *weird*. 'I don't care if it was meant for the fucking

65

pope! Why didn't they come to me for the job?' He gets up and snatches El Feo around the throat. 'This is still my territory, isn't it?'

El Feo makes a sound like Noah's flood trying to move through a single, shitty downpipe. Santiago lets him go. 'No one knew!' El Feo wheezes. 'It was a surprise.'

There is no such thing as a surprise in Ciudad Real. Not unless it comes from Tijuana. Oviedo's dog barks outside, as though to underline the point. Oviedo is his new bodyguard – smart enough to be ambitious but not show it. And compared to El Feo, Einstein brilliant. Maybe it's time to give Oviedo his chance.

El Santo walks over to his Mercedes-Benz 300 SL, lifts the door and gets in. He likes the smell of the leather; the contained world view inside the car when he closes the gull wings, masking all the problems, all the *chingadera y media* he has to face every fucking day. He likes the privacy he feels when he's talking on the phone. He even likes watching TV through the windshield. It reminds him of the drive-ins when he was a kid. It isn't just about showing off his taste. It is also a statement about his priorities. Speed. Class. Mechanical perfection. *Gleam*.

Besides, it doesn't take up that much more space than a grand piano.

They had to take the wall out to get the car inside. When they were rebuilding it, they found the bug. It must have been placed inside the wall when he had the hacienda renovated. It was a blessing that they found it, and it was only thanks to the Merc. Of course he made them put it back. They could listen all they want – as long as he knew when they could hear him. And when they couldn't.

El Feo gets in on the passenger side, pulls down the door, the barking vanishing as if by magic. Sure he's called El Feo because he's ugly, but he could also be called El Estúpido or El Idiota or El Pinche Pendejo. They're turning his turf into Beirut and El Santo has to hear the news on the radio? 'Find out all you can about this union guy. Find out who sent him here. Find out who wants him dead.'

'I'll pick him up myself.'

That's the way you normally *find out*. You pick someone up, and pretty soon they're telling you everything you need to know. 'Leave him alone for the time being. Find out the other way.'

The *other way* means picking someone up in Tijuana. That means one of his *sicarios* will have to show his face there. Risky, considering they're at war. Not only are they killing each other, they're killing each other's families. It's more than messy. It is fratricide of biblical proportions. It's coCaine and Abel. And it is everyone's fault. They have let it become personal, when it should always be kept professional.

Things degenerated badly over ten years before, when the Tijuana chief kidnapped a rival's family. They forced the wife to withdraw millions of dollars of her husband's ill-earned *dinero* before cutting off her head and mailing it back to hubby. It was so fucking *out there*, they even put it in a movie. Kevin Spacey wasn't playing a *narco* but he was certainly playing someone who was *totalmente loco*. But what they did next shocked everyone. They tossed both motherless kids off a waterfall in Venezuela. That one *came* from a film: *The Mission*. And it Pandora-boxed the whole fucking country.

You can't *unsmoke* a cigarette.

67

Once shit like that happens, the demons come out and there's no going back. It's not just take-no-prisoners time, it's take your time taking no prisoners. Ghastly murders were devised by men with a natural inclination for cruelty. Once it was *bang bang, you're dead*. Now executions were taking longer than a first-class letter from Mexico City. Only a genius like Amado was able to get things halfway back to normal again, and that was by focusing on business, not butchery. When revenue is up, revenge is down. They were operating 727s for Christ's sake. That's why Amado was called El Señor de los Cielos. The Lord of the Skies. Amado had owned over twenty Boeings, not to mention dozens of smaller planes. At first they stole them, then they just paid cash. Not having a plane ready for a flight cost more than buying one outright.

The money came in at an indecent rate. One billion became ten billion. They were on their way to the *Forbes* List. Donald Trump rich? Why not Warren Buffett rich?

The world had seen nothing like it since the Old Days of Cortés and Pizarro. The two biggest balls in a one-handed catch: Power and Riches. In a snap of the fingers, one empire collapses and another rises. The Colombian cartels losing the power of the powder; the Mexicans taking it all over. First border crossings, then general transportation from Colombia, then money laundering, then distribution inside the United States, then actual field production.

In less than two decades, they had gone from Middleman to Monopoly. Amado started using the *casas de cambio* to funnel money in and out. It was a beautiful operation.

Then Amado died, supposedly during plastic surgery. The body mysteriously nabbed and cremated before DNA tests could be carried out. The whole story was so ridiculous, and yet it had been quickly rubber-stamped. The alternative is too awful. That Amado is still out there with his billions, laughing his ass off in Rio or Marbella, while all the other *narcos* are stuck in the trenches, nursing colossal egos and even bigger headaches, paying millions in bribes while dodging pot shots.

And maybe now car bombs. The homicide rate like the Nasdaq Index: through the roof. The Lord of the Skies? With all the death he unleashed by selfishly disappearing, it should have been the Lord of the Flies. And Amado somewhere safe, laughing like fucking Nero while the whole country goes up in flames. It figures. Amado always loved playing Last Man Standing, and he even got his own El Santo moment; only when he removed his mask to announce his retirement, there was no face underneath.

And now the Ciudad Real cartel is at war with the Tijuana cartel – again. The bomb must have come from out of there. 'Send someone to Tijuana.'

'Who?'

Someone you won't miss if they get killed. 'Why don't you go?'

'I'll send my brother,' El Feo says quickly. 'Curro's reliable.' And expendable, apparently. El Feo looks at his watch. 'I'm late for church.'

'Jesus Christ, with all the time you spend there, it's a wonder you can do any work.'

El Feo stares at him with a hurt expression as he gets out of the car. 'That's not the way you used to think.'

He's right. El Santo used to be a believer too. All that *Santa Muerte* bullshit. But after everything that he's witnessed, he's come to his own conclusions. There's no such thing as God. And that's certainly good news because it means there's no such thing as the devil. He lowers the back of his car seat and closes his eyes. But, for the time being at least, locked inside his own huge, silver mask, there's still such a thing as Peace and fucking Quiet.

15

Padre Márcio

Padre Márcio carefully removes his fingerless lace gloves, so as not to break any scabs, and drops them in a bowl of cold water and table salt. After a few seconds he sees the first swirls of blood lifting from the gloves. He goes over to the basin and begins to wash his hands, rubbing his thumbs gently over the openings in his palms. He dabs at the wounds with a mild solution of water and hydrogen peroxide and then again, this time using Lugol's solution, toweling the wounds dry before covering them with light bandages.

Infection had always been a problem when he was a child. One morning he woke up and felt something ticking inside his hand, as though it were a bomb about to detonate. The wound in his left hand was throbbing. The lesion in his right hand was squirming; the skin undulating around his palm. He didn't know what it was; only that there was something alive in there. In a state of panic, he was driven to the bishop's personal physician, who lifted the folds of both wounds and discovered they were pulsing with maggots. The doctor told him he was lucky – the maggots had been eating away at nasty infections that otherwise might have gone unnoticed until it was too late. It could have developed into septicemia, or even gangrene. He could have lost both hands.

He would have been happy for the doctor to have taken an ax and amputated his hands – anything to end the direct physical connection between him and the maggots, to free him from the notion of worms feasting on his flesh, unaware that only part of his body was dead.

The doctor gave him a sedative, and then a local anesthetic, and cleared the larvae from his hands one creature at a time. After he fell asleep, the bishop performed a blessing on the infected wounds. He knew what the boy and the doctor could not: that the maggots had been sent by Satan to attack the holy wounds; to deliberately defile a miracle.

The boy recovered quickly, but that moment of awakening to a palpitating, living presence in his hands had filled him with horror. With self-loathing. The presence of something noxious and evil shifting inside him as it consumed his flesh was too close to memories he had hoped he would forget.

His stigmata had begun a year and a half after the first rape. The Little Brothers of Perpetual Succour was an order of teaching brothers made up of two kinds of vocational respondents. The first were men who had themselves been sexually abused as children. The second were naturally cruel men who had an intuitive grasp of where best to find their victims. They might have sold quack dietary supplements, or worked as pimps or stand-over men. They could have become neglectful nurses in old-age homes, stealing wedding rings from dying patients; or debt collectors, or gun runners. But instead they became brothers of a religious order devoted to caring for and educating orphans, where their victims were ideal.

Small and alone.

When he arrived at the orphanage in Ciudad Real at the age of five, Padre Márcio was still known as Vicente Salinas. His mother was a devout and naïve young woman taken advantage of by her local priest, who first noticed her when she arrived with the resurrection flowers one Easter Sunday morning. He was forty-seven and had grown bored with his housekeeper: both in the kitchen and in bed.

Vicente was a breech birth and nearly killed his mother. Father Felipe Hurtado waited many months, using Guadalupe in other ways. Ways she did not like, but accepted because her blessed father told her to obey, and because it was her duty. Finally, Father Felipe believed she had healed enough to be able to receive his normal ministrations. Neither the child nor the mother survived the second breech birth.

Father Felipe sent his bastard son to the Little Brothers of Perpetual Succour in the confidence that he would receive a good education and not be mistreated the way most of the children were. But he had miscalculated, as the vice-rector of the orphanage was the brother of Father Felipe's former housekeeper. Revenge was exacted the way it always is – on the defenseless; and after a week of hidings with belts, wooden paddles, bamboo canes and even books, the sexual abuse of Vicente began.

After eighteen months of repeated violations and beatings, Vicente was ready to kill himself. He had no fear of the consequences of suicide that the Little Brothers had taught him, for as far as he was concerned, nothing could be worse than the hell he and the other children woke to every morning.

Vicente remembered seeing the body of a young girl who had taken her own life by climbing over the top-floor bannister and jumping down into the stairwell. He had heard a rocking noise, like children playing in branches, and then glimpsed her body as it swept past the second-floor landing, clattering like a rain of shoes on the stone at the bottom of the stairs.

He had raced down with the other children, undaunted by the wet red stain flowering dramatically from her hair, or the unnatural splay of her arms and legs, her corpse forming a broken star. As the others turned their heads, he had stared hard at the soft repose of her face, finding an expression of calm contemplation there, as though she had just woken from a pleasant dream and, rather than opening her eyes, had decided to luxuriate a few more moments in the comfort of its memories.

At that very instant, surrounded by the rising hysteria of the rest of the children, Vicente felt different. He wasn't afraid of what he saw. He knew he wanted the same thing – bloody release from this life.

The more he dwelt upon it, the more Vicente yearned to join the girl, to share her lovely fate, better than peace or freedom. Oblivion.

But he knew he couldn't literally follow her into the void: he suffered from too acute a case of vertigo. He could barely approach the bannister, let alone look over it into the killing chasm below. Vicente may have feared heights, he may have feared life, but he did not fear losing blood; he did not fear the death that it would bring. He remembered the crown of red the girl had worn; like the aura of a saint. He looked for a weapon, and found one at last in a sharpened pencil.

After dinner, after mass and prayers and lights out; after that evening's rape, he picked up the pencil from its hiding place under the bed and began to work its tip into the palm of his hand, flinching at first from the pain, but then somehow moving beyond it, as though the knowledge that he would soon escape into the lonely eternity of death was acting as an anesthetic, slowly dulling his agony. He kept working the tip of the pencil into one palm, then the other, drilling away backwards and forwards, the soft warm bubble of his blood running cold and clammy down his wrists as he fell into a drowsy, unquiet sleep.

He awoke to outrage, the vice-rector throwing his sheet off violently and yanking him out of the bed by the wrists. The vice-rector slapped him across the face then ran him across the room and into the wall, the crack against his skull almost knocking him out. Vicente fell backwards, onto the floor, and that's when he saw them: two bloody hand prints like artwork on the whitewash; his mark – the proof that he was still alive. This was never supposed to happen. He wasn't supposed to wake up. He had assumed that he would simply bleed to death; that his blood would pump fast and free out of his self-inflicted wounds the way it had from the girl's fractured skull. But now instead of dying quietly in his sleep, he was going to be killed by slow degrees. The vice-rector dragged Vicente out into the courtyard and tied him to the punishment post, his hands burning with a deep, localized pain; an acute, humiliating pain: the pain of failure.

And at that very moment of ultimate despair, when all hope has vanished and one is finally reconciled to the brutal reality of life – that every moment is suffering or an unsuccessful attempt to alleviate suffering – as in every fairy tale, at that exact moment, a savior made a spectacular entrance.

The bishop of Ciudad Real.

His Grace was so astonished to see a boy with an egg-sized lump growing out of his forehead and bloodstains on his pajamas, tied to a pole in the middle of the quadrangle, that he did something he had vowed never, ever to do. He asked a question about the practices going on behind the closed doors of the Little Brothers of Perpetual Succour.

His Grace was informed that the child was an evil sinner and had deliberately soiled his bedsheets, but the bishop had already stopped listening to the flustered self-justification of the vice-rector. He was staring at one of Vicente's hands. He grabbed the child's wrist and turned the hand as much as he could against the rope that bound him to the pole, and managed to see the origin of the bleeding – an open palm wound. Quickly he grasped the other hand, and then crossed himself with a guttural prayer in Latin. He ordered the boy to be unbound and placed in his car. The vice-rector complied with a look of knowing malice. He had always suspected that His Grace harbored the same kind of evil proclivities he and his fellow brothers enjoyed.

Contrary to the brother's vindictive thoughts, the bishop was a kind and decent man, who would never have laid a finger upon either child or adult; a prelate who had learnt to repress his sexual desires under the comforting weight of numbing prayer, repetitive administrative duties and copious amounts of food and drink. But his lack of lust was not matched by a lack of gullibility, a fact attested to by the piece of the True Cross which he had purchased for an exorbitant amount from a traveling charlatan and which was now mounted above the painting of the Pietà in his cathedral, much venerated by the faithful.

Vicente was driven to the bishop's palace, where he was carefully bathed by two nuns, an elderly mother and a novice, neither of whom had ever seen the male anatomy before. As His Grace had requested, they were very careful with the wounds in the boy's palms. Vicente moaned piteously when the sisters

76

gently washed them. Afterwards, when the child was clean and had been dressed in the only available clothes – those of an altar boy – Vicente was brought before the bishop, who blessed his hand wounds with holy water and told him that he was a stigmatist.

Although Vicente had spent eighteen months in a parochial orphanage, His Grace soon understood that his religious instruction had been poor. Vicente knew very little beyond some rudimentary catechism – a few parables and common prayers, some of the Commandments, and snatches of liturgical response, learnt parrot-fashion. He hadn't even heard of St Francis of Assisi, let alone Padre Pio. The bishop sat down with the boy and told him that the wounds in his hands were a sign of his devout goodness. God had chosen him to lead the way through suffering.

The bishop could see that his words distressed the boy, which he found perfectly normal. A calling of this magnitude was bound to be alarming. He told the nuns to give Vicente a sleeping draft, but all they could find was some red altar wine, to which they added honey and spices.

Vicente spent three days in comfort, amongst kind people, without any threat of physical or sexual abuse. Three days in which he was told that he had been chosen by God himself to lead an increasingly secular humanity back to Christ. And then he noticed that his wounds were healing. At night he picked at the scabs, tears of pain in his eyes, but no matter what he did, he couldn't stop nature from taking its course. Over the next few days, the inevitable happened. The sacred wounds were no longer just healing, they were closing. For the first time in his life, Vicente prayed. Not the mindless chatter of repetition – more an exercise in oral agility than a heartfelt prayer – but words of his own choosing, addressed to a presence he had never believed in: God. Vicente asked God to make the bishop's words come true. Make him a holy boy. Make his holes come back.

But his prayers, like those of most people, were not answered. The wounds abided by nature's course, not God's, and continued to close.

It is always at our greatest moment of despair, when we have renounced all hope and given up completely; it is always then that we find that which we have stopped seeking: salvation. Respite.

Deceit.

Vicente was pacing his room, lost in his anguish, when he cut his bare foot on something sharp protruding from the floor. He bent down and touched the wooden planks to see what had caused the accident. A protruding, loose nail.

Sharper than a pencil. Easier to conceal. Vicente started to sob uncontrollably. Not out of fear or pain or sorrow as in the past. Out of relief. At last, he was saved.

16

Fuentes

Fuentes is standing in a corner of a Tijuana kitchen, aware of the potential threat to his jacket from two industrial deep fryers that are beginning to roil beside him, the shouts of the restaurant staff echoing off the white tiles as they strain to be heard above the anarchy of warring pots and pans.

His informant Adán, an ex-heroin addict who reformed when he found Jesus with his new Guatemalan girlfriend, looks up and down the kitchen gallery then shakes the water off his hands, layers of amulets and charm bracelets chiming musically. He dries his hands on his apron, then passes Fuentes a piece of paper from a child's exercise book, neatly folded along the blue ruled lines.

It is the first time he has held paper like this since it happened, and it hits him the way memories associated with bereavement always do. Unexpected. Hateful. They aren't just hard, the memories are harmful. His blood pressure plunges; vision blurs. For a moment the world exists, and then it doesn't, the way it must feel when you're having a stroke.

Fuentes squeezes the paper inside his fist, as though crushing to death all those emotions. He has just slipped it into his jacket's breast pocket when the wall opposite him erupts outwards in an explosion of white powder and tiny shards of porcelain, a lacerating cloud consuming his face.

The first thing he thinks of is an earthquake.

But then he hears it, hammering insistently in the suddenly hushed kitchen, and hearing it, realizes it was always the only explanation that made any sense . . .

Automatic gunfire.

He drops to the floor, spots the terrified eyes of the kitchen staff down there with him, hunks of tile continuing to shatter across them all as the gunmen rake the open kitchen indiscriminately, as though in a desperate hurry to run out of ammo. Unholstering his weapon with one hand, wiping the ceramic grit out of his eyes with the other, he elbows his way fast across the floor to the shelter of a retaining pillar and slowly stands and peers out into the restaurant. Muzzle flash in response within the newly imposed darkness; then the screams of trapped clientele hovering under tables. The open kitchen is a spotlight, drawing bullets like moths.

And he is a target illuminated on stage.

He looks around for a light switch and sees Adán, both arms slumped in adjoining frying vats, his head resting on the draining pan between them. Fuentes reaches forwards, grabs Adán's body by the scruff of the collar and hauls him backwards, freeing his arms from the scalding oil. And that's when he sees them, tumbling like battered shrimp inside the deep fryers, the perfect outline of two whole hands, the skin freed from the flesh, filled like gloves with the turbulence of oil, the fingernails crisping golden and dark.

Fuentes wakes from his dream with a start.

Tijuana, Baja California.

Sex and sea.

A terrain of cliffs and sirens, of shipwrecking rocks and pools of desire hidden within fast currents. A treacherous landscape negotiated by criminals and tourists alike. Every day, Americans leapt into the town's dark and urgent offerings and were carried, gasping and satiated, back up to the surface by local swimmers before being returned to the dry, flat world across the border.

A world of suburbs and family cars. A world of superiority. Their reality. Not Mexico's.

Tijuana. Where Fuentes fled after the car accident, losing himself in the murky tide of the city, the ebb and flow of crime and punishment. Cops and robbers. Kill or be killed. He was immersed in work. It made him feel safe because there was no time to think. And then the attack at Lolita's Restaurant; the way the melted wristbands had tightened and shrunk, cutting through to the bone, the remnants of Adán's flayed hands knuckles up on the floor.

Fuentes stepped out from behind the pillar and started firing. When the shooting first began, it seemed as though it had already lasted an eternity. It possessed all the heightened tension of ambush, that confused, then panicked awareness of attack, of the unexpected arrival of death that always prolongs time, freezing each action into a tortured pause of indecision; each response into elongated hesitancy.

But once full comprehension descends, the opposite always happens: time doesn't just unfreeze, it accelerates, helped by the screaming knowledge that in seconds, maybe less, the situation will be resolved. One way or the other, some people were about to die.

So you focused on the Now.

They were two.

He was one.

They had an AK-47 assault rifle and a 9 mm CZ 75 ST.

He had a Colt Python.

They were fueled by a carburetor mix of fear-induced adrenaline and drugs.

He was a sober marksman.

One, two, three quick shots.

Two dead gunmen.

Time resolved itself back into the mundane tick of twenty-four hours. It could have been a lot worse. No customers were injured. And only one kitchen hand killed; a man who, authorities were quick to point out, was a heroin addict and known to the police – defamation always being the first line of defense.

It was seven hours afterwards that Fuentes finally remembered the sheet of *cuaderno* paper Adán had given him. He'd had a lot on his mind. He kept thinking about Adán's hands, like bloated corpses, rising to the surface of the oil. He remembered the shock as his face was blasted by the opaque shrapnel from tiles obliterated by bullets. He remembered seeing the flames from the barrels light up the darkness in tortured strips of fire. He remembered the screams of the diners between bursts, and then the silence when his bullets had hammered home.

The paper Adán had given him revealed the address of a crystal meth lab on the outskirts of La Gloria. It also gave the location of a tunnel entrance in Castillo that came out on the other side of the border, under a house near Dairy Mart Road. Interesting information, if mundane in the general run of things. Nothing to lose both your hands over, let alone your life.

But when Fuentes saw the final piece of information, he felt the same dislocating disruption he'd experienced when the wall had leapt into powdery animation and burst all around him, as if for no reason. It was the name of the person controlling both the tunnel and the meth factory. Fuentes' immediate superior, José-María Sánchez Ribeiro.

A man he would have trusted with his life.

The man who had sent the *sicarios* to kill him.

The tunnel was the easy part. Fuentes simply picked up the phone and called Charlie Addsen, his contact in the DEA. He didn't even bother to ask Charlie for any favors in return. The lab would be dangerous but doable, even on his own. Meth factories had short shelf lives due to the combustible nature of both their product and their owners.

The hard part was Sánchez Ribeiro. His brother was an advisor to the governor of Sinaloa. His sister was married to a first cousin of Ramón Arena Gallardo, one of the most violent chiefs of the Tijuana cartel. His father was a council member at the *Ayuntamiento* of Rosarito.

In other words, Sánchez Ribeiro was untouchable. And Fuentes was now the exact opposite.

They say that Mexicans have a unique relationship with death.

It's not true. Mexicans die like everyone else. But what is true is that the Mexican *attitude* towards death is different; at least compared to that of their northern neighbors. Americans fear death the way they fear aging. It might happen to other people but it should not be allowed to happen to them. Mexicans fear death the way they fear hunger or unemployment. It happens to other people and it could therefore easily happen to them.

It was that logic that applied to Fuentes' decision. He had no choice. There was no alternative. He had to kill Sánchez Ribeiro.

He couldn't do it himself, he was not a murderer. And even if he were able to go against his nature and kill his own boss, he couldn't just rely on an alibi, no matter how steel-clad: he'd need to be so removed from the crime that his name would never come up.

Not at the funeral. Not at the wake. Not during the investigation.

Not ever.

And *not ever* was a concept that just didn't exist in Mexico.

17

Fuentes

He thought about his problem for a week and still had no solution. Fuentes was almost reconciled to the only action he could realistically take – inaction – when the answer presented itself to him with stunning clarity.

He called Charlie Addsen again. There was a favor he needed after all. Charlie was delighted to assist Fuentes. The only thing that helps a career more than doing a good job yourself is helping your fuck-up partners do a good job as well.

They arranged the bust on the meth factory for midnight, when there was a far better chance that his men would be reasonably sober than during an early morning raid. Fuentes had once seen one of his policemen shoot off three of his own toes during a dawn arrest.

Sánchez Ribeiro didn't ask a single question on the drive out. He was pleased to have the US TV crew along for the ride, showing the *gringos* that the Mexicans were pulling their weight in the War on Drugs.

Fuentes knew Sánchez Ribeiro wasn't stupid, so it could only have been hubris. He didn't even look worried when they turned into the street. And when they pulled up outside his meth house – well, it was all too late then. He tried to cancel, but Fuentes had made sure they were the last car, and the *gringos* were already filming his men going through the doors.

Even meth chemists have to sleep. The factory was unguarded

except for three kids who gave up without a fight when confronted with a dozen armed men wearing balaclavas, gas masks and body armor, backlit by TV klieg lights. Fuentes' men were filmed as they handcuffed the kids. They were filmed as they unplugged all the refrigeration and freezer units. They were filmed as they recovered nine hundred kilos of crank. Twenty-seven million dollars, the excited *gringo* journalist said into the camera. One of the most successful raids in recent times, and evidence of the growing co-operation between the two nations. 'This war can be won,' he said, turning to Sánchez Ribeiro, who tried to pull away from the camera. 'Tonight is proof of that.' Fuentes saw the look on Sánchez Ribeiro's face and almost felt sorry for him. It was a solemn look.

A familiar look.

A *Mexican attitude towards death* look.

The ride back was very quiet. Fuentes told Sánchez Ribeiro about something that had been tormenting him for days. The way Adán's hands had rolled and turned in the fryers, inflated by the boiling oil, the fingernails crisping at the top. What did he make of that? Was it normal to be haunted by such a scene, or was he just going soft? Sánchez Ribeiro said nothing, staring straight ahead, the lights of the dashboard floating ghostly across his reflection in the windshield.

Sánchez Ribeiro was killed two days later, coming out of his mistress's house with two suitcases loaded with cash, though by the time the suitcases made it to the evidence room they were empty. Fuentes paid a visit to Sánchez Ribeiro in the morgue. It wasn't pretty. Headshots. He'd instinctively put his hands up to his face. They looked like those of the crucified Christ.

Fuentes went to the funeral. How could he have avoided it?

He stood two rows back. The respect of a colleague for his boss; present but not too pushy. He watched everyone and was the only one to notice: he was being watched himself by Sánchez Ribeiro's brother. It wasn't a sideways glance. It wasn't a glare. It was what you'd expect from an advisor to a governor: careful; aware. Afterwards the brother broke from the family group and walked up to Fuentes, the cops around him going silent. He shook Fuentes' hand not in greeting but in assessment, as though searching for something. And not finding it. Fuentes felt like a guilty man who had passed a polygraph test.

Relieved and a little smug.

He knew he was safe.

A short time after the funeral, Fuentes got the call. Anti-union duties. He counted himself lucky and took it. It was the biggest fucking mistake of his life.

Fuentes peers outside his bedroom window, then lowers the curtain and walks into the kitchen. He stops in front of the refrigerator, staring at a piece of paper held there by a magnet. It's a child's crayon drawing of a house standing under a blue sky full of yellow stars and a crescent moon. A black cat sits on the rooftop.

He takes it off the refrigerator door and opens a cupboard, slipping it on top of a pile of other drawings. He slides another one out from the bottom of the stack. It's a picture of a man and a woman holding hands with a child. He puts it up on the fridge, making sure that the magnet holds. He runs a finger across the paper, tracing the outlines of the three figures.

Fuentes crosses to the kitchen sink and gets himself some water, leaving a smudge of colored wax on the glass. He stares out at the eastern horizon, waiting for the moon to build up enough courage to rise; to even dare to show its fucking face.

18

El Santo

El Santo is trying to find network coverage, scanning the night sky with his StarTAC. He needs to get his asshole broker on the line, and fast. Everyone's talking about a dotcom bubble. Even the local radio stations are on to it – and that means it's practically too late.

He has a stack of fucking phones at home, sitting on top of each other like poker chips, but what good are they if he can't even use them? They cost a bomb too. Every phone call he makes is a thousand bucks. Some spook who used to work in CIA told him never to make two calls on the same phone. Buy a brand new phone from an untraceable source; make a call; toss it. The way Jaime Santiago figures, the real crooks are Motorola and Nokia. And out here in the middle of fucking nowhere, trying to get a signal is like trying to get a hard-on for Mother Teresa. The last thing he needs is all this screaming in the background. He turns to El Feo. 'Can't you stop for one fucking minute?'

'It's not me – he won't shut up. I haven't done a thing to him for an hour.'

El Santo steps into the hot electric light of the barn, moths twirling around the overhead lights like they're dancing to the thumping rhythm of the generator. He stares down at the kid. Sixteen, max. Old enough to know when to shut up. The kid had shown up at the hospital after the car bomb to see how his friends were doing. El Feo made the snatch. Too easy, even for him. Moral of the story: never care about others. 'Did he tell you what you need to know?'

El Feo shrugs non-committally. 'Maybe he's lying.'

'No one keeps lying after that.' The kid's tied to a chair, his Levi's pulled down around his ankles. El Santo stares at the metal shims that have been hammered through the flesh and wedged between his kneecaps and his femurs.

El Feo sucks his frog lip in doubt. 'Once, there was this guy coming out of . . .' El Feo's voice rattles on, but El Santo has already jumped off the trolley car. All these old stories; always the same bullshit. *Narcos* are addicted to them, like families glued to their *telenovelas*. But if you tried explaining to a moron like El Feo that Jesús Malverde never even existed, he'd triple-cross himself, kiss his fucking scapular, then blow your brains out for blasphemy.

El Feo's into all the crazy legends. The *mariachi* walking out of the Sonora desert with a machine gun inside his guitar case. The *bandido* who claws his way out of a fresh grave and fills the empty hole with a village-load of corpses. The guy who peels off the faces of dead men and sticks them on his own like a mask, so no one ever knows what he really looks like.

There are even bullshit stories about Amado – how his dog sits on his tomb and howls at the moon, and kills anyone who approaches.

It's crazy. Amado doesn't even have a grave.

It doesn't matter. People like El Feo lap up the legends, the more insane the better. All of the best tales date back to before everything started going down the shithole. Before Nixon and Operation Intercept. Before the *gringos* torched the poppy plantations in Sinaloa and destroyed Rancho Búfalo. Before the fucking Colombians arrived. The 'Good Old Days'.

Before the cartel wars.

Before Amado.

Those days are long gone but no one has any new stories to tell, because that would take one iota of intelligence, and you'd be more likely to find that in the termite nests outside than in a *narco* like El Feo.

El Santo swears to God, sometimes it feels like the sun is that stupid fucking eye logo from Televisa, and all the people who pass under it every single day are just characters from the oldest *telenovela* in history – *Mámame La Verga* – *Go Suck My Dick*.

He turns back to El Feo, who is still talking. 'Will you shut the fuck up with that bullshit.' El Feo splutters in shock and starts to protest but he talks over him. 'He never existed.' He points to the prisoner. 'But this kid exists.' For the moment. 'What has he told you?'

'They were heisting cars, and one of them went boom.'

'The newspapers could have told me that. Who were they stealing the cars for?'

That look on El Feo's face. The one that says he forgot to do something important, like take a piss or chew his food before he swallowed it. Sometimes he'll catch El Feo just standing there, staring into space, and he has to hit him on the back because he knows El Feo has forgotten to breathe. El Santo turns to the kid. 'Who are you working for?' The kid's in so much agony, he can't even hear the question. Nothing exists outside his pain. El Santo crouches low and grabs an ear in either hand. The only thing that can break through the suffering of torture is the threat of worse to come. He juggles the kid's head with his hands, adjusting the level of his face until they're both finally looking at each other, eye to eye. 'Who are you working for?'

A flicker of fear. El Santo has seen this before. It's not fear of him, it's fear of what the kid has to say. The Truth. Something no one ever wants to hear. 'Tell me,' he whispers, 'and I'll stop all this now.'

'Padre Márcio . . .' He closes his eyes, ready to receive the bullet he knows his answer's earned him.

But the kid's got it wrong. It's the most unexpected answer El Santo could ever imagine, but it's *so far* off the wall, he believes him.

Father Holy Holes himself – just another crook.

It doesn't make sense – some fucking priest heisting cars. Even in *el mondo narco* it's too fucking weird. And the weirder something is, the greater the peril.

Jaime Santiago grabs the tip of a shim in either hand and has to yank, harder than he expected. He finally pulls them out with a scraping noise, their sharp edges bloody and gleaming with the yellow-blue sheen of cartilage and sinew. He tosses them to the dirt floor and turns to El Feo. 'I want you to put a tail on Padre Márcio and see what turns up.'

El Feo stares at El Santo as though his moustache were on fire. 'You don't really believe this kid?'

El Santo figured out the answer to a question like that a long time ago: the wilder a story is, the more likely that it's true. 'Take him to the vet's and have his legs fixed up.'

'But, boss . . .'

'Then give him five thousand pesos and put him on the bus to Santa Teresa.'

'He'll talk.'

El Santo leans down and looks into the kid's eyes. 'Do you ever want to go through this again?' The kid shakes his head, sending dried clots of blood flying into the air, slow as blow-flies. 'If you talk, this won't be an ending, it'll be a beginning. Understand?' The kid doesn't say a word but he doesn't need to; the tear that slides from his left eye, gathering dust as it streaks a grimy passage down his face, says it all.

'Where do you drop the cars you steal?'

'Enrique's garage, just out of town.'

He nods to El Feo, who drags the chair with the kid still on it across the stony terrain towards his pickup, then roughly lifts him into the cabin of the truck. The next thirty miles will be the longest trip this kid will ever take. Chances are El Feo will pop him and keep the five grand. El Santo doesn't really care. He has been just. He has acted with honor. He cannot be held responsible for what his *peones* do. El Feo is just another foot soldier on the slow slide to annihilation, only following orders when it suits him; getting killed when his betrayal is eventually found out.

The way things are going, that won't be long.

Maybe he should just get it over with. Oviedo is lean and mean. Oviedo is smart and hungry; ambitious. Of course, that means he is dangerous. Someone to watch out for in the future. But he has to worry about *now*, and Oviedo is looking more and more like the present – and El Feo more and more like the past.

El Santo watches the truck moving off into the night, leaving a sorrowful exhaust stained red with taillight. And then, after a small moment, there is nothing at all.

He glances all around . . .

It's always this way after a torture or a killing: that dislocating shift from one reality to another. Screams to silence. Mayhem to mundane. As though nothing has really happened, or whatever has happened will never affect you. It was like someone else's dream. And really: who gives a fuck about a dream that's not your own?

On the ground, ants teem around the shims in a frenzy of feasting. He kicks dirt over the swarm, then heads back towards his car, his hand held high, still trying to get that fucking signal.

19

Pilar

Pilar wakes in the car with a start. On the horizon, a henna light glimmers in the distance, radiant and warm. Pilar would consider it beautiful if she didn't know what happened beneath its sodium glow. Strange shapes begin to emerge, flashing past on either side of the road.

Women.

There are only a few at first, walking alone or in pairs, but soon more appear, in groups of three and four. Women coming from the opposite direction hold hands up to their brows as the car sweeps past, eyes glittering like those of wild animals caught in hunters' headlights. Dozens become hundreds the closer they get to the *maquiladoras*, the women ordering their passage, taking separate sides of the road. Women like her, mustering the courage for the ordeal of the night shift, who know their suffering will be rewarded when they emerge in daylight and relative safety, all taking the right-hand side of the road.

The ones who have endured their exhaustion and defeated their hours are now returning home, walking on the left-hand side, which runs below the shoulder of the road. They try to stay in groups. These are the lethal hours; the slice of night most people sleep through. The time of kidnap and murder, of desecration and the disposal of bodies. A nocturnal shield. The killers profit from the closed grilles and curtained windows, the pools of shadow and silence; the deserted streets and the hurried flight of cars with unseen, unseeing drivers.

After every murder, every violation, the sun rises with stupefied indignation, seeping yellow and sick across the ruined landscape, its fevered dawn light like a scythe, harvesting brutal crops.

The corpses of women.

Juan Antonio accelerates past the pedestrians, the women's faces slapped with the spotlight inquiry of headlights before being tossed back into shadow. Into heightened darkness. Pilar studies the expressions that glide past. They are familiar and humiliating, like bad memories unwillingly recalled then painfully expunged. Even though they have picked up three women, Pilar still feels sick with guilt. She rides; the others walk.

Juan Antonio begins to slow as the groups of women grow larger still, asserting their right to share the strip of macadam that slices across the barren land like a razor slash across a cheek, great crowds now converging round the thriving hives of the *maquiladoras*.

There are no buses to take them to work. No buses to bring them home. They have to walk. Eighty-five percent of the victims were from the night shift, women walking on their own, abandoned to their bloody fate by the municipality, by the factory owners. By their own community.

By the cold calculations of commerce.

Market forces as murder weapon.

Juan Antonio stops the rent-a-car in the parking lot, the three passengers in the back getting out quickly, relieved to have made the journey without incident, to be able to hurry inside to the relative safety of the sweatshops. In the cold desert hush, Pilar can feel the grind of machinery vibrating through the night, and the murmur of footsteps uncertain in the shadows. Juan Antonio gets out; lights a cigarette. Passes it to Pilar.

'Your name is at the door. Fátima Muñoz.'

'Fátima?' Pilar swears. 'Why not just *Blessed Virgin*! I know you pick these names deliberately.'

'I don't have time to torment you. Even if you deserve it.' He gives her a fierce hug. It's unexpected. It's alarming. It's too close to a goodbye. 'Be careful, *loca*.'

'I will, *cabrón*.' Pilar walks towards the gates, the only thing keeping her going the knowledge that they will be striking soon.

Factories will be shut down and concessions will be forced out of companies that historically have never cared about their workers.

Basic safety standards will be painfully negotiated; the bosses reluctantly conceding to the rule of law.

A pittance in pay will be extorted by the threat of more strikes.

The companies will lose more in two days of closure than they will in three years of concessions, but it's the principle of the matter. They can't be seen to roll over so quickly to the demands of a group of nasty women.

The collective punishment will come later, when the union leaders are all purged from the workforce; when they force the women to work overtime under the threat of relocating to China.

Still, that is all in the future. Right now Pilar has to focus on the immediacy of the strikes. There will soon come a time when she will be able to sleep. It won't be the sleep of the good, or the just, or even the exhausted. It will be the sleep of oblivion: the hardest to wake from.

20

Fuentes

Fuentes pulls up across the road from a small bungalow, half masked from the street by the clutter of two desert willows in flower. He glances up and down the street. Deserted. Windows barred. Doors locked.

Smart street.

This is a dangerous neighborhood. All the residents obey the two nocturnal rules of survival. No one comes in. And no one looks out.

Fuentes will be practically invisible.

Carrying a small leather tool case, he walks quickly across the road, entering the front yard by a creaking cast-iron gate. A dog worries the silence of the street then gives up – what's the use? No one really cares and anyway, half the time a bark is answered by a bullet.

Fuentes peers through a barred window. Nothing. He listens as he pulls on his gloves. Still nothing. He takes out a chisel and hammer and crouches by the lock, aims, and delivers one hard rap. The lock tube explodes inwards. There is a hollow ring as the cylinder rolls along the floor inside. Fuentes pauses, waiting for any kind of reaction from either inside the house or out on the street.

He levers the chisel through the door jamb to where the second lock is located and pulls. It's stubborn. Must be a mortise lock. He works the tongue of the chisel in still further, then yanks with both hands. There is the protest of cracking wood and the door pops open with a whine of relief. He enters, closing what's left of the door behind him.

Fuentes scans the room with a hooded flashlight, the narrow beam telling a story he expected. The place has already been tossed, the floor strewn with books and papers. Glass snaps underfoot. His beam finds what it's looking for: the back of a picture frame. He turns it over.

It is a snapshot of a woman in her thirties, with a knowing smile and peroxide hair. He recognizes her immediately. Marina. This is unexpected. He rescues the photo from the broken glass and pockets it.

The intruders have also trashed the bedroom. The mattress has been latticed with long slashes, its stuffing ventilated in the night air. Whatever they were looking for, it wasn't there. The contents of drawers have been scattered, the intimate details of Paredes' grooming, healthcare and sexual preferences fingered through and discarded.

Fuentes freezes. Shadows cross the window, the footsteps dying away as a group passes outside on the street: some kids walking their dogs; a reckless attempt at normalcy that Fuentes finds almost as touching as it is alarming.

He resumes his search, going into the bathroom. By the look of things Paredes had a lot of headaches. He opens one of the bottles, shaking the pills out into his fist, some of them bouncing off his palm and wheeling out of the bathroom into the hallway, spinning to a stop. He rubs the white residue across his gums. Legit. He checks inside the cistern of the toilet. The undercarriage of the lid is still ribbed with rubber bands. Someone has found a stash and removed it. But a stash of what?

Cash, a weapon? There is really only one answer. Fuentes hears the shriek of the outside gate opening. He kills his flashlight, watching from the shadows of the bathroom. A beam of light scans the living room, for a second exploding behind him as it hits the medicine cabinet's mirror and bounces back. There's a curse. Did they catch his reflection? Fuentes flattens against a bathroom shelf, a whisper, anxious and alert, carrying all the way through the house. 'What?'

'Caught my face in the mirror.' Speaking English. One of them is an American. Maybe DEA? 'Scared the shit out of me.'

'Now you know how Karen feels.' A Mexican voice.

Low laughter peppers the darkness. Someone kicks something on the floor, sending a broken cup skittering. 'Unbelievable,' the American says. 'Not even a piece of police tape in sight. *Official co-operation*, my ass.'

'We can forget about finding anything here.'

'I've got another idea.' The voices are much closer now. Fuentes has nowhere to hide. He hears a bedroom drawer slide open. 'A little calling card.'

'Are you crazy?' the Mexican says. It's probably a PJF–DEA arranged marriage. Doomed from the start to early divorce.

'We'll get Valdez on the phone, make him put someone outside and then inspect the place together in the morning.'

There is the silence of contemplation. 'How does that help us?'

'Implicates Paredes.'

'He's already implicated.'

'This'll prove it.'

'Prove what?'

'Paredes is innocent.'

Fuentes cranes his head in astonishment, staring through two sets of door jambs to where the men are standing, silhouetted inside the bedroom across the hall.

'Well, not *innocent* innocent,' the American continues. 'But he sure as hell didn't know he was being set up today. I mean, no one's that good an actor.'

'I thought he'd have a cardiac arrest.' The Mexican laughs. 'So why would they set him up?'

'A simple diversion. A Mexican cop caught with nearly a hundred pounds of coke crossing into Texas is one hell of a story. It's all anyone's going to be talking about for the next few days.'

'Tone squelch?'

'You got it. If you can't maintain radio silence – and we know down here that's impossible – it's the next best thing.'

'Got to be a huge deal.'

'Has to be.'

'And if they're offering up Paredes . . . ?'

'It's got to be someone a hell of a lot bigger.'

The Mexican's voice drops an octave. 'Valdez?'

Fuentes leans forwards, listening so intently that his shoulder brushes the shelf. A glass falls . . .

He catches it with both hands. Freezes.

Recovering his breath, he turns his attention back to the conversation outside, anxiety spreading through him at what he hears . . .

Absolutely nothing.

Finally, a whisper: 'What is it?' And the choking rasp of someone racking the slide of a Glock in reply.

Fuentes feels more than hears the approach of the armed DEA agent. He edges down towards the floor, his body trying to absorb shadow. There are footsteps coming towards him, and then the shatter of something exploding underfoot, the crunch echoing throughout the darkened house. The agent bends down to examine what he's trodden on, the crown of his head passing through the entrance into the bathroom.

In that instant Fuentes could have acted. He could have hit him across the head with the glass or even with the shelf itself, but what good would it do? He'd then have to deal with the Mexican, and under the circumstances, there would be only one way to *deal* with him. Besides, a blow to the back of the head rarely does what it's intended to do: knock someone out cold. Hit someone too softly on the head and all you do is enrage him. Hit him too hard and he's dead. Fuentes pays attention to biology. He strikes opponents in the head to sting and distract, never to stop. There are plenty of other, safer options to knock someone out.

'What is it?' the more distant of the two voices says.

There is a groan of protest at the salicylic bitterness as the agent tastes part of the tablet he's just stepped on. He shines the light into the bathroom, this time prepared for the presence of the mirror, using its reflection to examine the room. 'I thought I heard something.' He turns, the beam glancing across Fuentes for a fraction of a second. The agent doesn't notice. 'Someone bigger than Valdez,' he says, walking back into the bedroom. 'Someone *huge*.'

'You mean . . . ?' The silence of confirmation. A ringing phone makes Fuentes jump, almost dropping the glass. 'Hello?' The whole house simmers with intensified silence, as though it too were trying to eavesdrop. Fuentes can just make out the burr of a voice on the other end of the line and then there's the click of disconnection. 'We better get back.'

'What about Gomez?'

Fuentes' eyes widen with the need to hear more. Does Valdez know Gomez is an active suspect? Has he fed them Gomez to protect himself?

'I'm not losing any more sleep over him. He can wait till morning.'

Fuentes listens to them leaving, then steps out and watches them getting into the car. He has their faces, the model of the vehicle and its registration number as it drives away. By tomorrow, he'll have their names. The one thing he doesn't have is why they were here. What were they looking for? He can't be sure, but he has a feeling that, whatever it is, it concerns him . . .

He goes into the bedroom; opens drawers. Finds it straight away, which was the intention. A half-kilo of coke, probably heavily cut. But why? They think Paredes was set up, so what do they do? Try to set him up again. He pockets the cocaine, just to fuck with them. Besides, you never know when it might just come in handy.

21

Ventura

Ventura has just slipped her key into the lock when the door is pulled inwards with such violence that she falls forwards, almost toppling onto the floor. Carlos scans the street, then slams the door shut behind her. The anxiety that rushes through her slides away into astonishment when she sees the four suitcases huddled together. 'What's going on?'

Carlos stares at her with eyes she's never seen before: eyes that don't recognize her. 'Were you followed?'

'Carlos, what's the matter?'

'*Everything's* the matter. Webvan, SanMarTel. Nycos and Inktomi – they're fucked. Every single one of them is fucked!'

She grabs him by the shoulders. His cheeks are grimed from the trace of tears. He's never been this bad before. 'What are you talking about?'

'Nobody saw it coming. The IPOs were spectacular. And now they're collapsing. Just like that. It's over before it ever really began.'

Ventura can't mask the alarm in her voice. 'What's over?'

'Everything.' He grabs two suitcases, but then throws them across the hallway. 'Don't you understand? I'm finished!' He kicks the front door, making her start. 'It wasn't my fault. *Nobody* saw it coming. Try explaining that to them. It doesn't matter anymore. I'm dead.'

'Carlos, whatever it is, we can work something out. It's only money.'

'It's not just *money*. It's *where* the money came from. It's the people who gave me their fucking money.' He stares at her with those eyes again. Seeing but not registering. Familiar yet foreign, like her dog when she was a girl, just before they had to put him down. Eyes she had known and loved, transformed into a stranger's by fear, illness and the knowledge of the proximity of death. Eyes that broke her heart because they were no longer the ones she had loved.

'What people?' A stupid question, knowing there can only be one answer; especially here in Ciudad Real. She asks another stupid question, her voice dropping to a whisper. 'How much did you lose?' His silence says it all. *Everything*. 'I'm going with you.' He shakes his head, picking up the suitcases he'd thrown and opening the door. 'But I want to go with you.'

'I thought you'd understand . . . I thought you were smart. Why the fuck don't you understand?'

She follows, dragging the last two suitcases across the rutted concrete.

He stops in front of a car she's never seen before. 'I hired it. In your name. That'll give me an extra hour.' He puts the four cases into the trunk, then slams it shut. 'Have you got any money?' He snaps the question at her, as though he'll hit her if she doesn't answer. She rummages through her bag; gives him everything she has. 'That's it?' She stares at this stranger's panicked face. She tries one last time to take his hands. Something glitters on her wrist. He wants it. 'The Rolex.' The way he spits the word – brutal and commanding – makes her lose all notion of its meaning. He may as well have said *the rhino*. 'The watch, for Christ's sake.' She starts to unclip it, but he yanks it off, hurting her. 'Don't worry, I'll get you another,' he says, looking away in embarrassment at the paucity of his lie.

'I don't care about the watch. I care about you. I'm worried. We need to go to the police.'

He slaps her.

It's not the physical blow itself that hurts so much; it's the anger it unleashes inside her. Her disbelief at what he's just done. Her shock at something she never expected to happen. Something she thought he was incapable of ever doing. She loved this man. She thought she knew him. Self-disgust floods her. There's acid in his voice. 'Don't ever mention the police again.'

She takes a step away from him, surprised at how much better it makes her feel, rubbing her cheek not just to alleviate the pain, but almost to ensure that she's still there – that this is not a dream. Something is broken. Forever. It's like she's just let go of the rope and is watching a small craft drifting away, already disappearing into the night. She feels something. She doesn't know it yet, but it's an angry freedom.

She stares at this stranger for the first and last time, hating his tear-streaks. So weak. So narcissistic.

So male.

He gets into the car, slamming the door fast, as though expecting her to try to follow him. As though she ever would. Now. 'I'll call you when I get to Phoenix.' It sounds like a line from a pathetic song. The car starts to pull away, then lurches to a stop. 'Don't stay in the house tonight. Understand? It's the first place they'll look.'

Ventura watches the car slurring around the corner, and then it's gone, the night settling back into an uneasy silence. She looks around the street. Deserted. Curtains drawn across barred windows. Doors double-bolted. This has been her street – her home – for the past fifteen months. Now it's altered. She feels threatened. It's a physical reality. No money. Nowhere to go. And she's standing outside the first place they'll come to look.

A dog barks. She shivers and peers up at the sky. There should be stars up there on a night like tonight. She should be able to see them glittering, the way she did when she was a girl, staring out her window, listening to the regular pant of her dog beside her bed; feeling safe with his great, warm presence next to her, loyal and grateful for her love; protecting her as she slept.

But when she lay awake, unable to sleep, she was the one who was on guard, as though she could already see across the tunnel of years to the time when her beloved dog would be old and sick and afraid; to the time when Ciudad Real would lose its stars to the yellow stain of smog and factory fumes and the great flare of security lights that lit the periphery of the *maquiladoras*, and the exhaust of the highways that linked the north with the south in an unending river of traffic and money, balancing greed and false hopes – never ever stopping. It was a restless tide, surging or ebbing to the sea-change mood swing of *market forces*.

Tonight, like all the nights of these last few years, there is no room for stars, their celestial light leached out by the vagaries of progress. No stars, no constellations, no horoscopes. No future. No prognosis or predictions; no escape into the vast mysteries of space, existence and prophecy. She is grounded on this empty earth as surely as the asteroids that once pounded the desert; that led to the great extinction. She is locked into a gravity that holds her to the earth; that will never let her rise.

And she is alone.

Ventura is afraid. But most of all, she is angry at Carlos; furious at someone she has given her unconditional love to, someone she thought loved her in return. Someone she considered a good man, a true friend; a kind and honest person. A man who has struck her. A man who has run not just like a coward, but like a criminal. A man who has left her behind, knowing the risks she faces. How could she have let a man like that put himself inside her; how could she have accepted him as her partner?

She packs quickly, thankfully finding money in her other handbag. Not much but enough to get out, to escape. Can she really guarantee her own safety right now, in her hometown? The fact that she has to ask that question makes her sick with doubt; with rage at what her hometown has become. And fills her with contempt for herself for only confronting it now.

When she is vulnerable.

She sits down on the edge of their bed . . . *her* bed, and thinks about the injustice of the situation. She found this house for them on her own, when he was too busy to help. She has done nothing wrong. So why flee? She has just decided she is going to be defiant and spend the night in her own home when the phone rings. 'Who is this?' a man's voice says when she answers.

'Who is this?' she responds.

'Where's Carlos?' the caller demands.

She hesitates, just a moment too long. El Santo swears and hangs up before she can improvise a lie. They know he's gone. And she knows, right then and there, that she needs to go too.

As fast as she can.

22

Padre Márcio

When Vicente Salinas was a child, over half a century ago, magazine articles were warning their readers about the dangers of falling into 'bad habits' and offering advice on how best to avoid them. But for the future Padre Márcio, his habits – neither good nor bad but merely essential – were his salvation. Every morning, as soon as he woke up, the boy would start the day by picking at the scabs on his palms.

The pain had not really registered when he had first drilled the holes into his flesh with the pencil. He'd been in another state of distress – a terrified boy rushing towards a fatal door because death had to be better than what his life had become.

He realized many years later that his attempted suicide had been a ramification of the *metaphysical* pain that had sheltered him from all somatic suffering. And when he had discovered the loose nail squirming out of the floorboard, he had been protected from pain by his initial relief – no, joy – at finding a way of keeping his subterfuge alive.

But after those two moments – one of anguish and the other of elation – he had quickly found that his physical suffering could no longer be ignored. Vicente endured extreme agony for months and months, made all the worse by the fact that it was so deliberately and carefully self-inflicted.

After nearly two years, he thought he had started to master what the Little Brothers of Perpetual Succour might have referred to as the torments of the flesh; not realizing that he had begun to neutralize the map of nerves inside his hands, an achievement that was hastened by the destructive arrival of the nests of maggots.

Wounds, like people, are also creatures of habit. If you don't allow them to heal, eventually they give up and do what they've become used to doing: remain open and fester.

Thanks to His Grace's pious gullibility, the normal transitory period of small-minded suspicion that befalls even the most venerated saints, such as Bernadette or the Children of Fátima, was completely ignored in Vicente's case. There was an eschatological rationale to the bishop's stance. When he first found the boy, the wounds in his palms had already appeared. Vicente had clearly been ordained a saint by the very manifestation of the Holy Sign of Christ: proof that the child was blessed; his miraculous lesions nothing less than the confirmation of a divine confidence in an innocent soul. And perhaps an urgent Final Days message for those who believed.

Vicente was unaware of the finer points of this ecclesiastical logic. He only knew that he was going to bed without fear and on a full stomach. For the first time in his life he felt that comforting sanctuary every child should experience. But all fairy tales end when the infant falls asleep.

Being a fraud himself, the vice-rector sensed not just the deceit in Vicente's condition but also the opportunity. He visited the bishop with a bottle of Dimple Haig and a bowl of *escamoles* and spoke in a respectful yet authoritative manner. Vicente was a boy unlike any other, true, yet he was also undeniably a child, and as such required what all children needed most: a Christian education. It would be unthinkable to deprive him of such, just as it would be unthinkable to expose such an innocent creature to the temptations posed by fellow pupils of his own age. Vicente merited a private tutor, not the anarchy of the classroom, and the vice-rector was prepared to sacrifice his vocation to volunteer for the position.

The bishop accepted the pious offer with gratitude.

When Vicente found out what had been agreed, he sank into a terrible depression. He wasn't filled with rage, or even fear. It was far simpler than that. It was an elemental awakening to the knowledge that everything that had been given to him – everything which had saved him – had been granted solely to accumulate the devastation when it was all finally stripped away. For, truly, how can one know real damnation when one hasn't first known paradise?

His consequential fall was immeasurable. Vicente wasn't just in shock, he was rendered mute; comatose. Years later, when he was a student in the seminary and reading Dante, he would understand what had happened to him the day the vice-rector returned to his life. It was as though he had leapt from the First Circle of Hell straight into the center of the Ninth Circle. Like Satan himself, he had become frozen in his torment.

The bishop was so concerned by the sudden physical collapse of Vicente that he called in his cook and gardener, Pablo Grande, who – although only twenty-seven – was already a noted herbalist and *curandero* in the region. Some people might have found it amusing that this small, wiry man, with eyes the color of the *mole* he was famous for, was called Grande, but those who knew him did not think it odd. His Grace suspected that Pablo Grande, although a practicing Catholic, harbored secret ties to obscure occult rituals, but was prepared to overlook this as he normally got results, whether it was making a single chicken feed a table of ten, or bringing a half-dead garden or parishioner back to life. Besides, if the bishop was capable of giving communion to the mayor and the police chief every Sunday morning and turning his back on their activities for the rest of the week, he was certainly capable of doing the same for Pablo Grande, who was – unlike the mayor and the police chief – an honest man and, more importantly, a talented one.

Pablo Grande was deeply concerned by the condition of Vicente and secretly performed a sequence of *limpias*. He discovered through the magic of the healing ceremonies that Vicente was a victim of terrible crimes and that his worst tormentor lay close by, waiting for an opportunity to attack again.

Of course, Pablo Grande didn't share any of his knowledge with the bishop, whom he thought of as a kind, if naïve, person. His first priority was to lift the child out of his trancelike stupor. It was a severe battle that lasted several days. During the combat, Pablo Grande found and extracted a worm of malice, a spider of spite and a scorpion of violence, all buried inside the boy by his enemies.

He killed the first two, stomping on them with sandaled feet and then setting the crushed remnants aflame. The third invasive spell was much harder to extract and he almost lost two fingers from its stings. He smashed the evil creature with a club his grandfather had fashioned from a Montezuma cypress, then spat upon the powdery heap of shattered shell. His saliva bubbled into a hot froth, forming the profile of a face he did not know, but which he recognized five days later when the vicerector passed him in the gardens.

Pablo Grande of course identified the wounds in Vicente's hands for what they were: a desperate defense against a cruel world. He placed a tiny rock crystal of hope in each palm, knowing that hope never dies and that the crystals would keep the wounds open and raw as long as the boy lived. (Pablo Grande may have done an immense job of liberating the child from the curses of others, however he did miss two seeds that were in Vicente's chest, hidden behind his heart; seeds that were not invasive but of the boy's own making: anger and pride. By the time Pablo Grande became aware of them, it would be too late. They had already sprouted roots and could not be extracted from Vicente without killing him.)

The child began to show signs of improvement almost immediately after the *limpias*. Pablo Grande gave him various herbal teas to build up his strength, and radicles to chew on to induce the growth of a protective bark around his soul. That would at least provide some initial defense from predators like the vice-rector.

Pablo Grande watched the vice-rector the way *brujos* do, not out of the corner of the eye but the back of the head, and perceived slowly but irrevocably the manifold sins and crimes of the evil brother. He decided the best course of action for both the boy and the world would be to poison the vice-rector with *kieri*. He went to the part of his garden that lay forever in shadow, where he kept what he thought of as the *extreme* remedies: all the fatal plants.

In a corner, nestled between the wall of the church and a buried crow, was a datura plant; its blossoms hanging heavy and sentient as a sleeping bat, petals enfolded around the horns of death like webbed wings. Deadly nightshade. Belladonna, thorn-apple, moonflower. Devil's trumpet. The bell of madness. The common names given to *Datura stramonium* revealed both the wisdom of the ancients and their fear of a plant that rendered people mute and mad, that stole their senses and then their minds, that sent them flying through the air, contorting one moment in ecstasy, the next in agony. Devil's snare. Jimson weed. *Kieri loca*. The plant that promised enlightenment but instead bestowed the very opposite, trapping you in time and space, then sending you insane within the airless prison of invariable repetition.

The results of anticholinergic poisoning are always disturbing to behold, let alone experience. The multifold symptoms include frightening aural hallucinations of the most menacing sounds imaginable. Respiratory collapse. Renal failure. Hydrocephalus. Such extreme lobar and nuchal rigidity that the scapulae muscle can snap of its own accord. Paralysis so severe and terrifying as to cause death through panic attack and resultant cardiac arrest. Paranoia. Severe dehydration. Astral and time travel. Third sight. Transmutation of self into animal or plant or even demon. Flight and contact with the dead. Pablo Grande did not take lightly what he was about to do. He plucked a single stalk from the plant, containing five leaves, a flower and its seedpod, ready to rupture.

He macerated the stem, leaves and flower, put them in a pot with chili, garlic, onions, sugar, cilantro and sunflower oil and stewed the contents gently over a low heat for thirteen hours and eighteen minutes, that being the period of sunlight at the summer solstice. He then poured his concoction into a thick *mole* sauce that was served with extra cinnamon, chocolate and nuts, because he knew the added fructose would help mask the fibrous atropine aftertaste. He ground the seeds into a hazardous mixture of powder and husks and lightly marinated them in orange juice.

That evening at dinner, Pablo Grande informed the brother that he would be dining alone, as His Grace had succumbed to a stomach complaint – brought on by Pablo Grande putting immoderate amounts of olive oil, flaxseed oil, aloe pulp, molasses and prune juice into a spicy lunchtime soup.

After the vice-rector had finished his chicken *mole*, Pablo Grande served him a piece of caramelized lime tart topped with cooked slices of Seville orange that had been deglazed with vinegar and sprinkled with the crushed seeds. The neutering mix of sweet and sour would further conceal the poison's taste at this most delicate of times, when it started to repeat on the victim. During his meal the vice-rector drank four carafes of water and three bottles of beer, unaware that his unquenchable thirst was the first symptom of an onset of fatal polydipsia.

Pablo Grande watched silently out of the back of his head. The vice-rector sat satiated and stupefied at the table after his three-hour feast, feeling his salivary glands slowly withering like a premature coyote pup abandoned in the desert. The mucus in his nasal cavities and the natural lubricants coating his pharynx also began to desiccate, creating the distressing feeling that he couldn't breathe without tearing the lining of his trachea. Strangely, despite this acute internal dehydration, the vice-rector's body felt as though it were awash in fluid. Sweat beaded his brow and cheeks, pooled abundant under his arms, stretched wet and sticky across his back, making his damp shirt cling to his body like a parasite. His thighs were so wet, his feet so sodden, that he thought he must have pissed himself, fluid pooling inside his shoes.

He wanted to stand up, to go to his room and strip off his tormenting clothes and shower; he wanted to run the jet across his face, to gulp down its waters, to put an end to the terrible tightness in his throat which was already beginning to lock into sequences of choking spasms, but he couldn't move. His eyes stared at the decanter of water on the table, and he willed his hands to go towards it and fill his glass and raise it to his lips, but his hands, his entire body would not obey.

Paralysis.

Of a kind he had never known before; a kind he could never imagine: his mind feverish; his body dormant. And the sight of that water, together with his appalling internal aridity and external flooding, began to send him into a manic dread unlike anything he had ever experienced. Tears welled in his eyes, then were sucked backwards by his corporeal heat, evaporating through his tear ducts, proof of the internal combustion that was consuming all his moisture. His trousers and shirt began to steam as his sweat now vaporized, condensing into salt which stung his boiling flesh. He felt his bowels beginning to roast, his lungs humming with heat.

A ringing in his ears which had started while he was eating dessert was now so loud that he thought it had to be caused by something external – a fire alarm, or perhaps an ambulance arriving to save him.

He stood up, only he was still sitting in his chair, the carafe of water in front of him but wholly out of reach. He looked all around the room and saw Pablo Grande staring at him with eyes in the back of his head. He shrieked, and the only sound that came out of his mouth was the sound inside his ears.

He rushed across the room, and then realized he had no feet; no body – he was alone, just a shriek inside a cavern called death. Faces jeered at him, innumerable and familiar, their words obliterated by the horrible internal scream; hundreds of his victims pointing at the earth. He could see what they were pointing to: it was his own body, lying on the ground, his chest heaving so furiously with the effort to breathe that his ribcage exploded, latticing his sternum like two bloody rows of tomb-stones.

The vice-rector's transposed consciousness watched, aghast, from the other side of the room as Pablo Grande knelt down beside his dead body and placed a crow's feather inside his ear, and then he felt it rustling its way to the source of the blasting heat that was consuming him: his brain on fire.

*

The vice-rector woke from the appalling nightmare with a start, sitting up so suddenly that he rapped his head hard on the low ceiling. It took him only a second to realize he wasn't dead; that it had all been some terrible hallucination. But it took him longer, almost a complete minute, to fully understand.

He tapped the coffin's lid, then pushed and pounded and scratched against it, tearing his fingernails as he tried to claw through the wood, his terrible shriek now filling what was left of his universe: his piercing scream incinerating the last vestiges of oxygen.

*

Pablo Grande knelt over the newly turned earth of the vice-rector's grave, handing the marigolds to Vicente to place in the small cradle he had dug in the soil. The young boy paused a moment, his head tilted in reflection.

'What is it?' Pablo Grande asked.

The boy shrugged, going back to his flowers. 'I thought I heard something, but it was probably just the wind . . .' Above them, on the graveyard wall, a crow turned its head, then cawed.

23

Nomen Nescio #352 (Jane Doe #352)

The desert is silent at first. Then there is the distant mechanical menace of an approaching convoy. Headlights slash the night, rushing towards a strange, luminous glow behind the hills.

A cluster of farmyard pickups, expensive sedans, SUVs and truck cabins sits outside a fenced ranch house, which emits a hovering light through papered-over windows.

There is the sound of a scream from inside, followed by a burst of exclamations and a smattering of applause. A door opens and two men walk out and start to piss over the balcony, their faces covered in shadow. One of them laughs.

II

The Mirage of the Dunes

DAY 2

Victim 874
Nomen Nescio #352 (Jane Doe #352)

24

Nomen Nescio #352 (Jane Doe #352)

A garbage truck squats beside a wire perimeter fence as two municipal workers hook up an overflowing dumpster. One of them triggers the button and the bin rises with a jolt of protest before being mastered by machinery, dutifully mounting up to the lip, then bowing, its contents rolling into the truck with a hollow clatter. A naked body falls through space, free for a single instant before being buried again by refuse.

One of the workers cries out, and quickly hits the stop button just as the hydraulic blade is moving in to compress the trash.

He climbs up and peers into the hopper, then quickly jumps down, running away. His partner watches him heading down a road towards a phone box. He turns back to the truck, crosses himself, then looks inside. He falls backwards in shock, tumbling as he hits the ground, then scrambling back to his feet.

He leans against the wire perimeter fence for support, rocking there for a moment, then throws up.

25

Ventura

The bell clips the night, its coppery call soothing her after the torment of the last three hours. Ventura had left the house right after the phone call, driving out to the airport, but the only flights that evening were to Ciudad Juárez, Santa Teresa and Mexico City. Arriving late at night in the first two destinations would be even more dangerous than staying in Ciudad Real, and flying back to the capital was unthinkable – at least at this stage. She had given up too much to return so soon with nothing but a broken relationship, an empty bank account and an abandoned story.

So she drove back to the old town and was just pulling up outside the Hotel Los Arcos when she noticed a man standing in the shadows beside the door, staring at her with an unnerving alertness. She pulled away fast, watching in the rearview mirror as the man raced out onto the street, as though trying to read her license plates.

She kept driving, wondering if she should risk another hotel, and without realizing it, started taking the way home. She slowed at the crossroads three blocks from her house. The lights were on in her bedroom. She couldn't remember if she had left them on or not. There was a car parked outside. It might have belonged to one of the neighbors but she didn't recognize the blue Ford pickup.

Maybe it was them.

Anger and fear warred inside her as she thought of Carlos and what he had done to her. She turned left, leaving her home for the second time that night, the streets dark and unsettled.

She toyed with the idea of crossing the border. She had her passport and Border Crossing Card inside her luggage. But what if they had *narcos* looking for her at the crossing? They had plenty of people on the other side too. She headed back towards the center, and that's when she thought about Mayor.

She's about to ring the bell again when there is the scrape and stutter of old-fashioned bolts sliding free and Felipe Mayor is standing before her, resplendent in a thick bathrobe with navy and sky-blue vertical stripes. He takes a suitcase in either hand and leads her across the courtyard.

She starts to follow, then stops and goes back to close the exterior gate behind her, slotting home the bolts with the uneasy feeling that she is locking out a definite threat, but possibly trapping herself with an unknown one.

The lights in the downstairs entrance and living rooms are all on, but still there are shadows sitting in corners, obstinate as mules. It's all hardwood ceiling beams, whitewashed walls and polished terracotta tiles; furniture hewn from trees by men a century dead. There is no doubt: it is a grandee's home, and the former ambassador has the natural confidence to fill it. He goes over to a bar. 'Drink?'

Ventura shakes her head. 'I'm sorry if I woke you.'

'I'm like Balzac. I write mainly at night. Anyway, at this stage of my life, I hardly sleep at all.' He pours the amber liquid into a balloon glass, sniffing it appreciatively, then sits down in a leather armchair – more a throne – its massive silhouette outlined with cruel brass heads hammered into submission. He slides a cigar out of a box. 'Fidel sends me these himself,' he says. Even his rich voice sounds a little lost in the room.

'You're all alone?' she asks, sitting on the edge of a sofa.

'I keep a staff of eight. But there's no need to wake them. Unlike me, they actually work in the day.' He glances at her bags, like a jeweler looking at a poor widow's engagement ring, already assessing what he can get away with. 'When they awake, I will have them prepare a room. In the meantime . . .'

'It's just for tonight. I didn't want to be alone.'

'I'm glad you called. I don't want to be alone either.' He exhales a gush of cigar smoke, as though trying to mask his eyes behind the gray cloud. 'Surely it's better to share such moments than to endure them on one's own?' He puts his glass and cigar down and walks towards her. She stands up, but he's already there, taking her hands in his, drawing her towards him, into his scent of Aramis, smoke and cognac. She pulls away before he can kiss her. 'I made a mistake,' she says. 'I thought I could trust you.'

'That is no mistake. But you must enunciate your intentions.' He picks up his cigar, holding it speculatively. 'Normally a call such as yours in the middle of the night denotes a certain act. Do you wish to sleep with me or not?' She shakes her head. A slow-burn smile spreads across his face. 'One day we will argue which one of us regrets that decision more. Fine. You are under my protection. Anyone under my protection is safe. *Bueno*. Are you hungry?'

The question surprises her because she hasn't realized until now that she is. 'Just something simple.'

'That, unfortunately, is all I'm capable of.' He leads her into a kitchen that looks like it came out of a museum. Mayor chops purple onions and strips of beef and tosses them into a pan of hot olive oil, stepping out of the way as they froth and spit. He's already asked Ventura to peel the cloves of garlic, and now he quarters them, removing the green shoots in the interior, and tosses them in as well, with a fistful of red and green chilies. He lowers the heat. He plucks some basil and coriander from pots that line an interior window sill, breaking the leaves with his fingers and dropping them in. Rock salt. Ground pepper. Then he adds beans. Ventura starts to set the table in the kitchen. 'The dining room.' He indicates a darkened room. 'I never eat in the kitchen.'

Ventura hits a light switch. A ceiling lamp made from a wagon wheel illuminates a large oak table, with sixteen rigid chairs. She sets places in front of the chair at the head of the table and the one to its right, finding plates on a side counter.

Back in the kitchen, Mayor is turning the concoction with a wooden spoon. He hands two wine glasses to her, then takes the pan in one hand, an opened bottle of Argentine Malbec in the other, and leads the way into the dining room. He half fills both glasses over Ventura's protests, then goes over to the light dial and turns the intensity down low.

Mayor lights a single table candle so that the plates are lit with a soft, wavering glow. 'Unlike Hemingway, I'm not a fan of clean, well-lighted places,' he says, spooning a large portion onto Ventura's plate. 'I lived in Paris. Half the pleasure of dining there is the glitter of eyes in candlelight.' He toasts her, the crystal glasses reverberating in the silent house.

Ventura is taken aback by the soothing heft of the wine and the intense spiciness of the food. It's not that it makes her feel better; it makes her feel alive. 'Tell me your story,' he says.

She hesitates. There is a stillness in his gaze that is calming; that suggests surrender – not of her body but of her thoughts, for she is sitting all alone in the middle of the night next to a master of words. She starts to speak.

26

Fuentes

Fuentes stands in a doorway, staring across the room at a large bed. Gomez is asleep in it with a woman. Fuentes lightly taps on the open door.

Marina opens her eyes. She gazes at Fuentes for a long, surprised moment, her eyelids fluttering first in panic, then annoyance. She turns over and shakes Gomez. 'Your boss is here.'

'Partner,' Fuentes says.

Marina gives a short, sarcastic laugh. She shakes Gomez again, Fuentes catching a glimpse of her breasts as the sheet falls from her shoulders. 'Your fucking *partner* is here.'

Gomez rolls over, opens his eyes, focuses on Fuentes and swears. He gets out of bed, naked, and staggers across the room, past Fuentes, disappearing through a door in the hallway. 'Make yourself at home – fuck!' Gomez is pissing noisily. 'How'd you get in?'

Fuentes turns back to Gomez's bedroom. Marina is pulling on a pair of briefs. Their eyes meet. She indicates the door. Fuentes closes it, turning back to the bathroom. 'Through the kitchen window.'

Gomez comes out, a towel wrapped around his waist. He goes up close to Fuentes, his breath sleep-soiled. 'What the fuck are you doing in my house, man?'

Fuentes indicates the front yard with a thumb over his

shoulder. 'There is a *gringo* and a senior PJF officer sitting in a car outside.'

Gomez walks towards the kitchen scratching his chest. 'What the hell do they want?'

'You haven't heard?'

'It's too early in the morning for your games.'

Fuentes takes his time, lighting up a cigarette. 'Remember that partner of yours? Paredes?'

Gomez nods impatiently, pouring himself a glass of juice.

'They picked him up in El Lobo.'

Gomez glances through the window, pulling back when he spots the car across the road. 'What for?'

Fuentes watches his face carefully. 'As if you can't guess.'

'How much?'

Fuentes studies him. 'Forty-two kilos.'

Anger wars with disbelief in his eyes. Disbelief wins. 'No fucking way.'

'How can you be sure?'

'He was my partner for two years! A hundred grams here or there? Shit happens. But smuggling twenty years to life into El Lobo? He's not that crazy.'

Fuentes believes that people are never born crazy, it's circumstance that makes them that way. These days, circumstances are creating a population of lunatics. 'Maybe he was gambling. Maybe he owed money to people you should never owe money to.' Maybe he was desperate.

It's not so much that doubt has arrived on Gomez's face; it's more that the defiant disbelief has left it. He glances at the car outside again. 'Why are they interested in me?'

'Your former partner's just turned out to be a corrupt

fuck-up. They think you must be one too.'

Gomez swears, kicks a chair. 'Hypocrites!'

'Get dressed. We'll go out the way I came in. I've got the car out back.'

Gomez goes back into the bedroom. Hot, charged whispers come from the couple on the other side of the closed door.

Fuentes listens for a moment, then goes into the bathroom and flicks open the bathroom cabinet, checking the contents. He closes its door and moves into the large living room, taking in the expensive sound system, the professional racing bike leaning against the weight-lifting equipment. There's a corner full of hi-tech gadgets, some still in their original packaging. A bar stocked with expensive liquor – French cognac, single malt whiskey; the best *añejo* tequila. On the shelves of a bookcase are sporting and hunting trophies; girlie magazines totter like a makeshift coffee table by a leather sofa. It is a totally testosterone environment, filled with toys that Gomez could never afford; not unless . . .

He's as crooked as Paredes.

By the telephone is a framed picture of Marina. He takes out the snapshot he found in Paredes' place and compares it against Marina's photo. There is no doubt: it is exactly the same woman except now she is a brunette again. Fashion choice – or disguise?

The bedroom door opens. Gomez looks almost presentable. 'Let's get the fuck out of here.' The door is slammed behind him. Marina's still pissed. Gomez heads for the front door – on morning autopilot – but Fuentes stops him, leading him through the kitchen. He climbs out the window, dropping to the lawn in a crouch position, looking all around to make sure no one is watching. They are obscured from the street by the neighbor's house. Gomez lands next to him, loose change falling from his trouser pockets. He curses and drops to his knees, picking coins up.

Fuentes glares at him. 'Forget it.' He strides away, disappearing over a back fence. Gomez looks up for a second, then goes back to the ground, hastily picking up the last of the coins before rushing after Fuentes.

Fuentes walks through a backyard, past children half concealed behind washing hanging out to dry. He gets in his car, slides in behind the wheel and reaches over, popping the lock for Gomez just as he comes running up. Gomez looks over his shoulder nervously, then gets in.

'Now we know what it feels like.'

'Like *what* feels like?'

Fuentes switches on the police radio, static filling the car. He turns the radio down, glancing over his shoulder as he starts reversing down a lane. 'Being a criminal.'

Buses clog the roads, horns blaring, the radio humming into clarity, then veering back into static. Gomez is reaching to turn it off when the static fades and they hear snippets of a conversation. '. . . Near the airport?'

The response wavers on the radio, but the distortion is not enough to block the dreaded response: 'She was in a dumpster.'

Fuentes lurches forwards, turning up the radio, but all he gets is the whine of interference. Direction signs loom through the windshield. Fuentes turns right with a squeal, following an arrow pointing to the airport.

27

Ventura

They sit in silence, the bottle empty, Ventura's story told. It was painful when she started, but as she went along, recounting what had happened with Carlos that night, and digressing constantly with references to their earlier life together, she felt a lifting; an unburdening, so that now, with the first intimation of daylight, she feels strangely transformed.

'And what now?' Mayor asks.

Their conversation – *her* conversation – had reminded Ventura of her first confession: a monologue from her, answered by an occasional monosyllable. Mayor had been a famous early advocate of psychoanalysis in Mexico. Perhaps his brief comments – sometimes questions, sometimes prompts – were an echo of his own therapy. Perhaps Ventura had forgotten – or never knew – that all good writers are great listeners. 'I have to leave Ciudad Real. But before I do, I want to finish my story.'

He draws a pack of cigarettes out of one of the pockets of his robe. 'Did you ever hear about that case in Belgium?' Mayor asks, leaning forwards and touching the cigarette to the candle. There is a brief burst of flame. 'A man who kept young girls locked up in his cellar for use as sexual slaves.'

She draws back in her seat, alert. 'Why are you telling me this?'

'You'll understand in a moment.' The construction of that sentence alarms her. After feeling secure throughout the meal and her conversation, she suddenly feels vulnerable again. The way she felt when she first arrived and rang the bell. Trust is an odd thing. It's like love. A big emotion that grows out of nothing, that you take for granted but which devastates you when it disappears. She focuses back on Mayor, on the hateful story he's telling. '. . . He'd share these poor girls with friends. When he got tired of them, he'd simply kill them, and kidnap some more.'

Ventura shivers. 'A monster.'

'Finally this *monstruo* was caught and the surviving girls freed. Then came the rumors. That the people who had been sharing the girls were policemen and judges and politicians; that the kidnapped girls had been an open secret in the highest circles. The public became enraged by these rumors.'

Ventura's voice is a dry whisper. 'What happened?'

'A social revolution. There were strikes, demonstrations; mass protests. The government collapsed.' In the distance is the sound of a car backfiring. Or perhaps it was what it really sounded like: gunshots. Ventura looks around the vast, dimly lit dining room, unnerved. The hacienda feels threatening in an obscure and illogical way. As though she might vanish within its infinite shadows. She clears her throat, trying to recover her poise. 'And then?'

'And then . . . nothing. It just slowly faded from the minds of everyone. Except of course the families of the victims.' Mayor strikes a match, making Ventura jump, and lights her cigarette. He looks at her bare arms. She has goose flesh. He blows out the match, Ventura feeling his breath against her arm. 'No one imagined the Holocaust. No one foresaw Pol Pot or the Rwandan genocide. That's the nature of true evil: you simply cannot imagine it . . . *until it happens*. These are crimes of history. And they are always crafted by powerful people. That's a lesson we have yet to understand here in Ciudad Real. Think for one moment: hundreds and hundreds of women murdered and not one clue? Not one suspect? Not even an end in sight to the crimes – nothing. How is that possible?'

'It's impossible.'

Mayor gives a harsh laugh. 'Worse than that. It's preposterous. If you read about it in a novel, you'd reject the premise as outlandish. The reality we currently have in Ciudad Real is *beyond fiction* – and that is a very dangerous place to be.'

He gets up and walks towards the louvre windows, opening them one at a time, bird song beginning to fill the room from the garden outside. He turns back to her, his body silhouetted against the lightening sky. 'Ventura, this is the biggest cover-up in our country since the massacres of May '68. There is *nothing* like it. Not in Mexico. Not even in the world. And no one – not one person – knows anything about who's behind it.' The house creaks from the chill of the early morning air that shifts about them, curious and alien. 'You know what the police always say about a suspect? Silence equals guilt. If you want a credible suspect in these killings, look to those who have been silent the longest. The city authorities, the state authorities. The federal authorities.'

Above them, far away, is the low shriek of an airplane, troubling the sky with its drone. Ventura rushes though the open windows to the courtyard outside, fighting a wave of panic with deep gulps of cool air, the last eight hours catching up with her. She turns to Mayor, who has joined her. 'What kind of country allows so many women to be murdered and does nothing about it?'

'The obvious answer is, of course, *no country*, but here we are, living in that country.'

'I'm such a fool. I have no chance of getting any answers.'

'You're wrong. You have me, and I know people who can help you.' He escorts Ventura back inside, where he copies some phone numbers from a Berluti agenda onto a sheet of embossed paper. He passes it to her.

Ventura glances at the names on the paper. 'Who are they?'

'The first is a CTON union organizer. He's good. The second is a police detective. You can trust him. I'll let them know you'll be in touch.' He looks up as a maid appears at the door. 'Maya, can you prepare our guest a room please? She is tired and needs to rest.'

'I'm fine, thank you. I need to get to work straight away.'

'Believe me, you should take this opportunity, because once you get started on this story, there'll be no more time to rest.'

28

Pilar

The *cantina* hits Pilar with the asymmetrical assault of shade and noise as she steps in from the sullen, sun-blinding street, leaving her dislocated and vulnerable, male eyes turning in unison, quickly appraising her.

Fantasizing what they'd like to do to her.

They are young men, old men, middle-aged men. Men with whiskers and pot bellies and bad breath. Men with faces scarred by the elements or teenage acne. Some have bad teeth, many are balding, but they never think of themselves when they evaluate a woman's body, especially when she's a total stranger. It isn't just an idle dirty thought; it is their prerogative to judge, and they make sure they always assert it. The men are fast and crude in their assessments. Tits too small, ass too big. Or the other way around. It doesn't really matter, as long as they find fault. Thick ankles. Skinny arms. Long nose. Thin lips. If the woman is wearing make-up, she's a whore. If she isn't, she's a dyke. Either way the woman needs to be judged and found wanting.

In their fantasy world, women are not allowed to win. Perhaps that's why they play the game: because they are all losers too.

Juan Antonio sits alone at the bar, talking into a phone with a tone that alternates between desperate pleading and aggressive threats as he waves Pilar over through the cigarette smoke. In other cities, it could have been a lovers' argument on the phone, the tedium of saying sorry and not meaning it; doing whatever it takes to win the person back, at least for another night. But here, in Ciudad Real, a city too dangerous to ever think of romance, Pilar knows Juan Antonio is engrossed in work, not foreplay. He needs a shave; a change of clothes. His hair's a mess. Juan Antonio doesn't give a fuck about his appearance, but why should he? Men get away with lapses women are punished for. 'Twenty buses?' he says fast into the phone, making the question sting like a slap across the face. 'Only *twenty* fucking buses?'

He puts a hand over the mouthpiece and orders some coffee for Pilar and another beer for himself, a male voice whining at him across circuits all the way from Mexico City. The voice tells Juan Antonio that he should be happy to have buses from Guadalajara *and* Tijuana *and* Monterrey *and* Ciudad-fucking-Juárez and if he doesn't show some gratitude he can shove all the buses up his ass.

They both start laughing but Pilar's already stopped listening. This is the part she hates, the swagger of machismo banter in a world of women. Women working in sweatshops. Women abused at home. Women being assaulted; raped, murdered. Women fighting for other women. But everything controlled by men.

Her coffee's too strong. She used to drink it like this all the time, all day long. Now if she drinks more than one cup a day she can't sleep at night. They say it has something to do with getting old, but she knows it isn't physical. She doesn't need a stimulant. Her life's become one great adrenaline rush. Pilar feels exhausted not because she's only slept two hours since the end of the night shift but because she's slept, period. And she feels guilty. She should be with Maria and Lupita at the *maquiladora*, surrounded by women all working hard, not idling her time away in some lousy joint with a bunch of lazy men trying to wake themselves up with any number of stimulants.

She drops a sugar cube into the coffee and stirs it, glancing up at the TV behind the bar, announcers speaking with urgency, a graph behind them showing a bank of arrows all pointing downwards. The scene cuts to Wall Street and shouting, flustered traders, their faces full of fear.

They have no idea.

Real fear is being a woman walking home alone from work just before dawn, not knowing who sits behind the headlights bursting over the horizon. She sips her coffee, appreciating the irony of the televised fiscal panic. American companies have rushed to shut down factories in their own country and shift production to Mexico. Wage bills and production costs have been slashed dramatically, so you'd expect the cost of the products to drop as well. Companies that were already making a fortune suddenly can't afford not to make even more. Enormous profits become obscene profits, but still it's not enough.

It's never enough.

And now some opaque shift in the stock market instils the sudden terror that history has not ended, that profit is not limitless, that revenue may diminish. Pilar knows what such fears will trigger. Redundancies, factory closures, mergers and consolidations. Austerity. Downsizing. Global upheaval. The container ships are already in the harbors, waiting to set sail to China.

On the television, an announcer speaks about the percentage drop in the Nasdaq Index with dismay, as though he were announcing vast casualties in a terrible war. The disbelief in his eyes says it all – he's just another loser, gambling on a roulette wheel he only now realizes has been rigged all along.

Juan Antonio hangs up at last. 'I got a call from Felipe Mayor this morning.' The casual way he says it can't disguise his pride at dropping such a name.

Pilar read two of his books at school. She wasn't impressed. 'What did he want?'

'He's donating fifty thousand pesos to the strike fund.'

She's pleasantly surprised but doesn't want to show it. 'He could afford to give ten times that.'

'Don't exaggerate. It's an exemplary act.'

'Exemplary gesture, you mean. What does he want in return?'

This is why he has such respect for Pilar, such belief in her future, not just in the union but one day in politics. Her instincts are superb. 'You are such a cynic! Nothing,' Juan Antonio lies. 'He's even arranged for a journalist to provide extra coverage.'

'Let me guess. A female journalist?'

Juan Antonio grimaces defensively. 'I thought you'd be happy to have a *periodista*.'

'Who we have to babysit just because she's fucking Mayor?'

'Can it, will you? We're meeting both of them this evening.'

'I'm not.'

'You are.'

That's the difference between workers and bosses. Between women and men. One says *no* and the other says *yes*. 'He also told me we can trust that cop you spoke to yesterday.'

'Fuentes? He's not just any cop.'

Juan Antonio considers for a moment, turning his cigarette slowly so that the ash doesn't fall off. Then it dawns on him and he swears, the jerk in his hand making the tube of ash drop onto his jeans. He smears it into a blur. 'What *aren't* you telling me?'

'He recognized me from Tijuana.'

What a colossal fuck-up, Juan Antonio thinks. 'Really?' he says, his voice almost under control. 'When were you going to tell me this?'

'I was going to tell you yesterday, but . . .' But there was a car bombing, and she excluded everything from her mind to find the strength to start that night shift. She looks away from his red-rimmed eyes. 'He told me he wasn't here for the unions. He told me he was here for the murders.'

'And you believe him? A motherfucking, union-bashing cop?'

Pilar shrugs helplessly. She doesn't want to believe Fuentes, and yet somehow she does. 'How do I know? Mayor trusts him, you said that yourself.' She watches Juan Antonio finish his beer. 'You drink too much. Your eyes are always red.'

'Because you make me cry tears of frustration.'

'You shouldn't be drinking this early in the day.'

'It's only beer, and if you had to do what I have to do . . .'

There is a pause as they both think about what has just been said. 'Which you think is more important than what I have to do? Why is that – because you're a man?'

'Jesus, Pilar, when will you learn?'

'Learn what?'

'I'm on your side.'

'Sometimes it doesn't feel like it.'

'And sometimes the feeling's mutual.' He sings a phrase of a *ranchero* tune as he thinks about what to do next. 'We need to find out if he's really here for them . . .' The dead women, Pilar thinks to herself, are always *them*. 'Or if he's here for us.' Juan Antonio picks his car keys up off the bar counter. 'Let's go.'

'Where to?'

'To see the mother of Isabel Torres.'

139

29

Fuentes

Fuentes pulls up behind an ambulance, Gomez already out of the car, shaking hands and joking with the uniformed police. Fuentes watches him through the windshield, then gets out of the car, glancing around. 'Where's the body?'

A cop indicates the ambulance. Fuentes swears. He suddenly has everyone's attention. 'You had strict orders not to touch the body until we arrived. Who's in charge here?'

There's an embarrassed silence. A man steps forwards. 'Sorry, sir, but we couldn't just leave her lying there in the trash.'

Fuentes gives a harsh, scoffing laugh.

Gomez goes up to him quickly, speaking in an undertone. 'Come on, boss, they're just trying to do right by the girl.'

Fuentes ignores him, talking to the assembled cops. 'This is a crime scene, not a fucking dancehall. I want the dumpster and all the trash in it and the truck impounded as evidence and dusted for fingerprints. I want this area sealed off and checked for footprints and tire treads, the way it should have been done the moment you got here.'

The police all nod but stand there doing nothing. Fuentes goes over to the ambulance and pulls open the doors.

Inside is a zipped-up body bag. 'Totally compromised. Fuck!' He turns to a cop. 'Get her over to the morgue. Now.'

The cop shouts at the ambulance driver. The red light comes on, and the siren starts up, wailing in protest at the futility of its mission as it speeds away.

Fuentes walks slowly across the terrain, gazing at the ground. He crouches low beside the perimeter fence, examining something: rust-colored stains scabbing the dirt. Gomez crouches beside him, staring at them. 'Blood?'

Fuentes uses a wooden spatula to scrape the sample into a plastic evidence bag. 'Probably hers, but . . . it's about time we got lucky.'

Fuentes scans the area for other clues. Over by the terminal entrance, cars glint in the morning sun. A prop plane taxies slowly past them, sending trash whirling. Fuentes turns to Gomez, shaking his head. 'It's always the same. They're killed somewhere else and then they're dumped. Why do they do that? Why not just leave them where they kill them, or kill them where they dump them?'

'Witnesses?'

'What fucking witnesses? No one sees them being killed, but no one sees them being dumped either. The answer's simple.' Gomez stares at him with patient eyes. Not simple enough for Gomez. 'It's because they're killing them under controlled circumstances. Even though they know that by killing them somewhere else and then transporting the bodies, they risk accumulating evidence in their vehicles. Blood stains, hair; a lost earring – you name it. Why run those kinds of risks?'

Gomez looks at the police standing around the trash truck, still doing nothing. 'Because they think we're fuck-ups?'

Fuentes gives a deep, savage smile. 'Because they *know* we're fuck-ups. Because they know it's never going to occur to us to even think of looking for that kind of evidence in the cars they drive.'

Gomez says it as though it's never occurred to him before. 'Untouchables?'

'*Claro*,' Fuentes says, scanning the car park outside the terminal. 'And who's untouchable in Ciudad Real?'

'Cops?'

'And?'

'*Narcos*.'

Fuentes smiles, pleased with his student. 'Cops and *narcos* ... And let's not forget *gringos*. One or all of them is doing this and they know we're too stupid or too afraid or too greedy to go looking in their cars for evidence.'

'We're going to prove those motherfuckers wrong.'

Fuentes glances back at the airport parking lot. 'If we don't do it soon, we're never going to do it. It's like a football game. When you're down two–nil, even three, you can maybe fight back.' He gets in the car, still talking. 'But once you pass a certain point, the whole team gives up. For them, the game is already over. That's where we are right now. The whole fucking country. We're right on the verge of giving up for good.'

Fuentes starts driving back towards town. He glances up at the rearview. Through the curtain of dust rising behind them, he sees a sedan with Texas license plates following. He indicates the car to Gomez with a jerk of his head. 'They're the people who were outside your place this morning. They never saw us leave. The motherfuckers were tipped off.'

'They probably have a police radio.'

'They were tipped off.'

Gomez turns to Fuentes. 'You said you thought they killed them somewhere else for a reason ...'

Fuentes glances at his partner then at the rearview mirror,

the car dropping back but still tailing them. He shrugs. 'The way I've got it figured, it's some kind of ritual killing. A black mass.' He turns to his partner, who is staring hard at him.

'What makes you say that?'

'Makes sense, doesn't it? Murder in a controlled environment. How do *you* figure it?'

'Snuff films.'

Fuentes considers for a second. 'Have you ever seen a snuff film?'

'Who the fuck do you think I am?'

'A cop. Answer the question. Have you ever seen a snuff film?' Gomez shakes his head. 'Neither have I, and I've seen every other kind of film you can imagine. I've seen every perversity out there; ones I didn't even know existed till I saw them. But the only thing I have never ever seen is a snuff film.' Fuentes gives Gomez a challenging look. 'Why is that?'

'Restricted distribution?' Fuentes slams the steering wheel, moaning in frustration. 'It makes sense,' Gomez says defensively. 'Fear of prosecution.'

'You could say the same thing about pedophilia. But that's out there in *huge* volumes . . . I'll tell you why no one's ever seen a snuff film. It's because they don't exist.'

'Maybe you're right.'

'Fuck maybe, this case has gone on way too long for any more *maybes*. Maybe this, maybe that. Jesus, how about some clinical, precise detective work.' He looks at Gomez, the car slowly drifting to the side. Gomez reaches over and guides the wheel back. 'So how did Paredes figure it?'

'A loner,' Gomez admits, looking away, embarrassed.

'Eight hundred plus women and that's the best he can come

up with?' Fuentes gives a disdainful scoff. 'That's some mother-fucking hardworking loner. It's ten times as many as Camargo or López, in half the time frame. And they both killed under cover of civil war.'

'And that's not what we have here?'

Fuentes hates to admit it but Gomez has a point. 'What did you say to Paredes when he told you his loner theory?'

'I told him it was impossible. But he wouldn't listen to me.' His look is savage. 'He treated me like a kid.' The car's engine punishes the uncomfortable silence. 'My opinion didn't fuck-ing matter.'

'That's not the case with me.'

'I know. You're perfect.'

Fuentes lets the sarcasm settle. 'If that's not her blood, how do you think it got there?'

'Maybe she put up a fight before they killed her? Maybe he hurt himself transporting the body?' Gomez pauses for a moment, trying hard to think. 'Maybe he had a dispute with one of the other killers?'

'They're all possible. But you know what I think? I think he cut himself shaving. I think the motherfucker killed her, then got ready for work – shit, shower and shave – and dropped her off on his way to get some morning coffee. I think that's how casual it's become. And that's why we're going to catch him and once we have him, we have the others. There's no way one man's done all this.' Fuentes rubs the stubble on his chin, and glances at Gomez's five o'clock shadow. He gives a dark smile. 'At least we both have alibis . . .'

The radio quivers into life. Gomez turns up the volume, re-peating the address. He shakes his head. 'That can't be for us . . .

They've made a mistake.' He goes to take the mouthpiece from the dash but Fuentes pulls it from his grip, buttoning down hard as he responds. 'Affirmative.'

Gomez stares at Fuentes. 'You asked for this?' Fuentes ignores him, which tells him that he did. 'I don't get it. What the fuck do we want in a shithole like Anaprata?'

'Answers.'

30

Padre Márcio

Like a group of senior *matadores* fighting over who would be the *padrino* to a young prodigy about to take his *alternativa*, everyone wanted to consecrate Padre Márcio at his ordination. Two cardinals and the papal nuncio were forced to share the minor roles of sponsors as the former Vicente Salinas himself selected his mentor, the bishop of Ciudad Real, to perform the ceremony that transformed him into Padre Márcio.

The stigmatic's ordination received national coverage. María Félix attended wearing trousers, which created a scandal – not at the ceremony but only later, when her photos appeared in the newspapers, sparking grateful editors to life. But during the actual ceremony nobody noticed; their eyes were riveted not on the movie star but on the blood that flowed forth spontaneously just after Padre Márcio took his vows.

Even former President Alemán sent a telegram of congratulations, although it arrived a day late because the mayor had declared a public holiday in Ciudad Real to mark the occasion.

Padre Márcio spent the evening of his ordination in his quarters in the bishop's palace, reflecting on the journey that had taken him from abused child to exalted priest.

At first he felt pride.

Sinful pride.

But then he felt anger, and the more he let this most corrosive of emotions into his soul, the more it grew. It swelled into a painful tumescence which burst like a cyst. A simple thought had occurred to him for the first time: the positive changes in his circumstances had had nothing to do with the Mercy of God, only with a child's despairing cunning born from desperation. And yet all the distinguished guests at the ceremony had lauded Divine Grace instead of a small boy's guile. They had made offerings of thanks to the Lord, but there had been no acknowledgment of Padre Márcio's fearful ability to survive the unsurvivable.

To endure the unendurable.

To change the unchangeable.

As is always the case with the most intense and consuming anger, it was directed against God, though a certain part was reserved for himself. Enduring for the sake of survival was meaningless if it was not followed by vengeance. There had to be consequences to his survival; not for himself but for his tormentors.

He wondered why he had never thought of this before. Was it his pathetic relief at having been saved from the assault of the brothers which had made him so emotionally passive? Or was it his guilt at having escaped what the other children could not?

Perhaps it was something even more complex; the end of his deliberate subterfuge. The crystals that Pablo Grande had planted in his palms had worked their magic, maintaining his open sores without need of daily intervention. Like most imposters, Padre Márcio was beginning to believe his own artifice. Whatever it was, for the first time a crisp conception of the future took precedence over the painful blur of the past.

The morning following his ordination, Padre Márcio made his first apostolic decision: to request a surprise visit, in the company of the cardinals, the papal nuncio and the bishop, to the orphanage of the Little Brothers of Perpetual Succour. They were accompanied by an official delegation made up of the state governor, the mayor, the police chief and several others, including the editors of the town's three newspapers.

As Padre Márcio had expected, nothing had changed inside an institute solely constructed to facilitate the torture and abuse of children. He knew all the secret passageways leading to the punishment chambers and isolation cells. He escorted his appalled guests past victim and perpetrator, exposing all the procedures and processes of carefully organized rape performed under the guise of Holy Orders and in the Name of God.

He claimed Divine Intervention, citing a post-ordination dream that had instructed him to find and expose these horrors. His audience had no option but to believe him, because any other explanation was unthinkable. Several of the more corrupt, if naïve, amongst them wondered if the young priest would dream about their crimes as well.

Padre Márcio knew that if he had exposed the brothers' crimes just to members of the clergy, nothing would have been done. The brothers would have been dispersed to other parishes, where they would find new victims, their evil crimes continuing unchecked; a contagious plague of cruelty. But in front of this group, such concealment was not possible. Someone would talk and, more importantly, someone would listen.

Within two hours, all the brothers had been arrested and the children liberated into the care of medical staff. With outrage burning like a fatal fever, city authorities swore decimation.

Padre Márcio called a meeting in the late vice-rector's quarters, and it was there that he came of age as a politician. He urged discretion. A scandal such as this would not only destroy the orphanage, but the town itself. He reassured the troubled witnesses that they were not responsible, that they were above reproach. Why then should the guilt of a few sinners be allowed to tarnish social order and civic reputation? Not to mention the necessary ebb and flow of commerce.

He therefore volunteered to oversee the running of the orphanage, to cleanse it of its sins and restore it to a position of trust and decency. Above all he pledged to save the children from future harm. They had the potential to form a holy legion to spread Christ's word – to become soldiers in an army fighting for Jesus.

All the dignitaries agreed with a mixture of relief and gratitude. The brothers would be stripped of their ecclesiastical status and thrown into the state penitentiary of Absalom to await trial – in the knowledge that such a trial could never be allowed to take place.

The coup was complete. Padre Márcio had achieved the first step in his plan to take over the Order of the Little Brothers of Perpetual Succour, not just in Ciudad Real but in all of Mexico. And he had succeeded in his scheme to make the entire community – or at least its formal representatives – complicit in his plan. He was on his way to controlling the entire town, and with it the state. And there was only one man who could oppose him.

One man who knew a truth that could undo all his work.

Pablo Grande.

31

Pilar

Everything happened the way they had hoped. The two fuck-ups working as security guards went out to the food truck at eight, after the women had all arrived, and the manager – who was really only the son of the manager – was late as usual.

Pilar and three other agitators rolled down the front and back grilles, then bolted them to the ground. A cry of triumph went up from the thirty-four women barricaded inside. They had secured the premises.

The occupation had begun.

It was chance that had partly determined which *maquiladora* had been selected for direct action, but Pilar knew they couldn't have chosen a better one – or rather a worse one – to shut down in the whole of Baja California. The lowest rate of pay in all of Tijuana, which was saying something. A lack of hygiene so alarming that it constituted a health threat not just to its own employees, but to those of neighboring sweatshops. Most despicable of all, the product that it manufactured was a lie. 'Hand-made indigenous art' turned out on an assembly line. It wasn't just cultural appropriation, it was outright theft. Stealing revenue from the Yaqui, Hopi and Mayo peoples with mass-produced counterfeit silverware, woodwork, paintings and pottery. They were occupying the premises, but Pilar felt like blowing it up.

The lockdown went well at first. The women were united in

their anger about their working conditions; the arrogance and indifference of the young manager; the constant bullying of the guards, who were always trying to threaten and intimidate in the hope of sexual favors. That was how stupid they were. The women were even angry with themselves for their complicity in perpetuating a fraud. Most of all, they were angry with their customers: cynical market-stall hawkers, gullible tourists, and even gallery owners, who should have known better. The occupation quickly made the news. They were interviewed by telephone on a local radio talkback show. They waved through barred windows to supporters and a picket line as TV cameras filmed them. Thrilled with their success, they ate lunch together, laughing and singing.

Then one of them broke into the accounting section and found the money.

There were arguments. Juana, a popular woman known for her stinging tongue, said that the money belonged to them, the women who slaved over the machines, the people whose underpaid work made a fortune for the *pinche* young manager and his *pinche* fat father. She said that they might as well take the money because they would all lose their jobs anyway.

Pilar fought back. They were not like their bosses. They were not criminals; they were workers, proud women who were standing up for their dignity, publicly condemning scandalous conditions and outright fraud.

Juana said that the bosses wouldn't even miss the money. Insurance would pay for it.

Pilar said that they had a duty to all the other women working in all the other sweatshops. Just because the bosses were crooked didn't mean the women had to be. Unlike the bosses, they needed to behave with honor.

Juana said honor was a privilege of the rich.

Pilar said honor was the banner of the poor and dispossessed.

After much shouting and some sobbing, they took a vote. The money stayed where it was. Everyone felt proud, even Juana. They had proved to themselves what most people never get a chance to find out: that they were not thieves.

Not that it changed anything.

The police forced their way in just after 3 p.m. and arrested them all. For trespass. For vandalism. For attempted kidnapping. And for theft of monies in the accounting department. (The boss stole the money himself, but blamed it on the workers. Later he would claim it back from insurance. Juana had been right all along. No matter what you did, the bosses always won.)

The violence of the raid was excessive. Municipal police and, surprisingly, a *pelotón* of *rurales* behind them, had surged in with the aim not just of overpowering the women but of hurting and humiliating them. The police stood back, watching with smiles as the *rurales* tore tunics from backs, yanked at bra straps and ripped trousers. They pulled hair, slapped faces, punched breasts and pummeled asses. The women were dragged out, sometimes by their ankles, their bare arms and backs already tattooed with bruises. Pilar looked around with mounting fear as she was pulled and shoved outside. There were no picket lines, no supporters, no TV cameras.

No witnesses.

They were jeered when they were forced to board a bus. The women were silent at first when they started heading east, hoping that they'd take the first turnoff back to Tijuana. But instead the bus kept going towards La Presa. The women whispered uneasily amongst themselves as the landscape darkened with hills that lifted around the great dam, as though preparing to blot it out forever with their shadows. The skies grew somber, distant rain skirting the horizon with wisps of gray. Pilar looked out her window, watching the Jeep Cherokees shadowing them. 'Where are they taking us?' Juana asked. No one answered. There was the murmur of prayer, and the hot chokes of someone trying to suppress her sobs.

The bus pulled up in front of some stables half hidden from the road by a large ranch house. The wind moaned a warning across the arid land as the women huddled protectively beside the bus, watching the police shaking hands and joking with the *rurales*, money changing hands the way it always does; the ranch owner careless and indifferent as he handed out notes, the servile smiles of the police nodding thanks fading to resentment as they turned and walked back to their marked cars, abandoning the women to their fate.

Pilar looked back at the bus and caught the eye of the driver, who nodded towards the stables. She watched as some boys, no more than ten, started leading horses out, passing behind the bus towards an open-air corral. She turned back to the driver, who smiled, a huge gap in his teeth like an abandoned well, dark and threatening; hinting at a bottomless chasm.

The men started pushing them towards the stables, the women intuitively forming a circle, their backs to each other, the smallest of them protected in the center. A flash of sunlight burst across Pilar's face as a car turned fast towards the ranch house, its windshield going golden with the setting sun, masking whoever was inside it as it accelerated towards them.

The ranch owner stepped out of the group. She knew him from the papers. Raúl Abarca. A little man with big ambitions. He was an activist for the governing party in Lomas Taurinas and had been at the PRI rally when Colosio was assassinated. He was rumored to be involved in the counterfeit cigarette trade. 'It's better if you co-operate,' Abarca said. 'That way we won't go so hard on you.' There was impatient laughter from the men, amused by the false promise of mercy in a land without pity.

A gust of wind stirred the ash-colored soil, sending it undulating fast towards the corral, as though the earth was so insulted by what was about to happen, it had to flee.

'Isn't that why you brought us out here?' Pilar said. 'To go hard on us, as hard as you possibly can, you weak fucking cowards!'

Abarca turned slowly, staring at Pilar. 'We're going to start with her. We're going to ride her ass into the dust.'

Pilar turned to the other members of the *rurales*, who were staring at her with a mixture of curiosity and contempt. 'We are not anonymous. We are your wives, your sisters; your daughters and your mothers. Think about it!'

There was a long, unexpected silence that both surprised and heartened Pilar. The chief stared at her for a deadly moment, then slowly nodded. 'I've made a mistake,' he said. 'We'll be saving you for last.'

The men charged the group, grabbing the women by the back of the neck or the hair, one of them falling as he fought with Juana. Abarca lashed out with his boots, shouting to his men with despotic authority. Pilar broke free and rushed him, slapping his face with the force of her entire body, her shoulder aching from the blow. He staggered backwards, falling in a cloud of dust, then fumbled up on his knees, unholstering a Colt .45.

Pilar would have been shot dead right there and then if it hadn't been for the stranger who grabbed her by the shoulders and pulled her away, putting himself between her and the gun. 'Are you out of your fucking mind?' Fuentes said, glaring at the enraged man. 'Put that gun away or I'll shoot you myself.'

Abarca looked around. Three other cops surrounded him, hands on Berettas. A pause of humiliation, then reflection; then finally of survival. He holstered his weapon.

The woman Fuentes was holding in his arms squirmed. 'Calm down,' he said to Pilar, loosening his grip a little.

Then she twisted downwards and bit him on the wrist. It was the bite of a carnivore around its prey's throat. Ferocious. Furious. Unrelenting. 'Stop,' he whispered into her ear. She pressed down even harder, and then her jaw went slack, as though the rage inside her had suddenly subsided, like a tropical downpour, fierce one moment, gone the next; blood staining her lips.

He turned Pilar in his arms, so that they were gazing at each other, her eyes black with hate. She went to spit at him, but at the last moment stopped herself. Instead she pulled away from his grip, wiping his blood from her mouth as she walked back to join her sisters. Fuentes watched her as he held his wrist, his shirt sleeve going wet, the initial high ringing pain of the bite subsiding to a dull, thick ache. He took out his cuffs, and in one fast move, turned Abarca and snared his hands behind his back. He shoved the stunned man forwards, towards the stable, lifting his wrists while keeping his arms straight. Almost no one can bear the agony of that hold, especially a coward like his prisoner. Fuentes turned to the three other cops. 'Two of you watch his men, one of you come with me . . .'

Fuentes didn't need two cops to watch the *rurales*. They reacted as their forefathers would have done if they had seen their *hacendado* lynched by bandits or executed by Zapata's men. They folded their arms and stood away, disowning their boss in a second.

Pilar watched the trio disappearing into the stables, their figures slowly lost in the shadows. She shivered. The creaking darkness of the stables reminded her of something. The smile of the bus driver – that similar falling away from light. She didn't want to follow them, but knew she had to, and she forced herself to step into the gloom. It was the same kind of compulsion that drives some people closer and closer to the edge; an irresistible terror, combined with the burning need to know.

The stables were a maze of indistinct shadows, raw with the keening stench of manure, straw heaped underfoot as though scattered to mask a trap. Pilar felt as if the whole floor could give way. There was a terrible expectation, as though she were just one step from a frightening revelation she needed to avoid but had to see – at any cost.

A horse kicked impatiently against the wall as she passed, making her start. She finally glimpsed them ahead, already at the furthest end of the stables, disappearing round a box stall with its silhouette of a large horse. She nearly tripped on a discarded rake, grabbing hold of the edge of a box for support. She glanced into the stall.

Then screamed.

Footsteps hurried towards her as she tried to open the padlocked latch. She scrambled over the top of the stall, landing in a pile of straw. Lying in the corner was a young, naked woman, her hands tied to an iron hoop in the wall. Pilar struggled with the ropes, which were impossible to unknot. The woman just lay there, not reacting. Someone started kicking the stall's door behind her. It burst inwards, pieces of wood flying, Fuentes kneeling over the woman, listening for a heartbeat. He took off his jacket and covered the woman with it, exposing the hard blue metal of a gun harnessed near his heart. He used a piece of the shattered wood to lever the ring out of the wall, then lifted the young woman up in his arms, stepping over the shattered planks, the hoop dragging in the straw from her still bound hands as he walked towards the light.

Fuentes was almost out of the stables when he froze, his head inclined as though someone had just called out his name. He passed the unconscious woman to his colleague, then drew his Colt Python and aimed it at Abarca's mouth. 'How many others?'

Abarca stared at Fuentes, calculating risk. Fuentes cocked the gun, the barrel shifting as he did, now aimed much lower, at his paunch. Three days of agony, and only then death. 'I'm not asking you again.'

'Five,' Abarca said, then quickly, correcting himself, 'Six counting her.'

'Shoot him,' Pilar said, and it was like a siren call – the one thing Fuentes didn't want to hear and the one thing he felt he must answer.

The way God must react to our prayers.

Only one word came to Abarca's lips; a word he had heard so often that he had forgotten its meaning. A worthless word suddenly rendered valuable. A word he felt the force of for the first time in his miserable life. 'Mercy,' Abarca whispered. It was the worst thing he could have said; begging for the thing he had always denied others.

'Where are they?'

'I'll take you to them. All of them.'

Fuentes indicated with his head that Abarca should lead the way and that he would follow.

'You're letting him go?' It wasn't a question so much as an earthquake of disbelief. 'This pig?'

'There are more captives. I have to find them.' He followed the ranch chief back into the crypt-like darkness. Pilar started to follow. He turned to her, his voice disembodied in the gloom. 'Go back to your friends. Make sure none of them are missing. Get them all on the bus and wait for me there.'

'Wait for what, for more cops to kidnap us?'

'Wait to see if I come back alive.'

32

El Santo

'I pay these motherfuckers to work for me, not for the DEA or Los Pinos.' El Santo angrily pokes the coals of the barbecue with a long metal spoon, remembering what his mother used to say: *He who sups with the devil should eat with a long spoon.* He never did really understand why it had to be a spoon. If you were sharing a meal with the devil, wouldn't everyone be using a *fork*?

'But they *do* work for the DEA and Los Pinos.' El Feo shrugs the way he does when he has an opinion of his own. He's been shrugging way too often lately.

'Why do you think I hired them?' He shoves El Feo hard in the chest, feeling the reverberation of all that fat, like a shout in a tunnel, two seconds late. 'I don't give a fuck who pays their pension plan – there won't be any retirement if they don't come up with answers. Where the fuck is Mary-Ellen? Who the fuck is this cop, Paredes? And why the fuck was he driving her car?'

'Maybe he killed Mary-Ellen and ripped off her load.'

Honest to God, it makes him want to kill El Feo. It's not that he hasn't thought exactly the same thing – he has. It's just that he hates hearing it out of the mouth of a moron. 'Someone's jerking my chain and I don't like it. It's your job to find out who it is. I want results, not fucking opinions.'

'Maybe you need to pay everyone more?' El Feo suggests, not very helpfully.

El Santo feels like cauterizing El Feo's throat with the hot end of the spoon. 'What, now people think loyalty's for sale to the highest bidder?'

El Feo takes a step back, staring in shock at what El Santo's just said: it's not that people think loyalty's for sale; they *know* it is. El Feo's wondering if he should reconsider that offer from Tijuana. After all, how difficult would it *really* be to kill El Santo? 'They work hard for you, boss. Every piece of skinny they give up, it's always Tijuana or Juárez, never Ciudad Real. They're doing you a favor. Eliminating the competition.'

El Santo's been in this racket long enough to know that when people start justifying other people working *something on the side*, it means they're working something on the side too. Maybe he should ask Oviedo to start tailing El Feo. He glances through the walk-in doors leading to the kitchen. Oviedo's standing there, looking at them, sharpening a meat cleaver with a grooved honing rod. That's what he likes about Oviedo. Industrious. Never wasting time. The exact fucking opposite of El Feo. If only Oviedo could get that dog of his to shut the fuck up, it'd be a no-brainer. 'They keep squawking to the DEA and PJF the way they've been doing, pretty soon there'll be nothing left to give up.' El Feo looks at him as though he doesn't know what El Santo's talking about. He's going to have to explain it to him. Again. 'Don't you get it? They'll be giving *us* up soon.'

El Feo punches a fist deep into the ice crate and pulls out a beer. El Santo raps him on the knuckles with the spoon. 'Lay off the Noche Buena. It's months till Christmas and I'm already running low.'

'I was just going to pass it to you,' El Feo lies, rubbing his hand before snatching up a Pacifico with a resentful flourish.

He opens it with his teeth – if you can call them that. 'So what do you want us to do about them?'

'I don't know, sometimes I think we should tap them both and just start over with new recruits.'

'But . . . you can't tap them. They're protected.'

Unlike El Feo, El Santo is not stupid. Of course he knows that if he whacked either Byrd or Gordillo, he'd wake up the next morning covered in a heap of shit about the size of Tamaulipas. But no one has any right to tell him what he can or cannot do – especially some *pendejo* like El Feo. 'What's your problem? Because if you've got a problem, I can give the job to somebody else. Oviedo's got ambition. He'd love to help me out.'

'That sneaky fuck? Are you kidding?'

'He may be a sneaky fuck but at least he doesn't question my orders.'

'Neither do I, boss, it's just . . . complicated.'

'What about Paredes' partner? We could snatch him, sweat some answers out of him. No one would give a fuck.'

El Feo seems to brighten – if you could imagine a tub of tar radiating light. 'Sure, we could tap him along with his new partner, the jerk-off from Tijuana.'

'That way it'll not only be a warning, it'll make Gordillo and Byrd look stupid.' El Santo clinks his beer bottle against El Feo's. 'First problem solved. What about that fucking prick, Carlos. Any luck finding him?'

'We tossed his house. His girlfriend hired a car. We think they're heading to Phoenix.'

'How do you figure that?'

'We found an address book. He has relatives there.'

Yesterday was a fuck-up, but today is already looking better.

He manages a smile. 'Find both of them. I need to set an example no one will ever forget.'

El Feo preens. 'I'm on it, boss.'

'Any news about that union car bombing?'

'The guy who owned the car is working for the same organization that the piece of toast was working for.' The *piece of toast* who wasn't the actual target. 'The guy's the local boss.'

El Santo needs to follow this one carefully. They gave him a contract on the girl *sindicalista* and she got away. Later the same day her Red boss is targeted by someone else, who screws up too. At least their fuck-up makes El Santo's look better, but still it was disrespectful to go to Tijuana or Juárez for a hit in Ciudad Real. El Santo could tell them that he ordered the switch from the girl to the guy when he found out about the car bomb plan. He could make out that nothing happened in Ciudad Real without him knowing about it. He'd present the killing of the guy instead of the girl as a deliberate act; a mark of displeasure for handing a contract to an out-of-town hit team. That would truly strengthen him, and with Los Zetas and El Chapo and the others breathing down his neck, he needs to strengthen. One thing he better figure out fast is why the sudden interest in unions? What's at stake here – what do people know that he doesn't? He drains his beer, meditating on the mystery. El Feo's burp brings him back to reality. 'Last item. What about these cars the priest is heisting?'

'Padre Márcio,' El Feo corrects him.

El Santo doesn't like the reverential tone, although he could probably put up with it if it were being directed at him. 'Padre, pope – whatever the fuck you call him. He's heisting cars and selling them on. He has to pay taxes like everyone else.'

'Come on, boss. He's helping the poor.'

'I help the poor too!' El Feo's eyes flicker at the lie. 'I don't know why you've got a hard-on for this priest.'

'He's been marked by God!'

'So what? He's not the first guy with bullet holes in his paws. Probably put up his hands when the cops showed and they shot him anyway.'

'That's no way to speak. Those hands are sacred!'

He grabs El Feo's left wrist with both hands and forces his hand onto the hotplate. 'I'll show you fucking *sacred hands*,' he says, his voice rising above El Feo's scream. He lets go of the smoking hand, and El Feo plunges it into the ice, beer bottles tut-tutting as they rap into each other, floating away from his sunken, steaming fingers. 'A little fucking respect, is that too much to ask?' El Santo waits till the fingerprints sear, transparent as white onion, then scrapes the wafers of skin off the griddle and onto the coals, where they flare and cinder.

El Feo starts to blubber. It's got to be deliberate; El Feo knows if there's one thing El Santo can't stand, it's waterworks. 'Cut it out!' he shouts, grabbing a bottle of Noche Buena and breaking it over El Feo's head, glass skipping in agony across the hotplate. There's a rush of sudden silence, only disturbed by the sizzle of beer evaporating in the heat.

El Feo struggles to his feet, blood from the gash on his left eyebrow streaming onto his shirt. El Santo stares at the neck of the broken bottle he still holds in his hand, then tosses it across the lawn. 'See what you made me do? I have to wait till fucking winter to replace that one!'

El Feo says something. It sounds like, 'I didn't mean to . . .'

'If you don't shut the fuck up about that priest, so help me

God, next time it won't be your hand, it'll be your fucking tongue I'll be barbecuing.'

'Sinner.'

Something is wrong. El Feo is still talking after he's told him to shut up. 'What?'

'You fucking, dirty sinner.' El Santo hears the shot before he sees the smoke cough its way out of the gun. Then the next thing he knows, he's lying on his side, his face aching from being sucker-punched by the ground, El Feo's shoes doing an excited little dance just in front of his nose. It's as though there is no connection between the two events. First, *bang*; then lying here on the ground, like he's always been down here, bleeding.

'I am sending you to hell, you—' The ground jumps just a little; enough to slap him on the cheek, the spray of blood disproportionate to the tremor that he felt. El Santo crawls away from the twitching body of El Feo. Only one handgun could make a sound like that, let alone such a pulpy mess of El Feo. S & W Model 29. And only one of his *sicarios* is kitsch enough to make a point of always carrying the Model 29.

Oviedo.

El Santo scrambles to his knees. His crotch is wet. He panics, but it's only blood. His dignity is saved. El Feo's bullet has passed right through the solid silver buckle on his crocodile leather belt, traveling on through his pre-shrunk Levi's and the waistband of his Calvin Kleins, before calling it a day and stopping, exhausted and snub-nosed, in the shallow creases of his skin.

'You okay, boss?' Oviedo asks, with the same flat delivery of a shopkeeper saying *cash or credit?*

'Just a fucking flesh wound.' Flesh wound or not, this is serious. His right-hand man just tried to kill him. Word will get out. Before he knows it, everyone will be after him. Assassination attempts are like the clap – contagious as hell.

'You're pissing blood, boss. We better get you to the vet.'

El Santo gingerly explores the wound. Fragments of metal, leather and cloth have been driven into his skin in a livid splatter of debris, centered on a hunk of lead, the end of which is only just visible. He could almost worm it out with his fingers, but there's a risk he'd end up pushing it further inside that mysterious cavern known collectively as your guts. Then he'd be royally fucked. Plus the risk of infection. 'Fuck the vet. This needs a real clinic.'

'I know just the one.'

'Get some men. Get rid of this tub of shit. Make an example.'

'Sure, boss.'

'I want his whole fucking crew taken out.'

'I'll look after it.'

'Tomorrow. His family will be at the Heartbreak, for Curro's birthday. That's the time to do it.'

'You got it, boss.'

Shit. With co-operative killers like Oviedo around, why the hell did El Santo put up with El Feo for so long? Loyalty? Friendship? They're just bullshit myths, like Christmas and bad luck, invented to make you feel weak and guilty. 'Wait.' He grabs Oviedo by the arm, leaving a red mark on his white sleeve. 'Do you believe in God?'

Oviedo screws up his face. 'Who the fuck is that?'

El Santo smiles. 'My kind of man.'

33

Pilar

The makeshift home of the late Isabel Torres was deserted. Fuentes lifted the fiberglass sheeting at the back of the shack and looked inside, just to make sure no one was hiding. He braced a neighbor, who held out for twenty pesos. She said Isabel's mother had left with a young woman an hour ago. They were going to Rosario Flores' place. She nodded to the south, narrowing her gaze against the sun. He asked her who Rosario Flores was.

Wrong question.

Her eyes immediately cataracted. He was no longer there; and as far as the neighbor was concerned, neither was she. If she'd had one, the woman would have slammed the door in his face.

The response was an intuitive, almost physiological reaction to a terrible error of judgment: revealing information to people who shouldn't possess it. Information is the only thing you can own in a place like Anaprata. You don't sell it cheaply. And you never give it away. Normally it involves *narcos*. But sometimes, as Fuentes guessed was the case here, it concerns something on a higher plateau: something esoteric; maybe even divine. Ten to one, Rosario Flores was a *bruja*. The world of the *brujería* is like that of the *narcería*: you never ask for explanations, let alone specific information. You are either trusted enough to be taken in or else you are called into the world, as if by spirits.

Afterwards, Fuentes and Gomez cruise the streets of Ana-prata for half an hour until they get lucky, Fuentes slapping Gomez's arm hard, nodding down the street at Pilar, who is just stepping out of an illegal *miscelánea* with a fruit box full of groceries in her arms. They watch her walk down a gravel road, a bloom of torpid dust rising behind her. Gomez slows the car, putting extra space between them.

The makeshift houses she passes are built from peeling clapboard, unpainted cinder block or faded whitewashed adobe. Plastic and tar paper make up most of the roofs, rustling with regret in the hot wind. Trash litters the road, plastic shopping bags rolling lazy as tumbleweeds. A dog sleeps on a piss-stained mattress in the shade of a burnt-out car.

Two youths lounging inside an old Chevy whistle at Pilar as she passes but their hearts aren't in it. Pilar ignores them with dismissive indifference. Fuentes and Gomez sit in their car, watching Pilar disappear inside a narrow green entrance. 'I don't get it,' Gomez says. 'Why always her?'

'Know what I've noticed?'

'What?'

Fuentes pats his partner consolingly on the shoulder. 'There are a lot of things you don't get.' He steps out and walks towards the Chevy, Gomez watching him through his windshield.

One of the kids in the Chevy is fossicking in his jean jacket for a light, a newly rolled joint between his lips, when a hand appears through the window, offering a match. The kid leans forwards with a nod of thanks as he frowns through the smoke, sitting up fast when he sees it's Fuentes. Fuentes grabs the kid and hauls him through the open car window, onto the road. His friend springs out of the car and comes round the front with a knife in his hands, his eyes full of the fear that he might have to use it.

Fuentes shows his badge, pinned against his holster, mastering the situation with the threat of real violence. The knife drops to the ground. Fuentes kicks it under the car. The one he pulled out through the window slowly gets to his feet, both of them standing there, defiant but fearful, hinky eyes measuring routes for escape. Fuentes indicates the green entrance. 'Who lives there?'

The two exchange glances. Like many people in Ciudad Real, they suffer from short-term memory loss. Only seconds before, they were both trembling with apprehension. Now they are already reverting to their habitual stance of mannered defiance. One of them even shrugs. Fuentes moves fast, seizing a fistful of hair in each hand, bringing their heads sharply together. There is the hot slur of tires and the hammer of a door, Gomez already applying a headlock to one of the youths.

Fuentes bundles the other to the back of the police sedan and opens the trunk. Gomez is puzzled but joins him with his prisoner. Fuentes pushes the head of his captive into the trunk, shouting to Gomez. 'Take them out to the desert and shoot them.'

Gomez stares at Fuentes, totally confused, the youth he has captured sagging under his grip. Fuentes tries to bundle his captive into the trunk, the boy's voice muffled as he cries out. 'Please, wait!'

'*Now* you want to talk. Too fucking late.' Gomez looks around with anxiety. Neighbors are watching. Fuentes mouths: *Fuck them*.

Sensing Gomez's confusion, the other kid almost squirms free of his grip. He turns to Gomez, pleading, 'Don't do this, man!' Fuentes lets go of his captive, who tumbles to the ground. He grabs the other kid by the hair. 'Who lives there, motherfucker?'

'Rosario Flores.'

Something rustles behind Fuentes. It's the first kid, scrambling to his feet, his footsteps pounding fast away until they can't hear them anymore. His friend watches him disappear, wilting from the betrayal. Gomez is about to give chase but Fuentes shakes his head and turns his attention back to the remaining prisoner. 'I want more than a name.'

'She's a *bruja*. She talks to the dead.'

'Who's with her now?'

The boy's voice is barely audible. 'The mama of Isabel, the girl they found. That's all I know, man.' Fuentes nods and Gomez lets him go. He waits a moment, then puts out his hand. Fuentes stares at him. A second ago, he was threatening to kill the kid and now he's expecting a payoff? The kid shrugs. 'Information's information.'

Gomez slaps him across the ear. 'Get the fuck out of here before we change our minds.' The kid scampers away to a safe distance, and then turns and shoots them the finger. The street is motionless except for the neighbors' curtains all falling back. Fuentes straightens his shirt sleeves and starts walking towards the house of Rosario Flores.

Gomez follows, shaking his head. 'What are we doing here?' But Fuentes has already vanished inside.

Fuentes peers into the strange, flickering shadows that lie just beyond the entrance. He unclips his holster. Something bangs into him from behind. It's Gomez, who removes his sunglasses with hasty embarrassment.

They both move cautiously down a corridor lit by devotional candles, leading into a room aglow with dozens more. Women of all ages sit on the floor, holding hands in a circle as they softly chant. Fuentes allows his eyes to adjust to the dimness, glancing around the walls, which are covered with masks, feathers and sacred devices.

Sitting in the group is Pilar. She sees Fuentes and Gomez before they see her, rising to her feet, astonished. Other women in the circle turn and look, their chant dying away with the approach of the intruders. Fuentes scans the faces of the women.

His eyes settle on an exhausted, middle-aged woman with a face hollowed by the disbelief of the very early days of mourning. When things still aren't real. She wears a serape with an image of *La Guadalupana*. 'Señora Torres? I'm Inspector Fuentes.' For the first time, the small woman looks up at him, eyes inflamed from hours of weeping. 'And this is Detective Gomez. We're investigating your daughter's . . .' Señora Torres turns away from him, answering a secret call only she can hear. The women rejoin hands, closing the circle, and the chant begins again. Louder this time. Fuentes recognizes it now. The rosary.

Pilar motions for Fuentes to follow her out a back door. Gomez starts to join them but Fuentes shakes his head. Gomez pulls a face, leaning against a wall, watching as Fuentes closes the door behind him. He stares down at the women, first in boredom, then without even realizing it, becoming consumed by the familiarity of the chant, by its promise of assistance, if not redemption; falling into the nostalgic trance of detached early memory: the women of his home – their strength, their devotion, their protection; his lips automatically finding the words, moving with the innate, unthinking synchronicity of a child reciting multiplication tables.

It's cool outside, the narrow yard shaded by damp bed linen

hanging high and heavy. Pilar sits on an upturned milk crate, smoking. She doesn't look up at him when she speaks. 'You followed me?'

Fuentes studies her evasive gaze. 'We came to interview the mother.'

'Don't lie to me. How did you know she was here?' He doesn't answer. She looks up, making eye contact in her anger. 'You fucking followed me.'

'What's it matter how we found her? We need her help.'

'You won't get anything from her. Not before the funeral.'

'We can't afford to wait. Why are you here?'

'I'm a friend of the family.'

'You didn't even know their name yesterday.'

Pilar slowly stands, staring into Fuentes' face as though she were scrutinizing the blind marble gaze of a statue, looking for a flaw in the stone; its close proximity to reality only serving to heighten its inhuman remoteness. 'Today, every woman in Ciudad Real is a friend of the family.'

He sighs, turning away from the intense gaze. 'I want to stop the killings.'

'Just like you wanted to stop the strikes in Tijuana? You didn't succeed there either.'

For a moment Fuentes' face tics with anger. Then it's still again, impassive. 'We can work together, share any information we have.'

'I don't work with the police.'

'You can trust me.'

'Don't insult my intelligence.'

'Even if it's the police doing this, we're not all alike.'

'I never said it was the police.'

'But I just did. You're not stupid. You've heard the rumors. And I know you believe them.'

Pilar gives him a hard, penetrating look. 'Don't you?'

He offers her a card. 'One day you're going to need a policeman you can trust. Especially if the rumors turn out to be true.'

Pilar glances at the proffered card. 'You're always handing me things.'

'It's better than taking things from you.' Pilar slips the card in her pocket. 'If you need me, at any time; it doesn't matter: call me.' Fuentes goes back inside. Pilar stares after him, her eyes narrowing against her cigarette smoke, considering what he's just said.

Fuentes closes the door quietly behind him and stays there for a moment, allowing his eyes to readjust to the darkness. Gomez is where he left him, slouching against a wall as he mouths the rosary. Fuentes walks slowly around the perimeter of the room, trying not to disturb the circle of women. But just as he's passing, the chant stops, filling the house with silence. Fuentes freezes, looking back at the group. Señora Torres is standing, her arms outstretched towards him. 'Bring back my daughter.' Fuentes gazes into her eyes. They stare at him, but are unfocused. When she speaks again, her voice is louder, stronger; there is the lilt of a new chant in the way she says, 'Bring Isabel back.' The other women repeat the refrain, creating a soft, disturbing echo.

Fuentes takes hold of Señora Torres by the elbows. It could be for support. It could be to keep her away from him. 'Señora, I promise we will have your daughter's body back to you as soon as possible.'

Señora Torres seems mastered by the pledge at first, her eyes drifting away from Fuentes. But then she shouts, making

Gomez jump. 'Rosario? Is it true?' All the women in the circle turn to Rosario Flores, her fierce, ancient face framed by white hair pulled so severely back that it resembles the crust of a calcified skull. Rosario raises her hands in the air, her lips trembling.

A hush goes through everyone in the room. Even Fuentes feels its power. He lets go of Señora Torres, who begins a low sob. Fuentes and Gomez exchange unsettled looks, Gomez pleading with his eyes for them to go.

But before he can move, Rosario rushes up to Fuentes with a swiftness astonishing in one so old. She seizes his hands by his wrists and slowly turns them over, so they are palms up.

She stares at the palms in the gloomy light then lets out a long moan. Fuentes tries to free his hands but her clutch is fierce, her voice loud and fervent as she cries: 'I see death. I see death!'

She too begins to sob, falling to her knees, finally releasing her grip on Fuentes. The others crowd around her, supporting her as she rocks backwards and forwards. Daylight enters the back of the room. Fuentes glances up at Pilar, standing in the doorframe. She looks at Rosario then back at Fuentes, and motions for him to go quickly.

They hurry along the candlelit corridor, Gomez brushing a mask with his shoulder, almost knocking it off the wall. He adjusts it, then on a whim lifts it off its hook. 'Check this out, boss,' he says, glancing back into the room to make sure none of the women are looking, then puts the mask over his face. Something black tremors across the inner rim. He pulls the mask fast away from his face. Cradled inside is a red-knee tarantula. 'Holy fuck!'

He slams the mask back against the wall, the spider disappearing back into the crevice in the face. One of its legs quivers through an eyehole, hairs catching in the splinters of the lacquered wood. Gomez hurries after Fuentes, bumping into him again in the blinding daylight outside. They both pause to put on sunglasses.

'That was a cute trick with the mask.'

Gomez shivers. 'I hate spiders.'

'So why wear one on your face?'

'I didn't know it was there!'

'You didn't know because you didn't *look*. That's a serious fault of yours. Not looking.'

'Jesus, with you all the time it's a lecture. It's a lesson. It's a fucking parable! Don't blame me for all that creepy shit going on inside there. *I see death! I see death!* What the fuck was that about? I don't even know why we're— Oh man!' Gomez freezes in disgust. Someone's dropped a turd on top of the hood of their car.

Gomez glances all around the street: there is no movement, no sign of life. 'Check it out: the whole fucking street's innocent.' He turns to Fuentes. 'It was one of those *niños* you threatened to take out into the desert and kill. See what that attitude of yours gets us? Nothing but shit!'

'Not *us*. It's on your side. You clean it off.'

Gomez picks up a piece of cardboard and brushes the shit away, his nostrils tightened against the smell. He looks all around the deserted street, at the poor houses, the abandoned cars, the fucking dog still sleeping on its piss-stained mattress. He slams the roof of the car in frustration. 'Why the fuck are we even here?'

Fuentes opens the car door, then pauses. 'Because no one else wants to be.'

34

Fuentes

When Fuentes enters without knocking, Valdez looks up and swivels in his chair, using the great empty bulk of his desk to protect himself. It's an even bigger frontier than the border: that gulf between worker and boss.

Seated opposite Valdez are the two men who were in Paredes' house the night before. Valdez presents Fuentes to the unimpressed American, who clearly thinks he's the controller of the pair, and his Mexican partner, who is happy to let the *gringo* delude himself. 'I'd like you to meet our top man on the case. Inspector Fuentes was brought in from Tijuana to take over the investigations. Agent Gordillo from the PJF and his guest, Agent Bush . . .'

The American shifts in his chair. 'Byrd.'

'Agent Byrd, forgive me . . . Agent Byrd of the DEA. He's come all the way from El Lobo to talk with us.'

If the *gringo* understands irony, he doesn't show it. 'Texas. Have you executed any of my countrymen lately?'

'Should we have?' Byrd tries to share a smile with Gordillo, who's not interested. Byrd rubs his nose gingerly, as though testing to see that it isn't coming loose. 'We do whatever it takes to reduce crime.'

'As we all do,' Valdez says.

Gordillo turns to Fuentes. 'So have you made any arrests yet?' There is a moment's pause and then Byrd cracks up, coughing in a vain attempt to cover it up.

'You think that's funny?' Fuentes glares at Byrd. 'You know, when you come to my country, sticking your nose in other people's business, you should at least try to speak a little Spanish.'

'You come up to our side of the border and try finding just one Mexican who speaks any English,' Byrd says.

A pulse ticks in Fuentes' cheek, his smile full of ice. He leans against the desk, his back to Valdez. 'So, to what do we owe the pleasure of your visit?'

'As if you didn't know,' Gordillo says.

'Enlighten me.'

'Well, it's a . . . a fruit matter,' Byrd says.

Gordillo laughs, playing straight man to the *Yanqui*. Fuentes' eyes slowly travel the length of Byrd, measuring his worth – or lack of it. 'United Fruit?' His voice is low, hinting at menace without quite arriving at threat. 'What are you planning now, another coup?'

'Nothing so complicated.' Byrd shifts his weight away from Fuentes, shielding himself from the hostility. 'We found ourselves a bad apple.'

'And we're looking for the tree it came from,' Gordillo says.

'Then, my friend, I suggest you look in Cali or Medellín.' He turns back to Byrd. 'Or better yet, why not look in your own neighborhoods; in your colleges and nightclubs. In Hollywood.'

Byrd and Gordillo exchange looks, rolling their eyes in unison. 'We know where the tree is and we're going to rock it hard,' Byrd says. 'And all the rotten apples are going to start falling, and by the time we stop, my guess is there won't be anything left up on the tree.'

'Hardly an optimistic picture,' Valdez says.

'With all those raining apples, you should be careful you don't get hit on the head.'

Byrd glares at Fuentes. 'Is that a threat?' he says, thankful for the change to open aggression.

'Just a reminder of the laws of gravity.'

Gordillo leans past Fuentes, giving a vague kind of salute to Valdez. 'Thanks for your time, *el jefe.*' He and Byrd leave without another word to Fuentes.

'A pleasure sharing extraterritorial co-operation with you gentlemen,' Valdez calls out after them.

Fuentes watches them through the glass of Valdez's office. 'Shouldn't that be *extraterritorial humiliation?*' He turns back to Valdez, sitting down in one of the abandoned chairs.

Valdez shrugs, throwing his heavy feet up onto his desk. 'Paredes was a liar, a thief and a drug smuggler. Why should they trust us?'

'I think Gomez is clean.'

'Times have changed. *Think* is not good enough. Not anymore. *Think* is just another linguistic evasion. We need facts. We need to *know* Gomez is clean.'

Fuentes sighs. 'His place was staked out this morning. We were tailed to the airport.'

Valdez is suddenly sitting upright. 'By them?'

'What I'm wondering is: are they here to investigate us, or are they here to stop our investigation?'

Valdez studies him. 'What do you believe?'

'All I know is someone is in trouble.'

'Who could that be?'

'The person who guaranteed Paredes' safe passage.' Fuentes

gets up and goes to the door. 'That person is either dead, or about to die.'

Valdez calls after him. 'Where are you going?'

'To find out if we got lucky.'

35

Ventura

'Deserts . . .' Mayor mutters, switching on a ceiling fan. The stillness of the early afternoon begins to waver under the awakening blades. 'The only thing crueler than their afternoon heat is their nocturnal chill. No wonder I was so sick as a child.' He places the folder with Ventura's notes next to her coffee. 'But then again, I suppose I should be thankful: all good writers begin their careers as sick children.'

Ventura stares down at the folder, a few protruding loose papers fluttering in time with the fan. 'So what do you think of my angle?' she asks, trying not to sound too desperate.

Mayor sits down opposite her, refilling her cup from the *macchinetta*. 'When you were at school, did they ever tell you about the soldiers who died in the dunes outside of town?'

Ventura palms her hair away as she leans in to the proffered match. 'I don't remember.'

He gives a nostalgic sigh. 'It was quite a story. They were irregulars hoping to join up with Pancho Villa's troops, but got hopelessly lost amongst the dunes.' He pauses for just the right dramatic emphasis. 'When they finally found the soldiers' bodies, they discovered that their mouths, their throats, even their stomachs were full of sand.'

'They were caught in a sandstorm?'

'Except there is no record of such a storm. The answer to their mysterious deaths is something both obvious and incredible: they drowned in a mirage.'

'You mean they mistook sand for water?' Ventura asks, unable to hide her skepticism.

'It's more complex than that. When we accept one reality, by definition we exclude another. But mirages are a facet of the reality we accept, not an alternative to it. That's why they deceive and confuse. A mirage is like a mirror: an ideal paradox. It reflects *exactly* but *imperfectly*. Left becomes right and backwards becomes forwards. And so, within the logic of reflections, of Fata Morganas, a person who says *I love you* actually means *I hate you*. And life becomes death.'

He picks up a single cube of cane sugar and drops it into his cup, delicately stirring it into nothingness. 'Imagine the extreme conditions those soldiers found themselves in: lost in the desert, dying of thirst, in pain and despair. The victims from the *maquiladoras* were just like those soldiers. All of them encountered their mirage at the time when they were most vulnerable. They all found themselves unable to answer that most essential question: *which side of the mirror am I on?*' He leans over and taps Ventura's folder. 'You're on the wrong side of the mirror. You're following mirages.'

Ventura has just slept for seven hours straight. But instead of feeling rested, she has been anxious and irritated ever since she woke up. And now she has to defend herself against riddles. 'I don't even know what that means.'

'You need to stop looking inwards, mesmerized by reflections.'

Ventura gets up, going onto the terrace outside. At dawn that morning, the air was cool; invigorating. Now it's hot and humid and scaled with desert dust when she breathes it in. Ever since she started working, it has been this way: men telling her what to do, or men telling her that what she's doing isn't good enough. She turns to Mayor, who has followed her out onto the terrace. 'When I chose this story I knew I would no longer be a photojournalist but a war correspondent. That's why I asked you for help. I need allies, not people telling me I'm following fantasies. It may seem like that to you, but I'm a woman, and like all women here, I know what reality is: it's being unable to even guarantee my own safety. Just going out on my own at night is a risk. And now, thanks to Carlos, I can't even go home.' She grabs Mayor by the wrists. 'I need something concrete from you; something more than riddles.'

'That's why I've arranged this meeting tonight. These people will help you and what you learn from them will inform your story. And together all of us will protect you. It's normal to be afraid.'

She steps out of the shade of the terrace, immediately feeling dizzy in the sun. 'Has it ever occurred to you that women want a better *normal*?'

Mayor laughs, taking an old straw hat from the corner of a chair and handing it to her. 'Come. Let me show you how to save a dying lemon tree.'

She watches him cross the courtyard and pass under a terracotta arcade, disappearing into a citrus grove striated with black shadows and the gloss of green. 'Hey,' she cries out after him. 'What about my story?' She waits for a response but there's nothing except for the pulse of the sun and the distant throb of insects, calling her into the darkness.

36

Padre Márcio

Pablo Grande watched the sky, reading the movements of the clouds and the fast passage of the birds, their numbers revealing sequenced secrets. He felt the wind when it rushed through the leaves of the stone pines, humming with dark awareness of the past and warnings of the future. He listened to the bees pulsing with prophecy above the honey mesquite, and followed the scything ascension of the hawks, rising on great plumes of heat from the cliffs, cresting and cautious in the swollen heavens, then plummeting fast as a shooting star towards their hidden prey.

He was aware.

He was awake to possibilities.

And thus he was prepared.

So when the bishop's car appeared on the horizon, heading towards the ranch where he was working as a cook, he had already changed to a diet of garlic, lime, apple, honey and ginger. Fortified against the poisons about to be unleashed.

The driver's message was designed to flatter anyone with an ego but Pablo Grande was immune because his world was so large that his ego had been lost within its vastness. The bishop was dying, the chauffeur said; only one man could save him. Pablo Grande got into the car knowing it was a trap. He was like a pearl diver placing his hand inside a giant clam – trusting his reflexes to survive.

The bishop had aged poorly, the fate of all men of good will with weak natures. Pablo Grande saw instantly that His Grace was beyond cure but that his terrible pain could be alleviated enormously. He prepared a potion of activated charcoal and basil and then gave him a sleeping draft after his bowels were cleared. The bishop would have benefited from a *limpia*, but Pablo Grande knew the pious priest believed such healing ceremonies crossed the frontier into the territory of witchcraft. Besides, he had not been summoned to the palace to treat the bishop, but to be confronted by the most influential man in the state. Padre Márcio was a priest, but he was also a politician who understood that the only thing more powerful than a miracle was a public scandal kept private.

Padre Márcio had continued his dramatic exposés of the corrupt church he ostensibly served, taking over dozens of orphanages, schools and hospices for the dying, and punishing the criminals who had previously run them. Faced time and again with the crimes of the clergy – raping children, unmarried mothers and housekeepers; stealing money from building projects, charitable funds and even common poor boxes; driving limousines, drinking French wine and paying a fortune for renovating presbyteries – the civic fathers had continued to capitulate to the holy man. Padre Márcio's wrath was like Christ's in the Temple. He turned over tables, whipped the guilty, kicked in doors and let the light of day expose the hidden, suppurating crimes of vice and avarice.

The more horror and corruption he discovered, the more power the city's leaders ceded to him, for they lived in terror that he would one day turn his X-ray eyes to their affairs: their stuffed bellies, soiled bedsheets and swollen bank accounts in

Switzerland and Panama. Better to offer Padre Márcio every ecclesiastical head he demanded than to risk him running out of clerical victims and looking for secular ones instead. His ascension was a simple mathematical algorithm. The more the civic leaders capitulated to Padre Márcio, the stronger he became.

And strength is always measured in silence.

Padre Márcio owed much to the silence of Pablo Grande. Therefore it was essential for Padre Márcio to destroy him.

The weak can be subverted, but the strong must eventually be opposed, if not today then tomorrow, and Padre Márcio knew that although he had become dominant amongst weak men, he had not yet grown powerful enough amongst the truly strong. Pablo Grande was not only the mightiest man Padre Márcio had ever encountered; he also knew the secret behind his stigmata.

Padre Márcio's plan was brutal in its simplicity. He would poison the *brujo* and bury him face down above the vice-rector's coffin. That way his eyes would be forever staring at the past, not the future, and, freed of their knowing gaze, Padre Márcio would be able to embrace his destiny: to start his own Holy Order, the Army of Jesus, and take control of first the state, then the country, and then . . .

Arrogance is only the prerogative of the powerful or the ignorant. It was Padre Márcio's mistake to believe he could poison Pablo Grande. Pablo Grande accepted the coffee offered to him in the palace reception hall knowing that for any normal man, the dosage of white arsenic contained within would be fatal. But he had prepared for this moment. He gazed at Padre Márcio. 'I am not afraid of death,' he said. 'I am only afraid of lies.'

Padre Márcio held up his hands. 'You were not afraid of these.'

'They were not lies when I helped you. They were a manifestation of the truth.'

'A truth I have exposed.'

'And yet you wish to conceal the truth that resides in the drink you just gave me. The violence you have suffered has ended. And it has been avenged. That doesn't change your past, but it changes your future. Always remember, you didn't have to do this.'

Just then, a cloud raced across the face of the sun, causing the daylight in the reception hall to dip suddenly, plunging the room into momentary darkness before the sunlight returned, more fervent than ever.

Through that intense, dislocating instant of traveling shadows, Pablo Grande never took his eyes off Padre Márcio. He drank the cup of coffee in one gulp, then carefully placed the empty cup on the ornate service table between them. 'You have made a terrible error,' Pablo Grande said. 'I do not need you. But you need me.'

'I need no one, least of all a dying man,' Padre Márcio said, sipping from his own cup then returning it to its saucer with a gesture of delicate satisfaction, exaggerated by his fingerless lace gloves.

'We are all who we are – children born into this world with one purpose alone: to perish. I am not afraid of dying. Let us see if you are . . .' His eyes descended fast to the priest's cup, like the hawks he had watched for months, swooping pitilessly towards their prey.

Padre Márcio froze, the cup beginning to tremble as his hand holding the saucer started to shake with the horror of under-standing. Very slowly, he leant forwards and peered into his cup. There, at the bottom, amongst the dark silt of coffee, was the bleach-white stain of the arsenic. The saucer tilted in shock, the cup shattering the stunned silence of the room.

'For a man of some ability, you were surprisingly easy to hyp-notize. You must be able to feel it still; that pain behind the eyes, as though you've just bitten into ice? And a warm flush at the base of the neck, not unpleasant.'

Padre Márcio snatched Pablo Grande's cup from the cof-fee table, its interior thick and dark with the brown, even slur of grains. He leapt to his feet, knocking over the coffee table, panic rushing through him. 'It's impossible.'

'I simply exchanged cups when I put you to sleep.'

'You're lying...' But even uttering those words, Padre Márcio could taste the truth in the back of his throat.

Pablo Grande noticed the reaction and nodded. 'If you are as intelligent as I give you credit for, you will already have identi-fied the antidote.' He stepped out of the palace's reception hall into the garden that he used to tend with such loving care.

Fury unlike any he had ever experienced overtook Padre Márcio. Seizing a poker from the fireplace, he strode after Pablo Grande, sheltering his eyes from the sudden photophobia, the first advanced symptom of his poisoning. He looked all around the garden, the glare blinding him. And then he heard it – the call of a crow from a Montezuma cypress. Standing hidden within its cape of deep shade was Pablo Grande. Padre Márcio charged him, striking hard with the poker, leaving a furrowed scar in the tree's trunk. Pablo Grande had vanished. He scanned the sun-leached landscape in disbelief. Acute tinnitus left him feeling dislocated and queasy, as though he were standing on a floating dock with a rising wind sending dozens of halyards rocking and ringing in alarm. It wasn't just an internal aural phenomenon; it was a rupture in the fabric of the atmosphere around him.

He looked up and saw a crow break cover from the tree. The poker slid from his hand as he watched Pablo Grande flying away.

37

Fuentes

There was a strange, mournful atmosphere back at headquarters in Tijuana, as though the home team had just lost the Cup Final in the last minute of extra time. Faces weren't just brooding, they were hurting.

Twelve *rurales*, the bus driver and four stable boys were all packed into the largest holding pen. Fuentes watched their old boss, Abarca, sitting in the corridor trying to smoke, despite the angry coil of handcuffs tight around his wrists. Each time he gathered his fists to his lips to inhale, it looked as though he could almost be praying. Except no one could pray with such palpable rage on his face; not even Satan.

Fuentes knew the dark mood at the station wasn't because a handful of officers would have to be sacrificed: that was one of the only positive outcomes of the arrests at the stables. It gave the top brass the chance to purge disruptive personalities and overtly corrupt cops. And maybe try to settle scores with hotshots and troublemakers. People just like Fuentes.

Fuentes' superiors would have liked nothing more than to be able to blame everything on him, to put him under the spotlight of an interrogation room or the local TV station. But he had not only been exemplary in his conduct during the raid; more importantly, he had been impeccable afterwards. Normally they tried to get off on a procedural error. There was none here. Fuentes had smashed a kidnapping and sex-slave ring that had been festering under the nose of the authorities, saving the lives of six local girls, not to mention the female union activists, and he had the evidence to prove it. For the moment at least, he was untouchable. He was in fact that most contradictory and elusive of things in a Tijuana police station: a hero.

Of course his colleagues all hated him for what he had done. They didn't see girls and young women who had been saved. They saw money flying out of barred windows. They'd grown used to Abarca's largesse. He ran whorehouses and crooked card games. He sold weed and meth to tourists, and provided underage cocaine mules to the cartel. Through a winning mixture of law enforcement greed and incompetence, Abarca had been allowed to become a big man in a little town. As a consequence, he lacked all perspective, especially where he himself was concerned. He had thought he would always get away with whatever he wanted to do. He displayed the surly arrogance of a man without imagination.

Now he sat in a cramped posture, hunched over cuffs, muttering curses to himself like a greedy diner impatient for dessert. Well, fuck him. Fuentes kicked the old man through his hand-stitched cowboy boot.

Abarca looked up at him, his inflamed eyes framed by gray hair and white moustache. It wasn't the arrogance of the stare that annoyed Fuentes, it was the disbelief. He kicked him in the ankle again, harder this time. 'Wake up, *viejo*!' There was fury in the old man's gaze now, but something else besides, something Fuentes had been longing to see.

Fear.

At last, it was sinking in.

Fuentes grabbed him by the arm and paraded him past the

crowded lock-up, speaking to the miserable faces of the incarcerated. 'Make no mistake. You're all going to jail. But anyone who signs a confession stating that they were coerced into committing their crimes under threats of violence from this old fart will get an immediate sentence reduction for co-operating with authorities.'

Seventeen hands shot up. This was what Fuentes wanted the old man to see. Total mutiny. He was alone, and would die alone. He shoved him into a narrow cell at the end of the room. Abarca held up his fists. 'Free me.' It was not a request, it was a demand. 'Let him shit in his pants,' a voice from the holding pen shouted. Laughter filled the space between the cells. Fuentes felt the power of the collective humiliation pressing hard against the man, making him wilt. It was as if he had just aged five more years. 'That's what you did to the women. Jeered at them. Humiliated them. Tortured them. I want you to remember that when you're being tortured in prison. You think you're too old?' He shook his head with a savage laugh. 'Think again. Someone will know someone who had a woman out there today. And when it happens, remember you brought it upon yourself.'

He saw the emotional indecision ripple across the old man's face. He'd told him the reality of the incarceration he would be facing. Fuentes didn't care whether Abarca killed himself or not. One way or the other, Abarca was going to pay for his crimes.

Upstairs, the last of the striking women were being fingerprinted. Their ink-stained fingers fluttered like moths in the smoky air as they spoke and plotted amongst themselves, some in whispered conflict, voices harsh and low.

Normally Pilar would have stood at the head of the women, protesting that they were being treated as criminals and demanding an attorney, but like the others, right then she was just grateful to be alive. There was so much anger in her heart that she could feel it pressing inside her chest, as though it could burst like a rotten fruit in the sun; exposing everything she wanted to hide. Fear. Grief. Relief. And even, God help her, gratitude at their escape. Pilar knew how close they had come . . . She knew they had been rescued by a good man working for a corrupt system. As painful as it was, she acknowledged it, and having done so was able to let it go. 'Why are we being held?' she said to Fuentes. 'We're not criminals.'

'That's an interpretation of the law you'll have to leave to a judge.'

'What about the animals who did this?'

'They are all under arrest.'

'You know there are others.'

Of course Fuentes knew. Only the week before, a squad of mounted police in the capital had been arrested for exactly the same crime. At first they kept the women for themselves. Then they started selling them by the hour. Abarca had been doing the same. The question was: who were his clients? Fuentes aimed to find out. 'I'll do my best to see that all the charges are dropped against you and the other women.'

'And against the kidnappers? The rapists? I bet you'll see their charges are dropped too!' Pilar didn't really believe that. But she had to say it anyway. That was her role – to say and do the things that others were afraid of saying and doing.

'I give you my word.'

'The word of a Tijuana labor cop?' Her laugh was both contemptuous and fearful. He stared at her, his wrist ticking with pain. 'I demand to visit the kidnapped women.'

'So visit them, if their families will let you. You're free to go. All of you.' Then he turned and walked down the stairs leading back to the lock-ups.

Down in the holding section, Fuentes stared at the faces of the *rurales*. 'Who's the senior man here?' The men shuffled away from the question – and from one of the other prisoners. They didn't consciously mean to betray him. It was an instinctive response to danger, like a herd suddenly breaking from a watering spot. A force of nature. The police moved in a single wave, one of them unlocking the gate, the others tugging the isolated man out. He shouted for help and tried to hold onto the bars. One of the cops slashed at his fingers with a nightstick. The man screamed, his voice high in the ceiling, then low on the ground, clutching his hand inside his armpit.

Cruel fists lifted him up, struck him; threw him across the room. He hit a jutting counter with his ribs. They all heard the crack. He grunted, not from pain but from fear; of worse to come. Fuentes gestured for and received the nightstick – the magic wand of this interrogation. He slammed it hard on the counter, making the prisoner jump. He nodded to the cops and one grabbed the prisoner from behind in a choke hold, while the others held his good hand over the counter, like an offering on an altar.

Fuentes brought the stick down so hard he cracked the counter, the police all instinctively jerking away from the blow as he just missed the hand on purpose.

'I'm only asking once . . .' He plunged the nightstick into the solar plexus, the prisoner bereft of oxygen, then tapped the gasping head under the chin, forcing eye contact. 'The names of everyone who went to the stables.' Fuentes gave him a light tap on the collarbone. 'Everyone.' The prisoner muttered something and they dragged him to the deposition desk.

It took seven hours to verify twenty-nine names. After he read the names to the other prisoners, they all agreed to testify. It only took another five hours to get down all their statements. The rest of the interrogation was just to ensure, to the best of Fuentes' ability, that no one had been deliberately left off the list. He went through it one last time. Apart from a noted doctor, who worked for free in the hospital every Thursday morning and who had been called when one of the girls looked like she might be dying, none of the other names were that significant. Local party members who were only active at a municipal level. An exporter of limes. A local businessman. A primary-school teacher. An ex-radio broadcaster who was notorious for his binge drinking. Respectable enough people in the run of things. People you would trust to help out if the community were in trouble. It all made tragically predictable sense. And yet Fuentes wasn't convinced. These fish weren't big enough.

He called the first prisoner in again. A doctor had taped his broken fingers. They were a powerful negotiating tool for further down the line. Fuentes told him he needed the real names, and if he didn't give them to him, he was going to lock him up with Abarca. Incredibly, the prisoner still didn't talk.

He was even more scared of something else.

There was only one thing more frightening than death itself. *Narcos.*

But why would the Tijuana cartel be even indirectly associated with a worm like Abarca? Fuentes had a hunch that the answer must lie in the identity of one of the young women he had saved.

38

El Santo

El Santo sits with his legs dangling off the gurney, holding an increasingly wet and heavy compression pad to his stomach as the doctor cuts through his jeans.

He has sent Oviedo to the mall to get some new clothes, and now he's wondering if that wasn't a major fucking mistake.

His shooting might already be all over the *narco* grapevine. The problem with your average *narco* is that ninety-nine percent of the time, they're sitting on their asses, drinking beer, smoking crack, and gossiping about their bosses or their bosses' women; or even their bosses' women's women. It is just like school, only everyone has an Uzi and is *totalmente alterado*.

But now El Santo realizes that his quest for privacy has left him unprotected. Anyone could walk through the door and catch him literally with his pants down. He knows what would happen then. Shims under kneecaps would be the least of his problems. Just thinking of it makes his heart race, and that makes his blood run faster and that makes . . . 'How about another fucking bandage, I'm bleeding out here!'

The doctor sighs as he crosses to a cupboard and pulls out a diaper-sized bandage, the rip from the sterile strip being torn open making him flinch like fingernails on a blackboard. 'I said hold it *tight*.' He presses it hard against the wound, and takes El Santo's hand like he's a puppet, pushing it down on the bandage. 'You need to apply pressure.'

This doctor has a real fucking attitude – always the sign of a good surgeon, even if it makes you want to kill him. El Santo has forgotten what it's like to be talked down to. 'Lie down and try not to move.' The lights come on, showering him in their hot homogenous lux. He blinks up at the clusters of halogen lamps hovering inside the UFO-shaped dish elevated above him. In the background he can hear all the prep noises: the snap of plastic gloves, the rustle of paper face masks and hair nets, the bright metallic click of surgical instruments. A needle appears, its point pearled with a transparent bead.

He grabs the doc by the sleeve. 'No funny business!'

The doctor steps back, pulling free of his grip. 'Do you want that bullet out or not?'

Long pause. Even pissing blood, El Santo could leap to his feet and beat the surgeon unconscious. And what good would that do? He'd still be stuck with this copper-tailed slug trying to squirm its way further inside his guts, like a burrowing insect. He nods to the doc, consoling himself with the thought that he is superior to El Feo and all the other *narcos*, who live in the *now* because they have abandoned their past and sold their future. They are impulsive the way a blowfly is: never mind the smell, they always go for the hot shit. El Santo is like Amado. A planner. Someone who is in it for the long haul. Which means getting rid of this bullet.

A jab in his arm. Big fucking deal. He's up for this.

The cold squirt of Betadine across his body. Red, then orange. Shiver, tickle, shiver. Rub, rub, sting. Then the doc's holding a wad of cotton gauze at the end of some tongs. 'This is going to hurt,' he says.

He ain't lying. 'Shit, what is that?'

The doc doesn't say anything but El Santo can see the smirk through the mask. The surgical lighthead seems to glow stronger, as though it's in on the gag too. 'Now I'm going to inject the local anesthetic,' he says in a robotic monotone, the way they deliver safety instructions on an airplane. They know the plane's not going down and even if it does, no one's going to survive. No one's going to be able to reach for *the life jacket under seat*. It's just yabber-yabber filler until they can get on with the real work, and start serving lunch.

'You'll feel a little prick.'

Prick, my ass. The jab's more a stab. In the stomach. The tender spot. He remembers as a kid, hearing about the rabies vaccine and deciding he'd rather go mouth-frothing mad than take ten shots to the gut. Thank you, El Feo. If he weren't already dead, El Santo would murder him right then and there. Another jab, deeper still. More painful, if that were possible. 'Shit!'

'Don't move. I'm making the incision.'

'Ow!'

'You can feel that?'

'Fuck yes.'

'That's not possible.'

'Don't tell me what's not possible. I need a general anesthetic.'

'You told me yourself that you've eaten not an hour ago. You told me you've been drinking and ingesting drugs all day.'

'A little blow, so what?'

The needle gleams under the unwinking glare of surgery lights. 'Exceptionally, I'm giving you another shot.'

Exceptionally, I'm not putting a bullet through your head, El Santo thinks. Doctors are supposed to be healers. They're supposed to have compassion. More bullshit. They're just up-market butchers. 'Well? Are you giving it to me or not?'

'I already have.' Good news at last. 'Sometimes the reaction is delayed. Could be because of all the narcotics in your system.'

He wishes the doc would lay off with the lecture about drugs. 'It was just a little blow . . . Ow!'

'I can't do this if you keep moving.'

'I'm moving because you keep hurting me.'

'It's impossible that you felt anything just then.'

'I fucking felt it.'

'You must have a low pain threshold.' El Santo isn't sure what this means, but it sounds like an insult. 'I'm giving you another sedative.'

This time the shot hurts his arm. He tries not to react. Fuck this doctor and his low pain threshold. 'Why the fuck didn't you give me this before?'

'I did. Sometimes drug addiction can make you hypersensitive. Or else your system is so loaded with toxins, it's immune.'

'That's a good thing, right?'

'Try not to move, I'm making the incision.'

'Fuck me!'

There is a clatter as the doctor tosses his scalpel into a stainless-steel, kidney-shaped bowl. 'Listen. I need you to co-operate.'

'I'm lying here, trying to be as still as possible while you slice me open without anesthetic. What am I supposed to do?'

The doctor grabs El Santo's cheeks, squeezes open his mouth, shoves five or six wooden spatulas between his teeth, then pushes his mouth shut. 'Endure,' he says.

El Santo bites hard, until it feels like there's just a thin wooden membrane between his teeth. He gives a low, long groan as the doctor slices his gunshot wound open, his body flexed but unmoving. There is the cold tremor of clamps, going far inside him, and something white shifts fast behind his eyes, the doctor muttering curses to himself, wet flowing down El Santo's waist and thighs. Then something huge as a heart and heavy as a horse is extracted from his stomach and dropped against metal. It makes a sound like the gates of hell slamming shut. The doctor's already stitching. El Santo raises his head and peers into the kidney-shaped bowl. All this misery for that – a tiny fucking .22? Goddamn El Feo. 'I always knew he was a baby.'

'Consider yourself lucky. If it had been a .45 ACP, this would be an autopsy, not an operation. Don't move, I'm still sewing.'

El Santo hates the way this doc talks to him. At least they're alone so no one else can hear this disrespect. He's glad he sent Oviedo away to get some clothes. It was the right decision after all. He sits up with a grunt, shifting his weight and dangling his feet over the edge. 'Take it easy,' the doctor says. 'No sudden moves.'

If anyone comes through the door right now, El Santo will be able to respond. He could snatch up his SIG Sauer P226 9 mm and empty all fifteen rounds into them. He will not be taken alive. Things are already looking up. The doctor sees where his eyes are. And just that glance makes him feel better; stronger. Angrier. 'Call yourself a man of medicine?'

'You came to me dying. Now you'll live.'

'Don't exaggerate.'

'You would have bled to death.' He walks up close to El Santo, and that's when he notices that the doctor's face mask is speckled with blood – his blood. He looks at the bandages sitting inside the surgical waste: sopping with red. No wonder he feels light-headed. The doctor tears the mask off with a sudden rip, his voice no longer flat and muffled but direct and close. Judgmental. 'And if you hadn't, you would have developed septicemia and died.'

This fucking doctor's got one hell of an attitude problem. If he wasn't feeling so queasy, he'd teach him a lesson in manners. But fuck that. A saved life is a saved life.

All he wants to do now is settle the debt, clean the rest of the blood off his thighs and sides and stomach and walk out of here in new clothes. He reaches for his wallet – which is next to his P226 – and notices the doc flinch. That makes him feel better too. His usual world order has been restored. 'How much do I owe you?'

'Nothing.'

This is something El Santo was not expecting and he doesn't like the unexpected. 'Bullshit. Fifty grand should cover it.'

The room fills with the hiss and snapped release of gloves freed and discarded. 'I don't want your *narco* money. I spend enough time with your victims.'

The way things are going this will end very badly. 'You know something? I don't give a fuck what you want. You take the money I give you.' The moron shakes his head.

He stands. His bare feet look puny outside his cowboy boots, like an animal without its shell. He feels ridiculous, naked except for a blue paper operating smock tied up at the back, his ass exposed, the hem corroding and crenellating into papier mâché from his blood. This is the part where he's supposed to be threatening. 'Otherwise, I'm going to have to waste you.'

The doctor stares at him like *he's* the moron, then slowly

turns and points to a computer across the room. 'Have you ever heard of a webcam?'

As a matter of fact, El Santo hasn't, but he gets the drift. 'You filmed my operation?' He hurriedly fans his hands across his balls. 'Pervert!'

'Not perversion, insurance. Harm me, or my family, or any of my staff, and the film goes to the media.'

El Santo cocks his head in disbelief. Is this guy for real? 'There's nothing to stop me from stealing the film right now.'

The doctor points to this weird orb on a tripod next to the computer. 'It's a live feed to a secure storage site.'

He doesn't know what that means but he guesses that he's fucked. 'You didn't have to go to the trouble, I am a man of my word. A man of honor.' Something flashes across the doc's face that could be a sneer. He grabs his wallet. He may as well have picked up some prime tenderloin, it's so raw and bloody. Even the sanguine-puffed leather exterior feels like a slice of newly killed meat. The bank notes he takes out are actually dripping. 'A man like me always honors his debts.'

'And a man like me always honors his patients.' The silence in the surgery is broken only by the beading drops of blood from the bank notes. 'Give it to someone who needs it, someone who has never had anything to do with you. Give it to someone like Padre Márcio.'

That was almost worth a laugh. El Santo tosses the ruined wad of wet money into the kidney-shaped bowl. 'Wipe your ass with it, I don't care.' Just then Oviedo walks in, not even knocking. 'We all set?' he asks, tossing him a new pair of Calvin Kleins.

'Fuck yeah, we're all set.' He groans as he puts on his briefs.

'Say, do you know anything about computers?'

Oviedo shrugs. 'Typing's not my thing.'

'You know *anyone* who knows anything about computers?'

'Sure, boss.'

The doctor looks at him anxiously. He knows where this is leading. 'It's too late, there's nothing you can do.'

Bullshit, there's always something you can do – he's been doing it since he was a kid. He reaches for his piece, his stitches aching from the stretch, and shoots the doctor in the chest. The doc slams back into the wall, leaving a slurred trail of blood as he sinks lopsided to the floor. El Santo points to the computer set-up with his gun. 'He's been filming me. Find someone to figure it out and get rid of it.'

Oviedo goes over to the computer, rips out some electrical cords and hefts up the tower, balancing the weight against one hip.

'What about the screen and the camera?'

Oviedo shakes his head. 'We got all we need here. We good, boss?'

El Santo looks back one last time at the doctor, his glasses broken from his fall. 'Hell yeah, we're good.'

39

Nomen Nescio #352 (Jane Doe #352)

Fuentes enters into the shimmer of contained cold and an abattoir stench dampened by the high sting of chemicals. Gomez follows him into the morgue, crossing himself instinctually.

A corpse lies hidden under a sheet on one of the autopsy slabs. A hand protrudes from one of the corners of the sheet, charcoaled from forensics. They painted her, palmed her, printed her; then left the ink residue to dry, staining her. It wasn't just careless or disrespectful, it was negligent. Any evidence on her hands has been contaminated.

Perhaps that was the point.

Fuentes unfolds the sheet down to the shoulders, revealing the face of a woman in her late twenties. The skin is a blanched olive, the eyes dark-ringed in death. A gold crucifix lies cradled inside the hollow of her throat. Fuentes puts on latex gloves, then slowly, almost reverentially, unclips the crucifix and slides it into an evidence bag. 'She was christened once, when she was a baby. And now she's waiting to be christened again, aren't you, Jane Doe?'

Fuentes knows the parameters of what will happen next. A mother will visit in the next few days, praying not to find her daughter here. Or three months from now, she'll sit down in front of folders of photos at a police station in a different state. Or she'll write another pleading letter, hoping to receive a response in an envelope with a US stamp.

He lifts the dead woman's hair, revealing areas that have

been shaved along the temples, so that it could be worn either exposed or covered. She was no *maquiladora* worker, but perhaps someone who worked in an upmarket shop or an office; someone who was required to dress conservatively but who possessed a rebellious flair. A person keeping a secret; maybe leading a double life. Responsible by day, wild by night.

Her ears have multiple piercings through the lobe and helix, although there is no jewelry there. Some killers keep jewelry as a trophy, but the ones he's after are different; theft has never been a motive. They're disciplined, as though always adhering to precise directives. As though there might be consequences if they don't. The absence of jewelry most likely indicates that she was in her conservative environment when she was kidnapped, perhaps going to or coming from work.

A bank or law firm maybe?

There is a tattoo of the Virgin Mary on her right shoulder. 'Nice work,' Gomez says, 'real professional.' And easily concealed if need be. Fuentes folds the sheet down to her waist. Both nipples support silver barbell piercings, and the breasts show signs of recent bruising. They confirm Fuentes' hypothesis: public conformity – the crucifix; private mutiny – the piercings and tattoo. Fuentes delicately unclasps the piercings and drops them into a second plastic evidence bag. However unlikely, there could be latent fingerprints on them.

There's telltale scarring around the trans-axillary and peri-areolar regions and inside the inframammary fold. Breast augmentation surgery. Another unusual detail taking Jane Doe even further away from *maquiladora* worker. Tattoos tell stories, but scars tell entire histories and it's his job to interpret the chronicle being revealed to him.

She had money. She invested it in herself. Was the tattoo of the Virgin for contrition, or an *ex voto* offered up for an answered prayer? Perhaps the cash to pay for her breast surgery? He stares down at her face with a patient regard, as though awaiting a response to a whispered question.

Fuentes folds down the sheet to her knees. Gomez whistles. 'Check it out, boss.' There's an ornate tattoo of a butterfly on her shaved mons pubis. For her own sense of beauty or to excite a lover? Or maybe clients? There are no signs of the rashes, lesions and track marks you'd expect to find on the body of a *narco* sex worker. He is sure Jane Doe was leading a double life, but one she controlled herself. The butterfly speaks to him of something outside the pleasure of men. It speaks of transformation; of flight. He's thinking money laundering; maybe even blackmail. That would provide a motive. Compared to all the other victims she is atypical; asymmetric – in every way except the manner and signature of her death, which was identical to that of the other victims. She is their first link between two worlds. 'We need to photograph the tattoos and get them to all the parlors. Someone's bound to recognize the work. We need to get photos of the deceased to all the clinics that perform cosmetic surgery, even the ones that don't do mammoplasty. Someone referred her. Someone must know her.'

'What's the point?' Gomez asks, defeated by the work before it's even begun. 'We've got her prints.'

'Fuck the prints. Look at her. She's not someone with a criminal record. We need to be smart here. We need to do the rounds of her photo with every bank, every law firm, every chartered accountant in town.'

'You think she worked for the cartels?'

'I think she stumbled across information she shouldn't have. I think she's our breakthrough.'

The doors swing open, making Gomez jump. A doctor enters in a hurry, reading from a clipboard. 'She's O positive.'

'Have you heard back about the blood samples from the crime scene?'

The doctor looks up at Fuentes. 'A positive.'

Fuentes rushes out, slapping the doctor on the shoulder as he passes, speaking to Gomez in an excited rush. 'Ten to one we get prints on the jewelry. That's the way it always works: when you get one lucky break, you get them all.'

They push through the doors out into sunshine, brutal and punishing, traffic deafening after the silence of the grave. 'We get a photographer over, pronto.' Car keys gleam like a lucky charm, Fuentes pulling out dangerously in front of a bus, its horn pounding with murderous rage. 'We prioritize the toxicology tests.' Gomez leans out his window, gives the bus driver a colossal *mentada de madre*. 'We subpoena the medical records of every municipal employee, every state employee, every federal employee in Ciudad Real.'

Gomez turns back to Fuentes. 'Why?'

'Because the killers, or at least some of them, are cops.' He studies the look of surprise. 'You never figured that?'

'I've heard what people say, but . . . I never wanted to believe it.'

Fuentes adjusts his rearview mirror. The car with Texas plates is almost hidden by a truck behind them. 'You can believe it. The big question is, which cops?'

'Municipal or state?'

'Think again: Mexican or American.'

40

Fuentes

Gordillo dozes in front of the wheel of a parked car while Byrd watches a lit window through binoculars.

Gomez and Marina bustle in the kitchen. Gomez puts his arm around her, squeezes a breast. She drops her head to one side, kisses his arm. Gomez presses a cold beer against the back of her neck. She yelps silently, pulling away, laughing, then turns and holds him around the waist, her hands dropping to grab the cheeks of his ass, squeezing as they kiss. 'No wonder nothing works down here,' Byrd says, waking up Gordillo. 'Everyone's too busy fucking.'

Gordillo accepts the binoculars and watches as Gomez puts his hand up the back of Marina's T-shirt. 'What are we doing, staking out this moron? He's got nothing to do with anything.'

'The boss wants it done.'

'El Santo's full of shit. If you ask me, this is just some kind of distraction.'

'From what?'

'I have no idea, but neither does El Santo. These hits on union targets. They don't make sense. But something big is going down. And whatever it is, I want to be a part of it.'

That's the trouble with Gordillo. He wants to be a part of everything, which is not just greedy but impossible. Byrd stretches in his seat. His legs are aching from inactivity. Before he knows it, he'll have thrombosis. The sooner he can get back on a golf course, the better.

On the other side of the road, Fuentes stands behind an oleander, out of sight of a car with Texas plates that's watching Gordillo spy on Gomez. He turns, walking silently back towards his car, keeping to the shadows.

The drive to the last tattoo parlor on the list is long and depressing. Fuentes had stopped by Gomez's house to see if it was still under surveillance and had also witnessed the display of affection between the couple. Gomez and Marina reminded him of his own life. Before Ciudad Real. Before Tijuana. When everything seemed clear. Understandable. Normal. When he still believed in the bigness of little things: love and sex. Marriage and children. Family and the sanctity of the home. Trust. The nobility and purpose of a career. Being a cop and making a difference.

One by one, all those beliefs have been stripped from him until the only thing he has left is being a cop and the possibility – just the possibility – of putting a stop to one last thing. And his *one last thing* is the murders of the women of Ciudad Real.

It's just like Fuentes to have chosen the biggest thing he could possibly think of. But he knows from nine years in Mexico City and three in Tijuana that it never really matters if what you care about is tiny or huge; at the end of the day it's so hard to change anything, it requires such a massive effort, that you may as well aim for the big instead of the small. And if he is unable to effect change, to initiate something positive and fresh in a harsh world, at least he can still try to end something vast and ugly; something incomprehensible. So saturated in evil that politicians, police and the press will do anything they can to ignore it.

To maintain their silence surrounding the murders of hundreds of women.

It isn't the silence of the grave. It's the silence of an entire cosmology. A mute acceptance of an unspeakable ritual, which has been re-enacted not just over centuries but over millennia. Human sacrifice. Devil worship. The *tzompantli* demands of an insane deity.

Burnt offerings under a red Aztec sun.

It's an outlandish explanation. Inconceivable.

Preposterous.

But the only one that makes sense. The only explanation that can embrace the savagery and the horror of what has been happening in Ciudad Real.

The only one that stands up to logic.

He accelerates, flashes of worn earth torn up from either side of the road by his headlamps then discarded backwards into shadow, like graves being exhumed then hurriedly refilled. A car thunders around a curve, switching on its high beams when it sees him, slapping him with velocity and light. Fuentes curses and swerves, catching a glimpse of the car in his rearview mirror, a single red taillight flashing fast as a gunshot before disappearing back into darkness.

He pulls over, humping the car off the road, and gets out fast. Leaning with his hand on the open door, he throws up. It's sudden. Violent. It hurts him; sucks the breath from his lungs. Leaves him gasping and in pain. He's finally able to slowly straighten, looking up at the road ahead. Just in front of him, revealed on the stage created by his headlights, are hundreds of moths, swarming, flickering and colliding; frenzied by their desire to extinguish themselves within the burning light.

The tattoo artist is wreathed in swirls of ink and coils of color – his body landscaped by portraits, symbols and expressions of devotion. His fingers move slowly, heavy with rings, as they follow lines in an appointment book written in an elegant copperplate. 'Here she is.' He turns the book upside down so Fuentes can read the name: *Mary-Ellen*. There's a phone number beside it.

'Did she use a credit card?'

'I don't accept them. They fuck you over with their commissions.'

'What can you tell me about her?'

He lifts an eyebrow against the weight of a stud, thinking; remembering. 'Good taste in music. Rage Against the Machine. Chimaira. Stone Temple Pilots. We'd sing along sometimes. I remember the butterfly. I tried to talk her out of it, but . . .' He shrugs the way a sommelier would over an excellent suggestion that's ignored by a diner. 'She wasn't a *mariposa* kind of person, know what I mean? Yeah, Mary-Ellen . . .' The way he draws out the name, soft and spirant, gives him pleasure. 'Sorry to hear about her, man. Real sorry.'

'Did she come here alone?'

'House rules. It's only ever me, my client and the ink. That's the way I've always worked.'

'Did you ever see her in the company of others?'

He looks around the walls of his studio, covered with his artwork. Psychedelic. Totemic. Abstract. Pictorial realism. 'I don't get out much.' He taps his temple. 'I don't need to, understand?'

'Did she ever talk about a boyfriend? Any problems at work?'

The artist gives a sigh of disapproval. 'The thing about my studio? It's a sanctuary, man. You don't bring your problems inside, you bring your dreams. This is a space for creation. The negative shit stays out there. I insist on it and my clients prefer it like that.'

Outside, the sky trembles with the mustard-colored haze of sodium backlit smog. He feels strangely peaceful. Perhaps it is merely because he has thrown up something bad he had eaten. Something poisonous. Perhaps it is because he finally has a solid lead on a case that has eluded resolution for so long. Or perhaps it was the atmosphere inside the tattoo studio. A refuge for dreams and imagination.

A sanctuary in a city devoid of one.

He gets back into his car. When he arrived fifteen minutes earlier, he thought he'd be going straight home after this interview. He thought he was exhausted. But he won't be able to rest now. Not when he has a telephone number that will provide a family name. An address that might open a path and take him all the way to the killers. Maybe what the tattoo artist said about Mary-Ellen is true. Maybe she wasn't a *mariposa*. But she has already undergone one massive metamorphosis that evening. From Jane Doe back to Mary-Ellen. From a person without a past to a person with a history.

41

Ventura

Pilar and Juan Antonio sit opposite Ventura and Mayor in a restaurant booth, their table covered with empty plates, empty beer bottles; the ashtray a cemetery of cigarettes. A group of young men at the table opposite can't take their eyes off Ventura and Pilar. If it were only one man gazing continually at them, it'd be disconcerting enough. But their collective focus is powerful and intimidating. It implies both a right to stare and a need to dominate; to take whatever they want. Ventura glances at them, then turns quickly away.

If Pilar has noticed the youths at the next table, she hasn't shown it. In fact, she's reacted to very little throughout the dinner. The only moment she ever emerged from her exaggerated state of boredom was when she was first introduced to Ventura and was pointedly sarcastic. Now she's visibly wilting, her elbows on the table, nursing her left cheek in her palm, as though cradling the head of an infant.

Her obvious lack of interest must be vexing to Mayor, but he doesn't seem to mind. He has his audience. Juan Antonio is riveted, hanging on every golden word. And his words are devoted to one thing: selling Ventura. No wonder Pilar greeted her with hostility. Anyone's conclusion would be the same: she's sleeping with Mayor to get ahead in the world.

And, Ventura has to admit, how many other women has she known who have done something like that? Her best friend –

her *former* best friend – Antonia had slept with her supervisor in a clerical department of a law firm, after months of being subjected to his harassment.

Ventura was appalled. How could Antonia have fucked a man she hated, a man who had gone out of his way to treat her badly – not once, but every day. A man who had destroyed the love she'd had for her work.

Ventura railed at her at first but then Antonia started to grow angry, not with her boss but with her. Ventura persisted, pleading with Antonia to end the relationship for her own dignity. She explained that women were denied power and equality in the workplace precisely because it made them vulnerable. Antonia had to stand up not just for herself but for all female workers. But in the end, what business was it of hers who Antonia slept with? Yet still she felt Antonia had let herself down. She even felt that she had let Antonia down. It was so complicated, like having a friend who was the victim of domestic violence and not being able to get her to do anything about it. Powerlessness is contagious. So is self-doubt. They saw less of each other, and when they did, Antonia avoided the subject of her work.

The Christmas after she had started her affair, Antonia was the only one in her section to get a bonus. Ventura begged her not to accept it. They had a terrible argument. Ventura didn't see Antonia for several weeks. Then she got the news. Antonia's boss was leaving. He had been promoted to another section. And Antonia decided to go for his job. She asked him for a reference. He refused.

She didn't get the job.

Antonia had been Ventura's best friend since high school.

She loved her; she would have done anything for her. And then suddenly she was estranged from her. And nothing would ever bring them back together.

So Ventura understands Pilar's attitude towards her. Her suspicions. But she also resents them. Because she has seen the damage that Antonia's behavior caused. Not just to Antonia, but to her colleagues; to all women. Of course the odds are stacked against women in the workplace. They always have been. But that is no excuse. Above all else, in this masculine world, a woman needs to show solidarity with other women, and pride in herself. And it grieves her that Pilar refuses to grant her that based on a false assumption.

Mayor is finishing his pitch. 'Nothing else counts in this country,' he says, more to the attentive gaze of Juan Antonio than to the passive one of Pilar. 'Until we fix this, we won't be able to fix anything. Believe me, I know what I'm talking about. I know this country better than anyone.'

Pilar sparks up at these last words. 'You only *think* you know this country because you spend all your time explaining it to the *gringos*.'

'Pilar!' Juan Antonio exclaims, but Mayor calms him down with a wave of his hand.

'It's true,' the writer says, 'there's no denying. All of us who live here begin to accept things the way they are, just because we're used to them.'

'I don't,' Pilar says, draining a bottle of beer.

'But imagine if you had to start explaining *everything* to others,' Mayor says. 'The way we think. The way we believe. Why we live the way we do. *How* we live the way we do. The way we treat death. Impossible!'

Juan Antonio smiles compliantly. 'No one can understand us because we don't understand ourselves.'

'But we do!' Pilar protests. 'We understand we live in the shadow of a great power, we understand that our government and police are corrupt; that the poor will always remain poor. The problem is not that we don't understand ourselves; the problem is we understand too well.'

'Acceptance is not understanding,' Ventura says.

'Just as understanding is not acceptance.' Pilar stands up. 'I don't have time for philosophy, I have to work.' She turns to Juan Antonio. 'And so do you.'

'We'll continue this discussion,' Juan Antonio says to Mayor, embarrassed, as Pilar pulls him after her. 'Thank you for your support,' he shouts back to Mayor.

Mayor waves the words away as though they were wasps at a barbecue. 'I'm counting on you.'

'That was very rude, the way you left.'

'Boo-hoo. What's he counting on?' Pilar asks, pulling the door open and letting it slam shut on Juan Antonio.

'The girl.'

'There's always a girl where Mayor's concerned. And that was a woman with him, not a *girl*.'

'She's going to go to work with you tomorrow.'

'No fucking way.'

'She needs to see what it's like.'

'This is industrial action, not research.'

'She's a professional.'

'I've never heard of her. I ask for experienced activists and you give me a baby.'

'You said yourself she's not a girl.'

'We don't need her.'

'It's not your choice. It's mine, and I've made it.'

Fuentes is circling the plaza, his headlights lancing across couples and small groups talking, the beams suddenly strafing across Pilar's face.

He slows, watching her in the rearview mirror. She's with a man who has the lean, lethal look of a wolf; dangerous but patient. Knowing when not to attack. From the way they are walking, Fuentes can tell they're not talking about CTON business. He accelerates slowly across the plaza, Pilar's figure lost in the shadows.

'You've got to understand—'

'The only thing I understand is that you're in love with your own voice; just like Mayor.' She breaks away from Juan Antonio and embraces the three women who are waiting by the car for their lift to work. 'Sorry we're late. We were delayed by his ego . . .' She sees the look on his face. 'Go on. Say it.'

He opens his mouth to speak, then shakes his head and unlocks the car door. Pilar glances around the plaza. For most of the crowd, the night is ending. For her and the other three women, it's just about to begin. The pop of her door being unlocked sounds like a trap being sprung. So when someone grabs her arm, Pilar spins defensively. It's the girl. 'I'm going to help, with or without you.'

Pilar roughly pulls away, freeing her arm. 'I'm not stopping you.'

'You're doing everything you can to cut me out.'

Pilar hesitates. She doesn't know what Juan Antonio and Mayor have agreed between themselves, but clearly this *chica* is not going away. Better to control her than leave Juan Antonio in charge. 'We're going to need as many mourners as we can get at the funeral.'

Ventura brightens – inappropriately, given the subject matter, but she doesn't care. 'I won't let you down.'

'I won't give you a chance to.' Pilar gets in, resting her head against the window and closing her eyes. Juan Antonio watches Ventura pass through the headlights, walking back to the restaurant, then glances at Pilar as he swings the car out, heading towards the highway. She's already asleep. They're early. He'll let her sleep for as long as he can after they arrive.

42

Byrd and Gordillo

Byrd stares across at Gomez's house. The lights are all out. He turns to Gordillo, who is snoring lightly, then looks at his watch. He curses, fed up with this bullshit. In the general run of things, does it really matter if the ex-partner of Paredes is also involved in drug trafficking? Who really gives a fuck? Paredes is as guilty as hell. And so probably is Gomez. But then again, everyone's guilty down here, including Gordillo. It's unavoidable.

Byrd knows exactly what he's talking about: he fell for it himself, although he can no longer remember the exact circumstances. It was the usual trap – a slow-burn fuse: seduction then corruption. He saw stupid people with lots of money; more money than he'd ever seen before. Unimaginable money. Over time it seemed as though the stupider you were, the more money you could make. Look at El Santo, for Christ's sake. It's not like he's Steve Jobs.

And then the day came when he asked himself the question he'd been managing to avoid up until then: why them and not me? It's the kind of question you only ever ask when you already know the answer.

He went and got his hands dirty.

It still makes him shudder, thinking of what he had to do to start the ball rolling. But he did it; of course he did it. For the money. What other reason was there? And knowing everyone else did it made him feel more secure, even though it didn't ease the guilt . . . Or stop the nightmares.

That's why this shit about Paredes and Gomez is so weird. It's easy enough to implicate foot soldiers like them. Even Valdez and the general are vulnerable. When people get taken down, everyone knows who's behind it; *why* it needed to be done. There is always a logical reason. But this time there's nothing. Not to mention these union attacks. The uncertainty is troubling. Someone is trying to make waves. But who? Either someone on the other side of the border wants to destabilize the existing system for their own profit, or another cartel is staging a coup. Credit to whoever it is. The way they've set about doing it is perversely ingenious. Forty-two kilos is nothing – a loser's score these days. But forty-two kilos on a Mexican cop is huge. Bigger than the thousands they would have had to sacrifice otherwise to make the headlines. It's enough to alleviate suspicion and divert attention.

But from what?

The only answer Byrd can figure: from taking El Santo down. They had worked years to get their man close to El Santo. And when they finally realized their man was an idiot, it was too fucking late. At least El Santo can repeat basic information. But now El Feo has gone dark all of a sudden. That isn't like him. The challenge of handling El Feo has always been to get him to lie low. To stop him running to them every single day. To shut the fuck up. Byrd can't be certain, but it sure feels like El Feo has been silenced.

For good.

He starts the car, Gordillo stirring but not waking as he pulls out. He drives down an empty dirt track, the border corrugating the horizon, a dark welt emerging from the deeper shadow of the river. There's an old adobe ranch somewhere down here. El Feo said it was one of Oviedo's hideouts. El Feo hates Oviedo: the envy of an imbecile for someone half-smart. El Feo figures Oviedo is running coke on his own. A capital offense. A soldier never does anything on his own. He is meant to be a serf in the perpetual service of his master. Ambition is an abnormality; a warning sign.

Byrd catches something across the Rio Bravo – a small group of people clambering up the river bank and crouching in thin scrub. Then the signal of the coyote's flashlight, and a dozen more figures emerge out of the muddy waters, struggling up. He watches them for a moment in his side mirror, then decides to call it in. Normally he doesn't bother, but this will be an easy catch. He can tell from the difficulties they had climbing up the slope that they're either very young or older than normal. Either way, they're vulnerable; to the desert, to the coyotes; to shakedown and betrayal further along the line. An easy catch, and he'd be doing them a favor. He's just reaching for the radio when something runs fast across the road, ghostly and close in the headlights' beams. There is a sickening wallop.

'Fuck!' Byrd hits the brakes and the car squeals to a halt, Gordillo waking with a confused curse. Byrd gets out of the car, but stands still, waiting for the dust to settle, his ears straining; hearing nothing except the engine cracking in the cold night air. He slowly walks around the front of the car. A tan and white dog lies whimpering on the side of the road. He goes back to the car; opens the glovebox.

Gordillo sits up when he sees the gun. 'What do you think you're doing?'

'What anyone would do.'

It's always like this, when the graft you've been paying them finally requires an act that's more than just looking the other way. They panic, as though realizing for the first time what they've become, and that makes them self-righteous. And afraid. Up until that moment it's been an easy ride. A mortgage paid off, a new car; a girl on the side. All for doing literally nothing. But when the demand comes in for a *favor* – and it always comes in – then their cozy little world of denial, of *I didn't technically do anything illegal*, tilts in ways they never expected, and they reach for stability and normalcy, and life becomes all about the little things, because all the big things have been sold down a river of shit. 'Shooting that dog will attract attention,' Gordillo says. 'If you want to put it out of its misery, use a rock.'

Byrd stares at his accomplice; his tormentor. Just seeing Gordillo fills him with dread. Because Gordillo reminds him of what he's become. A craven accomplice in somebody's pocket, to be pulled out like a dirty snot-rag whenever required. He walks around to the dog, but it's already seen him coming. With a frightened shriek, it struggles impossibly up to its feet, limping away into the shadows of a ridge, heading towards the highway and the *maquiladoras*. Back towards civilization. As though seeking salvation. Byrd watches for a moment, aiming his gun as it crests the hill, but then it's out of sight. He gets back in the car. There are tears in his eyes. He had a dog that he loved, a long, long time ago. Before everything inside him turned rotten.

43

El Santo

El Santo watches as Oviedo preps the crew inside the eastern warehouse for tomorrow night's action. They're going to go in loud and hard, Oviedo tells them. Chances are not all of them will be coming back alive, but hey – that's what they do, right? A chorus of adrenaline-fueled agreement: *Fucking A!*

The morons.

But he has to admit that Oviedo's got it – that indefinable quality that makes men want to follow you into the worst kind of firestorm. Whether it's true or not, he makes the crew feel like he has their backs. The coke and the tequila and the cash stacked on the table in front of them don't hurt either.

Oviedo's cover story is so convincing that even El Santo feels his blood pressure rising, as though all five liters of his *sangre* were straining against his little black stitches, ready to burst out in a dark frothing tide. El Feo was a fink, Oviedo shouts – a fucking snitch to the Tijuana cartel. Boos all round. Thank Christ for our brilliant leader and champion bullshit detector, El Santo, who figured it out. Muted cheers, some frightened glances at *el jefe*.

Make no mistake, Oviedo hollers, you even *dream* of double-crossing El Santo, and *this* will happen to you!

Cue the ceremonial presentation of El Feo's severed head, pulled out of a green trash bag, matted with blood but recognizable. The look in their eyes. Freaked out but totally awed. A moment of power. It almost makes being shot by El Feo worthwhile. Everyone slowly turns to El Santo. Shivers of horror; chuckles of spite. Let's face it, El Feo wasn't the most popular of lieutenants. Most of the people here couldn't give a rat's ass that he's been killed. But they knew him. Some of them were talking to him only this morning. And now he's been turned into a three-dimensional Day of the Dead mask.

That's some spooky shit, even for these bad guys.

Expectant eyes stare.

El Santo's on.

He zips his leather jacket right up to the neck. He sure as hell hopes the bleeding has stopped. The last thing he needs is to start leaking in front of fifteen hyped-up gang-bangers. 'Who do you think deliberately fucked up with that hit on the *sindicalista*?' Uncomfortable silence. The cretins have no fucking idea. Oviedo to the rescue: 'That *hijo de la chingada*, El Feo.'

'You got it. And remember that fuck-up with the birthday party at the house yesterday? Who do you think let Los Toltecas get away?'

They're fast learners. 'That *hijo de la chingada*, El Feo!'

'Right! Now El Feo's brother is having his own birthday party – at the Heartbreak tomorrow. All of El Feo's crew will be there. This is a once-in-a-lifetime opportunity to take out everyone on the planet who's carrying El Feo's traitor genes.' Eyes flicker in confusion. 'We're going to DoA his DNA!' It isn't going over. El Santo's being too scientific. 'We're going to kill them all.' They get that part. Cheers. Catcalls. The heavy-metal music of weapons being racked. 'Tomorrow the rest of El Feo's crew joins him in the grave!' Not technically correct. After tomorrow's attack, the rest of El Feo is going to be hung from an overpass with a *narco* banner dangling from what's left of his neck. 'Tomorrow we make history.' He stares out at his men, their eyes not on him but on the stacks of money on the table. Whatever. He figures they're ready. He turns to Oviedo. 'Tell them about the clown.'

The joint falls silent. This is serious shit.

They're going to send in a death clown. That is only ever used for ultimate hits, like Colosio in Tijuana or Cardinal Posadas. The death clown rumors had started at the airport in Guadalajara in 1993. There were dozens of reports from people who said they saw them walking down the tarmac, laughing their sick asses off. Even flight crew and air traffic controllers swore they saw clowns hammering bullets into the cardinal's car. Oviedo surveys the silence. 'Green suit. Red hair. Classic. When you see him coming, get the fuck out of his way, because if he even looks at you, you're dead.'

The flutter of hands like startled birds, all making the sign of the cross. One or two even kiss a scapular. 'Now collect your pay and surrender your phones. You'll get 'em back tomorrow, after the hit.' Translation: we don't trust a single one of you. They don't care. They steal secret glances at El Feo's head, slam shots and snort snow. They're sliding into party mode, which is what El Santo wants, because come tomorrow, they'll all be in full hangover mode: morose; head-throb hurting. Nasty-minded and expendable: blindly obeying orders until it's all over and they can have their hair of the dog *clavo*.

But right now, the crew is all stoked. Too bad Mary-Ellen has disappeared. She would have ramped things up even more. No matter. The men exchange jokes and insults, slap each other on the back and stare at all the cash piled on the table, calculating how fast they could make it disappear. How fucking fast? El Santo knows the answer.

Finger-snap fast.

And so what? The way things are going, no matter how much you tried, you'd never be able to spend it all. The universe may be contracting, but the *narcocosmos*? That is one motherfucking expanding galaxy. And nothing – absolutely nothing – stands in its way.

44

Pilar

The repetitive slam and crash of machinery is deafening. Dozens of women work lined up along conveyor belts, sewing together a giant, collective jigsaw puzzle made of pieces of waffle tread, pre-cut leather and garish rubber heels.

At the end of this intricate and apparently random process, materializing like a magician's misdirected confabulation, appear running shoes. Shoes that high-school students will tug on without bothering to undo the laces when they're running late for class; that overweight executives will dutifully employ for an hour's walk every Sunday morning in an effort to atone for that second helping of dessert; that mothers will don before hurrying their children to soccer; that young female interns will use racing the chronometers of treadmills as they listen to Walkmans and formulate ways to avoid the devouring eyes of male bosses; that retirees will pull on sleepily at five o'clock in the morning so they can walk their incontinent, aging dogs, wondering how long they can delay the inevitable euthanasia, avoiding the implications surrounding their own slowly deteriorating condition.

These shoes encompass a universe of opportunities and choices – some wonderful, some mundane; most of them far outside the realm of possibility for any of the women bent over the production line.

Electric light sheens flatly off the whitewashed surfaces,

making the women's concentrated faces with rings under their eyes look like kabuki masks.

Two security guards stand half-aware of the scene, whispering comments about various women's asses as they smoke cigarettes, their eyes constantly drifting back to a TV inside their glassed-in office. It's switched to a European football game and the drone of the commentators is constantly spiking with excitement. 'How is it possible no one's scored yet?' one of the guards asks, watching a replay. 'That goalkeeper is not human,' the other guard says. Then the image cuts away quickly from the replay to the live action, one of the announcers screaming *penalty, penalty* as though it were the name of his daughter, trapped in an upstairs bedroom with the house on fire.

Pilar takes the hysterical shouting as her cue, and quickly moves down the rows, handing fliers to the workers she passes. Some of the women take them silently, folding them and tucking them away inside tunics. Others refuse them with a shake of the head, or the way they ignore a street beggar – staring straight ahead, repudiating the reality of the other's existence. Pilar glances back nervously at the guards. The striker scores, but is ordered to take the penalty again. 'Encroachment my ass!' one of the guards explodes. 'They're all on the take,' says the other. 'Refs are worse than fucking cops.'

Pilar risks the last row, but the women have all been watching her; they have had time to prepare a response – and, as anyone who has ever had time to do that can tell you, the response is always *no*.

Sensing a presence, Pilar glances up and sees the two guards now watching her. She hurries away, cutting back through the rows, the guards following. Pilar begins to run, crossing to the next room, but one of the guards grabs her.

Leaflets flutter to the floor. She is yanked hard into an office.

The guard who caught Pilar hands one of the leaflets to the night manager, who wears a blue dust jacket over a white singlet. He takes an incredible amount of time to read the flier.

Finally he looks up from the leaflet to Pilar, who is standing, disheveled, between two of the guards, the sleeve of her work tunic torn at the shoulder. The night manager's eyes are full of contempt, but they are also full of hot alarm. He knows someone's job has just been put on the line, and he's not thinking of Pilar. 'Empty her pockets.'

The guards pull out her cigarettes, the cell phone that Juan Antonio gave her. A palmful of coins. The night manager opens a desk drawer and sweeps them all inside.

'They're mine.'

He smiles at her, the way his father used to smile at him when he came home drunk. Right before a beating. 'Who sent you here?'

Pilar raises her chin. 'The women of this city.'

He slaps at her arm with the leaflet. It is an ineffectual gesture, as though he were brushing a bee out of his way. But it's still enough to open a door to the anger he's been able to contain until then. 'I'll ask you one more time. Who sent you?'

'Your wife, your mother, your sis—'

He strikes her hard across the cheek, then holds his hand as though the blow hurt him. 'Get this union whore out of my building!'

'I want my phone.'

'So you can call your communist friends?'

'I need a lift!' Pilar lurches forwards, trying to open the drawer.

The guard who first caught her pulls her with such force that he tears the ripped sleeve clean off her tunic. He throws her against the wall, then grabs her arms, twisting them behind her back.

The manager turns to the other guard. 'Search all the women when they leave. Fire anyone who has this propaganda.' The two guards exchange a look, satisfied with the orders. Maybe this worm of a night manager has a pair of balls after all. He senses the approval and calls out to them as they go. 'Who's winning?'

'Real Madrid.'

The night manager curses. 'Always the same – fuck the rich!' The security guards nod in complete agreement. The night manager sits down, his mind overflowing with hate – a trickle threatening to turn into a noxious explosion. Fuck Real Madrid. Fuck all its rich supporters who sit in their office towers in Monterrey and their condos in Miami and Dallas. Fuck their maids and their nannies and their drivers and their bodyguards. Fuck their villas in San Cabo and Acapulco and their spoilt children with their teeth braces and perfect English and ski holidays in Colorado. Fuck them all, while I have to work graveyard shifts and live in a house next to a polluted stream running like an open sore right where my children play. Fuck the *narcos* and fuck the cops. Fuck Televisa and their idiot fucking programs. Fuck the PRI. Fuck PAN and the PRD. Fuck the Church and its stupid Polish pope. And fuck that union bitch for making me think.

He slides open the drawer, pushes Pilar's phone angrily aside and pours pills into his fist. But above all, he thinks, fuck my fear of unemployment; fuck me and fuck my luck, to have nothing better in my life than this: being the tyrant of the night to women just like my mother and my sisters and my wife. He swallows the pills with a gulp of cold coffee, then puts his face in his hands.

45

Padre Márcio

Pablo Grande had of course been right. Padre Márcio had researched the antidote along with the poison and had thus been able to save himself. But it had been a traumatic, life-altering event. The tinnitus lingered permanently, a drone that resounded even in his dreams. His eyes had also been damaged, remaining hypersensitized to sunlight, so that everything he saw was leached one tone of color.

At first he was full of rage, but after several weeks his intellect overcame his anger and he realized that he had been lucky to survive an encounter with such a powerful *curandero*. He knew that Pablo Grande would not return for a long time; not after publicly demonstrating his therianthropic abilities. Only a *brujo* of very high degree could have enacted such a transmogrification, especially in daylight. Even a year after the poisoning, Padre Márcio might have pursued Pablo Grande, if only in an effort to understand and attempt to acquire his powers. But he abandoned the arcane and esoteric for the blunt force of market law when, the following Christmas, he first encountered Joaquín Lázaro Morales at the bishop's palace.

Joaquín's face had been calcified by desert sun, mountain wind and the multigenerational indifference of the government towards the poverty of its nation's farmers. But despite his calloused hands, *ranchero* clothes and the patina of silver-colored dust permanently ingrained into his boots, there was none of the groveling piety the poor normally displayed in the presence of his miraculous lesions. Joaquín possessed the stern dignity of an executioner, solemnly waiting to trigger the scaffold's chute. A small boy hovered in his shadow, silent but aware.

Joaquín explained that his son had lost his mother in a dispute between some warring *gomeros* in the highlands of Badiraguato. Would Padre Márcio see to it that Amado found a place in the orphanage in Ciudad Real, far from the dangers of Sinaloa? He pulled a large parcel wrapped in newspaper out from a woolen *moral* shoulder bag, watching with the sibilant eyes of a serpent as Padre Márcio slowly opened it to reveal wads of high-denomination bank notes.

Of course Padre Márcio would have said yes anyway, but he didn't offer to return the money. There was simply too much to seriously consider doing that.

It wasn't the amount that he thought about that evening when he dropped the boy off at the Army of Jesus orphanage in Ciudad Real. It was where the money came from. He was used to *clean* donations from guilty landlords and corrupt politicians seeking tax credits, not money from rural bandits and drug producers that was literally dirty from mountainous drives.

In 1961, marijuana and poppy plantations were not good business so much as the only business available to many of the farmers working the *ejidos*. The field work was hard; the risks high. The profit margins solid if unspectacular. But compared to the alternatives – working as a busboy in Dallas, or a fruit picker in the Salinas Valley, or a fisherman in the gulf – the money was monumental. More than the money was the prestige of being a respected local *gomero* instead of a nameless *peón* toiling in

Texas. Padre Márcio knew what the rich never could: that the poorer your background was, the more self-esteem mattered. And he could tell that it mattered a great deal to Joaquín.

Three months later, Joaquín returned with three more children – this time a boy and two girls, all under seven. Were they siblings? 'More cousins,' Joaquín said, a fluid notion in the sierras. 'Anyway, all orphans come from the same family.'

Padre Márcio should not have been surprised to hear such a sentiment expressed by a *gomero*; after all, he and Joaquín were themselves linked – not by grief, but by cunning. 'I never forgave the man who made me an orphan,' he said, perhaps not recognizing the spontaneous confession for what it was – the first sign of complicity.

'Tell me his name and I will take care of him.'

'Is that what you do, take care of things?'

'A man in my position . . .' More than anger, even more than jealousy; pride was always the hardest sin to conceal. Joaquín silenced himself with a knowing lift of the chin. 'I would be happy to take care of the man who made you an orphan.'

'God already has . . .'

Joaquín shrugged the way powerful men do – with feigned modesty. 'Even God needs help.'

'Resisting just one evil act advances God's work more than a thousand good deeds,' Padre Márcio said, thankful that hypocrisy was the easiest sin to hide.

'But if you had already committed a thousand evil acts, wouldn't that make your one good deed all the more powerful?' He nudged the children towards the priest. 'Please think of them as three good deeds.'

'How do you think of them?'

Joaquín smiled without warmth; without humanity. It was the smile not of a living person but of a graven image, pagan and remote. 'Isn't it better to threaten murder, rather than to actually commit it?' Just then thunder stirred in the distance, beyond the mountains that hid the promise of another way of life far from this desert reality of flaying heat, shifting sands and hostile borders. Padre Márcio sensed the thunder's significance, but couldn't tell if it was a warning blast or a solemn augury of future triumph. 'We both know that if you are chosen for a mission, there are sacrifices that must be made; crimes that must be forgotten, if not forgiven,' Joaquín said, handing him a weighty suitcase. 'It is not the way of God, but it is the way of the world . . . *our* world.'

Over the next ten years, Joaquín delivered many more children to the orphanages along with many more suitcases crammed with cash. Sometimes the children were the sons and daughters of men he had killed, or of men who had died fighting for him. But mainly they were passive hostages – a strategy aimed at bloodless conquest. What was it that made him break with tradition and seek to control rather than kill fathers, at the same time sparing the lives of their children? For in the land of vendettas, you did not take a man's life, you took a clan's. Otherwise, future reprisal wasn't a risk, it was a certainty. Was there surprising compassion within Joaquín, or a reckless pride that ignored the threat of revenge? Or was he simply an innovative strategist who realized it was easier to win hearts and minds than to brutally extinguish them?

As the 1960s collapsed into the 1970s, Joaquín's marijuana and poppy plantations grew in size and profitability. Drugs which had previously occupied a narrow band of traditional users bloomed into mainstream society on the other side of the border. America's hunger for drugs seemed even greater than its hunger for sugar and war. And every time Joaquín returned with more children, the donations grew larger. Until one day during Lent he came without any children at all. For the very first time, he came alone. 'I want to buy your palace,' he said.

Padre Márcio surprised himself with his own reaction. He was offended. 'This has always been the home of true servants of the Lord.'

'True servants of the Lord do not hide in palaces.'

The simple truth of the admonition was crushing. Padre Márcio had no response to either it or the inconceivable amount of money that Joaquín was offering; for this was not a donation. This was not even a purchase. This was laundering.

And Padre Márcio was about to become a master at it . . .

46

Pilar

Given the violence of the guards when they detained her, Pilar's expulsion from the actual premises is remarkably restrained. She is escorted through the gates without further physical contact. Not even a shove in the back, let alone a kick, which is always the final farewell – that cowardly concluding assault before the door of the police wagon or prison cell is slammed shut.

There isn't even a verbal insult as she's locked outside the gates.

She watches the two guards silhouetted against the light from the sweathouse entrance as they hurry back, disappearing inside; gone in seconds. Perhaps they want to get back as quickly as possible to their football game. Perhaps they have girlfriends or wives or sisters Pilar's age, working in other *maquiladoras*. Perhaps their fathers used to be union members, back in the old days when it still counted for something. Or perhaps they are simply anxious about becoming accessories before the fact. Expelling a lone woman outside in the middle of the night could easily sentence her to death. Being a witness is a terminal condition in Ciudad Real. The cartels punish talk, even on subjects that don't concern them. Terror of the *narcos* has rendered most of civic society mute. Censorship is preferable to sensory mutilation. Tongues are bitten off voluntarily when the other option is to have them torn out with red-hot pliers. And now that same fear is imposing itself across all commercial activities; even inside family homes. Silence is the first ally of the tyrant; the crueler they are, the more absolute the silence. The guards know this.

So does Pilar.

Or perhaps it is even simpler. Perhaps the guards are as afraid as Pilar of being alone at night.

She feels as though her very presence outdoors is like a scream of defiance, waking up the monsters feasting on the town: the killers and the *narcos*, the politicians and the factory owners; the fearful and the dispossessed.

Pilar looks around the deserted landscape. The only place she could flee to in an emergency is back to the very *maquiladora* that has just expelled her. She knows now why they locked the gates after her. It wasn't to keep her out; it was to keep out the thing that stalks the night.

The beast.

Pilar walks quickly along the road leading back into town. On one side is the river and the border. On the other side, she can see the great trucks of NAFTA torpedoing along the highway that connects two countries, two systems; two realities. One expansionist and confident; dominating. The other self-effacing yet full of guile; adept at survival. She can hear them on the near horizon; see the white of their headlights magnifying the dark, then ceding it forever, leaving behind the hypnotic coil of retreating red. There is no movement on the road she follows, no light except from the moon, cowering near the hills, like her afraid to show her face in this trembling landscape.

Pilar thinks she hears something. She stops and listens.

There is a sound she recognizes instantly; a sound she has

dreaded hearing but somehow always knew she would: an approaching car.

She glances ahead. Nothing. She looks behind and sees two headlights lancing towards her. Coming from the direction of the *maquiladora*. Is that why they let her go so meekly, then hurried away – to collect their cars and hunt her down on a lonely road? Away from witnesses.

Pilar looks for salvation on the empty road and finds it in a concrete culvert just ahead. She runs towards it in the blind night, trusting her feet, the sound of the car swelling towards her. She hurries down a ditch to reach the culvert opening, almost tripping on the stony ground. Just as she is about to enter, an animal darts out, brushing her leg – a rat or cat, or even a rabbit. Something small; just as frightened as her. She screams in shock, choking it back into her throat, hating herself for the betrayal of her location; listening to the newly heightened quiet.

Lights dart across the fields nearby. Pilar ducks her head inside just before the culvert's opening is engulfed by the car's headlights.

The car drives by very slowly, its engine vibrating in the nocturnal stillness. Pilar risks a glance as the Lincoln Navigator passes; exhaust coiling angry and red in the right taillight. The left taillight is broken.

She is staring after the car, trying to read its license plate, when it brakes with a shriek like an animal snared in a trap. She pulls back into the cover of the culvert, her breathing amplified inside. She listens.

Nothing.

The car glides forwards a few feet as if towed by the weight of the pending darkness just beyond its beams. Then it brakes again; the red light cycloptic and final.

A searchlight is switched on from the driver's side of the car. The beam darts across the scrap-strewn fields; a terrain devoid of shelter. Weeds bow, shamed by its inquiry. The light settles on a nest of trash. There's the tremor of movement – the beam holding intently until something undulates, then breaks fast for cover, the plastic bag escaping high in the wind.

The car inches slowly forwards . . . then accelerates quickly as though answering a secret call. Pilar waits, watching the car vanish into the velvet wall of night. She steps out of the culvert, trying to decide what to do next: move on, or wait in case the car comes back.

She gives it half an hour. They'll have realized by then she couldn't have traveled that far on foot. Perhaps they figured she'd cut across the fields to the highway. If they thought she were hiding, surely they would have come back before then.

That is, if they were really looking for her.

Pilar struggles up from the gully, steadying herself against the slipping rocks with her hands, climbing up onto the lip of the road, walking back towards town, alone except for the coward flash of the setting moon fast and insubstantial on the river's stagnant water.

She slows as she turns a curve. There's something on the road. A tan and white dog. She approaches cautiously, afraid that it might attack, but when she's closer she can tell by the way it's lying, by the misshapen curve of its hips, that it's hurt. Pilar speaks in a low, caressing voice and strokes its brow between the flattened ears. At first there's no reaction, just a gravity in its eyes. A knowledge. And a fear. Then it looks up with a gaze that seems to strain through the night for a final glimpse of something urgent and important, settling on her eyes. There's something breathless and faint that could have been a whine, and then the eyes roll backwards with a swift, effortless grace. She can almost feel the tangible release of life. A movement passing through her hand.

She starts to sob, a whisper of tears in the wilderness, then finally stands and lifts the dog up, placing it against a small boulder far off the road.

Pilar walks on towards the city, dazed by a cunning mixture of determination and self-deception, removing herself from awareness of anything except the next step, the next second; anything that will kill the moment and take her a little closer to the end. If she could see herself, walking in the dark, her feet and legs powdered with the dust that she has raised, she would be anxious. She would realize that she stands out more than she could ever imagine, a silhouette targeted across the bow of the road's horizon.

But she is no longer aware of the exterior world, of her external body moving across a hostile environment; of the stones teething through the soles of her shoes. She is focused on the internal: the suffering of thirst and exhaustion. Her anger. And the furtive fear that this time she doesn't have the resources to surmount her vulnerabilities.

Pilar remembers all the painful walks of her life. Going to school in the morning against her father's wishes, with only the flutter of the grasshoppers to keep her company. The inhuman drone of traffic on the way to catch the bus to university, men jeering at her in slowing cars. Moving down the prison corridors after her first sentencing, the blunt prod of a nightstick pushing against her trepidation. The graveled path of the cemetery road after her mother was buried, and the feeling she couldn't live with such grief.

The march towards riot police, gripping a banner in her hands.

She remembers these walks, not so much as specific memories, but as something more profound – recurring, internal emotions stockpiled within her very being; the way antibodies are stored. It is an immune-system response, not to disease but to suffering. Not to illness, but to defeat. And it is this organic reaction that keeps her on her feet; that propels her forwards, step by step. That prohibits collapse.

She is passing a long chain-link fence topped with razor wire. Behind the fence are rows of stacked drums covered in tarpaulin. She must be getting closer to town now. A guard dog pads along with her on the other side of the fence. Both are grateful for the company.

The dog whines, freezing in its tracks. Pilar stops, alert; frightened. The sound of a car wafts towards them, a magic trick conjured out of the confused and empty night. The next thing she hears terrifies her. It's not coming from the car, but from the dog: a low, deep growl.

The sound of fear.

Pilar ducks behind the abandoned wreck of a car, low to the ground and waiting, her heart beating against the corroded steel carcass, the approaching vehicle bearing down upon her, fast and certain. The dog starts to bark, a savage protest against what is about to happen.

The headlights slap them both, then rush past with a violent velocity. Something keens across the night with it, so frightful that it silences the dog and makes Pilar slowly stand, staring in horror as the Navigator absconds across the empty street, one taillight burning bright.

The scream of a woman.

She watches the killers escaping, the dog whining next to her on the other side of the fence, cleaved with anxiety. What Pilar does next surprises her.

She starts running after the car.

III

The Other Side of the Mirror

DAY 3

Victim 875 – Gloria Delgado

47

Gloria

Gloria pulls away from the man, trying the car door again, and that's when she sees Pilar, standing behind a wreck. She screams out to her, but then they have her by the hair and rip her down to the floor, their feet stomping, as though her body's on fire and they're trying to extinguish it.

She passes out.

*

Gloria only regains consciousness when they open the car door and lift her roughly under the arms, marching her across the terrain the way the police march demonstrators; half walking, half dragging her.

She screams, her voice resonant and loud, filling the night with her anguish. But no one comes to her aid, no one reacts. It's like a dress rehearsal in front of an empty auditorium.

They follow the beam of a flashlight past a strange rock formation, like steps leading up to a demolished building, the ground uneven with puny creosote bush and the crumble of abandoned ant nests.

On the other side of the rocky outcrop is a ranch house surrounded by parked cars. They pass through a perimeter fence. A dog barks from inside a truck, the Rottweiler's face pressed against the glass – a savage captive.

The house's windows are papered over but light still manages to ooze from them, like blood through bandages. 'Please!' she sobs. Her captors act as though they can't hear her.

As though she were already a ghost.

48

Pilar

Barefoot and wearing only a pair of shorts, Juan Antonio hurries out of the bedroom, the thumping at the front door getting even louder. He picks up a baseball bat lying in the corner, and leaning towards the door, passes its tip across the spy hole.

The knocking stops. He waits a moment, moving further away from the door. 'Who is it?'

'It's me, *cabrón*. Open up!'

Juan Antonio slides the latches, then turns the deadlock. Pilar rushes in, slamming the door behind her. Juan Antonio looks at his watch. 'What happened?'

'Motherfuckers!' Pilar angrily pushes past him, pacing up and down. He pours her a shot of tequila, trying not to stare at her dust-covered legs. Pilar gulps the drink down, coughing at the force.

'Pilar?'

'They caught me.'

'Fuck. Did they hurt you?'

'They threw me out. That's when I saw it. Walking back. The car.' Pilar's voice trembles. She takes a moment to compose herself, and when she speaks again, it's in a rush, trying to get it all out while she still can. 'They came looking for me. I hid until they were gone. Later, they came back. There was a woman. She was screaming . . .' Pilar starts to cry. Juan Antonio enfolds her in her arms, but after a moment she pushes angrily away from him. 'Don't fucking touch me!'

Juan Antonio backs away from her, giving her space. She begins to shudder with short, half-controlled sobs, speaking through her tears. 'I saw the car. It was them, the killers.'

'You said the car was coming after you?'

'It followed me from the *maquiladora*. I saw it coming back and I hid. I heard the woman screaming. I heard her!'

'Did they find out who you were?'

'What?'

'At the *maquiladora*. Do they know your real name?'

'Fuck the *maquiladora*! They've kidnapped a woman. What does it matter about my name?'

'If they know who you are, they'll find out where you live.' Juan Antonio is hurriedly pulling on trousers. 'We've got to get out of here.'

Pilar feels inside her hip pocket and pulls out a card. 'We need to find Fuentes.'

49

Fuentes

Mary-Ellen González. Born in San Diego in 1975 to a Mexican mother and a Colombian father. Life co-ordinates that just happened to form the *narco* Golden Triangle.

Fuentes skips the geometry and goes straight to the calculus: Paredes was apprehended in a car registered to Mary-Ellen. A direct link between a corrupt cop, drug trafficking and the murder of a woman. A murder that conformed to the exact pattern of the others in all but one respect: the victim was a college graduate, high-end escort with a US passport instead of an uneducated, impoverished *maquiladora* worker. She did fit the physical profile of the other victims, but . . . It was no mistake. Her killers wanted the police to think she was just another victim in an endless line of femicides. And they set it up so well, following the exact patterns of all the other rapes and murders, that it proves they were behind all the killings. Because no one knows what they do to all the victims at the end. No one except the police. And when was the last time the police ever kept a secret like that . . . ? Try never. The only logical explanation is that they are covering up their own crimes.

Fuentes slides back to the geometry part of the puzzle. It isn't just a *narco* triangle. This is a circle that's being drawn and its ends are closing. The *narcos* own all the geometric forms. They are the master masons in this criminal construction. Silent. Secretive. All-knowing.

In order to infiltrate a covert operation, you need an opening. And the only one he has is Paredes. He has to find a way to talk to him. Gearwheels of possibility turn in his head. None clicks. They'll never let him near Paredes, unless he can offer up something in return.

Something immense . . .

He pulls the drapes open. Eastern clouds bank, explosive with daybreak, as though the sky itself can't abide the notion of another day just like the one before. All the windows of Fuentes' apartment throb with celestial anguish, inflamed by the reflected dawn, the frustration of his new-found knowledge, and another sleepless night full of waking nightmares. The accident. Abarca's stables. The hands of Adán, tumbling in the oil.

And now Mary-Ellen will be added to that gallery of horrors. He'll need to notify US authorities eventually, but he wants to gain access to her home first. The car with Texas plates that has been tailing both him and Byrd might be connected to her. Might even be driven by some of the people who killed her. Only one thing is certain. Mary-Ellen isn't just a lead, she is now the key, and he isn't going to hand such a valuable discovery over to anyone he doesn't trust.

He slides a Glock 26 out from the hidden cradle he installed under the bookshelf, checks the mag, then slips the weapon into an ankle holster, the added gravitational tug offering some kind of stability in a world lacking any.

He takes his Colt Python from his bedside table and glides it into his shoulder holster. He slithers a four-inch knife into its belt sheath, next to his handcuffs, then pockets a couple of moon clips. This is his waking routine, as fixed as morning coffee. His promise to the day: get in my way and I'll kill you.

Fuentes looks around the room, like a traveler about to leave a hotel room, wondering if there is anything he has left behind; anything that could be fatal to forget. This is a difference between youth and middle age that could prove to be a lethal one – that moment when routine replaces instinct. He goes out to the kitchen and opens the cupboard. He takes the drawing at the top: a beach, the sun's yellow rays almost lost against the white paper. He puts it into the inside breast pocket of his jacket. Fuentes opens the front door, peers outside for any trouble, then closes it behind him and triple-locks it.

Parked cars. Passing early buses. Women on their way to work. He takes it all in slowly. He knows he's getting close. It's not just Mary-Ellen; it's something in the air. A sense of finality. That's when you have to be most careful. It's always in the home stretch when you fall. It isn't only fatigue, it is vanity; self-satisfaction – a sucker response.

It's never over till it's over.

He looks up and down the street. There are signs you need to recognize. Men reclining in the front seats of unfamiliar vehicles. Windowless vans parked within frequency distance. The backfire of an approaching motorcycle, the rider's helmet mirroring back your stare. Shadows fast on your peripheral vision. Anyone in uniform – any uniform. Uniforms stand out – which paradoxically is what makes them invisible.

His is a quiet street. Therefore potentially dangerous. Assassination is born in the mundane; it requires habit, not chaos. He opens the trunk of his car, takes out an inspection mirror and sweeps underneath the vehicle. No brake fluid leak. No wires. No tight cluster of detonators within nests of C-4. He doesn't bother with the hood. He always uses an exterior double brace to jack it down safe and tight. He is safe, at least for one more day.

And it's in that self-congratulatory moment – when he has lost his carefully cultivated sense of awareness to smugness – that he hears the footsteps behind him and their swift approach to target. He spins around, but there's not enough time to even draw his pistol before Pilar grabs his wrist and pulls him towards his car. 'We have to hurry.'

'What is it?'

Pilar tries to open the door. It's locked. 'She's seen them,' Juan Antonio says between gasps of breath. 'They tried to kidnap her.'

He doesn't have to ask *who*. Fuentes unlocks the car, fast. 'How much of a lead do they have?'

Pilar pushes past him. 'Almost two hours.'

'It's not enough,' he says, getting in.

Juan Antonio hesitates, then joins them in the car, slamming the door, Fuentes already accelerating dangerously away, talking to Gomez on his cell phone. 'I'll be there in five minutes.'

Pilar swears. 'You're wasting time.'

'He's on the way. Besides, we're going to need help, and . . .' Fuentes tightens his grip on the wheel, not looking at her. 'He's all I've got.'

50

Padre Márcio

Like the Vatican itself, everything that Padre Márcio possessed was thanks to a single crucifixion – or rather the physical manifestation of it. But the funds from the sale of the bishop's palace gave him the opportunity to go beyond the limits of his stigmata and forge a destiny of his own.

With the proceeds, he'd built orphanages in Ciudad Juárez, Tijuana and Matamoros. In all three cities he was received, if not quite as a savior, at least as a saint. Anxious to tap into his growing status, politicians and business leaders offered him support, contacts and access to donations. Even the most cynical amongst them were forced to admire the energy and effectiveness of Padre Márcio. He established orphanages that were safe and secure for the children, and hired lay professionals instead of clerical predators to teach and care for them.

Yet the revolutionary changes that he brought to the orphanages never satisfied him, because he was only partly driven by the notion of progress. What really consumed him was the idea of revenge. His goal was nothing less than the destruction of the Roman Catholic Church. He simply lacked a coherent plan for bringing it about. That began to change the day he encountered opposition from the archbishop of Santa Teresa, Cardinal Degoutta. The city already had an orphanage, His Eminence told him. If they opened another, it would only encourage homeless children from other parts of Mexico to throng there, with the inevitable rise in street crime and sexual promiscuity.

Padre Márcio was intelligent enough to know fraud was a double-sided glass. The more he practiced it, the more he began to believe in the lies he told others. That side was the mirror, which revealed only what you wished to behold. But if someone attempted to deceive him, Padre Márcio would instantly see right through them. That was the side which was a transparent window. The difference was very simple: looking in and looking out. He could delude himself, but no one else could deceive him.

Especially not another priest claiming to be speaking on behalf of God.

Cardinal Degoutta's family had fled Barcelona for Mexico at the beginning of the Spanish Civil War, not long after he was ordained. They were not nationalists, and they were certainly not loyalists. They were obscure, arch-reactionary Catholic monarchists to the extreme right of Alfonsism, who intuitively understood that no matter which side won, the family's morbid worldview would condemn them as zealots and doom them to the fate all radicals suffer during any civil war.

Luckily, the family had a relative living in Michoacán, where the young Degoutta found work in a local church and where he acquired a taste for alcohol, underage women and money. It was only a matter of time before he gravitated further north to the optimistic frontier of the new *maquiladoras* and their impoverished but hopeful female workers. Easy pickings for a corrupt cleric on the rise who knew how to share his taste for luxury with senior regional officials.

After only nine years he was promoted to bishop, and was seen by the Vatican as a rising star from the New World. He was an old-style fire and brimstone preacher who taught intimidation – not liberation – theology. The fact that he was European and not Mexican by birth helped him on his meteoric rise to cardinal, as did his medieval instincts. He sanctified the rich and persecuted the poor. He denied birth control to exhausted mothers and divorce to beaten wives; at the same time he arranged marriage annulments for movie stars. He even sold posthumous indulgences to the credulous widows of corrupt politicians and businessmen.

Cardinal Degoutta had the natural command and confidence only a sincere fraud can ever exude. He congratulated Padre Márcio on his stigmata and wanted to know how he 'did' his hands. If it wasn't too painful, he'd like to arrange the same for a pious nephew of his – and perhaps both feet as well. He'd make it worth Padre Márcio's while. There'd always be a seat for him at the cardinal's table – only in this Last Supper tableau, all the Apostles would be clutching bags of silver. Padre Márcio didn't take his leave of the archbishop's palace so much as expel himself from his company. A familiar hate flowed through him and it told him one thing only: the cardinal had to be stopped.

Padre Márcio contacted Joaquín, who naturally proposed a solution.

A few days later, one of His Eminence's very young 'chambermaids' paid her usual visit to his quarters after dinner, only to make a terrible discovery: the cardinal had hanged himself.

The alarming suicide note confessed to crimes so archaic that the police captain in charge of the investigation had to resort to a dictionary. Worse still were the allegations made against other members of Santa Teresa's elite. Scandal simmered, on the very cusp of conflagration – like a naked flame held above an open barrel of turpentine.

So when Padre Márcio proposed an emergency meeting with the Santa Teresa authorities, everybody came because every single one of them was in fear of exposure. A fish rots from the head down, Padre Márcio announced. Nervous eyes flickered about the room, avoiding contact.

Luckily, the sinful cardinal had severed his own head in time. The rest of the fish was still edible, so why throw it away when so many were hungry?

The group muttered excitedly amongst itself, sensing, if not divine intervention, at least damage control. Padre Márcio held up his blessed hands, calling for silence. He proposed a modern-day version of the miracle of the loaves and fishes; a feeding of the multitudes. If the assembly so desired, he would take on the onerous task of saving the reputation of Santa Teresa and its ecclesiastical resources.

The mayor meekly asked how they would ever be able to satisfactorily explain the suicide of the cardinal. Padre Márcio proposed that the coroner and the police chief, both of whom were present, should state that the cause of death was respiratory failure, which would certainly not be false.

Although Padre Márcio's plan was accepted by the assembled dignitaries, it was resisted by the Church hierarchy, which initially insisted on the right to appoint its own administrator until the Vatican announced a successor. But after a frank exchange with Padre Márcio about the consequences of such a stance, they approved the intervention of the famous stigmatic.

It took Padre Márcio several months to appreciate the scope of the cardinal's fraud. He had officially tithed ten percent of all charitable donations received by his parish to the Vatican, but only declared a tiny fraction of the actual amount. Padre Márcio now declared a quarter of the real amount, taking personal credit for the sudden surge in donations. He also doubled the tithe to twenty percent. Any lingering suspicions concerning his administration vanished with the increased revenue. As far as Mexican and Vatican officials were concerned, Padre Márcio really was a miracle worker.

He quickly sold the parish's vast real-estate holdings in the city center to Joaquín, along with swathes of parched land on the outskirts – worthless terrain donated to the Church for inflated tax write-offs. Land that was flat and close to the border. Using a Panamanian law firm which set up accounts with BCCI and Nugan Hand, a newly formed company was incorporated in Delaware with Joaquín as principal and Padre Márcio as minority shareholder. Joaquín was counting on Padre Márcio's skills to ensure their cheap desert land would be quickly rezoned, with paved roads, electricity, sewage and water facilities provided at the expense of the municipality.

Which of course it was.

The partners resolved to take the same course of action in Tijuana, Ciudad Juárez, Matamoros and Ciudad Real. By 1977, their company was renting land to more *maquiladoras* than any other landlord in the border region. But the revenue it made from rent was infinitesimal compared to the profit coming in from a new wonder export: cocaine.

51

El Santo

Enrique's garage is located on the knife edge between the waste-land limit of Ciudad Real and the solar flare of Sonoran wilderness. Mountains serrate the horizon like the battlements of an ancient Saharan fort crumpled by centuries, their blue shadows shifting uneasily away from the assault of the sun.

They drive under a time-blasted sign, lisping on its chains from the motion of their passage. Ahead are three large open sheds crowded with cars and a boxed-in office hiding out back. A chained dog sits with its massive head primed on two front paws, its eyes traveling secretly as El Santo and Oviedo get out of their truck and walk towards its master.

Enrique is standing over the open hood of a stolen 1997 Suburban, staring at the engine as though waiting for a response. He shakes his head with undisguised frustration and turns away, walking to greet the two unexpected visitors, his face going green from the refraction of the sun through the fiber-glass roof. 'I don't like automatic V8s. Too many problems with the crankshaft whip.'

'It's your age,' Oviedo says. 'You're a manual man.'

Enrique laughs, wiping his hands on a turpentine-stinking cloth. 'You selling or buying?'

'Collecting,' El Santo says, his voice sounding shaky, at least to him. The shooting, the surgery and the ride all the way out to this shithole are all taking their toll. Plus he can't remember the last time he slept. It feels like *never*.

Enrique stares at El Santo as though his face were a broken radiator and he's trying to decide if it needs fixing or straight-out replacing. 'Collecting what exactly?'

'Unpaid taxes.'

Enrique turns and spits into the oil-stained earth. 'I reckon you're going to have to take it up with my boss.'

'Padre Márcio?'

Enrique doesn't like that name coming out of a mouth owned by someone like El Santo. 'My boss is without name.'

'Right. How long you been working for Padre Márcio?'

'Long enough to know my respect for him is merited.'

'Sometimes respect is *merited*. Sometimes it's just imposed.' Oviedo grabs Enrique from behind. Enrique doesn't resist. 'How many cars do you turn over a week?'

Sullen silence for response. Then Enrique lifts his chin in de-fiance. El Santo's seen this so many times it makes him want to puke. It's ridiculous how many criminals think they've got the martyr bug and need to show it off: how tough they are. How fucking loyal. They think they can't be cowed. They think they can resist. Think again. It's the only rule El Santo has never, ever seen broken; the only law that's always respected. Silence never endures; not when you're still alive, at least.

Oviedo flings Enrique against the car. Behind them is the snap of a chain going taut as the Rottweiler goes into a frenzy. A car door opens. The hinge side slams shut on Enrique's hand. 'How many cars do you boost a week?'

Enrique speaks through sobs. 'My fucking hand.'

'It'll be your head next if you don't answer the question. How many?'

257

He spits the word out as though it were a core he was choking on. 'Five.'

El Santo gestures for Oviedo to open the door. Enrique's hand flops out and finds a nest under his arm, like he's trying to hide it from a pickpocket. El Santo goes up to Oviedo, keeping one eye on Enrique in case he tries anything stupid. 'This doesn't make sense.'

'Let me check it out, boss.' Enrique looks up from his bereaved fingers and watches Oviedo disappearing between rows of cars. 'You're trespassing,' he says, his voice watery from pain.

El Santo would laugh if he didn't think it could tear his stitches. 'We're not trespassing, old man. We're fucking invading.' The dog snarls behind him as it stands on its hind legs, choking itself with outrage as El Santo starts to examine the Suburban. One thing's been bothering him for the last few days – two things, actually, if you count being shot in the gut by El Feo, and even that falls into the other thing that's been bothering him: nothing in his world is making sense any more. Like this stupid lime-green Suburban. Why heist such a mediocre car? It's not a collectable; it's not even desirable. It's pathetic for parts, and so noticeably ugly to make it useless for a getaway or a hit.

They're definitely not boosting cars for resale. The volume's too low and the quality's not there. So the answer has to be hidden. It's not the cars but what they can conceal – and what does anyone conceal on this side of the border? It's got to be a classic Trojan Horse smuggling operation. El Santo starts to tap behind upholstery and peer under floor mats and cargo liners. He whistles to Oviedo, a single piercing dart that even shuts the dog up. Oviedo's head appears above a battered Ford Ranger. 'Check this out . . .'

Oviedo eases his way between the tightly parked cars, hopping onto bumper bars to get to him, the dog watching as he approaches, tensed against its chain, hoping he'll pass within mauling distance. El Santo opens hatches and displays panels with all the lazy confidence of a salesman taking apart a blender. Secret bays in the side. False bottom in the trunk. Hidden compartments under the seat. 'Even here, behind the fucking airbag. How did they do that?'

'Must have removed the valve and initiator.' Oviedo seems reluctantly impressed, his arm disappearing as he reaches up behind the steering wheel like a vet with a pregnant mare. 'No inflation mechanism whatsoever.' He looks up at El Santo. 'It's good work, boss. Real classy.'

Not just the workmanship; the entire concept. *Real* classy. 'Sure it's cute, but what about sniffer dogs?'

Oviedo shrugs. 'Vacuum pack, then can it?' That sounds about right. 'If you get caught, you get caught. But I'm telling you, boss, with this kind of work, this kind of *craftsmanship*, they're not going to get caught.'

'Particularly if they cross at Tijuana.' Oviedo raises his eyebrows in surprise, which only convinces El Santo even more that he's right. This fucking priest . . . El Santo has to give him credit. It's so simple. It's so smart. Heist and outfit family cars here in Ciudad Real, then drive them to the coast and cross at Tijuana; get it up to San Diego and LA and Frisco. Move it on to Vegas and Chicago. Or drive eastwards and cross at Brownsville. Get it into Houston, New Orleans and Miami; or up the East Coast, all the way to DC, New York and Boston. Doesn't matter where you sell it, just as long as you get it out of Mexico. 'How many kilos do you figure they can shift?'

Oviedo's eyes turn inwards, counting numbers inside his head. 'Forty sounds about right. That makes . . . two hundred and eighty thousand dollars on a fast offload.'

A fast offload is on an uncut basis; an adequate return – if you're a nervous freelancer; someone like Mary-Ellen. But if you're an organization, it's financially unacceptable. And financially unacceptable doesn't cut it with the cartels. Then it hits him. 'Jesus Christ!'

'What is it, boss?'

'It's not cocaine. They're working something else.'

'Something else?'

Oviedo is looking at him in a way he doesn't like. A skeptical way. A way that forces him to defensively admit what's really on his mind. 'It's cash. They're not shipping drugs, they're moving dollars.'

Oviedo squints at him, a dubious smile just one degree away from disrespectful hovering around his lips but not quite landing. 'But, boss, they could just wire it out, like everyone does. Route it via Panama or the Virgin Islands into Luxembourg or Delaware. HSBC every last penny.'

Of course Oviedo is right, but does that make El Santo wrong? He thinks about it. Why wouldn't they just wire it? Because no one knows they've got it. But that's impossible because everyone knows who owns what in *la tierra narca*. Even the government knows; it's just paid not to do anything with the knowledge. This is something different. They're planning something big; something massive.

El Santo doesn't understand what's going on, but he certainly wants to be a part of it. 'Imagine. Forty kilos of hundred-dollar notes. That's a million bucks a trip. Five trips a week. And how long has this been going on?' It feels like that priest has been around forever.

'I don't know about this cash thing, boss.' El Santo doesn't really know either. 'If they want to cut it and go for the long haul instead of the fast offload, forty K of coke is worth almost five million. Why turn down the possibility of making five mil?'

Good question. Who in their right mind would do that? Unless . . . 'What if they don't care about making money, they just need to transfer what they've *already* made?'

'Don't care about making money . . . ?' This time he lets the smart-ass smile land. 'Come on, boss. It's always about drugs. Just look at that fucking cop, Paredes. Bet you his car came from here. They picked him up with forty kilos of coke.' Forty-two kilos actually. 'Nothing else makes sense.' El Santo has to agree with Oviedo. But his gut – or what's left of it – says otherwise. Fuck sense, this is about dollars.

He walks over to Enrique. 'What are they shipping in the cars?'

The old man raises his face, but this time in defeat, not defiance. A slow, plump tear slowly slithers its way out of his eye like a worm painfully emerging from a corpse. 'Bibles,' he gasps. 'For China.'

El Santo has to give it to Father Holy Holes, he's terrific at selling the big lies. This poor slob mechanic with one fucked-up hand truly believes he's batting for the Christian Cubs.

El Santo walks across to the office at the back of the shed. Even at that hour of the morning, it's already baking hot and stinks of the old man's shitty world of kerosene, black tobacco and honest sweat betrayed. There are wooden crates crowded with stolen license plates and some clipboards hanging on the wall with names, driver license numbers and insurance details. Looks like old Enrique hasn't heard of *never mix, never worry*. The recklessness of keeping all this cross-contaminating evidence in the same place tells him one thing: they're certain no authorities are ever going to come snooping. He's just started leafing through the first clipboard when he hears the shot. He ditches the papers and goes for his gun.

Stupid, fucking careless.

They didn't bother to really case the joint. There could be ten men out there, with guns all pointing at the office. In the sudden rush of amplified silence that always follows an unexpected gunshot, all he can hear is the whine of the dog. '¿*Oye?*' he shouts.

'It's all clear, boss.'

El Santo pokes his head out, gun in hand. Oviedo is standing over Enrique's body. 'Why the fuck did you kill him?'

Oviedo shrugs. 'He tried to make a run for it.'

It doesn't look like it was much of a run. 'Fuck me, I had more questions for him too.' That dumb shrug again. Could be he's wrong about Oviedo after all. Could be Oviedo is just one minuscule level up on the evolutionary scale from El Feo. It's not like anyone is really expecting a turbulent rise in the Henchman IQ Gradient. 'There are documents in the office. We need them.' Oviedo goes inside, gathering up papers from the floor and clipboards off the wall. At least he's compliant. None of El Feo's excuses about a bad back.

Stepping around the blood, El Santo goes through Enrique's pockets. He soon wishes he hadn't. There's nothing there but a couple of religious cards, a wrinkled photo of two teenagers, and a well-used snot-rag. He wipes his hands on Enrique's jeans.

Oviedo's already back, the papers in a cardboard box under his arm. El Santo feels rather than hears the low growl behind them. Its intensity is alarming, as though it were coming from a pack of hyenas. 'Take care of the dog.'

'But, boss . . .'

'You can't leave a fucking dog tied up in the middle of the desert. It's not right.' Saying it makes him feel better about Enrique, lying there outlined by his own blood in the dirt. Not that he really cares. But he likes to think of himself as someone who is kind to animals – at least who presents as being kind. He doesn't approve of cockfights for instance. He hates them. But he doesn't stop them either. Profit's profit.

Oviedo goes up real slow to the Rottweiler and lets it smell the back of his hand. The growling stops. There's the jingle of chains against metal, and the collar is off.

'What the hell are you doing?'

'I'm going to take care of it, boss, just like you told me to.'

Oviedo is being a dick – that's not what he meant, and he knows it. 'Why fucking bother? It's just another mouth to feed.'

'You don't keep dogs to feed them, boss.' Oviedo grabs the dog by the scruff of the neck and starts leading it towards the truck. 'You keep them to take care of the scraps.'

El Santo follows the henchman and his new dog back to the truck, the earth underfoot running a temperature in the sun. At least Oviedo stows the dog in the back cabin, where it can't tear out their throats if it gets a mind to. Maybe El Santo should look into getting a dog himself? He'd call it Héctor or César; some ancient name that speaks of nobility and courage. It might even help calm all the anxiety that's been coursing through him these last few days, like he's forgotten to do

263

something important and can't remember what it is.

Oviedo is slipping the cardboard box with the documents onto the floor in front of the passenger seat when something catches his eye through the windshield. Slow as a hunter, he takes out his knife, the blade flicking open with a cruel whisper. El Santo watches as he moves across the yard, stalking a Lincoln Navigator. He slips the knife in under one of the taillights and snaps it off with a deft flick, then strolls back to the truck, tossing the taillight into the air and catching it, pleased with his prize. 'My brother-in-law's is broken,' he says with a smile. As if Oviedo couldn't afford to walk into a parts shop and buy a new one. But why buy anything you can steal? The golden rule for all criminals; one he lives by himself. 'What do we do now, boss?' Oviedo asks.

'We go pay a visit to old Father Fraud before we hit the Heartbreak, and find out what the fuck he's up to.' Because, whatever it is, it's huge. And El Santo's never been known to say no to *huge*.

52

Pilar

Fuentes slows as they approach the wrecked car. 'You're sure it's here?' Pilar stares at the car and then the chain-link fence behind it. In the distance she can see the dog, flattening itself in a patch of shade inside the yard. It raises its head as they pass, as though recognizing her. 'Absolutely,' she says.

Fuentes accelerates in the direction of the *maquiladora*. Pilar watches the landscape that terrified her only hours before now transformed by daylight into a mundane, defeated wasteland. 'Tell me where you stopped running.'

'It was after the turnoff to the highway . . .'

'We're already there.' He looks at the odometer. 'Nearly three hundred meters. And you're sure they didn't take it?'

'I've told you already!'

'Calm down,' Juan Antonio says softly. 'They're just trying to do their job.'

'Then why don't they do it? We have to find her.'

'We will, I promise.'

How can Fuentes even say that? A promise made is a lie revealed. Gomez's phone rings. He listens intently. 'A black Lincoln Navigator with the right taillight out . . . Of course detain! And the suspects are dangerous, so watch your asses, okay? *Bueno.*' He sighs the way someone who has to deal with fuck-ups on a daily basis always sighs, not even aware he's doing it, and turns to Fuentes. 'The roadblock is up at Juárez,' he says.

More incompetent bullshit. 'You mean it's only gone up *now*?'

Gomez stares at her, his eyes dark with mounting irritation. 'It's only been fifteen minutes.'

'Fifteen minutes now. Two hours earlier. What does it matter? It's too late. We'll never catch them.'

'Pilar, calm down.' She wants to slap Juan Antonio but instead pulls away from him, furious with his patronizing attitude. She nestles against her window, remembering again what she saw earlier that morning. She fights against the sorrow and the horror welling within her. It's not that something inside would break if she started to sob, it's that the broken parts that are already there would rise up and rip her to pieces if she ever did lose control. Juan Antonio tells her to *calm down*. He has no fucking idea what that means. It feels like she's spent her entire life trying to calm down.

'Even if they drove without stopping, we'd still probably get them at the roadblock,' Gomez says, as though explaining to a child.

'What good is *probably*?'

'*Probably* is the best we've ever had,' Fuentes says. 'So I'll take it. Besides, I don't think they're going to Juárez.'

Gomez gives him a look. It could be surprise. It could almost be fear. 'What makes you say that?'

'Ciudad Juárez is way too far for the patterns. They're much closer to home.'

'That's what I've been telling you: the car came from the *maquiladora*.'

The car hurtles forwards, as though trying to escape the tension inside. Pilar glances at the speedometer. Something rushes past outside: a flash of sunlight on the river. A memory. The coward moon, peering behind the hills like a witness behind a curtain, not daring to answer the victim's scream for help, but unable to find the courage to tear its appalled gaze away from the crime. 'There it is,' Juan Antonio says, pointing to the *maquiladora*, looming low and ugly to the north. They comet past the main gates. Pilar looks back in confusion. 'You're not stopping?'

'I have two cars on their way there right now.'

'Two cars of what – the same police who have spent years not finding the killers?'

Gomez grunts. 'Pilar, enough!' Juan Antonio says, his face creased in anger.

The car humps across a cattle guard, vibrations protesting through the chassis with a grinding hum. Fuentes swears, the car slurring to a stop. He's already out. Gomez strikes a match hard, lighting a cigarette between cupped fists before joining him. Pilar gets out of the car, the sudden standing making her dizzy. Three days with so little rest. She sways, the ground shifting out of focus for an instant. Fuentes has her arm. 'Take it easy.'

She pulls away from his touch. 'Don't worry about me, worry about her!' Gomez passes him a phone, as though trying to block her out. Fuentes listens for a moment, his face flayed with annoyance. '*When* will it be available?' He kills the call. 'Tomorrow.'

'Lying assholes.'

'No helicopters available,' he says to Pilar, then turns away and studies the horizon. 'That way is too close to the border. Too big a chance of being noticed. And that road leads back to the highway.' He points straight ahead. 'We have to keep going.'

53

Fuentes

They drive through a landscape which has slowly abraded itself with desert winds and brutal sunlight into an ochre blur. What is left is not so much a terrain as a fading stain. Juan Antonio sighs. 'How much longer is this going to take?'

Gomez turns in his seat, a malicious smile on his face. 'Didn't your *gringo* friends teach you that time is a different commodity on our side of the border?'

'I don't have any *gringo* friends.'

'Really? I thought the *gringos* would be falling over themselves to help an agitator like you.'

'Tell him to shut up,' Pilar says to the rearview mirror. But Fuentes doesn't hear her. He's not even aware of the arguing all around him. He's already seen it.

He saw it as soon as the road started descending into an arid basin ribbed by rose-colored hills and the sun-crazed flicker of quartz: a dirt-track turnoff, leading through a low canyon. At the other end is a ranch house, hunched low in shadow as though trying to hide.

He brakes, everyone bowing forwards in unison, like pilgrims arriving at their destination. He grabs the binoculars out of the glove compartment. The ranch house is protected by a perimeter fence. There's a black SUV parked in front, next to a red pickup. He passes the binoculars to Gomez. 'That's it,' he says, his voice on the verge of breaking from his effort to contain his emotions. He is almost overwhelmed by recognition. This is a moment he has always wanted but was never sure he'd ever get. Yet now that it has arrived, there is no time to savor or even acknowledge it. It is already passing into the next stage: swift and violent action.

Pilar gets out of the car with the others and stares down at the eroded vista. Even if she had noticed the house, which was unlikely, she wouldn't have thought anything of it. It is perfectly camouflaged just by being so unremarkable. She feels a reluctant respect for Fuentes, who is already on the phone. 'Tell them not to use sirens, and stay off the radio,' he says. 'That goes for the ambulances too. And that's an order.' Fuentes opens the trunk of the car. There are three shotguns in the back: a Mossberg and two Remingtons. He loads the Mossberg, then starts filling his jacket pockets with shells. Gomez whistles when he sees the guns. 'Where the hell did they come from?' he asks, taking a Remington and racking it.

'From people who don't need them anymore.' He offers the other Remington to Juan Antonio. 'Know how to use it?'

Juan Antonio takes a step back, staring at the shotgun as though it were being aimed at him. Pilar snatches it from Fuentes. 'Careful!' Gomez says, as he jumps out of her way, feigning being scared. He puts his hand out to take the gun from her. Pilar keeps hold of it. 'Come on, what the hell do you know about guns?'

'I know not to short shuck,' she says, pumping the slide action with a single fluid movement.

Gomez whistles. 'Check out the Queen of the Pacific.' He turns to Fuentes with pissed-off eyes. 'So why are you arming civilians?'

269

'To defend themselves. In case something happens to us.'

'Please tell me we're waiting for backup.' In the silence that follows, Gomez can hear the wind sighing through the windows of the car; moaning a warning. 'The cars from the *maquiladora* will be here in fifteen minutes, twenty tops!'

'We can't risk it.'

'But we can risk getting killed?'

Fuentes points down to the ranch house. 'They don't know we're here. How long will that last? You know I believe police are involved. You think so too. We have to go in now. While we can still surprise them.' He turns to Pilar and Juan Antonio. 'When we get there, stay in the car. Keep down.' He looks at Pilar as he slams the trunk shut. 'And do not use that unless you absolutely have to.'

They speed towards the turnoff, the deep silence inside the car one more of meditation than fear or anger. It is a constructive silence, respectful and aloof, like a prayer beside the bed of a dying stranger.

Fuentes takes the turnoff fast, following a rutted river bed with a higher eastern bank. Gomez swears. 'Watch it, you're trailing dust!'

Fuentes looks in his side mirror and slows. Pilar peers up at the high river bank on their right. Something catches her eye before disappearing. She stares back and sees it again; movement at the top of the ridge. But before she can react or even shout a warning, the turkey vulture launches itself into the air, flying with ponderous disbelief across to the other bank. Gomez watches Pilar watching it disappear, then gently pushes her barrel so that it's pointing perfectly upwards towards the roof again. 'Nervous?'

She glares at him. 'You?'

He gives a cynical laugh. 'I'm never nervous when I'm forced to do something crazy.'

The car stops just before they leave the protection of the river gully. 'You stay here with them,' Fuentes says to Gomez.

'As if that's going to happen.' Less than fifty meters away, they can see the red pickup parked outside the fence. Fuentes gets out and creeps around to the front of his car, peering across the clearing. The other car is obscured by a strange rock formation, like a ruined cathedral stepping up into the void of the empty sky. Beyond is the house.

Gomez turns to Pilar. 'Stay down. And if the police arrive while you're still here, do not let them see that fucking gun.' He opens the door and slips out silently, stopping next to Fuentes. 'Is it the Navigator?'

'I can't tell. It's behind those rocks. We'll use them and the cars as cover to approach the house.'

Gomez races hunched and low to the outcrop. Fuentes covers him, then waits for any movement or noise. Nothing. He joins Gomez, both of them with their backs to the rock. Gomez scans his side, almost level with the rear of the pickup. There's no sign of any movement. Fuentes peers out his side. The Lincoln Navigator is empty.

Juan Antonio and Pilar watch through the windshield as Fuentes and Gomez disappear from sight, heading in the direction of the ranch house. There is a pause. Then Pilar gets out of the car.

'Pilar!' Juan Antonio's whisper shrieks across the desert silence. Pilar puts a finger to her lips, then dashes to the red pickup. Juan Antonio swears, looks all around, then follows her all the way to the passenger side. 'What the fuck are you doing?'

She doesn't answer, but goes to open the door. Juan Antonio's grip on her wrist is fierce. 'What if there's an alarm?' She pulls her hand away as though she's received an electric shock. Pilar slowly creeps up to the front of the pickup, watching the house over its hood. Juan Antonio scans the landscape. They're protected from the ranch house, but totally exposed from the river. He curses silently.

Fuentes and Gomez have rushed over the crumbling terrain of exhausted creosote bush and ancient termite nests, raising a shallow bloom of red dust behind them. They pause behind the Navigator. The fence gate is closed but there's no sign of a padlock. The windows of the house have been papered over and there's glare on the windows. They look at each other . . . Then run.

The gate is locked. Gomez passes his shotgun to Fuentes, then hoists himself over the fence, somersaulting down onto the other side, landing in a crouch. Fuentes passes him both shotguns, then climbs over, slower than Gomez, tearing his jacket as he drops to the other side. He takes his shotgun back from Gomez, both keeping low as they move towards the steps, eyes scanning the windows for any movement, listening intently for any sound.

Gomez motions with his head – he's going around the side of the house. Fuentes watches him disappear, then slowly mounts the steps, listening for the betraying creak of wood or a footstep behind him; or the cocking of an unseen weapon.

Pilar watches Gomez moving fast along the side of the ranch house towards the back, hunched low as he passes under the windows. He vanishes from view. She leans further out, watching Fuentes reaching the front door. Juan Antonio tugs her back behind cover. 'They'll see you!' She shifts the shotgun from one hand to the other, wiping her palms dry against her jeans.

Fuentes stands close to the door, his ear against the wall, straining to hear inside. There's a murmur, low and indistinct; rhythmic. Voices. Maybe music.

The shotgun blast is so sudden that he jumps away from the wall and hits the floor of the porch, not even sure at first if it was aimed at him. There is the answering shot of a handgun and then the sound of footsteps coming fast towards the door.

Fuentes braces himself on one knee and targets the front door. Someone explodes out of the house, a Walther P-38 in one hand. He jumps down the steps, losing his balance as he hits the ground, rolling and spotting Fuentes for the first time as he gets to his feet. There's another gunshot from inside the house. Fuentes aims his shotgun at knee level. 'Drop it.' The man raises his arm to shoot. Fuentes fires. The blast takes the man's legs out from under him and spins his upper body forwards, catapulting his chest and face into the earth.

Pilar stares in shock, Juan Antonio hovering behind her. They watch Fuentes enter the house, sweeping his shotgun from one side to the other. A moment later there's a shot, and a bearded youth bursts through one of the covered windows on the side, landing hard on his knees in a rain of glass, dropping the gun in his hand. He stands up, swaying for a moment, his face lacerated, then snatches the gun from the ground. He looks back at the smashed window and fires twice into the house, then starts running towards the back of the building.

There are more gunshots inside. Juan Antonio pulls Pilar to the ground, pushing her under the pickup. There is the tang of contact somewhere above them and then the sing-scatter of broken glass. Pilar covers her head with her arms, breathing in the rich dank smell of desert sand and fear.

Fuentes shelters behind a door jamb. There is another exchange of fire from the back of the house. Someone bolts towards him, a gun in his hand, his face falling apart when he sees Fuentes, who stands and fires, going for another low blast, the force of the shot sending the gunman smashing backwards through a wall, disappearing inside a puff of plaster powder. Fuentes peers through the hole in the wall, then kicks the room's door in. There's a woman, tied to a bed. The gunman is trying to crawl away from Fuentes on his elbows, his broken legs rolling impossibly then catching together, feet pointing the wrong way as they drag a smeared trail of blood and gristle. Fuentes raises his stock and brings it down on the gunman's collarbone. There is a sharp crack, then the silence of coma.

Fuentes checks the woman's dorsal pulse. She's alive. There's an explosion of automatic gunfire behind him, holes punching high through the wall, sunlight spotlighting the ceiling. An AK-47. Someone's reached an armory. That means their chances of getting out fast and unharmed just plummeted.

Fuentes cuts the unconscious woman's bindings, then lifts her off the bed and places her down in the corner in a recovery position. He upturns the bed so that its frame and mattress offer some protection. He takes the gunman's Beretta, engages the safety and slips it behind his belt in the small of his back. Then he heads towards the gunfire.

Only when he's outside the room does he realize the gunfire's no longer coming from inside the ranch house, but somewhere further away. He racks his shotgun, then returns to clearing the house. He kicks in a door, sunlight rushing into the hallway. The room's window is shattered, torn scraps of newspaper swarming in the wind like disturbed insects. He checks the next room. Also empty. He moves slowly towards the kitchen – the last room. Two bodies. One with a .38 Long Colt, the other with a Ruger M77 rifle. Both killed by shotgun blasts. There's no sign of Gomez. He grabs the Ruger in his free hand and peers through the back window at a blockade not twenty meters away.

A youth squats beside a doorframe, his beard matted with blood. He fires again, raking the house indiscriminately. Fuentes ducks behind the stove. Something jumps in the room: one of the dead bodies, taking more rounds. Silence. Fuentes hollers Gomez's name. A shotgun blast in response. Gomez must be outside, maybe pinned down by the kid.

Pilar is just emerging from under the pickup, trying to catch any movement from the front of the house, when a burst of gunfire makes her drop down behind one of the wheels. Juan Antonio pulls her towards the back of the car. 'We have to go.' But a second, prolonged burst of gunfire sends them both diving to the ground for cover. They lie there, searching for an answer in each other's eyes about what to do next.

Fuentes can see the kid through a bullet hole just above the skirting board. Everything shifts back into the containment of training, Fuentes emptying his mind as he automatically works the bolt and adopts a preferential shooting position, lying on the floor, his legs spread, ankles inward, his elbows firm against the ground, his right cheek inclined as he sights, the stock heavy against the muscle padding of the pectoralis major. He exhales. Takes the first pressure. Fires.

The kid disappears with the recoil.

He waits, watching until he has a sign – the tremor of one of the kid's shoes shuddering into stillness. 'Gomez?'

'All clear out here.'

Pilar looks up at the ranch house, hearing Fuentes' response. 'All clear in here.' Gomez steps out from behind a velvet ash tree, in the posture of a hunter, the shotgun aimed at something she cannot see. He disappears from sight behind the house. Seeing Gomez makes her realize she doesn't have her shotgun. She runs back to the pickup and slides under the chassis. It's still lying there in the dust.

Fuentes kicks open the back door and slowly walks towards where the youth has fallen, the rifle at his shoulder, covered on his right by Gomez, who is moving in behind the stockade.

They both gain full sight of the body at the same time. There's an entrance hole in the kid's forehead. 'Jesus Christ, you must have—' Gomez's voice fades. He's heard it too.

They both slowly turn, looking up at the hill, two police cars speeding towards them, the urgency of their flashing lights mocked and eliminated by the glare of sunlight; the sirens not so much a shriek of urgency as a howl of outrage against the incompetence and treachery of the officers inside the cars, deliberately disobeying orders. 'Those motherfuckers,' Gomez says.

Beside the pickup, Pilar has retrieved the Remington and is getting to her feet when the sound of a car starting sends a shudder through her. She spins and from behind the rock formation sees the Lincoln Navigator accelerating towards them.

Pilar steps out from behind the pickup and aims at the man behind the wheel.

Fuentes and Gomez split up when they hear the shot from

the front, running on either side of the house. Gomez gets to the fence first, vaulting it with one hand, the Navigator already crumpled into the wall of the gully where it crashed, the back wheels spinning with a still-powerful intent, as though trying to burrow through stone.

Fuentes jumps down the front steps. The gunman he wounded is no longer there and the gate is open. Fuentes follows a blood pattern across the earth to where the Navigator was parked.

Gomez approaches the vehicle, glancing back at Pilar. 'Take cover.' Pilar doesn't react. Fuentes tugs the shotgun out of her hands and guides her behind the pickup. On the way back, he notices Juan Antonio sitting on the ground, blood streaming through his fingers from his forehead.

Fuentes approaches the passenger side of the Navigator. The gunman is slumped against the wheel, a deflated airbag gathered around him like a carelessly placed shroud. Fuentes slowly eases the barrel of the Mossberg through the window, until it touches the back of the man's head. No reaction.

Gomez reaches for the door handle, then opens it and springs back fast. The body falls out, Gomez kicking the hands clear. Fuentes jumps over the hood, landing on the other side. He turns the man over onto his stomach and secures both hands, feeling for a pulse. He looks up at Gomez, surprised. 'One tough son of a bitch.'

The sirens are bearing down hard on them. He looks back at Pilar, who is trying to staunch the bleeding from Juan Antonio's scalp. 'What happened?'

Juan Antonio tries to laugh. 'No idea. Maybe she shot me ...' He runs a finger along the ridge of his forehead, pulling it away in pain. 'Or maybe it was the glass when she shot the car.' He squints up at her. 'All I know is you're a goddamn *loca*.'

Gomez reaches inside the Navigator and kills the ignition, freeing them from the relentless grinding sorrow of the turning wheels, the sirens' song of pain consuming everything as the police cars brake hard, dust fountaining behind them. The cops get out, pistols drawn, their faces hard with adrenaline and panic. 'Holster your weapons,' Fuentes shouts. The cops comply reluctantly. Two of them run over to Pilar and Juan Antonio, roughly yanking Pilar to her feet. 'Don't touch her, she's a victim.' The cops let Pilar go so quickly that she stumbles and nearly falls. 'Where are the ambulances?'

'About five kilometers behind us.'

'Send a car back to the main road. Make sure they don't miss the turnoff. No one is allowed access except for police and emergency services, got that?' Fuentes calls out to Gomez, 'She's inside. She's still alive.'

Pilar starts to follow them but Juan Antonio blocks her way. 'She needs my help.'

'Pilar, let them do their job.'

'They wouldn't be here if it weren't for me.'

'If it weren't for Fuentes too. He was the one who knew where to look.' She tries to go around him, but again he stops her. 'This doesn't concern you anymore.'

She pushes past him. 'You have no idea how wrong you are.' She runs after them, Fuentes stopping when he hears her coming up the steps. He takes her in his arms. 'Trust me, you don't want to go inside.'

'I need to see her.'

'You will. We're bringing her out now. But you can't go inside. It's a crime scene, do you understand?' Pilar turns and sits down on one of the steps. She hears Gomez swear inside the house just as she's trying to light a cigarette, but it's no good. Her hands are shaking so much, the match goes out.

54

Padre Márcio

The last time he saw him before he disappeared, Joaquín Lázaro Morales was accompanied by a slim young man with dark eyes. Not eyes full of resentment or fear, like most young men's, but with a hunger for knowledge and power. They were eyes just like his own.

'This is my son.' It took Padre Márcio a moment, but then he recognized Amado. The active, intelligent silence of the boy he had raised in the orphanage for eight years was still evident in the young man. All grown up. Unharmed. Undamaged. It was a moment of satisfaction; almost sinful pride. Amado was the first child placed in his care. The first he had been wholly responsible for. A vulnerable child sent to an institution that provided for him, cared for him; educated him. Did not molest him. Already there had been thousands more like him. To the children Padre Márcio was San Martín de León; a protective cloak. To the Church he was San Miguel, wielding a fiery sword as he sent his enemies tumbling down to hell.

'Amado is to represent me now.' Padre Márcio was surprised. It meant Joaquín was either about to go into hiding or about to die. One thing was certain: a man like him would never allow himself to be captured. 'Everything he does, everything he tells you to do, is performed in my name and with my authority, now and forever. Can you accept that?'

Padre Márcio recognized the moment perfectly. He could

neither acquiesce nor protest. He had to wait until the offer was made. 'In return—' Joaquín continued, but Padre Márcio interrupted. 'Not in return, in partnership. It has to be a partnership. Not necessarily of equals, but of brothers. Otherwise I must walk away.'

'I could have you killed. I could have Amado do it.'

Padre Márcio turned to the young man, who stood there staring at him with the stone-cold patience of a killer. 'You could. Or we could prosper together in new and extraordinary ways.'

Amado took a step towards him, passing through a ray of sunlight, the unsheathed blade flashing with the cruel gleam of intent. His father placed a hand upon his son's shoulder and he froze, his eyes never leaving Padre Márcio's. 'What could a priest do for me?'

'Make you the richest man in Mexico.'

'And what would that do for you?'

'Make me the second richest.'

'How would you do it?'

'For the purposes of tax exemption, I have already registered the Order of the Army of Jesus as a charity in the United States of America. I will borrow money from both the Mexican Church and the Institute for the Works of Religion . . .' He saw the look of incomprehension on Joaquín's face. 'What the papers call the Vatican Bank . . . And then I will start buying property on *both* sides of the border using blind trusts set up in Panama, Luxembourg and Delaware. Trusts we will jointly control. Trusts that the Church will never know about.'

'What do you have planned?'

'The Church is eager for me to expand the Order. I will identify a dozen properties to purchase in the US and request funds to buy them outright. But instead the funds will be transferred to a BCCI account in Karachi, and thereafter funneled to the Virgin Islands and Liechtenstein. We will launder your cash by using it to place a deposit of ten percent on a hundred and twenty properties, borrowing the rest from savings and loan establishments in the southwest, using the Church as guarantor. We will renovate these properties quickly and sell them on for a profit, avoiding capital gains thanks to our tax-exempt status. We will then return to the same savings and loan establishments, borrowing ten times the previous amount and purchasing thousands more properties. We will sell the mortgages of all these properties on to a holding company for cash, thus laundering even more of your money. This holding company will issue two sets of bonds. We shall be secured lenders, but the unsecured lenders – the future unsecured debtors – will end up being the Church.'

'Why would the banks agree to such a scheme?'

'The savings and loans are currently paying more in interest rates to the Federal Reserve than they're receiving as fixed-term payments on their home loans. They are all massively in debt. Yet they still trade, in the hope of buying time until the rates eventually reduce. But in order to keep doing so, they have to hand out increasingly risky loans. It is unsustainable and it will collapse. But for the moment it is legal. The trick is to act fast and to avoid the consequences of the inevitable failure of the institutions.'

'There must be someone in the Church who would see through the fraud?'

'These are parish priests we are talking about, not chartered accountants. Elderly cardinals who dress in ermine gowns and satin slippers, not hardened business tycoons. They have willfully removed themselves from the world. Why would they know anything of its workings? Particularly when they involve complex financial structures.'

An enchanted smile of possibility. Even a *narco* like Joaquín, grounded in the searing reality of the sierras, in the bone-breaking land of his ancestors, was as easily seduced by the modern El Dorado of *la tierra gringa* as any bewitched teenager from the *barrios ñeros* of Mexico City. 'It won't take them long to ask questions.'

'Not if I ensure that there is always a trickle of revenue passed on to them every month. It will be additional income. That's all that matters. The trick is to make them believe in the magic of money.' Padre Márcio understood the thinking of the tyrant. A fistful of coins flung at beggars from a passing coach was enough to keep the tumbrils of revolution at bay.

'And when they find out that the funds have been diverted and their bonds are worthless?'

'It will take decades for them to comprehend the fraud. By then both you and I will be gone.' He turned back to Amado, relieved to see that the naked blade had disappeared. 'It will be a question for the next generation to resolve.'

Joaquín did something rare. He laughed, exposing yellowing calcium phosphate sown between golden crowns. It looked more like a leering threat than an expression of joy. 'It sounds tempting, so there must be a catch. What else do you want, Father?'

55

Gloria

The ambulance pulls up, Fuentes jumping out ahead of the medics, swearing when he sees the television cameras grouped around the entrance to the hospital. He quickly tugs the top sheet over Gloria's face, trying to block the cameras with his hands as he escorts the trolley through a media gauntlet, Valdez standing solemn outside the hospital, the lenses pivoting to him as the procession passes. The trolley bursts into the hospital, the press blocked outside, their shouted questions suddenly muted. Valdez stares at Gloria, then looks up at Fuentes. 'You said she was alive.'

Fuentes wants to tear his head off. 'She won't be for long if images of her face are broadcast.' He folds the sheet back down onto Gloria's shoulders, the procession rolling fast along a corridor, doctors running towards them. 'I said no fucking press!'

'You know what they're like.'

There's the flap and slam of the trolley being pushed into the emergency ward, leaving the two of them stranded alone outside. People have often told Fuentes he's a good cop, but they're wrong; totally wrong. A good cop is controllable. Reasonable. Malleable. And he is none of those things right now – which makes Fuentes one bad fucking cop. 'It was supposed to be a covert operation!'

Valdez grabs his arm. There's surprising strength in his grip. 'Bullshit, it was an *unauthorized* operation. You placed her life in jeopardy with your reckless actions.' Fuentes has never seen Valdez like this before; transformed from a laconic, cynical bureaucrat into something sharp and dangerous as broken glass. He tries to free his arm, but can't. 'So watch that mouth of yours or I won't just suspend you; I'll break you.'

He releases Fuentes as though he were disgusted to realize he was still in contact with him. 'A full report, on my desk, today.' It doesn't sound like a request, or even a demand. It's more like a sentence of execution. 'Now follow me.'

They step back out into the ambulance bay, the press gathering around. Valdez ignores the first shouted questions, signaling for silence. 'Today three men were killed in a carefully orchestrated police operation linked to the kidnapping of a number of women in Ciudad Real over the past few months.'

A number, not hundreds. A choice of words that reveals not the lie in a sentence but the lie in an entire language. A lexicon of contempt and cover-up. For the first time, Fuentes feels the true power of Valdez; a man who could take not just his job away from him, but his reputation and maybe even his liberty. A man who is rewriting history during an impromptu press conference. A trio of serial killers, not a city-wide, maybe even a national conspiracy. A few months, not years. A man who wouldn't hesitate to crush Fuentes; not as punishment but merely as a warning to others. He has been blinded by his dismissive presumptions about Valdez. When he first arrived in Ciudad Real, he quickly identified Valdez for what he was: a cog in a corrupt system. But Fuentes thought he was merely ornamental; a diverting, shiny component that would simply spin in place, inching more important matters slightly forwards, when in reality Valdez is a hammering cogwheel, a brutal turning mechanism designed not to progress but to crush anything that passes beneath it. Fuentes has been duped by his quick assumptions; his lazy reading of a highly dangerous and duplicitous man.

'Their captive was liberated unharmed.'

'What's her name?' a reporter cries.

'Her family has asked that her privacy be respected. She has obviously been through a terrible ordeal, and is currently being cared for by hospital staff. There will be a full press conference at six this evening. In the meantime, I wish to thank all my men and supporting agencies who carried out this successful rescue operation with professionalism and valor. This raid was the culmination of a long investigation and a meticulously planned tactical strike that has neutralized the kidnappers.'

Kidnappers, not rapists and killers.

Journalists shout questions over each other. '*Ya me cansé*,' Valdez mutters, looking back one last time at Fuentes before disappearing into a sedan, his face a mixture of cold anger and cool triumph: the lofty disdain of a deity. Of course Valdez contacted the press himself. Why else would he have been there, awaiting the arrival of the ambulance like a foreign minister on a tarmac receiving a head of state? That isn't necessarily suspicious in itself. The man is a politician within the department. Even his knowledge of the operation; the way he was able to spin its details with such short notice is typical of the flagrant careerism of a successful bureaucrat boosting his profile. What troubles Fuentes, what sends every internal warning bell erupting into a five-fire alarm, is the fact that he has mentioned nothing about the two wounded suspects.

Either he doesn't know about them, which is practically impossible.

Or else he already has them in custody – his custody.

Fuentes grabs one of the doctors exiting the room, who delivers boilerplate diagnosis. The prognosis is encouraging. She's in shock, of course, but her vitals indicate she's strong enough to receive a heavy sedative – essentially a medically induced coma, which will be maintained for at least twenty-four hours. 'What about DNA samples?'

'We've been instructed not to proceed with them for the moment.'

'. . . Why not?'

'Firstly, she hasn't consented. Secondly—'

'How can she consent when you've just put her in a coma?'

'*Induced* a coma. Secondly, we don't have consent from next of kin. We don't even know her identity.' So Valdez was lying about making contact with her family. 'Thirdly, we have no information to suggest she has been sexually assaulted.'

'There were sperm stains on the sheets.'

'Which may have occurred at an earlier stage.'

So now he's an attorney as well as a doctor. 'Can't you just proceed with the assumption she was sexually assaulted, given the circumstances of her abduction?'

Irritation creeps into the doctor's voice for the first time. 'We don't even know what the circumstances of her abduction were.'

'She was kidnapped, restrained and raped. I've just given you reasonable cause to proceed.'

'Captain Valdez made it clear to our chief physician that he alone was in charge of this case and we were not to follow orders issuing from any other police authorities.' Fuentes digests the implication of the news: Valdez has removed him from the case. 'Look,' the doctor says, 'we're not the enemy here. On the contrary, we're doing our best to help the victim. But that's all we can do. If you have issues with Captain Valdez, you have to resolve them yourself.'

'I need your help.'

'I just told you—'

'Not with her, with two other patients, gunshot victims. Both men have serious leg wounds. I haven't seen them come in yet.'

The doctor sighs, glancing at his watch. 'I'll see what I can find out.'

While he's waiting, Fuentes calls Gomez. 'How's forensics doing?'

'They've found a ton of prints. No ID on the girl though.'

'What do you know about the gunshot victims?'

Fuentes doesn't like the puzzled pause. 'They were in the ambulances that followed you. Why?'

'They haven't shown up yet.'

'Try the ballistic trauma unit at San Vicente.'

Fuentes sees the doctor walking towards him. With all of that morning's events, he still hasn't had a chance to mention Mary-Ellen to Gomez. 'I'll call you back.'

The doctor shrugs. 'They're definitely not here. I asked around the other hospitals. No one knows a thing about them.'

'Did you try San Vicente's?'

'That was the first place I tried.' The doctor studies Fuentes' face. He finds something there that allows him to do something he ordinarily would never do: go out on a limb. 'Have you thought of contacting the morgue?'

56

Ventura

After Ventura returned to the restaurant the evening before, Mayor had invited her to spend the night at his place with the assurance that she would pass a peaceful night – code for promising not to attempt to seduce her.

She had agreed to go to Mayor's house under the pretext of picking up her car, which was parked there, safe and out of sight, almost ignoring the real reason: she was a woman on her own in Ciudad Real, and she was afraid. And she was seeking protection from a man more powerful and knowledgeable than her. It shamed her but it reassured her too. Now she had decided to take control of her own work, she might be able to once again take control of her life. A control she had gradually lost with Carlos.

All that morning, she kept recalling her last moments with Carlos; how he sobbed as though he were a victim, not a perpetrator. As though he were the one being abandoned. For many women, it is a moment of unbearable anguish – to see the man whom they loved break down and cry. Even for strong women, it is often the one thing they simply cannot bear: the tears of their men; men they thought of as capable, indestructible – and often foolishly as their equal – suddenly reduced to sobs. No longer acting like *men* but crossing over to the realm of women, used to the crucible of tears, of suffering; of mourning. Burdened by the weary weight of martyrdom.

But Ventura isn't one of those women. She hates tears, in women and especially in men. They aren't just a sign of weakness, but of manipulation. Of capitulation. Of surrendering custodianship of one's own anguish and bequeathing it, unwanted, to another. So often, it is an opportunity for exploitation; especially with men. How many times has she seen men cheat on their women and then come crawling back, voices quivering with emotion, eyes watering, searching for pity like a scolded dog. Usurping the tears of the women they have betrayed. How many times has she seen male neighbors sobbing as they cradle their wives in their arms, covering black eyes and bruised arms with kisses, saying they didn't mean to do it, it wasn't their fault. They were drunk. They were jealous. If only the women could understand the stress they were under. As though their violence was the fault of their women; women like her own mother.

Evil domestic memories are disinterred from her childhood. Her father explaining to her mother that if she really didn't want him to punish her, she wouldn't have done whatever it was he was accusing her of: dressing up like a whore; looking at some man in a way she shouldn't; spending too long at work; speaking that way to him in public. Why wasn't his food on the table when he came home? he'd demand, the shock of his fist making empty plates leap, mocking the use of the word *home*. Surely home should be a refuge, not a dwelling shared with an unstable, violent monster.

Dark thoughts tumble out from the past as she showers and dresses. Tears hover, then are stubbornly suppressed as she walks alone across a carpet of jacaranda flowers in Mayor's garden, thankful for the color in a city of black and white; for the solitude in a time of sirens. She is remembering her first boyfriend, explaining in a high, trembling voice that he hadn't meant to hit her – but she had no right to say the things she had, before breaking down into sobs of self-pity, as though *he* was the one who had been hit. Leaving him that day had made her the woman she'd become. A woman capable of saying no. Of walking away to protect herself and her dignity. A woman able to take care of herself in a world of masculine advantages. Her work had gotten her noticed. She lived the life she wanted to lead. She got to choose her partners, not the other way round.

She had chosen Carlos.

And he had damaged her sense of self-worth.

Is it true what they say? That all children are condemned to repeat the mistakes of their parents. That all girls marry their fathers and all boys their mothers. That the loop of failure can never be broken? What does that say about her? What does that say about the whole country?

Her anger at Carlos washes over her like a drowning tide, tugging her down into cold currents of contempt. For him. And for herself. For the entire nation. She can taste it on the back of her tongue: metallic. Iodic.

Toxic.

Carlos hasn't bothered to contact her since he fled, and for that she is relieved. She can't bear to think of the cartel people finding him; enacting *narco* revenge. And if they can't find him, they'll try and find her. She hates him now, but only two days before she still thought she was in love with him. Such a schism is too traumatic to think about. So she has put all thought of him out of her mind, until this morning. Now she knows that she has to do the inevitable: escape like Carlos. She has to run from all of her past. From this inherited legacy of male violence, betrayal and infidelity.

From being afraid and at risk, simply because she is a woman, alone.

It was a mistake to leave Mexico City and return to Ciudad Real; a colossal error of judgment. She had allowed Carlos to dictate the terms of her life because of tax advantages to his business. Because of his needs, not hers. And now because of that decision, she is being hunted; but at the same time, she is strangely free.

Free from a man who lied about his love; who was reckless enough to try to defraud professional killers.

Free to leave her hometown and this time never, ever return.

But before she leaves town, before she starts running from her past towards a new future, there are three things she has to do.

She wants to complete the research for her story, because it is her duty as a woman to tell it.

And she wants to help with the strike at the *maquiladoras* because the union people are right as well: women will never be safe until they enjoy the same advantages as men. Economic equality. Protection from exploitation.

Her having to hide in Mayor's house proves that. Juan Antonio said it at dinner the night before. The only way to make the women of Ciudad Real safe – to make all working women safe – is by improving their living and working conditions and giving them the economic independence to choose how they want to live, and with whom. So if they ever want to walk away from domestic violence or just an unhappy relationship, they can.

But most of all she wants to shoot everything; not as reportage but as testament. This isn't just another story, this is something far bigger. And she will be there when it unfolds; on the right side of history. Her side. She has faith in her work. She has faith in her instincts. She has faith in her talent. And most of all, she has faith in her ambition. If everything coalesces, this will be her legacy.

Just three things, she thinks, and then she will be free.

57

El Santo

El Santo has never liked going to church. It isn't just that it's mind-numbingly boring. He can't see the point. Wasting your time worrying about what's going to happen when you die? As if he doesn't know. The answer is dumbass simple. Absolutely nothing.

Eternal life?

Immortal souls?

El Santo has seen inside more people than your average heart surgeon; he's opened up living bodies while their owners called out to God to save them. And guess what? God never did. El Santo knows from firsthand experience, there is no such thing as a miracle, much less a soul. There are only muscles, sinews and indecent amounts of blood. It's the same with church. Empty. If you *really* want to forget your earthly worries, go to a disco.

The whole concept of churches still does his head in. There's all that stone, which makes you feel like you're in a castle, which is kind of cool. But then they spoil it by throwing in all that glass. Invulnerable meets breakable. What's that all about? The only thing he doesn't mind is the artwork. Not the gory crucifixes, as phony as a George A. Romero flick. What he likes are the *retablos*. All those little tin squares painted with stories of help, salvation and devoted thanks. When he was a kid he read them like they were comic books nailed up on a wall. How El Santo Niño de Atocha came to the party with a basketful of food. How the Virgin's tears put out a fire. All those crazy Sacred Hearts floating in the sky like flying saucers, beaming healing rays down on poor sick kids. His favorite *lámina* was one with the devil, slick and blue as Mister Fantastic, getting tossed into a volcano by a royally pissed Santiago. Those pictures and the stories they told were all kind of cool.

Then came the House of Death, and there was no more time for stupid dreams and *naïf* drawings; for churches and blah-blah about salvation.

So it's weird that he's back in one now, talking to an old man who looks like Jerry Garcia, only with holes in his hands, who might be insane or, more probably, just cunning as a shithouse rat. One thing's for sure – he ain't no fucking saint.

'Fifteen percent is outrageous,' Padre Márcio says, although he doesn't sound outraged at all. In fact he seems bored out of his mind. Maybe being in a church does *his* head in too.

El Santo gives his *tell me about it* shrug. 'That's the usual rate.'

'I'm not the usual customer.' El Santo can't argue with that. 'I do enormous good with all the money I raise. Why would you want to take food out of the mouths of poor orphans?'

'Why do birds shit white? It's the way of the world, Father.'

The priest sits down, right there on the altar steps, clenching his hands together, not in prayer but in computation, like a bookie hesitating on expanding the odds. 'Your world, perhaps. Not mine.'

El Santo and Oviedo had arrived at the cathedral just after lunch. Not that he could hold anything down. Not even a glass of Noche Buena. The way things were going, that slug to the gut was going to cost him at least five kilos, and let's face it, he was already a couple of kilos under *slim*. His mother's goddamn metabolism. She knew. She was always at him to have a second helping, while fat fucks like El Feo, who could audition for the Michelin Man, put on weight just driving past the *panadería*. The last thing he needs is to end up looking so gaunt, people will think he's using. Bosses who abuse their own product are like a curbside needle jockey sitting in a puddle of piss. Beyond redemption. To be put out of their misery to save embarrassment at the first opportunity.

When they arrived at the church, some battle-ax nun flapped around, trying to get them to leave. She had picked them out as sinners as soon as she spotted them stepping through the incense smoke. But wasn't that the point of a fucking church? To welcome the good and bad; the rich and poor; the healthy and the dying, and people like him who have a say in who is who?

But when Sister Hitler got a sniff of the money El Santo was waving in her face, she ran off to get the old bleeder. He listened for maybe a minute with a look on his face like El Santo was standing on the other side of an eight-lane highway, trying to shout out an order from a Chinese menu. It wasn't until Father Holy Holes noticed Oviedo standing by the baptismal font that he decided to give him the time of day. El Santo remembers what Amado used to say: respect is born out of intimidation. He could go one further. Intimidation is born out of enforcement. El Santo could snap his fingers and Oviedo would murder Padre Márcio right here in the cathedral. There'd be a shitstorm like no other but . . . That's what makes people fear *narcos* so much. They don't give a fuck about the consequences of their actions. They do things as though they're batshit crazy, and these days most of them are. So seeing Oviedo standing there in the shadows, the old priest's attitude has finally readjusted. He's focusing on El Santo. 'Why are you here?'

'What are the compartments for?'

'Compartments?'

'You can't bullshit a bullshitter, Father.' He feels the intimidating weight of Oviedo's presence stepping up behind him. It even gives him a little chill. Imagine what it does to the priest. 'You know exactly what compartments I'm talking about.' Padre Márcio's eyes flicker up at Oviedo, then nervously dance away. Oh yes, the fear is working its magic now.

'The automobile compartments?'

This is why he can't stand priests. They never go with simple words. They use *deceased* instead of just plain *dead*. *Excommunicated* instead of *out on your ass*, and *salvation* instead of *saving it*. 'What are they for?'

'Contraband.'

There he goes again. 'The way I figure, it's cash. I suppose it could be drugs, but I doubt it. Whatever you do, don't tell me Bibles.'

'What is being smuggled is of no concern to you.'

'This is where we have a major problem. Everything that crosses that border concerns me.'

'I am prepared to pay you fifty thousand dollars a crossing.'

'I want fifteen percent. That's one hundred and fifty thousand a crossing.' Or three million a month if his calculations are correct. Again with the wringing hands routine. No wonder they bleed all the time. 'Who are you working for?'

'You understand that I can't tell you.'

El Santo knows a phony statement when he hears one. 'I think my friend here thinks otherwise.'

Padre Márcio glances up at Oviedo, as though he's finally

realized how much a guy like Oviedo would love to hurt a priest like him. Because Oviedo is a man of faith's worst nightmare. A devout believer. Not in God, or even the devil, but in the devil's by-products: torment. Everlasting pain. He can already hear him, sharpening his knife with the honing rod; that slate-scratching catch in the grooved stainless steel that makes your blood run cold.

He recognizes the beat-up look on the priest's face. Surrender. Or, as the priest would say, *capitulation*. Well, that was fast. 'I will pay your exorbitant tax but I cannot tell you the identity of the person I work for.'

'Then I will have to kill you.'

'Then you will never see your money. Free will. That's what makes humans different from the animals. I've made my choice. Now you need to make yours.' He has to admit, that's pretty ballsy for a guy who never uses them. This priest is a good talker. He remembers that from his First Holy Communion lessons. Fuck it. He'll take the money now, get the information later. 'We're not done yet,' El Santo says.

The priest smiles. El Santo almost misses it, because it's not the kind of smile you'd expect to see in a place like a church, even for a non-believing *narco* like him. An evil smile. 'Not by a long shot,' Padre Márcio says.

58

Gomez

Gomez is still at the ranch house when he gets the call from Fuentes. The two wounded gunmen have just shown up at the morgue. Fuentes is seething. Gomez couldn't give a fuck. Fuentes is acting like it's part of some great, overarching conspiracy but Gomez saw the state of both of them at the ranch house. The legs of the one in the bedroom were basically only attached to the body by congealed blood. And as for the *güey* they pulled out of the Navigator, it was like he only survived the shotgun blast so he could experience the thrill of driving a speeding car into solid rock.

They're both dead, and as far as Gomez is concerned, that is a better outcome than pissing away money on a trial just for a couple of years in jail, with the risk of a counter-suit against the department for excessive and unnecessary force leading to permanent disability. No one made the two gunmen shoot at him and Fuentes, just like no one forced them to kidnap and rape the girl. Fuck them. The moment you show remorse for lowlife killers is the moment you better hand in your badge, because in Ciudad Real, every *sicario* carries three bullets marked *pity*, *hesitation* and *regret*.

The first time Gomez killed someone, he couldn't stop thinking about it. For months. In the first week after he pulled the trigger and watched a junkie with a knife spin fast and drop slow, he couldn't get the scene out of his head. His first ever partner, Ortega, had carefully approached the body, aiming at the head while a woman shouted some hysterical shit from a window above. Ortega kicked the knife out of the dead man's hand and sent it whirling into a fire-blackened doorway. Then he turned to Gomez with a hateful smirk. 'You just became a man,' Ortega said, as though Gomez were a teenage nephew he had caught sneaking out of a Chatarrita whorehouse.

After he'd shot the junkie, everything had gone silent for an instant, then the woman had started yelling from the window. It was the memory of those shouts – like a banal song you can't get out of your head – that always launched the involuntary recurring sequence. A perpetual memory which dominated his waking hours, and infested his mind during hypnagogia. Even when he was able to sleep, he'd soon wake from the force of those screams hovering above his head. He'd try and remember what the woman was shouting: a warning? A cry for help? Was it just a manifestation of hysteria or fear, or simply hateful invective – the universal curse delivered to any approaching cop with a gun in his hand? It didn't matter. For him it had long ceased to be communication. It was a soundtrack to a nightmare that no longer bothered to distinguish between day and night; lucidity and unconsciousness. All his thoughts were fused to that single moment of murder: it was a fatal synapse, one that changed him; that began to threaten his sanity.

Then after a month, the burden of that brutal synthesis lifted without him even realizing it. He was pouring himself a beer after work one day when it hit him: he hadn't thought about the shooting since the night before.

He was free. What everyone had said was true. The memory

300

had gone with the simple passage of time. He thought he was over that first killing.

He thought wrong.

It was as though he had weeded an infested garden, and convinced himself he had removed the problem. But seed-pods must have broken sometime during the clearance because he kept flashing back to the shooting. It wasn't like before, a constant weight that obliterated all other thoughts; all other emotions. Now it was something active and unpredictable that would alight at the most unexpected of times, chiseling away at his supposed *recovery*. He actually preferred it before, when it so dominated his mind that there was nothing he could do but muster his strength and try to live with it, even though he knew it would linger like an opportunistic infection. Now it would take him by surprise. Ambush an instant; leave him stinging and in shock. It made him doubt himself. It made him wonder: was he capable of defending his life again if he had to? That in turn led him to the most uncomfortable question of all, one he had been avoiding until then: did a junkie with a switchblade on the other side of the street really constitute a mortal threat?

Other killings followed in the line of duty. Other reactions too. They were never as severe as that first shooting. But there was always something extra deposited afterwards. Something that hurt but helped. It was like he was growing a new layer of skin. Ballistic-proof and one size too tight. It changed him. It made him harder.

It made him feel as though he didn't give a fuck.

And then came the moment when Paredes and he had chased down two serial muggers. Junkies turned maimers. They had blinded one of their victims; crippled another. It

301

wasn't *malicious intent*. It was worse. It was selfish disregard; brain-dead incompetence. They needed money for their next hit, and they got it any way they could. And now he and Paredes had them cornered. They looked at each other, and without any noticeable signal passing between them, executed both of the motherfuckers right there and then.

And after that, there were no more regrets.

No more memories.

No more doubts.

Not about that execution, not even about the first junkie he ever shot. The shouts from the woman were finally silenced. He became a cop who did not give a shit about what happened to all cops' enemies: criminals. Violent death was a part of his world. There were shootings all the time and someone was always going to die. Maybe even him.

So Gomez has no qualms about the two men he killed at the ranch house, or the man Fuentes shot through the forehead, or the deaths of the two injured gunmen. The girl is alive. Forensics are gathering evidence. And Fuentes is wrong. There is no conspiracy. Innocents die because there are too many bad people out there, forcing their evil on the world. It makes a difference when they are taken down.

It usually saves someone.

This time it was the girl. Gloria Delgado. He found her ID in the ranch house. Fuentes told him not to tell anyone just yet. Fuentes is fucking paranoid.

He drives back to town. Fuentes wanted him to stay at the ranch house, to make sure forensics didn't screw up. Weren't being controlled. Fuentes has it all backwards. It isn't forensics, it's the people with oversight of the evidence. People like Valdez, who get to choose what is retained and what is *misplaced* or simply destroyed as *contaminated samples*. Powerful people. More powerful than any street criminal.

People you never want to cross.

Gomez drives straight to the hospital. The staff see him coming. They point the way to the emergency ward like he's a panicked parent. As though they've never seen a cop there before.

Fuentes comes out of a room just as he's turning into the corridor, his face dropping into an ugly mask when he sees Gomez. Here it comes. Anger and then the lecture about disobeying orders. He's had it with Fuentes. After the insanity of that morning; after the *puto* unnecessary risks. And he's striding towards Fuentes, about to tell him where he can shove his fucking indignation, when he sees them – two municipal policemen, coming up fast from the other end of the corridor. Heading towards the room Fuentes has just come out of.

Sicarios.

Gomez unholsters his weapon. He sees the look of doubt on Fuentes face, and then the understanding as he too draws his weapon and turns, the two municipal policemen freezing, running odds through their heads; coming up short. They turn. They run. They knock staff out of the way. Equipment goes crashing.

Sunlight slashes across their faces then vanishes with the slamming fire door. Gomez and Fuentes pursue them out into the delivery bay and the dazzle of high noon. The crack of two shots, the lisp of a near miss; the slur of a ricochet too close for comfort. And then the squeal of a getaway car. Fuentes races after the unmarked black sedan, his gun raised in contemplation of a shot, then slowly lowered, the car already distending then disappearing behind blacktop rolls of heatwaves.

The girl really is in danger.

Fuck Fuentes. He's right.

Again.

Gomez follows him back to the girl's room. Fuentes whispers his discovery over the rhythmic gasp of a ventilator and the pulse of a monitoring machine playing bass in the corner. The Jane Doe from yesterday is Mary-Ellen González. No rap sheet but almost certainly a high-end escort and experienced drug mule. She was a dual national and that's what makes her important.

'Important *how*?' Gomez asks.

Fuentes explains his plan. Gomez gets the chills just listening to it. It's genius. It's *out there*. It might even work. But that's not what gets him sweating. It's the consequences. Save one life by destroying an entire kingdom. It would be the apocalypse and Fuentes doesn't seem to care. Not about his career, not about his freedom, not even about his life. And certainly not about the careers of others . . . about *their* lives. Fuentes has flipped. All he wants is just this one moment of brilliance. Of defiance.

Of redemption.

He is going to save one innocent life and one is better than none. But the cost will be devastating to both him and Gomez.

Gomez stands there, sucking deep breaths in time with the ventilator. 'Well?' Fuentes asks.

Fuck it. 'I'm in.'

59

Pilar

They take a taxi to Mayor's hacienda, Juan Antonio peering out under the bandage that covers his eyebrow, trying not to show how impressed he is as the gates open for them.

'This is a stupid idea,' Pilar says, slamming the gate behind her. Ventura and Mayor watch from the shade of the verandah as she and Juan Antonio cross the courtyard, the mosaic pavement hot underfoot. The two speak to Pilar in a soothing rush, saying words that mean nothing. *Glad. Safe. Terrible.* 'I don't want to talk about it.' They retreat from her, nodding, chastened, then turn to Juan Antonio. 'How bad is it?' Ventura asks, touching his bandage as though it will help him heal faster. Pilar interrupts Juan Antonio's self-deprecating response. 'Not bad enough. He can't think but he can still talk.' Ventura laughs, Juan Antonio poking his tongue at her.

They enter the century shadows that have prospered inside the hacienda, ceiling fans hushing them into a respectful silence. 'Thank you, Señor Mayor,' Juan Antonio says, diminished by the reverence in his voice.

'Why thank him?' Pilar says. 'This is stupid. We're not in any danger.'

Juan Antonio sighs like a man whose dog has just pissed on his host's Persian rug. 'Now you're being irrational.'

'*Irrational?*' Her inflection mocks not just Juan Antonio but the very existence of the word. 'Of course, that's what men always say to women who oppose them.'

'Jesus Christ, Pilar, stop pretending that nothing happened this morning.'

Her voice breaks as she speaks. 'Don't patronize me. I know more than you could imagine about what happened this morning.' She goes over to a bookshelf, glancing at titles.

'Then you know that we need protection.'

'This isn't protection, this is hiding . . .' She turns to Mayor. 'Not a single book by a woman?'

'Keep looking. You'll find the works of Woolf, Matute and Mansfield. Lispector and Meireles. Campobello and Castellanos. Atwood and de Beauvoir . . .'

'You're perfect. Is there one female writer you *don't* have?'

'Ibárruri.'

Her laugh is more a choke of outrage. 'What would a man like you know about *La Pasionaria*?'

Mayor fixes her with a hard gaze. 'Too much.'

'The rich judge. It's what they do instead of work.'

'Pilar, please.'

She glares at Juan Antonio. Ventura goes up to her. 'Let me show you your room.'

Pilar pulls her arm away from Ventura's touch. 'I'm not your friend, so don't pretend you're mine.'

'Whether you like it or not, we're all allies,' Mayor says. 'You're safe here. You should rest.'

She turns to Ventura. 'Does he tell you what you need to do too?'

'He's right,' Ventura says gently.

'You're both witnesses,' Mayor says. 'And you know what happens to witnesses in this town.'

'Exactly,' Juan Antonio says. 'They've already bombed my car. We have to be careful. If anything happens to you it will jeopardize tomorrow.'

'We're safe here,' Ventura whispers. 'And it's nice to feel safe for a change.'

Pilar stares at the three people gazing at her – not so much to intimidate but worse, as though they were trying to understand a puzzling mind. She walks through the enormous dining room with its feudal table out into the kitchen. A maid turns when she comes in. 'May I get you something?'

Pilar sees an empty glass upside down beside one of the sinks. 'I'm old enough to get myself a glass of water, thank you.' But the maid insists on taking a fresh glass from a cabinet anyway. A decorative tumbler. 'Would you like sparkling water or plain?' Pilar reaches for the glass by the sink and fills it up with tap water. 'Please. That's not a glass for guests.'

Pilar shuts off the tap, turns and faces her. 'Who is it a glass for?'

'The staff.'

Pilar shakes her head, disappointed that she guessed the answer so quickly, and drinks from her glass. The maid is startled to notice Mayor in the doorway, watching. 'I'm sorry, Señor Mayor.'

He smiles at her, speaking so softly that it is difficult for Pilar to hear every word. 'It's not your fault, Maya. She's not being deliberately rude, she's just upset.' Pilar stares at him with mounting outrage. 'You may go upstairs and help the others with the bedding.' Maya turns to Pilar with a look of curiosity before she goes.

It's a rare moment for Pilar, to have to gather her thoughts before she can speak. 'Any woman for you is just a—'

'Shut up and listen for once in your life. You may learn

something, although I doubt it with your ego and arrogance.'
Pilar's body goes rigid with anger, her face scarlet; her eyes
fierce and furious. She lifts the glass as though she's going to
hurl it across the room. 'If you break that glass, I'll call Maya
back and make her clean it up in front of you.'

'You pig!'

'I don't care what names you call me, but never humiliate my
staff again.'

'I did nothing of—'

'The arrogance of people like you—'

'You know nothing about me!'

'I could put someone like you together on an assembly line
with my eyes blindfolded.'

'You disgust me!'

'And you repeat yourself. All the time. Now shut up please and
listen, because unlike you, I'm not used to repeating myself.'

Pilar stands there, debating whether she should hurl the glass
across the room anyway, or better yet, aim it at Mayor's head.

'Eight people work full-time in this house. Twelve if you
count the gardeners. The gardeners live out at the back, but the
eight domestic staff live here with their spouses and children.
Take a look around. It's a big house with large grounds. But still.
Do you really think I need twelve people to look after it? To
look after me? I could live here happily on my own.'

'You have twelve servants because you need to play the feudal lord, the great cattle baron. The *criollo*!'

'The reason you're absurd is because you know nothing of
the lives you claim to represent.'

'And a man born into privilege and wealth does?'

'I let my staff get on with their work. And they let me get on with my writing. Everyone is happy. It's not just economic co-operation. It's more. It's community. It's a functioning society. It's something a professional political activist like you knows very little about. And when I do have guests, my staff enjoy it, because it gives them something extra to do, to prove their worth, to show that they are capable of doing as good a job for ten as for one. They don't need some conceited little *apparatchik* to storm in here and preach a revolution they don't want, that will leave them and their families homeless.'

'Your logic of domination is perfect; just like the plantation owner's. Preaching liberty through slavery.'

'I am a writer, so of course you don't understand me. I rely on the power of words. You rely on slogans.'

She goes to slap him. He catches her hand. She flings the glass to the floor, filling the kitchen with the detonation of exploding crystal and the singsong of scattering shards. Ventura runs in, staring in shock at the couple joined by a hand around a wrist and surrounded by broken glass. Maya hurries in after her, taking in the scene. 'Don't worry, Señor, I will clean it up.'

Pilar turns to her, her face drawn. 'I'll do it.'

'This is my kitchen.' Maya's voice is haughty; unforgiving. 'I don't want your help. You've already caused enough damage.' Maya drops to her knees and starts to sweep up the glass. Pilar picks up the larger pieces, but the other woman pulls away from her. 'I said I'll do it on my own.'

Pilar steps over the rest of the glass, walking back towards the library.

Ventura waits a moment, then follows her across the dining area into the den. And by the time she notices her, curled up on a corner sofa, Pilar is already asleep.

60

Fuentes

Gomez wasn't happy. Join the club. But in the end, he saw the logic: extreme measures were the only ones that would ever be effective in a society of extremes. Extreme poverty and extreme wealth. Extreme corruption.

Extreme evil.

The set-up was simple. He gave Gomez Mary-Ellen's address. All he had to do was try and retrieve her passport. The rest was up to Fuentes.

There was a full rotation of staff at noon. The doctor he had spoken to was gone. The emergency room staff didn't know exactly what had gone down, except that someone had tried to kill a patient guarded by police, and shots had been fired outside. San Vicente was safer, Fuentes said, signing a form. Nobody argued. She was just another Jane Doe. NOK unknown. And now a target.

The girl was transferred in an ambulance, her slim medical file in Fuentes' hand. No police escort. It would only attract attention, he said, and this time he wasn't just dissembling.

On the way to San Vicente he gets the call from Gomez. They're on. He shouts across the two medics to the driver at the front. Change of plan. They've just IDed the patient. She's a US citizen wanted by the cartels. A wave of fear rises hot above the air conditioning. That means only one thing. A potential cartel witness. A potential cartel ambush.

Fuentes tells them to take her straight to the border. The ambulance siren rises in frequency, as though wailing the question of all the medical staff inside: *Why us*? The rest of the trip is spent setting up the ambulance to meet them on the other side, while listening to the curses of the driver, desperate to evade traffic so he can unload his potentially fatal cargo as fast as possible. Fuentes has done three medevacs in Tijuana. He knows the drill. He has his credit card out before they've even asked him.

Gomez is waiting at the border and takes possession of all his weapons and ammo. Then he hands over Mary-Ellen's passport. He even has her health plan. That will assist with admissions but it will also compound the crime. Criminal fraud in addition to impersonation, facilitation, transportation and illegal entry. Possible people smuggling. Human trafficking, if they really want to hammer Fuentes. He passes Gloria's file to Gomez and tells him what to do.

'You promised this would be it.'

'You just have to drop it off at the desk.'

'They know me.'

'I'll take the rap if there is one.'

'You bet there'll be one and I'll make sure you fucking take it solo.' He storms off. No goodbye. No good luck. And why should there be? He'd worked it out only recently. Gomez is *way* smarter than he is.

61

Pilar

Pilar sleeps for an hour. She dreams that she's lost something but can't remember what it is, and it is only when she comes across a pool and looks into it that she realizes it's the moon. It hovers like a crown above her hair, a crescent of blue and white light. Then she wakes, still within her slumber, and rests for ten minutes, until her heartbeat regulates and her vision fully focuses and she is able to stand without fear of fainting.

She has a long shower, changes into the clothes that she brought to Mayor's, then goes downstairs. The kitchen is empty. The floor gleaming. No sign of fury; no sign even of life. She prepares some food from the refrigerator. There are footsteps behind her, coming to an abrupt stop when Maya sees her. Pilar opens her mouth to speak, but Maya is already gone.

She eats her food outside in the hot air. Then she washes up her plate and glass, goes upstairs and gets her bag. 'What are you doing?' Juan Antonio says as she starts to cross the courtyard. It isn't a question. It's an accusation.

'I'm going to work.'

Juan Antonio stands in her way, blocking the sun from her face. 'Are you out of your mind?'

'Don't talk to her that way.' It's the new girl, watching from the shade.

'She's being absurd. And you stay out of it.'

'Don't talk to *her* that way.' Does Pilar even care how he

speaks to the girl, or is she just on autopilot?

Juan Antonio stares down at her. 'You haven't slept in over two days. The strike is tomorrow.'

'That's why I need to work.'

'There's nothing more you can do. Please, Pilar, just this once, be reasonable. Save your strength for tomorrow.'

Pilar walks around him. He watches her go, his face a mixture of exasperation and admiration. 'You are the most stubborn person I have ever had the misfortune to know.'

'And you are the most repetitive,' she says, closing the gate behind her. The gate reopens quickly. She turns, ready for conflict, expecting Juan Antonio, but it's the new girl. The new *woman*. She catches up with Pilar, so that they are walking side by side.

'I'm going with you.'

'I don't need your help.'

'But I want to help.'

'So what? I don't want you with me.'

'You can't stop me,' Ventura says.

'I can do whatever I want.'

'Well, so can I.'

Pilar sighs and increases her pace, calling back over her shoulder, 'Then keep up with me. And if you want to make yourself useful, give me all the change you have.'

Ventura fishes through her camera bag, coming up with a fistful of coins. Pilar takes them all, sliding them into side pockets. 'Why do we need so many coins?'

'Because we're going to do a bus marathon . . .'

62

Paredes

Thanks to Fuentes' tip-off about the tunnel and the meth factory, and the resultant exposure of the DEA's liaison in Tijuana, Charlie Addsen had been transferred to Washington. It was a promotion, but for Addsen it was also a Great Escape. Charlie missed the climate, but it was a small price to pay for a safe desk job, good schools and a big enough raise in salary to afford them.

In San Diego he wasn't remembered as a hero; more as a selfish colleague who sold out the cause to become just another DC bureaucrat. But in El Lobo he had the kind of pull Head Office always has with the smaller branches. They complained behind his back; insulted him. Resented his interference. But they did what he told them to do, not because he was, after all, a much-decorated, distinguished former field agent, but because he was their last resort. El Lobo's budget had just come under attack. Again. And Addsen pulled purse strings in the allocation office. So they did the favor for Addsen, knowing – expecting – he would do one for them.

Of course the El Lobo authorities weren't crazy about the idea of letting Fuentes see Paredes. Addsen's statement that he was an honest Mexican cop looking for a lead on a big murder case didn't cut it for any of them – but there were three things in Fuentes' favor. He was so new to Ciudad Real that nobody knew anything about him. He had reservations about Byrd, who was under secret surveillance, suspected of corruption. And most significantly of all, he had just saved a US citizen from death by torture.

The War on Drugs was as black and white as the newspaper headlines it generated. But the terrain the war was fought on was another color entirely and El Lobo DEA knew how to do gray. They gave Fuentes thirty minutes in an interview room. He knew they'd be behind the two-way mirror, recording everything that was said, which was fine with him. They'd be listening, not understanding. His conversation with Paredes would be all about nuance, not *narcos*.

By the time Fuentes arrived, Paredes was already on seventy-two hours but his lawyer had asked for a continuance so he was still being held in county jail. The transfer to a federal facility would have killed any hopes of a visit.

Fuentes had played it fast and smart after the two wounded gunmen from the ranch showed up toe-tagged at the morgue. It would have been easy enough to let them both bleed out. Hell, it might even have been unintentional, although *accidental* wasn't Valdez's style. Fuentes knew what was going down. Valdez wasn't tying up loose strings, he was snipping them off. He and Gomez had saved Gloria Delgado at the hospital once, but they'd get her in the end. The real question was who was next: Gloria or him. He had to figure a way to get her out. And that's when he thought of Mary-Ellen González.

Gloria and Mary-Ellen were similar in age, weight and height. Their eye and hair color matched. If you worked on it, you probably could have passed them off as cousins, if not quite sisters. But an unconscious woman with facial abrasions riding an ambulance gurney back into her own country, accompanied by a pouched US passport attached to a hospital clipboard and with only an IV stand as NOK, blurred scrutiny. Sympathy was always the best disguise. No one was going to look too closely. They probably wouldn't even realize till after Gloria regained consciousness. *If* she regained consciousness. Fuentes even had an immigration lawyer standing by to request emergency asylum, just in case they went for a knee-jerk deportation when they did find out. Nothing would save his career, but Fuentes was going to do everything possible to save Gloria's life. And destroy the lives of the people who were trying to kill her.

Paredes knew Mary-Ellen. That could be problematic later. But Fuentes had no choice. He had to play up the fact he was her big savior if he were to win the confidence of a man he didn't trust. If he could make Paredes feel obliged to him, he might not even need Gloria.

*

Paredes is good. Paredes holds himself together tight. He is contained. Skeptical. Professional. They understand each other. They communicate silently. His eyes tell stories. They say: I know the DEA's behind there, listening, so let's keep this all in code. They say: I was set up and I think you know it. They say: I might be guilty of other things but not this. 'Do I need my attorney?' – strictly smokescreen.

Fuentes shakes his head. 'I just want an informal chat.'

'Nothing's admissible then, right?' he asks, already knowing the answer. Fuentes nods. Paredes smiles. His eyes say words that Fuentes understands. Tijuana. Cartel war. Cover-up. His eyes say they are both fucked.

Paredes opens his mouth and tells the story that is meant to be overheard. He's a good talker. He fell in love with Mary-Ellen when he first rousted her in a disco, for doing a line at the bar. He was bored and in need of distraction. But when she looked up at him? Lightning bolts. And who could blame him? Of course he never made the arrest. He kept her off the records – then and later. He did her favors. She was worth saving. She became his lover. She became his snitch.

Mary-Ellen was half *chamaquita*, half *gringa*, half *Colombiana*, and two hundred percent party girl. Her specialty was high-volume short runs. Fifteen kilo minimums, twenty-five max – so she could kick up a fuss about being ripped off over excess baggage charges. 'It costs more than the fucking ticket, you crooks!' got her noticed, which was what she wanted. Not that she would have gone unnoticed anyway, traveling in cut-off shorts and tube tops one size too small. She'd check in early, go to the lounge, get pretty drunk and pretty loud, which was, let's face it, pretty normal for her, and then buy up big in duty-free.

More drinks on the flight, some suggestive chit-chat; team up with some unlikely escort. Customs were more likely to focus on a straight suit accompanying her than on Mary-Ellen. Reverse psychology, plus a little touch of nasty envy.

She was usually staggering by the time she went through customs, and it wasn't just because of her six-inch heels. And if they stopped her, which was quite often – not because they suspected her but because they just wanted to have some fun – she'd fuss around for her ID and receipts and 'accidentally' drop her duty-free and then start crying over the broken bottles of Cristal and Chanel No. 5 until one of the customs officers made a joke about spilt milk, and this was the moment when she really got to act, and part of it wasn't even acting because she was half thinking, What if they wise up to me today? And that thought led to the only possible answer: *twenty years to life*, and the tears came so naturally that sometimes it almost awed her and she wondered: Is this what they do – the method actors?

She had tried this routine in over twelve different airports and the customs officers were always embarrassed, or apologetic, or thought it was all some big joke and laughed about the dumb drunk bimbo and although every one of them mocked her, truth be told none of them would have said *no* if she had asked them to take her home.

That then was her secret; that and always having shitty luggage, because if they see you coming with your Louis Vuitton or your Briggs & fucking Riley they're going to know you have more money than you know what to do with and the attitude of sick entitlement that always comes with it. And they're going to search until they find the luxury item you're trying to smuggle in without paying duty.

So it was always shitty luggage, saturated with coffee, because the dogs couldn't smell the cocaine if there was enough coffee spread around. Was it true? Who knows, but it always worked for her.

And all the time, she was snitching for Paredes.

So yes, professionally it worked out very nicely, but personally? He tried to put off the break-up for as long as he could, but it was just too obvious. She was *loca*; as in high-octane, high-maintenance crazy. He cut the ropes. He had to. She was surprisingly relaxed about it. He had expected some big scene, but in their hearts they knew it was for the best. They still fucked occasionally but it was really business masquerading as pleas-

318

ure; a professional courtesy extended by both sides. Paredes never accepted a peso from her. Ever. But she paid him in info like no informant ever had. Prime details. She kept him up to speed in the confusing, rapidly changing universe of *los narcos*. She gave him the skinny on the insane new head of the Ciudad Real cartel. El Santo was *loco*, but he was also no moron. It was thanks to Mary-Ellen that Paredes was able to half-turn his right-hand man, El Feo.

El Feo had lost the plot. He had gone over to the dark side, making secret moves with El Chapo, with Tijuana, with El Chayo. Even with Los Zetas, for Christ's sake. Fast eyes flicker to the two-way mirror. With a crooked DEA agent named Byrd. El Feo is in way over his head. His days are numbered, but El Feo is so stupid he will never realize that.

Paredes worked El Feo hard and fast, because he knew the End Days before an execution foretold are always a time of revelation. It's like morphine to a terminal patient. It isn't the promise of The End that is the allure, but the promise of an end to pain. It is an instant of glorious appeasement; a moment of denial and euphoria. It loosens doubt and with it, mouths. The false sense of immunity that it bestows breeds complacency. Paredes wanted to suck all the info out of El Feo before he was finally taken out to the desert, before his body was lost to the dunes and the ravenous crows.

El Feo thought Paredes was a crooked cop. Why wouldn't he? There are enough of them on both sides to line the border, shoulder badge to shoulder badge. Someone set Paredes up. It wasn't Mary-Ellen. She would never ever have done it. And El Feo is too dumb. El Santo? Tijuana? Who knows? He is innocent. His lawyer will prove it.

A flicker in Paredes' eyes. Of divulgence. Focus, the eyes say. Nothing else matters but what he is about to say next. Paredes has a great lawyer. Yale. The best. Ever heard of that *Yanqui* club, Skull and Bones? That's him. Juvenile, but it works. They force you to do some secret initiation shit, but after that, you're locked into the system for good. Law partner, judge. Supreme Court. His lawyer's got leverage. Contacts everywhere. Keep him in mind. You never know, Fuentes might need him one day. His eyes harden. The interview is over. 'How did Gomez take the news?'

'Hard.'

Paredes gives a *what-the-fuck* shrug, like a non-smoker offered a cigarette before his execution. 'He'll get over it. Is the asshole still fucking my ex?' His dirty smile covers the information in his eyes. Marina is the key. 'Have him send me a photo of her. It gets lonely in here.'

Fuentes gives him a contrived look of disgust, making sure he is facing the two-way mirror so they can all see his reaction. His mother taught art at high school. He remembers her advice to her students: if you want to see a flaw in a portrait, hold your drawing up to a mirror. Fuentes gazes out at a familiar composition: two Mexicans surrounded by iron bars, being judged by hidden *gringos* who have no idea what has just gone down. His work is balanced. Coherent; its structure possesses a certain integrity. It will stand up to scrutiny. He turns to rap on the door, but the lock is already slotting open.

'What did you want from him anyway?'

'Confirmation.'

The DEA agent shakes his head, pitying Fuentes' naivety. 'He's as guilty as hell. And he'll roll for a deal.'

'What are you going to do about Byrd?'

'We've already pulled him. As soon as he mentioned Byrd, we had to yank him. They should be reading him his rights about now.'

'The car with Texas plates. It was following him.' Actually, it was following Fuentes. 'Yours?'

'That's need-to-know.' Operational code for *go fuck yourself*.

Fuentes had ridden in with the ambulance. They dropped him at the border. He thought he caught a glimpse of Byrd, in the back of an unmarked car with Texas plates, crossing the other way. Yin and Yang. Give and Take. Gloria for Mary-Ellen. Byrd for Paredes. Blood for money. For a moment he is overwhelmed with emotion. Not sorrow; regret. Paredes isn't just good. He is exceptional. He solved the case on his own. That's why he was set up. They knew he knew. Mary-Ellen was nothing more than a mere brush fire; a burning-off to prevent a major conflagration. A convenient means to a sinister end. And that end is the silencing of Paredes.

They will kill Paredes as soon as he is transferred out. No one will even think twice. A corrupt cop inside. A lucky break for any one of a hundred inmates. He knows he is dead, so he has transferred his knowledge. Paredes had not sought Fuentes out, but he recognized him as soon as he stepped into the interrogation room. A cop smart enough to have talked his way in. A seeker of truth. Maybe even an honest one.

Fuentes walks back home across a smear of stagnant water passing for a river, feeling eyes on him from both sides of the border. Shadows hover on his peripheral vision. Not those of stalkers but that of a massive, encroaching vacuum. An absence of light. Of oxygen. Of space and time. The hourglass is filling.

Whole dunes are tumbling down upon him. Suffocating him. Only the narrow neck is left. A few last gasps and then . . . Extinction. He sees the future clearly. Paredes today. Fuentes tomorrow. He can hear the whispering sands around his shoulders, hushing him, easing him gently but firmly towards the inevitable Silence.

63

Pilar

The dog that Byrd hit the night before lies swollen and stiff in the ossifying sun. A bus roars by, its blast forcing the flies milling around the corpse's eyes to break from their host for a startled instant, before regrouping and swarming back again.

Inside the bus, Pilar stands halfway up the back, addressing the female workers. This is how she and Ventura have spent the last three hours. Preaching on buses. Pilar's smart enough to know that she couldn't get a job in another *maquiladora* so quickly, and it wouldn't be any use anyway if she did. With the strike tomorrow, the time for reason is over. It is now time for emotion, for stark and violent agitation. Ventura has followed her patiently, lending quiet support. She would never admit it, but Pilar is glad to have another woman, however untested, by her side.

Especially after last night.

Most of the female workers on the bus listen blankly, but a few whisper sarcastically at the back. Pilar is used to bored or puzzled expressions but these sour faces tell her she's going to have to excel to get the reaction she wants: the glorious ability to focus on the possibilities of a better future, and not stay blinded in a crushing present.

Ventura sits in a seat across from Pilar, shooting discreetly, not really listening to what is being said, her professionalism isolating her within its own concerns of fast shots, focus and framing. '. . . So if we all stick together, they'll have to listen to us.'

A worker, whose name badge on her company tunic says *Lucía*, gives a mocking laugh of disbelief. 'I've been working here for over twenty years and let me tell you, in Ciudad Real *nobody* sticks together.'

Ventura shifts her camera towards Lucía, not because of what she's said but instinctually, because of what she feels in the air – dissent. But Lucía feels something too: unwelcome attention. She slaps with lightning speed at the camera, almost knocking it out of Ventura's hands. 'Get that out of my face, bitch!'

Ventura cries out in shock more than protest. She snaps the lens cover closed fast. 'I'm trying to help.'

Help is a concept like *hope* and *freedom*; never to be mentioned to people who've been denied it. 'Look at them.' Lucía points to Ventura, then Pilar, her hand trembling with rage. 'Who the fuck *are* these bitches?' She turns to the other passengers, who have fallen silent as a jury. 'Has anyone seen them before?' The women shake their heads, confirming what they already knew, psyching themselves up for the inevitable riposte. Pilar watches what's happening, alarmed and alert. She's attended too many meetings not to recognize these signs: the mass resentment swelling dangerously into something physical – something which demands release. Except that normally she's the instigator of such wrath – not its target. 'Why are they taking our photos? Who are they working for?'

Pilar holds her hands up in a soothing gesture that manages to hush the women. It's like a magus calming the waves. She's a professional; a master speaker adept at putting her audience at ease – or at least diverting their seething resentment to a target of her choice. 'Please, *amigas*, there's nothing wrong. We're just—'

'Who are you?' Lucía roars. 'Police? Company spies?' Most of the passengers are standing, already screaming insults at Pilar and Ventura, or shouting to each other, trying to figure out *what the hell is going on*. The bus driver turns impatiently, telling the *chicas* to shut up, but no one pays him any mind. They're riveted on their twin targets. On their hate. 'This is the way those bastards work. Taking our photos and then firing us.'

'*Amigas*, please, stay calm.'

'And let you steal our jobs? You lying bitch!'

A dark wave explodes inside the bus, hands striking Pilar; cruel fingers damaged by factory work tugging at her hair. Two women try to wrench Ventura's Leica from her hands. She bends down, gathering it to her body, guarding it like a parent sheltering a child, fists hammering hard on her back, nails scratching at her face, searching for her eyes.

The bus brakes hard, some of the women falling to the floor with the sudden lurch, the driver standing in his seat. 'Listen to me! We don't move again until you stop this fucking scene.'

Eyes turn and stare at him, unnerving him with their intensity; their fury at yet another man in uniform threatening them. Lucía's voice is a sharp stick, prodding for weaknesses. 'Don't talk that way to us, *cabrón*, or we'll cut your fucking balls off.' Both menace and fear fume in the uneasy silence that follows. She points to Pilar. 'Get these bitches off the bus before I kill them.' Hands grab Ventura, hauling her to her feet, still trying to yank the camera from her. She defends it, her hunched body tugged down the aisle by her hair. Someone lands a hard kick against her ass as she passes, jeers and insults raining like spit upon her as she endures the gauntlet, each bus seat another Station of the Cross.

Pilar tries to shelter her from the blows. Someone swings

a plastic bag at her head, the can of drink inside striking fast and hard above her ear. There is the eruption of skin, the fast-traveling stain of blood, shoes kicking her on her way. The bus driver watches, the false smile on his face masking his growing concern for his own safety, the chaos making the vehicle shudder. He opens the front door and Pilar and Ventura are pushed out, landing on their hands and knees. The whole bus cheers. And then the door snaps shut.

The driver turns to address the women, but he doesn't exist; the women are all jeering through the windows at the figures of Pilar and Ventura still on the ground, as though trying to hide inside the cloud of dust they've raised. He sits down fast and pulls away, not daring to even glance in his rearview mirror, the women cheering as they leave Pilar and Ventura behind on the side of the road.

Ventura helps Pilar to her feet. Blood pulses through her hair. Pilar watches with both despair and anger as the bus draws away, folding itself into a plume of diesel fumes. She turns to Ventura, who is shooting the bus as it abandons them. 'It's all your fault!'

Ventura slowly lowers her camera, amazed. 'Pilar . . . It's nobody's fault.'

'Bullshit! Taking photos right in front of their faces. Like they're animals in a zoo.'

'It wasn't like that.'

'What were you thinking?'

'I was just trying to help.'

'Help? Don't you understand?' Her voice rises into an anguished cry. 'No one can help us. No one even *wants* to help us. We're way beyond help but you're too fucking stupid to see it.' The sob rips through her body, forcing its way out against Pilar's effort to swallow it. Ventura touches her, and Pilar pulls away fast. 'Why do I even bother? I must be as stupid as you.' She starts walking back towards the city center, leaving a soft trail of blood after her. 'Where are you going?' Ventura calls out. Pilar stops and turns. 'It's over,' she says.

'For those women, maybe. But there are thousands of others. That's what you said. That's what you've been saying all along.' She hails a passing bus. It roars past, blasting them with grit.

'What do you think you're doing?'

'I'm going to finish the job we started.' Ventura steps out onto the road and tries to flag a car down. It accelerates, using its horn as though it were a club as it rushes past, only just missing her. Pilar wheels on Ventura, her hand pressing against her temple, shouting above the furious noise of the traffic.

'Don't be stupid!'

'If you can do it, so can I.'

'You're nothing like me.'

'I know. I don't give up.'

Pilar goes to strike her, but controls herself. 'You're pathetic.'

'And you're not?' She holds up her camera. 'At least I can do my job.'

Pilar opens her mouth to respond, but then just shakes her head and starts walking back towards town. Ventura watches her go, anger creasing her face. She runs after Pilar, shouting over the traffic.

'What makes you think you're better than me?'

'Shut up.'

'My job is the most important one there is.'

'Selling beauty products in magazines? Making women look

good enough for poor bored men to fuck? Very important.'

'My job is telling people what's really happening,' Ventura says, running in front of Pilar and blocking her way. 'Giving them the truth.'

Pilar waves futilely at the buses roaring past. 'What *truth*? That workers are getting screwed? You think that's news? Who needs someone to tell them what every single worker knows? People care about the food on their table and the education of their children and the health of their parents. No one gives a fuck about abstracts like *truth*.'

'I do, and I'm not the only one. There are millions like me.'

'Millions like you who don't work in the *maquiladoras*, who live in gated communities with cars instead of buses, and maids and nannies instead of bosses. But there are tens of millions, hundreds of millions like us, who do the shit work because we have no choice and who pay for your private schools and vacations and dental work.'

'I'm not like that.'

'It doesn't matter – you *act* like you are! And you attract attention – look at Mayor, he can barely keep it in when you're around.'

Ventura grabs Pilar's arm. 'The people you want to help just tried to kill us.'

'Because they're poor and afraid.'

'Because they're ignorant.' She lets go of Pilar. 'If they had the facts; if they knew what was really happening to this country...'

'And an amateur like you is going to enlighten them? It's laughable.'

Ventura's voice rises above the shriek of vehicles. 'I'm going to tell this story, whether they want to hear it or not.'

Pilar looks at her, at the way her whole body is trembling, poised for fight, poised to defend her camera. Her work. Her values. She sees something she's never seen before in Ventura; something that astonishes her.

She sees herself.

Pilar has never lived a life of moderation or restraint. Her fury deflates as fast as it rose. She feels the shame of her anger. 'It's okay.' She moves towards her but Ventura steps back towards the road, speaking with a trembling voice. 'I'm going to tell them. You'll see!'

Pilar takes her wrists and pulls Ventura slowly away from the road. 'Then don't say it, do it.'

Just then a car horn sounds, loud and close. The two women turn, startled. A white pickup has stopped in one of the lanes going back to town. The driver leans out of his window with a gap-toothed, happy smirk. 'Hey, sweethearts, you need a ride?'

Pilar glares at him, then shakes her head.

A bearded man in the passenger seat cranes forwards. 'We'll even let you suck our dicks.'

Ventura whirls on him, brushing hair from her eyes. 'If you need it so bad, why don't you keep it simple and suck each other?' Both women burst into laughter. The leers of the two men vanish, unveiling what was on their faces all the time: violence. The driver points his hand at them like it's a gun. 'You're already dead.' The truck accelerates with a screech, nearly hitting a motorcycle as it pulls out into the traffic, does a U-turn and speeds away. It turns off into a gas station two hundred meters down the road.

They wait until they see the men going round to a garage at the back. And then they both start running.

64

Ventura

Ventura stands behind a payphone. In the far distance she can still see the gas station. Pilar hangs up. 'He'll be here in fifteen minutes.' She points across the road to a little church. 'It'll be safer to wait over there.'

The interior of the church is dim even when the daylight follows them inside. Ventura quickly closes the door behind them, then glances around the internal gloom. Behind the altar, a flickering fluorescent light forms half a crucifix. The horizontal tube is dead. A framed reproduction of *La Tilma* is displayed in a modest side chapel watched over by a brace of small votive candles. Mainly stubs; all long extinguished. Ventura lights them, one by one, watching their reflection flickering on the dusty glass protecting the portrait of the Virgin, like stars in a veiled sky, not radiant but straining to be seen; hovering rather than glowing. Her camera whispers inside the church, a gentle, reassuring murmur of approval.

Pilar sits in a single column of sunlight on the edge of a confessional box, on the ledge where people normally kneel, smoking a cigarette. The thought is absurd to Ventura, but she can't help thinking it even though she would never say it aloud: You shouldn't be smoking here. Only where is *here* – a bleak and lonely place with dead leaves and plastic bags gathered against the base of the altar railing, blown in by the rush of cars or a sudden storm and then left to slowly decompose out of sight, like a retirement home at the edge of a village. *Here* could be just another embarrassed failure of belief; a monument to superstition, manipulation and the fear that ignorance always engenders. Or *here* could be a refuge – both spiritual and, in their particular case right now, physical – that gives up its mysteries to the faithful who have the courage or simplicity to seek them. Ventura can't be sure, but she feels the puzzling duality of *here* is on display right at this very moment. *Here* for her is *there* for Pilar, and vice versa. 'Do you ever go to church?' she asks.

'Not since my mother's funeral. And you?'

'Only at Easter and Christmas, although not for the last few years. Sometimes, I stop at the cathedral and watch the people praying and take their photos.'

'Do you pray, or just watch?'

Ventura caps her camera and sits in a pew in front of Pilar, her legs joining the sunshine. 'I sort of pray . . . sometimes. I try to remember to say thank you for what I have, but I always end up asking for something. How about you?'

'I prayed when my mother was dying of cancer. When she died, I stopped.'

'Do you miss it?'

Pilar laughs and offers a cigarette to Ventura. Her inner voice says *don't* but she takes it anyway, only noticing then how badly her hand is grazed. It must have been from when they pushed her out the door, and she fell protecting her camera, not herself. The match flares, creating a nimbus around the shadow of Pilar's head, and then it's gone, the silhouette too. Ventura holds the cigarette towards the door, but the smoke snakes like incense back into the church.

Pilar pulls a leaf of tobacco from her tongue, contemplating whether to share an intimacy with someone who is, after all, a stranger to her world, but perhaps the proximity to the confessional works its dark guilt-magic. 'When I was in Tijuana, we did a lot of work supporting people with AIDS. Junkies. Sex workers, both male and female. They prayed too. Most of them died.'

'You're saying everything's hopeless?'

'I'm saying I don't expect God to do my work for me. I'm saying it's more important to get NRTIs to patients and condoms to schoolgirls and needle exchange programs started than it is to spend hours in anguish in front of fucking candles.'

'I understand that. But what I was asking was do you believe in God?'

Pilar gives a short bitter laugh, gazing at the smoke from their cigarettes, wafting through the single beam of sunlight. 'How many women called out to God to save them when they were being kidnapped – when they were being raped and tortured? All of them. And how many did he answer? Not one of them. If that's God, then why believe in him – and it has to be a *him*, because a *her* would never have stood by and done nothing.'

'My mother died when I was eleven. The only thing that kept me going was the belief that she was watching over me in heaven, sitting by my bed while I slept.'

'It's nice for children to have such things. Children need reassurance.'

'Of course, but the thing is, I still have that feeling. It stays with you, even as you grow older, even as you learn about life and let go of all the other childhood beliefs. It's like an inoculation against fear of death. If I didn't have that sense of an afterlife, I don't know how I could go on. It's that powerful.'

'You don't realize it, but you're exaggerating your dependence. You'd be able to go on without it. You're like me, you're lucky – you love your work. You don't need to pray. That's why all the women in the *maquiladora* pray to the Virgin – because their work is killing them. Faith is the only thing left for them: the promise of a happy future – in a happy afterlife.'

'But if you don't believe in God—'

'If you don't believe in God, there are only two ways in which to conduct your life. The first is to enjoy yourself as much as you can – fucking, drinking, dancing! – without regard to the rules and constraints of society. Of course seeking pleasure solely for oneself is socially irresponsible. If you carry such selfish desires to their logical conclusion, it means having no regard for anyone else; seizing pleasure at the expense of others, whether they want to give it to you or not. The murders are the ultimate outcome of this way of thinking: *I demand pleasure and I will take it if you don't give it to me* becomes *the only pleasure I have left is harming others as I take it . . .*' Pilar sucks on her cigarette then sends it spiraling out onto the porch. 'Most people are selfish, but luckily for us, most are not natural psychopaths.'

'And the second way?'

'The second way evolves out of the first, when you're tired of servicing your own pleasure; when you're looking for something more than your own ego. It's when you decide you have to try to make the world a better place, because there's no God to do it for you.'

They hear it at the same time: a car pulling up outside. 'He's early,' Ventura says.

Pilar is already on her feet. 'If it's him . . .' She looks around, then snatches a large prepared candle of *La Santísima Muerte* that's propped against the wall, and holds it like a weapon. A card slips from the top: *el corazón*. She motions with her eyes for Ventura to go over to the shadows on the other side of the porch entrance.

The door swings inwards, blinding Pilar with sunlight. One hand goes up to her eyes, the other raised to strike. The door flaps shut, slowly concertinaing the dazzle of daylight. 'Bless me, sisters, for I have sinned.'

Pilar lowers the candle with relief. '*Cabrón!* . . . What took you so long?'

'Please don't overwhelm me with your thanks, it makes me sentimental.' Juan Antonio turns back to the door, holding it open for Pilar, letting traffic noise in. 'Where's the girl?'

'Ventura? It's safe.'

Ventura steps out of the shadows and follows Pilar out, the door banging slowly, listlessly to a halt, like a spring rainfall ending before it even began, robbing the church of sunlight, leaving only the hesitant flicker of candles, and the rustle of something behind the altar.

65

Padre Márcio

Joaquín Lázaro Morales didn't disappear; he didn't just run away and vanish. That implies something which is there and then is removed. This was not just nullification, it was more an evanescence, a cessation of existence, both future and past. It wasn't *gone for good*. It was *never there in the first place*.

His son, Amado Lázaro Mendez, showed up one day, picking up the conversation where his father had left off the last time. And that was it. As a manifestation of the transition of authority, it was comprehensive and terrifying. Padre Márcio realized then the enormous forces he was up against. It wasn't so much evil power or even absolute power; it was the only force that truly exists, for it annihilates everything else – the *brujo's* ultimate intent: sovereignty over reality.

In the first years of his reign, he and Amado laundered billions. When first Nugan Hand and then BCCI collapsed, they created alternative laundering routes by funneling cash into a host of small *casas de cambio*, then wiring the money overseas in confusing loops to accounts across Europe, via respectable institutions. They used the US branch of the Order to continue to launder money via high-end property purchases. They 'borrowed' money from the Vatican Bank at will, playing on the goodwill and naivety of the increasingly infirm Polish pope. Padre Márcio calculated that if his fraud continued at the current rate, the Vatican would be completely bankrupt by 2019.

Then one day Amado drove him to a ranch outside of Ciudad Real, close to the border.

They were unaccompanied and a sense of dread descended as Amado turned off the road and followed a dry river bed. The isolation felt immense, as though the landscape had swallowed all life; dispensing with any need for movement, let alone humanity. They passed a crumpled rock buttress, like a staircase rising up to a ruined pulpit from which a sermon had been delivered to the damned before it had been struck by lightning. A Rottweiler prowled the other end of a perimeter fence, rapping its snout in a rhythmic display of aggression.

'Why have you brought me here?'

'To see the future . . .'

The ambiguous response would prove to be typical of the enigmatic nature of Amado, but he didn't know that then; it was as if he were being led to his execution. So he felt a large degree of relief, tempered somewhat by shock, when he saw a prisoner tied to a chair in the center of the kitchen, his bare feet stained with blood. There but for the grace of God . . . except it was by the grace of Amado that Padre Márcio was standing and the prisoner was sitting in a puddle of his own piss and blood.

He was still alive, although that was not immediately obvious to Padre Márcio. Amado explained that the captive was an American citizen, a former agent of the Central Intelligence Agency of the United States, who had become aware of Padre Márcio's dealings with several banks under the direct control of the agency. He had foolishly threatened blackmail. Fortunately, Amado had quelled his initial impulse to murder him, and subjected him to sustained interrogation with interesting results.

The American spoke of a cash reserve of $16 billion that

covert US operatives had assembled via drug smuggling, kidnapping, extortion, people smuggling and illegal arms sales in Central America and the Middle East. The money had been destined to fund the Contras as well as death squad operations in both Central and South America, but had been siphoned off by three associates of the American, Roberto D'Aubuisson, Pablo Escobar and Manuel Noriega. The cash was spread across at least 117 different locations. Amado had already seized funds from two of the locales.

Silence ruled the room. Padre Márcio and Joaquín had been partners for many years – but partners *after* the fact. Now Amado had done something his father never had; shared intimate knowledge of one of his illegal operations prior to committing the act. It made Padre Márcio an accessory.

More importantly, it made him an equal.

After what seemed like an eternity of introspective contemplation, Amado finally spoke. 'Times are changing. New rivals are appearing. There is a war coming, the consequences of which we cannot know. This is why I want to keep this windfall separate from our other operations. We need to retain this as hard cash.'

'We could smuggle it into the United States, launder it through the Order as charitable donations. Protect it from the IRS.'

Amado smiled, and he was saturated with relief. Up until that moment, he hadn't been sure he would be walking out of the ranch house. 'How would you get it out of the country?'

Padre Márcio had no idea. He wasn't a smuggler. Anything he suggested would reveal him as an amateur; even expose him as a liability. Amado had set a trap, and his vanity had led him into it. He could feel the trigger mechanism under his foot, hovering in its eagerness to snap shut. And then an otherworldly voice, as though from the grave, slurred its way across the hot kitchen air. 'Shit, if I have to sit here until you two come up with the only logical solution, the least you could do is pour me a drink.' The American spat a voluminous mix of saliva and blood. Something sat atop the squall of sputum, before slowly sinking from sight: a tooth. He slowly raised his face, staring at Padre Márcio through the eye which wasn't swollen shut. 'Hollis Earl Jeetton. But you can call me Tex.'

66

Fuentes

Not snuff films, not a black mass, but a forced initiation ritual. Ultimate blackmail. And somehow, Marina – Paredes' one-time lover, now with his ex-partner – holds the key . . .

Fuentes pulls up outside a row of cinder block buildings with barred windows. He gets out, dogs sentrying the evening with their sad, futile howls. He pauses, looking up and down the street; his second illegal entry in three days. But he doesn't feel like a criminal.

He feels like a target.

He goes up to the front door and listens. There's pleasant laughter from the neighboring house. The sound surprises him, almost as though it has no right to be there. People start singing 'Happy Birthday'.

It's a cheap pin tumbler with a protruding cylinder. He places the head in a vice grip, waits for the applause at the end of the song, then twists and pulls. A credit card takes care of the latch. The door slips open. Fuentes is inside. He closes the drapes, crosses the living room to the kitchen, then hits a switch, fluorescent tubes stuttering in confusion, disturbed by the un-expected intrusion. He begins checking all the likely hiding places, starting with the cupboard under the sink. Cockroaches scuttle in panic. Pots, pans, cleaning products. Dregs from a sad domestic life in need of cleaning or, better yet, simply tossing.

He enters the bathroom, a naked lightbulb glaring down at

him. Eyes glide across surfaces. Fuentes almost misses the fresh mastic on the access hatch around the bathtub. The rest of the tiles are sealed with a grouting gone gray with mildew. He gets a knife from the kitchen drawer and sets to work, peeling away at the secret.

It's surprising how few real hiding places there are in the average home. The back of furniture. The rims of high shelves. The underside of drawers and the interiors of curtain rods. Puny treasure is carefully concealed behind heating grilles or skirting boards; locked away inside the mechanical mysteries of air-conditioning units. Or simply shoved under mattresses. But for highly illegal articles – firearms, narcotics, vacuum-sealed wads of cash – plumbing is always the hiding place of choice. The proximity to sewers and drains; to murky, stagnant water, and the steady drip of guilt, anxiety and greed.

He jiggles the hatch open. The stink of mold and grit of rust. The dark stain of corrosion and the grave. He wraps a dirty towel around his hand, grabs the light cord and gently tugs in the direction of the wall switch. There is mild resistance, then the rip of rotten plaster, the electrical cord unzipping the ceiling, creating a trail of dust as it frees itself, running down the wall and halting at the bank of tiles. It gives him more than enough length to peer inside the hatch. Lining the dead space between tiles and tub are two shoeboxes, taped shut and sealed inside heavy plastic.

He pulls them out, stacks them on top of the washing machine and is just about to slit through the wrap when a woman's loud moan makes him jump. He hasn't even checked the bedroom yet. He spins in the direction of the sound, the knife raised defensively. Nothing. Then another, longer moan – not from the bedroom as he first thought, but from behind the bathroom. The other neighboring house.

He listens intently, and then he hears the rhythmic creak of a bed tapping insistently against the wall; a Morse code message of hard, fast fucking. Birthday celebrations on one side, sex on the other. And Fuentes stuck in the middle in a damp-fudged room. He slices open one of the shoeboxes and peels back the plastic skin to reveal stacks of photos.

He holds the light cord over the contents . . .

Fuentes curses and slams the lid back on the box, as though there were a scorpion inside, dropping the light. He hears it shatter against the washing machine. It takes a while to register that he's in the dark. He stands there, trying to control his breathing. In the distance, the sound of automatic gunfire rattles the night. From the direction, it sounds like it's coming from Chatarrita. That's where the heroin is sold. That's where you find the crack and meth houses full of blistered lips and vacant eyes; lice infestations and human shit in dark corners. AIDS, HB, HC and ODs. Daylight stabbings and nighttime shootouts. Chatarrita is a barrio where hope and junkies are treated as equals: both placed on a butcher's block and pounded to a red and stringy pulp.

The talk about the War on Drugs is always from the American perspective. But the problem is more domestic than anyone wants to admit, especially the local authorities. In the old days, Mexican black tar was strictly for export. There are now five times as many heroin addicts in Mexico than there were only ten years ago. The same with crack; with crystal meth. Lives are being ruined, families destroyed, neighborhoods marginalized, politicians criminalized, police neutralized. Cities are falling to the inexorable logic of addiction. Democracy is becoming narcocracy. Violent crime has gone through the roof; set fire to houses, turned towns to ash. What has happened to Chatarrita is already spreading to the rest of Ciudad Real. Left unchecked, it will eventually engulf the whole nation. Cortés destroyed an entire civilization once, just for gold. And it's happening again. Only no one dares admit it. It is a form of collective narcolepsy; a communal denial in the face of a single brutal truth: the country has been sold wholesale to the *narcos*, and as long as they get a lick of the salt block of profit, no one in power really gives a fuck.

He stands there, in the darkness, amongst the shards of the broken light, listening to the hammering of the bed climaxing, then slowly falling away into silence. He picks up the two filthy shoeboxes and walks out of Marina's home, not even thinking as he slams the door behind him.

67

El Santo

The Heartbreak Hotel had gone up in the early 1970s as an ode to optimism and a sly wink to Vegas. It was the International without Elvis, the Sands without the crap tables. It was the place where government fat cats and porker businessmen took their mistresses for a steamy afternoon that sometimes got out of hand. That's how it picked up its nickname: the Heart Attack Hotel.

But after the December peso crisis of 1994, it became a lot harder to lay off an afternoon tryst as a business expense or claim it back as petty cash, and no one wanted to spend money on what they could get in an empty evening office or the back of a car. Vacancies grew. Maintenance slid. Paint peeled and concrete cracked. Five stars became two. Now the Heart Attack Hotel is the venue of choice for budget wedding banquets. Afternoon bingo and a bridge club take turns sitting in the oversized ballroom. Indoor plants wilt, surviving on the charity of ice cubes from guests' glasses emptied amongst cigarette butts and pistachio shells. The whole joint has the disorientated look of a grandma who has managed to do the makeup on only one eye before slipping out the door to go wandering. You still kind of love the place, but it breaks your heart enough to make it easier to stop thinking about it all together. Whatever you once imagined Mexico could be, this is what it has become.

Sad.

So it makes perfect sense for El Feo's cheap-ass family to book the Heartbreak, and on a midweek discount too. El Feo and his brother, Curro, are famous for being penny-pinching with their families but lavish on their own needs. Hookers, drugs, flashy clothes and jewelry. Cars. Donations to the Church. El Feo and Curro figure they're worth it. But their kids go to local schools, their wives work in the supermarket and a big night out is a family dinner at TGI Friday's.

El Feo's brother breaks protocol and rings El Santo himself. 'You know you're not supposed to call.'

Curro hums and haws like a priest at a baptism waiting for his envelope. 'It's just Teo's not answering his goddamn phone.' Teodoro to Teo to El Feo. Not a stretch. 'He promised he'd split everything fifty–fifty and now I'm liable to get stuck with the bill.'

All unhappy families are the same – it's always about money. 'I wasn't supposed to tell you this, but El Feo is in Tijuana,' El Santo says, 'risking his neck so his jerk-off brother can afford to puff out some fucking candles.'

Long pause. Curro has noted the tone of reprimand. He knows that El Santo considers him a shitty little cheapskate, but he can't help himself, because that's exactly what he is. 'Still . . . it's a lot of money to put out on your own.'

'Tell you what: I'll go halves with you.' Sullen silence. Curro's been around this block before. The boss makes a promise, but then the boss doesn't deliver.

Question: Who's going to call the boss out?

Answer: Are you for fucking real?

So when Curro sees El Santo coming through the hotel doors for the party, he's servile but surly. Acting all sad and put-upon, like a slum landlord who has to turn on the water to put out a fire. If there's one thing a *narco* can't stand, it's having to pay for something not connected to his dick or his nose. 'Just got a call from your brother. He'll be back before ten.' Curro cracks a smile not of joy but relief. 'Now where's the Noche Buena?'

Curro's forehead furrows in fear. 'Seeing as it's May and . . .' His voice fades away, undone by his puny excuse. El Santo grabs him by the lapels, pulls him in close. 'I'm going to tell you something that I never want you to forget. Christmas comes but once a year. So once a year you stock up on Noche Buena. It's easy. When you see the nativity scenes and *las posadas* and the *piñatas* and the fucking poinsettia growing out of everyone's ears, that's when you know it's time to stock up. Now is that simple enough for a moron like you?' Curro nods nervously, like a bobblehead dog in the back of a pickup.

Why did El Santo even bother? Curro's not going to make it through this evening, let alone next Christmas. But the irritation of his short conversation with Curro makes El Santo feel better about what is going to happen next. When you're going to kill someone, it's important to believe that they deserve it.

He looks at his watch. Five minutes and counting. He crosses the crowded dance floor, avoiding the entreaties of the men who are all trying to push their wives and mothers into his arms and force them to dance with the boss.

Thanks but no thanks.

A roar goes up from all the dancers and for a crazy instant he thinks it's already begun. But it's just some second-rate singer starting up a new song, a *narcocorrido* about El Feo and Curro, for Christ's sake, *los hermanos chingones*. Bad-ass brothers? More *fat-ass* brothers. He's running a temperature, it's so hot

345

around the dance floor and the Heart Attack Hotel sold its air-conditioning units for scrap years ago. He was expecting maybe twenty guests, but there's more than one hundred. El Santo had no idea El Feo and Curro knew so many people, but then again, it's hard to say no to free food, music and an open bar. Not to mention the coke and the strippers that will turn up once they finally get rid of the women and children.

He steps off to the side of the band, crappy music blaring then fading, the world going dim after crossing the spotlights. El Santo takes a seat away from the windows in the shadows, his shirt wet from sweat, the stitches itching and burning at the same time. He can barely touch the area around his wound. It's bright red and slightly puffy. He doesn't like the look of it. Let's face it, Life on its own is just one colossal fuck-up after another, but Life plus this kind of Pain? May as well put a gun to your own head. The only thing that keeps him going is knowing he's going to feel better soon. And he isn't just thinking of the stitches coming out. Vengeance always puts a spring in his step.

Some fucking old man with a vaguely familiar face shambles towards him, his pants hanging around his hips like Cantinflas on a bad day. El Santo waves him away with a bank note. 'Go buy yourself a belt.' The old goat gets the picture – he gives him a *mentada* as he shuffles over to the bar. Up yours too, Pops – chances are he just saved what's left of his miserable old life.

El Santo looks at his watch. Two minutes. He slots in earplugs and slips on a pair of polycarbonate glasses. The whole joint goes dark. Then he takes out a Glock 17 with a taped grip, and racks the slide with only one hand the way Oviedo taught him, pulling his elbow backwards with a harsh, sudden tug, keeping his arm parallel to the ground, then thrusting it forwards as fast as he can. Fuck! He feels more than a reload, he feels something like a rip. That was a big fucking mistake. He checks his bandage under the shirt. No bleeding – yet. He glances up, his glasses nearly flying off in shock. The fucking clown has already appeared. Either his watch is slow or the clown's early. He may be wearing an Omega but the clown's wearing a crazy red leer; and it seems to be telling everyone: *time's up*.

The clown goes over to the singer and gestures to take the microphone. The singer likes the sound of his own voice too much to comply. The clown slaps him hard across the face and tugs the mike from the singer's hand. The music wavers as two or three of the musicians down their instruments, wondering if this is part of the show or if they shouldn't just kick this clown's ass. If any of the guests notice, it doesn't stop them from dancing. There's the screech of feedback and then the clown's shouting: '*¡Ahora! Venga, venga, venga!*'

And all hell breaks loose.

First thing El Santo notices is that the crew are all wearing plastic Hulk masks. They look like a gang of fucking Martians. And they're suited up in ballistic vests, which is kind of unfair because the only protection he's wearing is a fucking bandage over a gunshot wound. He can tell which one is Oviedo – he's dressed like the Terminator, in black leather jacket and biker's boots. All that's missing are the red rays shooting from his eyes.

He thought he had picked a place out of the line of fire. He thought wrong. Nowhere is out of the line of fire. Even with the earplugs the barrage is insufferable, like one continuous howl of death. Glass and shit goes flying everywhere; plumes of muzzle flash burst across the room in meteorite storms of fire. His glasses don't seem to filter the bursts of light; instead

347

they magnify them, disorientating him – like he's driving into oncoming traffic on a wet, dark night with broken windshield wipers. Then he realizes he's breathing so hard, he's fogging up his own lenses. He's hyper-fucking-ventilating. The gunfire increases in tempo, if that were possible, rising in register to an ecstatic death wail, salvo upon seething salvo. Relentless. Implacable; the air going misty with heat haze and splatter spray.

This must be what it's like in war, when you're galloping your horse at the assembled armies of Emperor Maximilian or Porfirio Díaz; your heart beating as fast as your mount's hooves, and the bullets raining down on you from a hot lead sky.

Detonations. Destruction. Shattering mirrors; the floor vibrating and the ceiling weeping plaster tuff for tears.

Upturned tables.

Collapsing fucking walls.

Bottles dancing then exploding in relief. The sluicing ignition of tracer trails combusts all the oxygen in the room, leaving a choking, impossible panic. There's screaming, hollering; the yowl of orphaned children. The thud and whack of wood taking multiple hits. All hell breaking loose again. Not just shock and awe. This is profligate. This is scandalous. *Total y chingadamente loco y tonto*. And an unlikely thought occurs to him; one that would normally never occur to a man like El Santo, whose nature is not given to such self-reflection: *Have I gone too far?*

The unrelenting gunfire hammers home the answer: *Fucking A, I have.*

A ringing, shocking sound whips through the room, making him want to heave from its force. It's like he's never heard it before in his life: silence.

He takes off the glasses, everything sliding into sharper, sur-

348

real focus as he looks around the combat zone. Waiters lying dead, their white shirts red. Barmen slumped over counters. Musicians over bullet-scarred instruments. Wives and mothers and children toppled over fallen chairs and collapsed tables. The dance floor sheened into a red-gloss mirror. It is unspeakable. It is impossible. It was never supposed to be *this* bad.

Carnage writ large.

A fucking bloodbath.

The worst part? It isn't even over yet.

What the fuck was he thinking?

A panic rises inside him, fusing fast with anger. This is all because of that asshole, El Feo. The clown strides through the mayhem, a ball-head hammer in his hand, like a slaughterer at an abattoir, smashing the skulls of the wounded. El Santo raises his firearm. The clown jumps in the air with the force of the shots then falls backwards, knocking over the last standing drum on the stage: a classic comic pratfall; a showman to the end.

Oviedo marches up to El Santo and says something. El Santo rips out his earplugs. 'What?'

'We better get you the hell out of here, boss.' He takes El Santo's arm and leads him through the debris; the mayhem. The massacre. Some of his *sicarios* are already emptying jerrycans of gasoline. He looks back one last time, and then thank Christ he's outside, and it's like he's fallen into a swimming pool. The smash splash of reality. He's awake. Compos mentis again. He gets in the passenger seat, listening for sirens. There aren't any.

'Ninety percent success,' Oviedo says.

'Why ninety?'

'You were there. People saw you. Someone tried to kill you.

That's your alibi. Everyone will blame this on Tijuana. On Los Toltecas. All of El Feo's people are dead. All of them. Plus you killed the death clown. You're a hero.'

'So why only ninety?'

As if in answer to his question there is a low detonation, and a fireball rolls through the broken windows, flushing his face with heat. Oviedo steps on the gas. 'Casualties look set to be excessive, even for us.'

El Santo glances back. The fire's raging through the lobby, just behind the last of his men who rush out of the Heartbreak, laughing hysterically; one step ahead of exploding glass. On the floors above, people are leaning out of windows, screaming for help. El Santo swears, then turns to Oviedo.

'What do we do now?'

'I'll tell you what we do, boss. We escalate. We make this look like a church picnic. We make them forget this ever happened. They won't even bother looking for us after tomorrow.'

Smoke cyclones from the hotel's roof. In the distance he can hear the first sirens finally approaching. 'How the fuck could we ever do that?'

'Simple. Today there were at least fifty fatalities. Eighty or ninety tops. Tomorrow, we make it hundreds. Why not even a thousand?'

The thing about Oviedo is the way he speaks. His flat monotone makes him sound reasonable. Knowledgeable. Totally reassuring. But the more El Santo thinks about it, the more he realizes that most of what Oviedo says is totally fucking insane. Maybe it's time to terminate him before his advice gets them all terminated. 'It doesn't make sense.'

'It does if we blame today on Los Toltecas and tomorrow on

Los Zetas. We make it look like it's all-out war between Tijuana and Juárez, and poor fucking Ciudad Real is stuck in the middle, just a battlefield, not a player; you know, like Belgium.'

Belgium?

'So the government is forced to go after Los Toltecas and Los Zetas and leaves us the fuck alone.'

El Santo's beginning to get it. 'And so Tijuana blames Juárez...'

'And Juárez blames Tijuana... And they all kill each other, and that includes El Chapo and El Lazca, and we get to pick up the pieces at the end.'

For a lunatic idea, it is kind of brilliant. 'What do you have in mind?'

'There's going to be a big strike tomorrow with a march and a funeral and the whole box and dice. They're bringing in professional agitators by the busload. It'll be easy as hell to infiltrate.'

El Santo turns in his car seat, the twist at the waist making his wound throb. Behind him everything's going black from the smoke. A burst of noise and light shoots past them, the first of the fire engines arriving. He wonders if their ladders are high enough to reach the top-floor windows. 'I don't know...'

'Leave it to me, boss. I'll handle everything.' A phone rings. Oviedo answers it super-fast, then hangs up, military crisp, ambulances roaring past. 'They've just put El Feo up on the overpass,' he says. 'The *narcomanta* claims it on behalf of Los Toltecas.' He turns and stares at El Santo with an intense, sundering stare, profoundly familiar, like a dream about prehistoric times when you recognize your ancestors. Sometimes Oviedo feels too good to be true and sometimes he gives you the creeps. This is one of the latter times. He turns away, staring back at the road. 'Besides, it will distract attention.'

'From the Heartbreak?'

Oviedo turns and stares at him, and damn it, the intensity of his gaze sends a shiver down El Santo's spine. 'From you killing that doctor. It's all over the internet . . .' He nods down at El Santo's wound. 'You're bleeding, boss.'

El Santo touches his side. It smarts like hell. He looks at his fingers, all covered in blood.

IV

Los Caminos de la Vida

DAY 4

The Burial of Isabel Torres

68

Fuentes

Fuentes works at his kitchen table, the shoeboxes on chairs beside him, their plastic ripped away and heaped upon the floor. He hadn't wanted to bring the photos back to his own house. It wasn't just because it was reckless. He can feel their contamination seeping into his home. Spores of evil and cruelty settling within the folds of curtains, thickening the grime inside drain pipes, saturating his clothes. His life is already infected by unimaginable horror. He doesn't need more.

He doesn't need *this*.

But it is the only way to end it.

The phone rings again. He takes it off the hook. If anyone came through the door right now, they wouldn't even have to set him up. He would have incriminated himself just by being in possession of such evidence. How could he explain it? He doesn't even know how Paredes came across the photos in the first place. But he knows why Paredes hid them. The photos would never be secure at the police station. Someone would be bound to find them, no matter how well they were concealed. Then they'd be impounded, and locked away in a place where they'd be sure to meet with an accident. An electrical fire, or water damage from a mysterious leak. Simple, elemental solutions were always the first response to potentially lethal evidence.

He finishes covering the table, the shriek of plastic wrap tearing across metal teeth the only sound disturbing the silence apart from the regular tambour of a leaking tap. When he's done, he covers it with a plastic sheet, taping the edges under the bottom of the table. Pulling on a pair of latex gloves, he carefully unpacks the photos, handling them by the edges only. Some are in black and white, most in color. Many of them are Polaroids.

He hasn't worked up the courage to separate them into categories, let alone examine them.

All he's doing right now is counting them.

Isabel Torres was victim 873. Mary-Ellen González had been victim 874 and was still officially Jane Doe 352. Gloria Delgado was victim 875 – and the first known survivor of an attack. Those numbers attached to their files weren't abstracts or mathematical theories, but they weren't solid physical realities either. They were something else entirely – a numerical challenge, because how do you count a loss? They weren't aggregates, they were massive absences; stars inexplicably extinguished in a sky already veiling over with clouds. The immensity of the loss would only become apparent when the heavens finally cleared again. And when would that be?

He finished the count. Nine hundred and eighty-nine. More than they were aware of. Or possibly there were some repeat photos. He still couldn't bring himself to confront the images. But he was aware of what a colossal undertaking it would be. They'd have to cross-reference every photo against every known victim. That way they might be able to establish a chronological order. They would have to pay particular attention to correlating the Jane Does. An item of jewelry or clothing might be the key to a name. Then they'd have to cross-catalogue the photos according to any details apparent in the background. How many different crime scenes could they establish? Would any clues emerge that could point to actual locations – a specialized object or item of furniture linked to a specific profession; a glimpse of a landmark through a window?

And there was the actual forensic value of the photos. Fingerprints. DNA. Hair or fabric traces. Blood, saliva. Sperm. It would be months of work, and the only person he thought he could trust enough to share it with was Gomez. But no one else seemed to trust Gomez.

Could he?

There was one alternative. He could take it all across the border. Put his faith in their superior forensics. Their police forces. Their FBI.

Sell his own country out.

It could get him fast results. Or he could simply be giving the *gringos* an easy way to extort a neighboring country. Could he really trust the Americans not to consider doing that to their so-called ally in the War on Drugs? After decades of public give and ambiguous take, why wouldn't they see this as just another policy option; one to go along with the threat of withdrawing funding or imposing sanctions. A shadow route for that time when an extradition is required or negotiations hit a wall – *la frontera*.

He isn't a traitor to himself, or his country. This is our problem, he thinks, and we have to deal with it ourselves. We didn't ask for it, just as we didn't ask to be the neighbor of a rich nation with an impossible level of addiction and an intelligence service that exploits this to fund covert operations. Whatever the causes, whatever the obscure motives, it is our problem.

Only Mexico can solve it.

He steadies his breathing, then starts to examine the photos. Shots of naked or semi-clothed women tied up. Often unconscious; always having a sex act forced upon them. Even with restraints, bound with gags or blindfolds, their faces contort in silent screams of disgust, horror; fear and rage.

Terror and disbelief.

In each photo there is a clear, identifying image of a man committing the act, their faces clearly visible. Trophy shot and blackmail material all in one. He can't be sure, but there appear to be no recurring photos of any particular victim, nor of any of the killers – meaning that possibly each female victim was raped by a different man. When Fuentes had first arrived in Ciudad Real he had been appalled by the anarchic state of the DNA collected from the victims. There were literally no matches. He had put that down to incompetence, technical failure, contamination and deliberate criminal obfuscation. He was wrong. But could hundreds of different rapists all have murdered their victims in the same way? That would be impossible. Paredes had suggested an initiation rite. Which in itself suggested entry into some kind of secret society. A gang, like Los Toltecas. Or a cartel. Or possibly some kind of black magic cult. That in turn could indicate a single controlling entity – a high priest; the implicit killer who controls as the keeper of tradition by honoring an historical culture of sacrifice, of lustratio: Huitzilopochtli; Xipe Tótec. Paredes had even said it himself once to Gomez: a lone killer.

Maybe he knows.

Fuentes' thoughts slur to a stop with one photo, brutally similar to the murder of Isabel Torres. The victim is tied to a bed, naked except for a bra, her blindfolded face frozen in a scream.

In the bottom corner he can see her ankle, and the black band of the strap of her shoe. A man is standing by the bed, holding the other shoe in his hands. The self-mutilating look on his face terrifies Fuentes. If he found this man, he knows exactly what he'd do. He would interrogate the rapist until he had all the answers. And then he would shove his head against a wall, put a gun barrel to his temple and blow his brains out.

He takes a deep breath, trying to control his thoughts, then continues working through the photos, his habitually impassive face contorting for an instant before realigning itself at every photo that passes through his gloved hands. This is business. It has to be kept professional, otherwise Fuentes will snap, and he knows if he does, there will be no coming back. These images don't put him on the edge of his faith in humanity, they take him way past it, out into a place without light or hope: a claustrophobic tunnel flooded with a mephitic cloud of despair. He knows he has to be careful. He is a man in a diving suit, walking along the bottom of the ocean when his oxygen starts to run out. Panic and he's dead. Stay calm and there's a possibility he might survive.

He picks up the next photo and studies it. Then, very slowly, he does something he hasn't done in years. He crosses himself. He's not even aware he's doing it.

Fuentes leaps to his feet and throws two hard punches into the bookcase, books and framed photos falling; glass breaking. Now he fucking gets it. He gets it at fucking last.

69

Pilar

Juan Antonio had promised buses from Ciudad Juárez, Santa Teresa, Matamoros and Tijuana. From Monterrey, Guadalajara, and even as far away as Iguala. But that had been before the Heartbreak Hotel.

The first phone call came in just after midnight. Buses were turning back or simply not leaving. It was too inflammatory; too dangerous. It was just plain inappropriate. The nation was in shock. The city was in mourning. And the CTON had members amongst the dead.

It wasn't a suggestion.

It was an order.

Now was not the right time to go ahead with a disruptive strike that would tax the resources of authorities trying to deal with the aftermath of something they have never experienced before: total *narco* war.

Pilar didn't learn about any of the events until the following morning. She had gone straight to her room when they got back to Mayor's and had fallen asleep soon after. Not so much repose as a suspension from reality; a disconnect from time. Her body was punishing her for the arrogance of three sleepless days.

She plummeted beyond the realm of dreams into a potent and dangerous state inhabited by totemic mysteries. Archetypes. Pre-memories. She was wandering in a rainforest, the canopy so high that she could barely glimpse the sky through the swaying branches. Animals leapt from tree to tree, fifty meters above her, squealing and crying to each other with short, communicative barks. They were warnings, not threats. Exclamations of fear. She could smell the smoke clouds lofting above the jungle, the fire announcing itself the way catastrophe always does; harmonic chords ascending towards a fiery crescendo.

Ignition. Combustion. Detonation. Eruption. Conflagration.

She sat up in bed. Esteban was sitting next to her; afire.

Pilar wakes from the nightmare, breathless, her body damp from sweat.

She gets up and has a shower, leaning with her hands against the tiles, feeling the luxury of the regular hot beat pounding along her spine.

Pilar soaps her body until she smells of lavender, touching herself for a lingering moment; enough to feel a soothing warmth she hasn't felt for days, before turning on the cold water, strong as a sierra stream, her pores closing from its assault, protecting her from the intruding fog of her thoughts; her denied anxieties.

Her fears about today.

She dresses, surprised to see it's nearly six. After making her bed, she goes downstairs, feeling her way along the dark steps, following voices towards the only room in the house that's lit: the kitchen. She hesitates before entering, relieved to see that Maya isn't there. The way she reacted yesterday shames her, but what can she do? It's a reflection of the way she wants to live – uncensored; which these days too often means being brutally honest. No one said it would be easy, but it was still harder than she had ever expected.

So she doesn't attempt to hide her irritation when the first thing she sees is Ventura pouring coffee for Juan Antonio and Mayor. 'Aren't the men old enough to make their own coffee?' Ventura smiles, embarrassed, and is just about to reply when Pilar cuts her off. 'Or are you afraid they're going to ignore you if you don't?'

Ventura turns the coffee pot so the handle is facing Pilar. 'I was just making myself useful. The cups are up there . . .' Ventura goes over to Mayor, who hands her a cell phone, explaining the buttons.

It was a nasty thing to say, and on another morning she would have apologized. But this is a morning unlike any other, which is why she recognizes the silence all around her so quickly, and why its significance alarms her so much: bad news. 'What's happened?'

'There was a shooting last night. Dozens are dead.'

She sips her drink, watching Mayor over the steam rising from the cup's rim. 'I'm sorry. Anyone you know?' Mayor shakes his head.

'But there are already consequences . . . grave consequences,' Juan Antonio says.

The ring of porcelain startles her as she puts her cup down too quickly on the saucer. 'Don't you dare even think about it.'

'The orders are from HQ. This is not the right time to act.'

'It's *never* the right time to act – that's why we *always* must act. You taught me that yourself.'

'The CTON won't support us. Not after what happened last night. It's too sensitive.' Pilar swears. 'They want to be seen to show consideration for the victims. Some of their own members have been killed.'

'Besides, they know they will probably have to deal with Vicente Fox in July.'

Pilar turns to Mayor. 'Bullshit! Why would voters throw out the PRI just to elect PAN? Fox won't win. The Alianza will win.'

'They'll vote out the PRI to punish them,' Mayor says. 'Who they vote *in* doesn't matter.'

She's seen this before. Mayor is distracting them all with sophisticated political theory; with the possibilities of the future. She has to focus on action; bring them all back to *now*. 'We brought the strike forward. We all made sacrifices. We can't just cancel it.'

'If we're lucky, there'll be four or five buses. If we're lucky, we'll manage to close down one or maybe two *maquiladoras*. And that will be seen as a defeat.'

'They're right,' Ventura says.

Ignition. Combustion. Detonation . . . Eruption. 'Who the fuck even cares about your opinion?' Pilar explodes. 'You think one day makes you an activist?'

'Not one day, one life. My life. A woman's life.'

'You are so full of shit.'

'Pilar, please.'

She wheels on Juan Antonio. 'Don't *Pilar please* me. What about the funeral? We promised we'd be there for the family.'

'The authorities won't allow a demonstration. It's a question of public order after last night.'

'One night does this to us? What about these last eighteen months of preparation, all that hard work? What about more than eight hundred unprotected women raped and murdered?

What about *my night*, when I saw another woman taken with my own eyes?' Her voice breaks. 'A woman who could have been me. You're saying one night negates all that? One night negates *everything*?'

'We'll regroup. We'll reorganize. We'll strike in the future.'

'After the elections?' she cries. 'When nobody gives a damn. Are you crazy? It has to be now. Please, it's got to be now.'

'Pilar, be reasonable. It was a massacre.'

'And what's happening to our working women *isn't*? This has got nothing to do with last night. It's about fear. They're all afraid of China. The CTON, the workers, the factory owners, even the *gringos*. They're all terrified of a country on the other side of the ocean. Everyone is staring so far into the distance that no one can see what's happening here, right in front of their noses!'

'For fuck's sake, Pilar, it's not China they're afraid of, it's the cartels.'

'And yet Pilar is right,' Mayor says. 'Fear's fear. If you can't act in the face of fear, you'll never be able to act in the name of truth.'

'I don't know what the fuck that means, and I don't even care.' Juan Antonio turns back to Pilar. 'Be disciplined. Accept it. It's over. They called it off.'

'How many times do I have to tell you?' Pilar cries. '*They* are not *us*!'

'There's got to be some kind of compromise.' Ventura looks across the room at Mayor. 'Do you have any ideas, Felipe?'

'If the strike is rescheduled for after the election, it will never take place. The CTON is going to be in a very awkward situation with Fox, effectively negotiating not just its relevance but its continuing existence. Fox is an unknown. They'll want to put on a moderate mask for him.'

Pilar stares at Juan Antonio. 'See? Even he understands.'

'Don't condescend to your friends,' Ventura says.

'You're not my friend and neither is he.'

'You're right, you don't have any friends. And no wonder, the way you talk to people—'

'Ventura, it doesn't matter, as long as she can still listen to reason.' Mayor turns back to Pilar. 'If you dare go ahead on your own, there will be consequences. Ordinary people are outraged by what happened last night. They'll want to take out their anger on someone, and they can never reach the *narcos* . . .'

'But they can reach us,' Juan Antonio says. 'That's why they canceled the buses. Surely you see the danger, Pilar?'

'*Claro*. But I also see the danger of inaction, and it is far greater.'

'I think you should call off the strike, but maintain the demonstration. March in solidarity with the funeral; not as demonstrators, but as mourners.'

Pilar turns to Ventura. 'Can you explain just who the hell gave you a voice in this?'

Ventura stares at her for a searing moment. 'You did.'

Her initial impulse is to slap Ventura, but passion has two faces: anger and love. Pilar pulls a seat out from the kitchen table and sits down. She knows it's going to be a long day. 'So what's your plan?'

70

Gomez

Gomez is escorted to Valdez's office by two plainclothes detectives. The only thing missing is the blindfold and cigarette. Valdez motions him in without looking up from the vast terrain of his empty desk. It's as though it's a mirror and he can't pull himself away from the intensity of his own gaze. 'Where's Fuentes?' It's not a question. It's more a lament. Gomez can still smell the smoke from the Heartbreak. Even though he took thirty minutes out to shower and change before coming here, he can still smell it in his hair. 'And don't tell me you don't know.'

Gomez turns options over quickly. There aren't any. That's what working with a man like Fuentes does – it defoliates all potential cover. 'I don't know . . .'

Valdez slaps the desk so hard that Gomez takes a step back. Not in fear, in shock. He's used to the sardonic Valdez. Not the man who finally looks up at him, his face full of hot-marrow fury. 'According to the hospital, the witness was transferred without my authority and died during transportation to another facility.'

'An attempt was made on her life.'

'You deliberately disobeyed my orders.'

'I wasn't there.'

'Don't lie to me. You were seen at the hospital. There's even CCTV images.'

'I meant I wasn't there when you gave the orders.'

'I went to the morgue myself. Interestingly, her file led me to a cadaver that had already had an autopsy performed upon it.' Gomez tries to shrug but it's more an admission of guilt. He can see where this is leading. Fuentes promised he would take the rap. But this isn't going to be just a rap; this is going to be a nuclear strike. 'A cadaver that, according to hospital authorities, was not that of the witness who was being treated there yesterday morning . . .'

'Are they sure?'

'I will give you a chance to withdraw that question. Now tell me, what happened to the rescued victim?'

'That was the first thing I noticed, boss. You call me in here, and you don't say a single word about the Heartbreak, even though I've spent the last seven hours there. I mean, it's like you don't even care about the biggest massacre in history? You only care about a missing witness. Why is that?'

There is a long pause, as though Valdez is trying to remember a phrase in a foreign language. Then he slowly stands, pushing himself up with his hands spread wide on his desk, as if he fears he might slip and fall. 'What happened to her?'

'She's in the US. She's been granted asylum there.'

The ashtray comets across the office, leaving a surly dust trail of ash and debris before shattering into an explosion of crystal asteroids. 'What fucking game are you playing?'

Gomez brushes glass fragments from his hair. 'Your fucking game, boss.'

'You're suspended. And as soon as I find Fuentes, I'm having him placed under arrest. Now get out of my sight.'

Gomez pauses at the door to the office. He has nothing more to lose, so he may as well play his hunch and see where it leads.

'It's only a matter of time, boss.' Valdez stares back at him, betrayed by his silence. 'You know he's got you, right?' Still silence. He smiles, and slams the door behind him.

One of his colleagues, Hernandez, calls out to him. 'What the fuck was that all about?'

'Just letting off steam. I think he knew the manager at the Heartbreak.'

'That explains it.'

Gomez takes the cigarette that's offered him. 'Explains what?'

'Why he hasn't said a word about it. Not even to the press. It's like it never happened.'

'Cut the guy some slack. He's got a lot on his mind.' Gomez starts out saying it facetiously, but by the time he has completed the sentence, he recognizes the truth. The only explanation – the people responsible for the Heartbreak are responsible for the women of Ciudad Real. Valdez works for them. And soon he'll end up like El Feo did last night, a headless corpse with a *narco* banner, hanging from an overpass.

71

Pablo Grande

Pablo Grande had been living in *la tierra celestial* for the last forty years. He had spent all of those four decades honing his abilities. He had run with the *naguals* and danced with the lunar goddess during an eclipse. He had sat on the lip of the highest cliff shelf at Las Barrancas del Cobre, his legs dangling two thousand meters above the Copper Canyon, and listened to the earth reverberate as it turned on its orbit with a hollowing cosmic chime.

Pablo Grande had spent fourteen thousand nights watching the stars emptying themselves from the sky and falling to earth as phosphorescent crystals. He had sung the ecstatic song of the leaves at the summer solstice, and explored the secret tunnels that looped the past with the future, and the living with the dead.

Pablo Grande had witnessed the creation of the universe, but had turned his weeping eyes away when faced with its destruction.

For the most part, he had remained silent, patient and courageous in the face of wonder, and had been rewarded with an understanding of the spirit world that suffuses our earth with its veiled munificence. He had acquired the strengths of reticence, observation and humility and become an expert on spagyric medicine and second sight.

In short, he had assumed his responsibilities as a celestial being; which was why he had started walking to Ciudad Real forty days ago, for he had a rendezvous there with a man whose life he had already saved once before – Padre Márcio.

Pablo Grande had earned his celestial wisdom and it had come at a price. He had grown prematurely old, advancing forty years in a single decade. Augmented knowledge always leads to accelerated aging. Nothing compares to the exhaustion of the *brujo*, who must remain forever vigilant; using not just the two eyes he was born with, but the eyes that he develops in the back of his head. Never dormant. Alert not just to every movement but to the suggestion, the mere prospect, of motion; of differentiation. Disparity and similarity are opposites in the physical world, but in the spiritual world they are invariable: measurements of growth, of existence. They are harmonious dualities, like night and day, life and death. Fire and water. If not exactly identical, then complementary forces.

After that first decade of enhanced aging, the accelerated process suddenly stopped. His body became like the finest mountain ash caulked by the sun; immune to generational corruption and erosion – an enduring monument to polished strength. He was that rarest of things: a vital elder, destined to survive another half-century of wisdom, effortlessly capable of walking fifteen hundred kilometers on a quest to save a saint.

He descended the mountains a *kupuri* spirit and re-entered a world of brutality. While he had been absent, the drug cartels' evil had migrated to Ciudad Real, like spiders ballooning across restless skies inside the camouflage of silver gossamer trails, landing with the blister char of a haboob. Evil spirits sheltered sullen in the shade, watching Pablo Grande walk with immunity across the town's melting macadam.

Pablo Grande followed the call of electricity cables that formed a teslatic path to an orphanage at the edge of town. Rendering himself invisible, he observed Padre Márcio's kindness to the children; and witnessed his severity with the staff for having dared to cut back on food supplies, medicine and books. He listened to Padre Márcio as he explained to the lay workers the simple mystery of children: the more you give them, the more you receive.

Pablo Grande was pleased with this side of Padre Márcio; his just amalgam of kindness, concern and wrath. The priest had grown in unexpected ways. But he could observe the dark metallic flush of anger and pride still rooted inside the stigmatist's thoracic cavity. He also quickly discerned the ephemeral shadows of assassination that followed Padre Márcio like footsteps in a low tide.

The ancient *brujo* knew his serene vigilance would be tested, for, as any shaman can tell you, it is far easier to save someone who only deceives others than it is to save someone who also deceives himself.

72

Pilar

In the end only three buses made it, two from Guadalajara and the last from Iguala. They had already traveled so far that when they finally got the news, they decided to keep going anyway. They were only half full of activists, mainly students from university and technical colleges, even a few from *preparatoria*. The students were brimming with idealism and a need for adventure. Brief romances would be born over the next few days; lifelong friendships forged. In their later years, they would be able to look back with pride on marching alongside fellow students and workers, defending universal rights; standing fast as they were gassed and clubbed by police. Virginity would be lost. Songs would be sung; protests chanted. Factories would be closed, strikes enforced, streets barricaded. Arrests would be made, bail posted, fines paid and sentences suspended. They would travel back home in the buses, transformed into more compassionate, complex adults, their righteous zeal softened by reality, their tolerance ripened by experience.

At least that was what normally happened.

But *normal* is no longer a concept in Ciudad Real.

The body of Isabel Torres is carried out of the church in a modest plywood casket with a silver-plated cross that will be passed to her mother during the interment. Juan Antonio is one of the pallbearers because Isabel's brother hasn't shown up. He went out drinking the evening before and never came back. He wasn't there when his mother needed him most. His own desire for oblivion was just too strong. In his absence, the women are left to fend for themselves, just like always.

The activists march silently behind the family, the hearse barely advancing, a low purr amongst the drumbeat of footsteps, Ventura's camera fluttering gentle as an ascending dove. Their banners and placards are at the end of the procession, not because they want to draw less attention but because they are aware of the power of the mourning mother; a more pragmatic than modest decision. Besides, the last thing they want is for the police to disrupt the most sensitive component of the demonstration: the mask of the funeral.

Afterwards, when Isabel has been buried, and the sobs of her family have faded, there will be plenty of opportunity for disruption. For protest.

For battle.

Some of the students wear orange high-visibility jackets with reflective strips and red bandanas, acting as parade marshals, shepherding traffic a safe distance away from the mourners; from the concealed activists. The out-of-town buses and two more from Ciudad Real follow, their windows covered in slogans. Cars slow, some of them tooting their horns in support as though it were a wedding, not a funeral. There are also whistles and catcalls, and a couple of shouted insults, but the most common response is silence. Not the silence of respect.

The silence of indifference.

The cortège reaches the highway and begins the crossing, heading away from the bridges and the border, the marshals stopping traffic. This incites a new response. Irritation. Buses idle patiently at first, their drivers sitting high on their thrones and, when the passengers start to grumble, gesturing grandly to the procession. This time the fault lies not with the individual drivers, or the bus company, or the goddamn municipality. Or even that most convenient and ineffectual excuse of all – the weather. Now the delay has a clear cause: the young people parading slowly by, arms linked in solidarity: not with the workers whose commute they are delaying, but with the dead. Passengers who only minutes before crossed themselves at the sight of the hearse now complain angrily; intimidated drivers easily swayed into revolt, blasting the passing demonstrators with horns, gassing them with black fumes belched across desert air that was last clean decades ago.

The agitators pass leaflets through the windows, chanting to the women workers inside: *March for jobs. March for justice.* Ventura shoots the scenes, capturing the various reactions on the faces of the women in the buses: curiosity. Annoyance. Anger.

Fear.

Pilar walks at the head of the procession, right behind the family, because she cannot bring herself to witness the puny demonstration at the back. She had envisaged thousands, even tens of thousands. She had imagined walkouts from dozens of *maquiladoras*; blockades of all the roads leading to the industrial estates, barricades across the bridges. Huge delays crossing the border. Tumult and passion. For her it wouldn't be industrial action, it would be industrial war.

And now they are a glorified honor guard for a woman who died because the basic elements she needed for survival – safe transport to a secure working environment with honest standards of payment and conditions – did not exist. Their march will mourn Isabel's life and death, but it won't change the circumstances that led to her murder, and that was the whole point.

Tears come to her eyes, and as soon as she is aware of them, it is already too late. She is weeping. Juan Antonio glances at her. He knows she has spent time with the family, and thinks that Pilar is being overwhelmed by their grief. But he is wrong. Pilar is weeping because at last she understands the dimensions of her own failure.

73

Fuentes

A lock slides free and Gomez rushes in, slamming the door behind him, heading towards the bedroom, when he freezes and slowly turns . . . Fuentes is standing at the kitchen counter, drinking a glass of orange juice. 'How the fuck did you get in?'

Fuentes jerks his thumb over his shoulder, towards the kitchen window. 'Same way as before.'

'This is becoming a bad habit.' Gomez kicks a coffee table over, sending magazines skating across the floor. 'Get out of my house.'

'I need your help.'

'You're always asking for help, but all you ever give in return is trouble, you selfish son of a bitch.' He starts to pick up the magazines, then gives up and kicks them under the sofa with a wail of frustration. 'Where the fuck have you been, man? It was pandemonium at the Heartbreak and you weren't there. I called you like a hundred times.'

'I took the phone off the hook.'

'I even sent a fucking car to get you.'

'You seriously expect me to answer my door at three o'clock in the morning?'

Gomez slumps onto the sofa, his anger giving way to fatigue. 'It was mayhem. I've never seen anything like it. We don't know how many more bodies are there. They haven't even started checking the upper floors. Too dangerous. Structurally unsound.' He closes his eyes. 'I can't get rid of the smell.'

'I said I need your help.'

'Fuck help. Nothing's going to help you. Or me for that matter. That asshole Valdez suspended me.'

'What about me?'

'They're putting a warrant out for you. Valdez is going to arrest you, man. And I'm going to be the one handing him the cuffs.'

'You can't. You're suspended.'

'Fuck you. I'm resigning. It's bullshit anyway. We don't make a difference. You should have seen what they did last night. Women. Children. Last night was a fucking war crime. And the only thing that *pinche pendejo* could talk about was Gloria – or Mary-Ellen, or whoever she is now.'

'I've got something to show you . . .'

Gomez leaps to his feet. 'I don't want to see it.' Fuentes walks towards him, holding a large manila envelope in his hands. Gomez pushes him hard in the chest. Fuentes topples backwards into a display case, cracking the glass, trophies rocking and falling on their shelves inside. 'Get out of my house before I throw you the fuck out.'

Fuentes pulls a sheet of paper from the envelope and holds it up in front of him like it's some kind of protective talisman. Gomez stares at it, then staggers backwards as though hit by its force. 'That's right,' Fuentes says. He drops it on the floor, then pulls out another. 'Remember Byrd?' He tosses it across the room towards Gomez. 'Or him?' He walks up to Gomez, holding the color photocopy right up to his face.

Gomez looks at it sideways. 'I've seen him somewhere . . .'

'It's that asshole manager at the *maquiladora*, López. The victim looks like half his workforce. She looks like Pilar.

377

Remember what he said when he fired her? "There are thousands like her, just waiting to take her place?" He should know. He's been helping kill them.'

Gomez snatches the paper from Fuentes, staring at it hard. 'I remember this motherfucker . . .' He rips the paper in half then tears it again and again, bunching the torn ribbons into a fist and squeezing as though it were a telegram announcing the death of the only person he ever loved. He hurls the damp ovoid of hate at Fuentes, tears in his eyes. 'What is it, snuff films?'

'Blackmail hiding behind an initiation rite. You want to make money, you want to get ahead in this town? Then join the club. But the entrance fee is taking a woman's life in front of a camera.' Fuentes leads him to the kitchen table and starts pulling out all the photocopies from the first envelope. 'Blackmail. Control. And guaranteed silence.' Gomez leafs through some of the sheets and cries out. 'Nepo Dossena! Fuck me, we all knew he was corrupt, but this? He was a state fucking senator.'

'Retired?'

'Dead, maybe five years ago? Who knows. No one gave a shit.'

'Listen, you've lived here all your life. I need you to look through all of these, tell me who you recognize. Who you can name.'

Gomez opens the freezer compartment and slides out a bottle of vodka. He pours some into Fuentes' juice, then takes a long swig from the bottle, shuddering.

'This is fucked up. We should be putting together a team.'

'Everyone's working on the Heartbreak. Besides, I'm through with the Force. You know that.'

'That won't last long.' He takes another slug, wiping ice from his lips. 'Wait till Valdez . . .' Fuentes passes him a photocopy. Gomez's whole body jackknifes in an involuntary spasm. He rushes over to the sink and throws up the vodka, shuddering as he starts to dry-heave. He turns on the tap, scoops water into his shaking hands and brings it to his face. '*Dios mío ayúdame*. We are so royally fucked.' He straightens, his hand shaking as he picks the bottle up by the neck and takes a short sip. 'So Valdez knows the killer?'

'Valdez *is* the killer. One of many. But he knows who's behind all this.'

Gomez takes another sip, longer this time. 'Tell me everything.'

'Where are my things that I gave you at the border?'

'Why, you don't trust me?' Gomez gets up and goes over to a drawer in the living room, taking out the two handguns, the knife, cuffs, ammo and holsters, slamming them on the counter top. 'You afraid of me now?'

Fuentes removes his jacket and slips on his shoulder holster. 'I'm afraid of the next thing that comes through that door . . .'

Gomez takes his own service weapon out and puts it on the kitchen table. 'Where did you find these photos?'

Fuentes waits such a long time to answer that Gomez steels himself with another sip of vodka. 'Marina's . . .' Gomez slowly gets to his feet. 'Paredes hid them there. The only place he thought they'd be safe.'

Gomez stares in the direction of the bedroom. 'Where is she?'

'On a bus to Dallas. She'll be safe. She has friends there.'

Gomez pulls a seat out, the legs scraping against the tile floor. 'We'll never see each other again.'

'She's safe, I swear it.'

Gomez stares at him, his eyes luminous. He takes another long swig. 'I wasn't talking about her, man.'

379

74

Ventura

Things had progressively deteriorated after the interment when, despite the protests of Juan Antonio, the mourners continued to march down the streets, this time without the cover of a coffin.

Ventura had stayed within ranks during the funeral procession and listened to the arguments between Juan Antonio and the outsiders, debating terms like *social utility*, *deontology* and *momentum* and employing labels as though they were insults: *utopian*; *reactionary*. What struck her most was the total absence of Pilar from the dispute. She stood in a place Ventura had never seen her occupy before – the sidelines: not so much distracted as bereft; abandoned not by the others but by herself.

The outsiders forced a vote and of course they won, moving past Juan Antonio with raised, triumphant fists, as though he were the enemy. Banners were relocated to their rightful position at the front of the march, the demonstrators escorted by their buses – both protective and intimidating.

Given the changing circumstances, Ventura feels free to break from her assigned role of mourner and roam ahead for her shots, framing the heroic activists against the desolation of wasteland and distant border. She chants their brave slogans as she walks backwards, her camera channeling all her intelligence and instinct.

Pilar has lamented the numbers but Ventura thinks they are

perfect: large enough to impress but small enough to retain a sense of individuality; of intimacy. She feels joyous and alive moving through the presence of a group of young people like herself, all clamoring for change. It sends a message out to the city, the entire country: this is what is needed most now. Not cynicism. Not anger or hate. Idealism and commitment.

Hope.

'It's a fantastic turnout.'

Pilar studies her face for irony. 'There's only a few hundred.'

'That's all Garibaldi had to start with.'

Pilar looks away. Garibaldi was a fantasist from a paternalistic, feudal society. He had about as much relevance to today's *maquiladoras* as a harrow. 'They promised us thousands.' The subtext is left unspoken, which is always the way with implicit truth: they lied.

Ventura disengages, standing off to the side, one of the buses almost brushing her as it throbs slowly after the demonstrators with the menacing heft of a bodyguard, alert and anxious. Juan Antonio follows on the heels of the procession, like Pilar more an observer than a participant. 'Children . . .' He says it the way other men say *women*. 'Being led into a trap.'

Ventura lowers her camera. 'If that's what you believe, you have to stop them.'

He gestures to the marchers with a dismissive lift of the chin. 'I tried. They wouldn't listen.'

'Make them.'

'That's not the way it works.' He takes a cigarette and offers one to Ventura, who declines. 'Every demonstration quickly develops its own destiny. Once it is formed, it is impossible to change.' Fire leaps, is sucked in; blown out. 'My uncles were at the Plaza de las Tres Culturas in 1968. The flares dropped from the helicopters weren't a signal for the massacre to begin, like people think today. It was more a simple confirmation of what everyone there already knew, because everyone – not just the soldiers and the presidential guard and the secret police, but the students too – everyone knew that evening would end in terrible bloodshed. I asked my uncles, "So why didn't you leave when you had the chance?" And you know what they said?'

Ventura shakes her head.

Juan Antonio stops in his tracks, fixing Ventura with an intense stare, a look of transmission that sends a shiver through her. 'They said, "Because we were trapped within history."'

He laughs, breaking the solemn spell, and starts moving again, trailing a procession he doesn't believe in. 'I didn't know what that meant until many years later, in 1995, when I was in Aguas Blancas to support the Campesina de la Sierra. And one morning we woke up and what my uncles had spoken about was there, surrounding all of us; a sense of dread combined with a powerful – no, an *irresistible* – inevitability. It was an overwhelming force, as though every possible narrative had already been written, and the blood had already been shed. It was transformative. We were no longer sentient beings, we weren't even spectators. We were puppets; archetypes dancing to a song that had been sung since the beginning of time. *Sacrifice.*' He freezes, staring not at Ventura, but at something on the far horizon of his memory that still adheres to the stanchion of his soul. 'My entire career has been predicated upon didactic logic, but there are moments, like chasms in space, when rationalism no longer exists and one is compelled to face the greatest mystery there is: the extent of human savagery.'

He nods to Pilar, moving listlessly with the group. 'She feels it too; she has the experience; the innate awareness. She and I are meteorologists. We feel the change in air pressure before it even happens. But the students here are innocent children at a picnic. They will feel it eventually, but only when the lightning is already in the treetops. And then it will be too late . . .' His hand trembles as he takes the cigarette out of his mouth and crushes it underfoot. 'The secret allure of martyrdom is not that it's irresistible. It's that it's inevitable.'

He picks up his pace, quickly joining Pilar and linking arms with her. Ventura watches them catching up with the others, joining the students, losing themselves in the mass of demonstrators. Further down the road she notices for the first time the flashing lights of a police roadblock. Without even knowing why, she runs after Juan Antonio and Pilar, searching for their faces in the crowd.

75

Fuentes

Fuentes had made three photocopies of every photograph before he had gone to find Gomez, forcing the night staff of the print shop to leave the room for three hours while he worked. The first set he had already Fed-Exed to the immigration lawyer he had retained for Gloria in El Lobo, with instructions to forward them to Charlie Addsen at DEA in Washington, DC, in the event of his disappearance or death.

The second lot he had secretly stowed inside Marina's luggage with a note before he drove her to the border. If he had told her about it, she would have given off all the wrong vibes crossing over. She would have been stopped and the photocopies would have been located and seized. She would have been detained as an accessory and somewhere along the line – probably during transfer to a federal facility seventy-two hours later – she would have been removed to a dark corner, where she would have been interrogated until she named names, and then killed.

The copies with Marina were addressed to an investigative journalist in Mexico City, Ruíz Coronel, who wrote for *La Jornada*, the *Guardian* and *Le Monde*. Fuentes knew him from his time in Mexico City when Ruíz Coronel was under police guard following a story he had published on the death of Amado Lázaro Mendez. The journalist's home was firebombed. It didn't stop him. His police guard was withdrawn due to 'necessary strategic and logistical redeployment'. Total bullshit, but he kept writing anyway. Fuentes recognized the journalist's tenacity in a cellular way – after all, they were both the sons of the same moral parents: the massacres of 1968.

The third and final set of copies was for Fuentes and Gomez's own investigation, to allow them to identify as many of the perpetrators as possible. The actual photos themselves would be delivered later that morning to the only person in Ciudad Real capable of keeping them safe, with the understanding that they would remain sealed for forensic purposes.

Gomez was satisfied with the arrangements. Their only other challenge was how to gain access to, and remove, the files of all the female victims. This had to be done before Fuentes' possession of the photographs became common knowledge and the files seized and destroyed. The operation was hampered by the fact that all of their current colleagues appeared in the photos.

'Hernandez. I accepted a cigarette from that motherfucker only this morning,' Gomez says, his voice raw from the vodka and coffee that have kept him going through the first inventory. They have identified 280 perpetrators. Another 130 are known to at least one of them – usually Gomez – by sight though not by name. In less than twenty-four hours, they have gone from the unknown to the classified; from supposition to confirmation.

Of course Fuentes knows that the battle is not yet won, but if they target the first arrests correctly, and coerce cooperation from those initial suspects, they will create an irreversible process: for fission always takes place when a large nucleus – in this case the conspiracy surrounding the murders of the women – begins to fragment; the effects of the disintegration providing massive energy to the investigation and an irresistible, accumulating impulse to continue to divide, to the point where a chain reaction finally occurs.

For the first time, Fuentes can see the end game.

But the entire Ciudad Real police force stands in his way. Gomez's phone rings again. This time he answers. He listens in silence, then hangs up. 'Insane . . .'

'What is it?'

'Valdez is taking everyone off the Heartbreak and putting them on sentry duty outside the *maquiladoras*. All because of some fucking strike.'

Fuentes starts shoving the photocopies back inside their envelopes. 'This is our chance.'

'My chance. If he sees you, Valdez will have you arrested.'

'He's not going to see me, because he'll be out of the office.'

'Since when has Valdez ever done field work?'

'Since he's been scared . . .' Fuentes opens the refrigerator door, slides out the crisper shelf and pulls out the photos, bundled inside plastic evidence bags, that he'd hidden under carrots and corn. Gomez stares at him. 'You fucking hide them in my place without asking permission?'

'What would you have said, *no*?'

'That's not the point. The point is to ask.'

'There was no time to ask.'

'That's exactly the time when you should.'

Fuentes lifts the corner of a curtain, peering up and down the street. 'If I had known you were this touchy, I never would have taken you on as my partner.'

'Fuck you too. Do you have the shotguns?'

'We won't need them.'

'That's where you're wrong. Do you have enough ammo?'

'Sixteen boxes.'

'That's a lot for someone who's not going to need them.'

'Always be prepared.' He slides open the kitchen window. Gomez curses. Fuentes glances back at him. 'Why take chances when we're this close?'

'You know what I hate about you?'

'That I'm always right?'

'That you make even the easiest things difficult, man. Why do you do that?'

'A natural talent?' Fuentes drops from the window.

'More like an affliction,' Gomez calls out, climbing up onto the sill, then disappearing from sight.

76

El Santo

It got worse, if that were even possible, when they started finding the bodies upstairs. Who would have thought that the Heartbreak doubled up as a hostel for illegal immigrants? Not that El Santo really cares – how could he with this pain in his guts. The soft puffiness that had slowly inflated around the stitches yesterday has solidified overnight into a bulbous tumor, as though some fucking ostrich has laid an egg inside the bullet hole.

Oviedo gets all domestic, slipping on dishwashing gloves before he removes the bloody bandage. Just the weak tug of the plaster being lifted from his inflamed skin causes swooning agony. Oviedo gingerly touches the purulent cords around the wound, like a fisherman testing to see if the eel in his trap is dead, pulling away as if bitten when El Santo bellows. 'It's golden staph, boss. You're totally fucked.'

Not exactly music to his ears. 'So now what?'

'You got to drain it fast, otherwise the poison and the pus will be sucked up by your organs, like a milkshake through a straw. If it gets down there, it'll melt them all to shit.' Obviously Oviedo has never done a course in bedside manners. 'After that, we got to put you on special antibiotics to stop it coming back.'

Coming back? 'You just said we have to drain it out.'

'That's to stop it killing you now. But then we have to stop it killing you later. This kind of infection is like a counterfeit note: once it gets in the system, it just keeps coming back until you put it out of circulation.'

Goddamn doctor . . . He probably did it on purpose. Not to mention that live-streaming stunt. The press is all over it too. Oviedo hands him a shot glass. 'What's this for?'

Oviedo helps him to stand up. 'The pain, boss.'

El Santo groans as he drinks, just the lifting of his arm making his stomach feel as though it's stretched to bursting. But the tequila works its sullen charm. He holds the empty glass out for another shot. 'What about this plan of yours, this Belgium shit?'

'I got it covered, boss. We're going to massacre all these fucking agitators today; you don't even have to worry about it.'

That's where Oviedo's wrong. If there's something that El Santo has learnt in the last three days, it's that all you can ever do is worry. Worrying is part of the human condition, like money, power and drugs. You can never have too much of it. 'You heard the radio this morning. One hundred and forty-two dead! Even the president of Honduras is sticking his nose in, like it's some act of war.'

'But that's exactly what it is, boss, war . . .'

There he goes again, from loyal lieutenant to psycho paramilitary. Oviedo must be bipolar or something, but whatever it is, El Santo makes up his mind then and there: as soon as he gets over this infection, he's taking Oviedo out. He's through with crazy people who want to be Napoleon.

'Wrong. That's exactly what we don't want! We need to lie low, not escalate.'

Oviedo stares at him with those pagan eyes of his. They're not so much like a god's eyes but the eyes of a victim of a vindictive god's punishment. It's as if he's been staked face up on top of a sun pyramid until he's gone blind. The apparition vanishes and then Oviedo gets all sulky, and goes over to the kitchen and starts sharpening knives again. Sure, he gets points for being industrious, but for fuck's sake, how sharp is *sharp*?

'I did some calculations, about shifting the cash in the cars.'

El Santo's happy to change the subject. 'What number did you come up with?'

'Sixteen billion dollars . . .' He says it with all the emotion of someone buying a bus ticket to a neighboring village.

El Santo crosses to the kitchen. Funny how his stitches don't seem to hurt right now. 'Sixteen *million*?'

The rasp of blade against sharpener extends the silence, protesting against the slow unfurling of time. Finally Oviedo looks up at him. 'Billion, boss. *Billion*.'

'Fuck me.' Oviedo puts down the sharpener and then starts chopping garlic cloves in half, not bothering to shell them. Thank Christ, the shriek of sharpening was making his blood run cold. 'Jesus, imagine if we could lay our hands on some of that?' He actually laughs at the thought and is too excited to acknowledge the blister-burst of pain the laughter gives him.

Oviedo starts raking the garlic cloves up and down the grooves of the honing rod, grating them into milky obliteration. 'I already have.' He puts the sharpener down and goes to the Sub-Zero wine cooler, taking out a bottle of Cristal. The cork fires fast from his fists, making El Santo jump. 'Remember that ex-spook who told you how to use your phones?'

'That crank? Who gives a fuck about him, tell me about the money. How much did we get?'

'It was Tex who led me to it – all of it.' Oviedo offers a glass to El Santo.

'*All* of it?' That's insane. So fucking crazy that another truly insane idea occurs to El Santo; one that has never been conceivable, let alone possible, before: retirement. He can see it now. A beach house somewhere close but far away, without extradition treaties. Brazil, or Nicaragua. Just like Amado. Toss it all in and disappear, for good. Oviedo raises his own glass and they toast. 'To sixteen bil,' El Santo says, finishing the entire glass in one gulp. It burns but in a manageable way. Oviedo refills him. El Santo stares at the amber-colored champagne rioting inside his glass, bubbles detonating on the sleek surface. 'Jesus, look at this drink. It's the closest we'll ever get to swallowing gold.'

'Poetic, boss. And prescient . . .' Whatever that means. He can tell Oviedo is shifting again, going over to that other side of his; the dark shore. He puts his glass down and returns to what he was doing before, grating garlic up and down the honing rod in the same methodical, almost robotic manner he does everything else: cleaning a rifle; picking a lock. Preparing a fuse.

'So where's the money?'

He looks up at El Santo with a dull, almost hostile expression, as though he's annoyed to be interrupted. 'All over the place, boss. A lot of it is in the States.'

'Wait a minute, you said before you had it.'

'Sure, boss, I *have* it – I just don't have it in my hands yet.'

'But you will . . . ?'

Oviedo laughs – a short rolling chuckle that fades to black. He shrugs modestly.

'Listen, we need to focus here for a second . . .'

Oviedo freezes what he's doing. 'Sure, boss . . .'

El Santo peers at the tiny pieces of garlic caught within the serrated surface. Apart from being distracting, all this cooking preparation is stinking the place up; tainting his champagne. 'What's with all the fucking garlic, anyway?'

'It's to induce blood poisoning. In case the wound isn't fatal.'

'What?'

'Not that you need help, what with your problems, but . . . Old habits, right?' Oviedo takes one step towards El Santo and lifts his left arm up at the elbow. It's almost a polite gesture, as though he were excusing himself brushing by in a crowded bar, and then Oviedo drives the sharpened end of the honing rod under El Santo's arm, into the yielding pouch of skin covering the armpit. 'Never use a blade.' The rod travels far. 'People always panic when they see a blade. Always.'

El Santo looks down on the ground. He's standing on his tiptoes. He stares at his feet, wondering how the fuck that just happened, as though he's been elevated, and then he sees them, the beads of blood slowly tambouring onto the kitchen floor.

Now that he's gained entry, Oviedo pivots his weight suddenly, straightening up at the knees and using the additional force to drive the rod through the thin opening between two ribs and on into the thoracic cage. 'Plus blades snap against bone. Happens all the fucking time.'

There is a slight resistance as El Santo makes a sound like he's winded and the glass in his right hand drops and breaks. Then the rod travels on, a wheezing noise like a bike tire losing air passing between them as the left lung collapses quickly.

Oviedo knows he's almost home now. He pushes hard, and the rod enters El Santo's heart.

El Santo stands there, his left elbow still raised, his right hand moving slowly through the contracting light, then gripping Oviedo's wrist, trying to defend himself as Oviedo begins to twist the handle of the rod, struggling at first, then gaining traction. El Santo lets out a sigh like an old person stirring in their sleep, his right hand twitching violently.

Oviedo steps away, and El Santo sways for a moment, steadying himself against the counter, blood pooling inside and around his shoes. 'You were just a fucking kid with a gun and a mask. Ballsy and bright.' El Santo stares at Oviedo's face, but it's already beginning to blur. 'Now look at you. You remind me of a bolt-shot steer still on its feet, too fucking stupid to even know it's dead. What the fuck happened to you, *hombre*?'

El Santo's eyes widen in recognition and one word escapes his lips. '*¿Amado?*'

77

Pilar

The entire morning has been a requiem for Pilar's defeat; her neat betrayal at the hands of professional male activists who have long since traded ideals for favors and personal power – all of them adept at the opaque barter of industrial action: the tenuous balance between threat and withdrawal.

She's navigated this terrain many times before, but had convinced herself that Ciudad Real would be different, tethered as it was to the femicides. She was wrong and it has hit her harder than she could ever have imagined. But the sight of the police blocking the road ahead jolts her out of her apathy; her shameful self-pity. Pilar's old defiance is reawakening. Police deployed to stop a demonstration, but never to save a woman's life? She recalls the mantra of her early student days, the fierce warning of Victor Hugo: *police partout, justice nulle part*. It is as though nothing ever really changes . . . except that things have a way of getting worse.

And that is no longer acceptable.

She strides to her rightful place, at the front of the procession, ripping a bullhorn out of the hands of an astonished young man. 'Protection for the women! Justice for the victims! Protection for the women, justice for the victims!' Scattered voices take up the call, hesitant at first; others joining in, finding the cadence that is always present in any spoken truth, unifying at last the hundreds of students and the handful of local activists in their common goal: provocation.

Juan Antonio looks all around, feeling the power of that instant of coalescence. He curses, knowing what it means; what it will lead to. How much it will cost. In front of them, not a hundred meters away now, are the riot police, their visors glinting from the reflected sun, batons resting against shoulders and thighs. Fuck it. This is what he does. This is what he will always do. He pushes his way to Pilar's side, one hand holding hers, the other punching the air with a clenched fist, his cry joining the others, the chant a single harmonious voice: 'Protection for the women, justice for the victims,' shouted so loud, it drowns out the police as they charge.

78

Fuentes

The station is deserted except for the front desk, the officer rising in her seat when she sees Fuentes and Gomez. 'Valdez has been looking everywhere for you,' she says. Code for letting them know she's been ordered to call him as soon as they appear. 'Ten minutes, *guapa*, that's all we need,' Gomez says. It isn't condescension so much as complicity. Gomez and she are or have been lovers, and Fuentes didn't even know. He isn't really surprised. Focus like his blinds him to everything else. But it's now time to shift that focus a little – from investigation to survival.

Numerically it's enormous. Eight hundred and seventy-five victims, but most of the files are surprisingly thin. Over half of them hold no more than four documents: incident report, autopsy findings, death certificate, release to next of kin. Eight boxes. Fifteen minutes. Two men. That's all it takes to transport 875 lives to the trunk of Fuentes' car. 'What do I say?' the desk clerk asks Gomez, beginning to dial Valdez's cell phone.

'Tell him we came in together, and when we found out he wasn't here, we went out looking for him. Tell him we were pissed.'

She pauses, something passing between her and Gomez. Regret. Maybe farewell. 'Be careful,' she says, then punches in the last two numbers.

Gomez is shifting the boxes, trying to make them all fit in the trunk, when he sees the Ruger M77. He whistles. 'Someone's been a bad boy.'

'I borrowed it.'

'Like those shotguns you *borrowed*?'

'They came in handy, didn't they?'

'That's not the point. You're compromising evid—' He slams the trunk shut. 'Fuck it, we need all the help we can get.' Gomez gets in behind the wheel. '*Órale*. Where to?'

Fuentes doesn't even have to think about the answer. There is only one place where they could seek refuge now.

79

Ventura

It isn't the way she imagined. A prolonged battle like you see on the news, with tear gas and rubber bullets. High-pressure water cannon and dogs. It is elementary, and it is over before it has ever really begun. She feels almost disappointed.

The police charge, and the students turn and run. Batons swing wildly. A few students go down. Some are kicked. Others dragged away. Then it is over, the demonstrators slowing, looking back, stopping to examine each other's injuries, abandoning a dozen or so of their companions who are being led to waiting police cars.

She has shot a roll of thirty-six with a fast shutter speed but a maximum aperture of only f/5.6 and is changing film, hoping for the best, when it finishes. The whole incident lasts maybe two minutes. No one challenges her as she stands there taking photos. It's like the police don't even notice her as they walk past and board the buses, speaking to complacent drivers, who sigh as they start the laborious process of turning around and going back the way they came, the police motioning to them in side windows as they reverse onto the fields, even halting traffic to let the buses swing back onto the road.

The buses don't get very far, pulling over to let the students board, and Ventura has to run to catch the last one just before its doors spring shut. It isn't even two-thirds full, but the mood inside surprises her. There is laughter and excited voices talking over each other. She walks to the back, sitting down next to Pilar, the two of them riding along in silence, staring out the window, jumping in unison in their seats every time they hit a pothole.

'What we needed were professional agitators, not babies,' Pilar says too loudly.

There's a long, uncomfortable pause. Some of the students towards the back of the bus have heard her. Like them, Ventura has no doubt she would be included amongst the *babies*. A young student stares at Pilar with a mixture of defiance and curiosity. 'Where would you find someone crazy enough to fight riot police?'

Pilar shrugs. 'Homeless shelters. The streets . . . Psychiatric hospitals – you did say *crazy*. The political fringe, both left and right.' She stands, raising her voice, more faces turning towards her. 'You look for certain types. Radical anarchists. Punks and bikers. Boxers. Bouncers. Illegal immigrants. Moonlighting cops. Former prison guards. Off-duty soldiers. Out-of-work laborers, dispossessed farm hands. Ex-convicts.'

She recites the list as she moves down the aisle, all the passengers turning, listening to her. 'What you want are angry men. Desperate men. Men with scars on their faces and their fists. People who don't give a damn what happens to them anymore.' She lowers her voice for dramatic effect. 'Drunks and drug users . . .' She turns back to the youth who asked her the question in the first place. 'What you're searching for is simple and brutal: men who like to hurt. Men who don't mind being hurt . . . Men who *enjoy* being hurt.' There is nervous laughter. 'In any city, in any country, you can always find men ready to battle police.'

She points accusingly at the youth. 'But they're not the people

I'm referring to when I speak about *professional agitators*, because they're amateurs, not professional. And they are disrupters, not agitators.' Her voice rises as she scans the faces staring up at her. 'I'm talking about people who are disciplined, who create a plan and stick to it; who eschew improvisation. People who show integrity to the cause, loyalty to each other, and fearlessness for their own safety. I'm talking about the women I have trained and organized and worked with for the last fifteen years.'

The young students listen to her, enthralled, crying out encouragement, some of them rising in their seats. 'I'm talking about the future of this country, the future of women, when they can live in dignity, secure in their equality. Respected in their work. When they can walk the streets alone at night without fear or anguish. I am talking about change. Listen to me, all of you, isn't that what you want?'

There is a chorus of agreement, of something approaching adulation. 'Is that why you're here today? Are you ready to turn your dreams into acts?'

The roar is so monumental that some fruit pickers sitting in the back of a flatbed passing on the other side of the road look up as one, staring after the bus.

Juan Antonio is in the lead bus, too far away to hear the cry of approval. He is standing with his back to the road, talking to the driver, when something catches his eye and he sees Pilar's bus swerve and take the turnoff heading towards the *maquiladoras*. He swears, watching the bus peeling away from them, then turns to the driver. 'Take the next turnoff.'

The driver nods. 'Where are we heading?'

Juan Antonio watches Pilar's bus disappearing in traffic. 'Somewhere we were always supposed to go.'

80

Pilar

They are too early for the afternoon shift. It doesn't matter. Her bus drives through the gates, wire exploding inwards, the other buses following. Four guards come out, not in aggression but in confusion. Disbelief. One of them smiles, as though it were the circus coming to town. The demonstrators stream out and charge through the main doors, sweeping the guards aside. Pilar strides in their midst, the patchwork light, the noise, the rows of bent-over women like a childhood dream suddenly remembered.

She takes the steps two at a time, the women standing away from their work benches, their watchful silence in contrast to the unyielding hum of the machines; devoted to their eternal duty.

López leaps up from his desk, and when he sees the numbers rushing in, reaches for a drawer. Pilar kicks it shut on his hand. López howls in pain and is wrestled to the floor. She wishes this was something else; not a strike but a civil insurrection, a bloody *coup d'état*, and she could be free to take the revolver he had gone for and shoot him through the heart. But that would be against her nature, and the nature of the movement. They are not revolutionaries; they don't want insurgency, they simply want reason. A state that is normal and just; equal opportunities. An end to corruption and privilege. Their needs are moderate; which is what makes them so dangerous.

There is a dense mechanical clatter and then all the lights go out, and the *maquiladora* falls silent. Pilar steps out of the office and gazes across the quilt of solar illumination and ice-cold shadow, the sunlight squared by economic imperatives. 'Sisters, today we have buried one of us, Isabel Torres. We have already buried hundreds, and we will bury hundreds more unless our demands are met. We have negotiated. We have signed petitions. We have boycotted and we have asked for outside help. No one has listened, because our voice is too small. Today we need to shout to be heard, and the only way we can do this is to close the *maquiladoras*.'

Pilar pauses, listening to the quality of the silence. Silence has many meanings: rejection. Contempt. Anger. Capitulation. Fear. Awareness. Both prey and predator are silent before they meet. Which silence is this? Pilar listens, trusting in her instincts. It is the silence of a *maquiladora* which has been captured and shut down.

It is the silence of victory.

'I invite you all to join us. And I invite you to remain if you so wish, and continue your work . . .' The students who stand around her exchange confused looks. 'I invite you to follow your conscience; your instincts. The economic necessities of your life; of your household. No one will be forced to come with us. No one will be criticized for staying.' She gazes down at all the faces of the women, and sees Maria and Lupita on the factory floor, staring up at her, tears in Lupita's eyes. 'For today we all possess that most precious of commodities . . . choice.'

Pilar begins to descend the staircase, a few claps building into applause. She walks over to Maria and hugs her, then turns to Lupita. 'What is it, *amiga*?'

Lupita glances nervously at Maria, who takes Pilar's arm. 'It's Esteban. It was on the news this morning. He's dead.'

'He was murdered in a hotel.'

Pilar holds her friend close to her, remembering the death threats she and Juan Antonio have been receiving these last few weeks; recalling last night's dream and certain now that Esteban died because they were looking for her. It makes her want to weep, to scream with outrage and guilt. But not right now.

There is work to do.

She gets on the first bus, which is already full with students and female workers, everyone on board applauding her. 'Come on, *compañeras*,' Pilar cries. 'Let's shut this town down!'

81

Padre Márcio

When Padre Márcio saw Amado standing with El Santo by the baptismal font in the cathedral the day before, he had felt the coming change. Not the natural change of evolution but the wresting one of cataclysm.

Extinction.

Amado's face had not just been transformed, it had been transmuted, stripped of what little humanity he had managed to retain during the course of his criminal career, and rendered into a death mask – some fierce fetish which occupied the savage border zone between existence and extermination; both mocking the living and defying the dead. Even his eyes had changed color, the earnest *mole* of the child lost to a chemically induced marbled gray. Amado was physically unrecognizable . . . but the silence of the man, the power of his malign intent was unmistakably unique. Padre Márcio had never truly believed in God, but that moment in the cathedral had been his epiphany, because he knew, watching him lurking there, that Amado was the devil.

He had been spending less and less time in Ciudad Real and had convinced himself it was because of his manifold interests across the border and in other countries. But it was simpler than that: he couldn't sustain the proximity to such evil. An evil that he had helped create and hone. An evil which had returned for its final reckoning.

Padre Márcio had dared to believe the extravagant notion that Amado had really died. He had appropriated billions from their partnership over the last four years, financing orphanages, clinics and schools in over one hundred nations. There were billions and billions more left, in property, in stocks and bonds. In businesses and warehouse stock. In cash. But he had betrayed Amado by naïvely assuming that death had severed their partnership, when both men knew that it was never really a partnership, but a dictatorship.

And now the moment had come. Padre Márcio had looked up from his papers and Amado was standing there, watching him. 'I'm not like one of those bishops who send the pedophiles away to another parish – passing the problem along,' Amado said, crossing the study and standing over his desk.

Padre Márcio had no idea how he had gained entry: both doors were locked. And the alarm was on. He rose to his feet in fear. 'How did you get in?'

'I tend to my garden. You've always known that. And now it's time to start pruning.'

'You went away. I had choices I had to make.'

There was a flash of teeth – perhaps an indication of something approaching amusement. 'Lucifer told God the same thing. You remember the shitstorm that caused?'

'Your father gave his word. Equal partners.'

'My father had two weaknesses. One was his word. The other was thinking he was smarter than me . . . Let's go, Padre,' he said, passing him a chalice brimming to the top with a red, viscous wine.

'Where to?'

'Come on, Padre, don't make this any harder than it has to be.'

Padre Márcio held the chalice in his two bleeding hands, the wine spilling over the lip. 'Where are we going?'

Amado shook his head, disappointed in the priest. 'Golgotha ... Where the fuck else?

82

Pilar

She should have known. She should have listened to Juan Antonio. But she has always been like that: not impulsive so much as visceral. Aware not of the voices in her head but of the fervor in her heart.

And now they are trapped.

The second *maquiladora* was 'liberated' with only middling results. That was to be expected. It had never been identified as a target, or subjected to the usual organizational protocols, but it was on the way to the next designated objective. She thought it would be worth the risk.

All the striking women and the students and the agitators are standing by the side of the road, state and federal police watching them behind riot gear, balaclavas and sneers, gun muzzles pointed their way. Most of them are alarmed. Pilar isn't. There are television crews. There is even a helicopter. As long as they are seen, they are safe. It is only when you are taken away from the public gaze and locked inside interrogation rooms that things get ugly. Like the stables outside Tijuana. So she is calm; almost optimistic. She saw Juan Antonio on his phone before it was ripped out of his hands. The two of them even exchanged their usual looks. The first one was reproach from him and acceptance, if not apology, from her. The second told her that he had communicated what had happened. Lawyers would be waiting back in Ciudad Real. Medical staff would be standing by. Human rights and labor organizations would be notified. The idea was simple but effective: make their arrests phosphorescent – simply too hot to handle. Their story might even be picked up by the international press.

It might not be such a disaster after all.

When the municipal police arrive, Juan Antonio steps forwards, speaking directly to a state police commander. 'They have no jurisdiction here. We're dealing with federal and state laws, not ordinances.'

The commander nods to a municipal police officer, who strikes Juan Antonio across the face. Juan Antonio staggers backwards but regains his footing. He knows the rule: the ground is your enemy. Once you go down, chances are you stay down.

Journalists are escorted back to their cars. Papers are swapped and torn up. Hands are shaken. Weapons are ostentatiously racked. Engines are started. Dust settles after the departing convoys. The prisoners stare back at the municipal police. 'You will all get on the buses. Anyone who resists will regret it.'

Looks are exchanged; not so much a communication as a page shared from a history of the twentieth century. The activists start to comply with the order, but a young student is suddenly yanked out of a bus, falling backwards down the steps. Police encircle him, rifle butts pummeling him with a mounting frenzy, his body kicked under the chassis of the bus. The prisoners all take a collective, unconscious step backwards into horror.

'Women only in the first three buses.' Maria helps Lupita onto the bus, followed by Pilar, who notices Ventura sitting all alone. She sits down next to her as the bus starts up, Ventura's breathing surging with anxiety. 'Don't worry,' Pilar lies, holding Ventura's arm. 'It will be all right.'

83

Ventura

They seem to be heading in the general direction of Juárez, but Ventura can't be sure. It's not a road they're following but more a cleared track, etched between shadowing canyons, the rock face purple with shadow on one side, blinding ochre with sunlight on the other. It's as though they're hewing two extremes: fire and ice. No one speaks. No one dares to within this foreboding terrain. The only thing that gives her any hope at all is that the convoy of buses has been maintained.

They are still all together.

She notices the driver and a few of the women trying to get a signal on their cell phones. She tries again on Mayor's phone, even though the battery's nearly dead. There's nothing out here.

They begin to rise, a nauseating loop of cutbacks amidst the crumble of curves and the plunge into scree. And then they come out onto the plateau. It's like they're entering a military exclusion zone. The buses are waved through a roadblock into a huge loading area, with camouflage nets pulled over storehouses and vehicles. At the opposite end of the plateau is a tarmacked landing strip that only comes to a stop at the edge of a cliff. Ventura can see something gleaming through the heat haze.

She takes out her camera and fits the 90 mm f/2. Trembling like a mirage in the distance is the border. Far beyond is the white splash of settlement. El Paso.

'Put the camera away,' Pilar hisses. 'If they see it, they'll kill you.'

Someone thumps one of the windows from the outside, startling her. There's a shout and then the bus lurches forwards, trundling towards the runway. Ventura looks back. Only two buses follow – the other ones with the women.

The division has begun.

She sees the men stepping out of their buses, hands on their heads, municipal police pointing guns at them . . . Then the view is lost as they pass the storehouses, the netting undulating in the wind. There's a radar antenna at the end, turning like a windmill, and three men talking, staring up at the sky expectantly. One of them is on a phone . . .

Ventura glances at Mayor's phone. 'There's a signal,' she cries. 'We have a signal!'

An excited stir breaks out all around her; the electronic ping of numbers being punched, the murmur of connection, then the shout of quavering voices. Crying. Pleading. Fast with confusion and fear.

84

Padre Márcio

The last thing Padre Márcio remembered from this world was sipping the bitter red wine. Then he dropped into a deep and narrow well. There was a dreamy, expectant mist hovering on the surface, followed by an unexpected sense of flying.

His landing was surprisingly soft; as though he had been consumed within a soothing embrace removed from all light.

Darkness reigned, ponderous and powerful. When the sound first came to him, it did so with a slow reassurance, pulsing into a steady and unmistakable presence, growing in timbre; the echo of a gentle tapping coursing around the constraining walls of the well, rising in volume as he himself drifted upwards into consciousness.

As the persistent hammering increased, so too did his perception of something wholly unexpected and unwelcome: pain.

Padre Márcio's eyes sprang open, his scream emptying his lungs. He was lying down, staring up at a sky that contained no pity, the red Aztec sun watching him with a practiced, sacrificial stare.

He tried to move. Impossible at first. With a monumental effort, he raised his neck and stared down his naked body to his mutilated feet. He had no doubt that if the nails were removed, they would tumble from his legs like oversized shoes.

He turned his head towards his tormentor. 'They talk about the palms of the hands, but you have to respect anatomy,'

Amado said, driving the final nail's head flat against the wrist. 'You wanted the stigmata? Well, your prayers have just been answered.'

85

Fuentes

Fuentes talks Mayor through the documents' failsafes without naming names. It's not that he doesn't trust Mayor; it's just good business practice to let him know he's not alone; that he couldn't bury it even if he wanted to; even if Fuentes were killed. Even if Mayor had a gun pointed at his head.

He stresses the forensic importance of the original photographs, and the charges of criminal possession that Mayor will face if they ever find the victims' files in his possession. Mayor could live with that. Fuentes has the feeling that Mayor has lived with a whole lot worse. Mayor has a Xerox machine in an office at the back. He'll make copies of both the files and photocopied photos and have them all sent by diplomatic bag to his agent in Barcelona and his publishers in Milan and Buenos Aires. He still has connections. That way he'll have his own failsafes.

He's smart. And he is happy to help – after all, it is paperwork, and he is a writer.

Gomez comes into the library, holding up his cell phone. 'They just put El Santo up on the bridge. The *narcomanta* claims it on behalf of Los Zetas.'

'A war between Tijuana and Los Zetas ... Why here?'

'El Santo was sitting on the fence?'

'Makes sense. And it gives us a distraction.' He turns back to Mayor. 'I'd like you to look through these photocopies of the photos now, and try to identify anyone you can.' Mayor takes a step back, holding the bridge of his nose as though trying to regain his balance. 'Are you okay with that?'

'There's no one else you can ask?'

'I'm afraid not at this moment, Señor Mayor.'

'Very well . . .' He accepts the package from Fuentes and slides the first page out, then gasps in shock and takes a step back.

'You may wish to do this sitting down, Señor Mayor . . . Perhaps in the privacy of your study?'

Mayor walks into the adjoining room and sits down behind a massive oak writing table as though seeking shelter. Gomez studies him, then turns back to Fuentes. 'You sure we can trust him?' Fuentes nods, taking the cigarette Gomez offers. 'I don't know . . . Do you think it's true what they say, about him fucking all those actresses?'

'Who even cares?'

Gomez shrugs defensively. 'After all, gossip's a form of information.'

'Like cotton candy's a form of nutrition? What they say about you is true. You can't take your mind off fucking.'

'That's not true. I think about eating three times a day . . .'

'Well, put that fevered little mind of yours to work because we need to think of a way to fuck over Valdez.'

'Wait, we're not letting him off the hook – are we?'

'We need our first roller and he has to be huge. Valdez knows everything, including the consequences of even being suspected of informing. He'll roll in seconds. And what's more, he'll know exactly who else will roll.'

'Fuck that. I don't want to cut a deal with a scumbag.'

'I don't see that we have a choice.' There is a cry from the study, and both of them turn as one. Mayor is wincing away from the image in his hand, as though it were a newspaper announcing appalling news. And in a way that's exactly what it is: the big reveal. Every corrupt and rotten set-up he has ever imagined is true, only one thousand times worse. He is receiving the Gospel of Saint Jude, the patron saint of the impossible, and what it preaches is: the impossible has become our reality. Felipe Mayor, a founder of magic realism, has just landed on the other side of the mirror.

Fuentes turns back to Gomez. 'We need to work this out fast. We'll only get one shot at Valdez, and if he eludes us, all three of us are dead.'

'So what do you have planned?'

'We make an arrest.'

Gomez's laugh is more a choke of outrage. 'That's original. For what?'

'Byrd dropped a bag of coke. I found it.'

'It'll take more than one bag of coke to arrest Valdez.'

'Not Valdez. Hernandez. *Then* we brace Valdez. We tell him we have the photos. We tell him Hernandez is in them. Valdez will know that Hernandez will be desperate to make a deal. He'll know the first name Hernandez will give up will be his. Valdez's only chance will be to roll faster than Hernandez.'

'*Chido*. It could actually work.'

'It *will* work. All we need is one minute alone with Valdez. And then a safe house for his testimony.'

'Where?'

Fuentes pulls a face. 'You know where it's got to be.'

'And let that *pendejete* go into witness protection?'

'We lose Valdez, but we get everyone else. Are you really

415

going to say no to that trade-off?' As if in answer, a phone rings in Mayor's study. 'Besides, we have options. After the arrests, after the convictions. Once the dust has settled. You know it yourself. No one *really* disappears. And, if someone kills Valdez five or ten years down the track, no one will mourn him.'

'I know you. You're no killer.'

'I don't have to be. I just need to know the right people.'

Mayor strides into the library, tugging a phone on a long cord behind him like a stubborn dog on a leash. 'It's a friend of mine.' He thrusts it at Fuentes. 'She's just been kidnapped.'

86

Padre Márcio

Pablo Grande had gone to the crossroads at midday and waited under the contracting shade of a flowering eucalyptus. A battered J2000 Jeep pickup with a broken grille guard was the seventh car to stop for him, but the Huichol family inside were the only people to seriously consider his request. The man behind the wheel was younger than the car, although the couple sitting next to him were far older than Pablo Grande.

He told them what he needed, then stood back politely, allowing them to debate his request in Coyultita. The old woman got out and scanned the skies, while the old man sat quietly inside, watching Pablo Grande out of the back of his head.

Then the woman got back inside the pickup and appeared to fall asleep.

An hour later, the driver got out and offered Pablo Grande a gourd. The *agua* was cold and had the metamorphic alkaline taste of all sierra water. The driver said they were in no particular hurry and would be glad to assist him in his quest.

They drove for the rest of the afternoon, and it was sunset when they stopped the car.

Pablo Grande stepped forwards cautiously, smelling on the air the distinct scent of ozone – the confirmation of a recent lightning strike.

'We're too late,' the driver said, transfixed.

'We can still save him,' Pablo Grande said.

He hurried to the base of the crucifixion. Sinking to his knees, he began to remove the rocks grouped around the base. The driver watched for a horrified moment, then began to work by Pablo Grande's side, heaving stones away, the base already beginning to tremble.

Pablo Grande looked up at Padre Márcio. 'Hold on, old friend. You put yourself here, but now together we will get you down.'

87

Fuentes

They drive in silence through canyons that are hostile with secrets. The mountains speak of struggle and defiance . . . and defeat. They are like liberated Titans, imprisoned for eons under the earth's dark mantle before finally erupting in triumph, only to find themselves staring into the Gorgon's eyes, fossilized before they could even celebrate their freedom. The mountains are like us, Fuentes thinks, fighting for something that has already been lost. 'You know the chances of us coming back?' he says to Gomez.

Gomez turns and stares at him with a look Fuentes knows: a *Mexican attitude towards death* look. 'What's there to come back to?'

The track begins to wind upwards, in a series of hairpin bends. Fuentes once had an answer to Gomez's question, but that was before Ciudad Real. Before Tijuana. 'Nothing . . .'

The track begins to level out to what looks like a plateau.

Gomez shucks the Remington. 'So what are we waiting for, *caballero* . . .'

88

Pilar

Pilar watches the darkness running across the distant treetops towards them; a high tide of night. Out here in the arid hills, there is no pollution, no reflection from security lights. Out here the stars rise in triumph with the setting sun. She remembers the stories her mother told her; how she pointed out and named the constellations. All forgotten with the carelessness of childhood. If only her mother were still alive; if only she were with her, she could ask her the names, and this time Pilar would remember.

Headlights lance fast down the track, and the bus is overtaken by a Jeep, a mounted machine gun in the back, a man holding on to it. It's the second one they've seen since they left the plateau. Ventura stands, snapping as it passes. 'Don't take photos!'

'They didn't see me . . .' The bus shudders over a ridge and they all lurch in their seats. Ventura turns to her. They've hardly spoken since the abduction; since Pilar lied to her. 'How bad is this going to be?'

It is the end, Pilar thinks – it's the only way it could ever have ended. 'I've seen worse. Much worse.'

The bus thunders through the night as though trying to escape Pilar's lie. Pilar gazes up at the stars blooming in the desert sky. So close, so brilliant.

So far away.

Ventura sees the tear traveling down Pilar's cheek. It's like it's always been there; a jewel revealed at exactly the right moment. Ventura knows what it signifies. She starts to sing, plaintive at first, wavering in uncertainty: '*Los caminos de la vida*'. Her voice rises up like an offering, slowly joined by other voices. It's as though the bus was dead and is now being resuscitated, all the women joining in with their song about love and loss; obligation and memory. Singing a song about their lives, fighting their terror, everyone singing now . . . Except for Pilar. She is watching Ventura, who is struggling not to cry as she sings.

Pilar takes her hand. 'It's fine to cry,' she whispers. 'When we have nothing left, when everything is taken from us, we still have our tears.' Pilar doesn't have to tell Ventura the rest; she knows it in her own heart, the way every woman knows it: they are not tears for oneself, but for all women.

Acknowledgments

Enormous thanks to Xochitl Zepeda Blouin, without whom this novel would never have been possible.

Very special thanks also to Ernesto Zepeda, Dominique Blouin de Zepeda, Catalina Zepeda, Miguel Angel Chávez, José María Lumbreras and Gerardo Medina.

Very special thanks to Oscar de Muriel for his guidance with the Mexican Spanish usage in the book, and to early readers Julie Baker and Harriet O'Malley.

Deep appreciation to all at Faber, especially to my editor, Angus Cargill, whose guidance was as invaluable as ever, and to Samantha Matthews, Sophie Portas, Lauren Nicoll, Alex Kirby, Jonny Pelham and Ruth O'Loughlin. Thanks also to copy editor Eleanor Rees for her sterling help.

Very special thanks to my agent, Tom Witcomb, for his great instincts, and to all at Blake Friedmann, including the late Carole Blake, Isobel Dixon and Hattie Grunewald.

My deep appreciation to my brother, Chris Baker, for his generous support and assistance.

Thanks to the following for their support throughout the writing of the book: Gabriela Arnon, Harry Avramidis, Lily and Bella Baker, Wayne Jowandi Barker, Clare Barry, Alison Benney, Natasha de Betak, Stefano Bortolussi, Ricardo Bravo, the late Liam 'Billy' Burke, Kent Carroll, Matthew Condon, Val Coy, Helen Curtis, Rosemary Curtis and Peter Horsam,

Daniel Dayan, Emmanuel Dayan and Rachel Rosenblum, Yves Yang Diep, Colin Englert and Susan Wells, Josephine Ferrer Frogley and Janet Ferrer, Andrea Soler Ferrer, Maha Ismail, Jing Jin, Fiona McQueen and Beverly Oliver, Frank Moorhouse, Janica and Mike Nichols, Keith Nixon, Herbert Ochtman and Dominique Peguy, Harriet O'Malley, Steve Potts, Paolo Roversi and everyone at NebbiaGialla, and Hal and Arlette Singer.

Special thanks to les Berlugans: Yves Berthelot and Dosithée Yeatman-Berthelot, Delphine Berthelot-Eiffel and Alain Touchard, Arnaud Arches, Daniel Berger, Sylvie Bilardello et Frédéric Duprey, Stefanie Brandt and Pietro Alberti, Raymond and Gabrielle 'Mounette' Carli, Paulo and Eliane Chaves, Rino and Laura Corazzari, Massimo Di Paola and Stefania Orlandi, Fabrice Gaquerel, Gilbert and Aimée Garziglia, Yves Garziglia, Roger and Sylvie Garziglia, Philippe Huguet, Irena Kazaridi, Jeremy Lagarrigue, Laurent Lobby and Maria Nesmes, Laurent Millat-Carus, Anthony and Patricia Pharaoh, Adrien Plesu, Claudine Reinach, Quentin Richard, Christophe Rinaudo, Andreas Sirio, Bertrand and Béatrice Stevens, Christophe Tari, Olga Tchernychov, Bruno, Sylvie and Noémie Valois, Laurent Voulzy and Alain Souchon.

Enormous gratitude to my family for their support and encouragement: my late parents, Colin and Lorel Baker, Steven and Anna Baker, Nicholas Baker and Maryanne Blacker, Michael and Margaret Baker, and in particular Chris Baker. Above all, thanks to my wife, Julie, and our son, Nathaniel, for their sustaining and inspiring belief.

Also by Tim Baker

ff

Fever City

Shortlisted for the CWA John Creasey New Blood Dagger Award and nominated for the Private Eye Writers of America's Shamus Award

Nick Alston, a Los Angeles private investigator, is hired to find the kidnapped son of America's richest and most hated man. Hastings, a mob hitman in search of redemption, is also on the trail. But both men soon become ensnared by a sinister cabal that spreads from the White House all the way to Dealey Plaza. Decades later in Dallas, Alston's son stumbles across evidence from JFK conspiracy buffs that just might link his father to the shot heard round the world.

Violent, vivid, visceral, *Fever City* is a high-octane, nightmare journey through a *Mad Men*-era America of dark powers, corruption and conspiracy.

'Packed with tough-guy poetry, deeply felt emotions and startling images . . . A superb debut novel. A direct hit.' Jeff Noon, *Spectator*

'A noirish storm of corruption, violence and depravity . . . In this ambitious debut, Baker gives us a bare-knuckle take on the president's murder and adds two other plotlines, connecting them solidly with the equivalent of a jab-jab-cross combination.' *New York Times Book Review*